RAVE REVIEWS F

GATES (

"This book is a jewel—riv
packed. The twists and tu
page-turner to the very last. . ..gmy recommend *Gates of Hades*."

—Fresh Fiction

"*Gates of Hades* is a suspense-filled novel."

—*Midwest Book Review*

THE JULIAN SECRET

"I could not put this book down! Loomis has woven three time periods into a plot tapestry of twists and curves and connected them through the lives of a gritty American and a stoic German. I was sure I had the mystery figured out, but as usual, Loomis kept me involved and surprised until the end. This sequel to *The Pegasus Secret* is a highly recommended read."

—Fresh Fiction

"*The Julian Secret* is thought provoking and Loomis lets his readers form their own conclusions. This is a lively and stimulating thriller you do not want to put down. The surprise ending is great—a light moment from the serious questions on life. Dan Brown's fans will find *The Julian Secret* a delight."

—I Love A Mystery

Anthony Aracich
50 Glenwood Ave
Jersey City NJ 07306

"I'll take that, Mr. Reilly."

Lang turned slowly. Leather Jacket and another man stood just inside the door. Each held an automatic obscured by a silencer.

The two men were a good five feet apart. No chance Lang could draw the SIG Sauer from its holster and fire before at least one of the intruders could shoot.

Lang slowly raised his hands, his fingers manipulating the envelopes so that one was squarely behind the other. "What can I do for you, gentlemen?"

Leather Jacket motioned with his weapon. "The envelope you have in your hand, Mr. Reilly, put it on the counter and slide it towards me."

The question was whether these two intended to take what they had come for and leave or make sure Lang did not trouble them further. The silencers on each gun did not suggest a happy ending. It was unlikely a man would risk carrying something that bulky if he had no intention of using it.

If Lang was going to do something, now seemed about the right time.

But what?

GREGG LOOMIS

THE SINAI SECRET

Dorchester
Publishing

This book is for Suzanne.

DORCHESTER PUBLISHING

March 2011

Published by

Dorchester Publishing Co., Inc.
200 Madison Avenue
New York, NY 10016

This is a work of fiction. Names, characters, places, and incidents are either the product of the author's imagination or are used fictitiously. Any resemblance to actual persons, living or dead, events, or locales is entirely coincidental.

ISBN 13: 978-1-4285-1141-5
E-ISBN: 978-1-4285-1106-4

The "DP" logo is the property of Dorchester Publishing Co., Inc.

Printed in the United States of America.

Visit us online at www.dorchesterpub.com.

THE SINAI SECRET

PROLOGUE

Mount Horeb
Sinai Peninsula
March 1904

Sir W. M. Flinders Petrie was astonished but certainly not pleased by his discovery.

His expedition had been funded by the Egypt Exploration Fund for the purpose of revisiting and mapping the area of mining activity by the ancient Egyptians between the gulfs of Suez and Aqaba. Like so many explorers before him, he had found something quite different from the object of his search.

Although this was supposedly Mount Sinai, the mountain from which Moses had brought down the Ten Commandments, Petrie had no particular expectations. The place was in the area he was surveying, so the expedition had struggled up the sharp outcrop to its summit. Instead of more craggy red sandstone boulders, scrubby brush, and a surplus of scorpions, they were viewing something totally unexpected.

Jutting out from what was clearly a man-made cave were remnants of walls of ancient handmade brick. The southern side of the walls had long ago been abraded by sand blown by millennia of wind, the consistent gritty, hot breeze Petrie had come to think of as the breath of the desert. The northern side still displayed a patina of the painted plaster that had once covered the crude bricks. In the plaster were inscriptions, hieroglyphics that Petrie recognized as possibly dating back to the Twelfth Pharaonic Dynasty of about 2600 B.C.

Long before Moses.

This presented a problem.

The articles of association of the sponsoring Egypt Exploration Fund were quite clear: One of its objectives was excavation and exploration for the purpose of confirming or elucidating the Old Testament. This was the mountain where Moses had spoken with God in the form of a burning bush; from which he had brought down not one, but two sets of commandments; and at the base of which he had burned the idolatrous golden calf.

Petrie's discovery was tantamount to betraying his friends and sponsors, something no English gentleman could countenance.

Making the find public would certainly lose future financing from the fund. It could well lead to disgrace, even his loss of privileges at the Explorers' Club in Mayfair.

He wished he had never seen this wretched mountain.

Still, he and his exploration team were here, and not even investigating the site would be wasteful indeed.

By sunset the shifting sands had yielded an impressive collection of tablets, statues, and tools typical of a temple. Petrie was confident the next day would reveal an altar and other evidence of worship of the oft-depicted Hathor, the goddess of love, tombs, gold, and song, and from whose milk pharaohs gained immortality. There was no doubt about the god pictured: No other deity had cow horns and a solar disk on its head.

By the time dinner was over and the native porters had erected tents for him and the three other Englishmen,

Petrie had decided to simply submit his findings and let the Fund decide what use to make of them.

A bother, that. He had planned to publish an account of this exploration himself.

By the next afternoon loose sand had been removed from a number of halls and chambers. Reliefs of various pharaohs and their favorite wives, sons, and chamberlains were uncovered, but not the main altar.

What had been discovered was a series of rectangular and round holes carved into the sandstone, each hole larger than a bathtub. Petrie had never seen anything quite like them, and their possible function eluded him. The discovery of a metallurgist's crucible and perhaps several pounds of an unidentified white powder beneath a stone floor was equally puzzling. Perhaps it was the strange object frequently mentioned in the inscriptions on the walls and surrounding stelae. He certainly had no other idea what the word referred to. He had never seen it before. Even more mysterious was why a crucible would be in a temple in the first place.

It was referred to again in a portrayal of Anubis, the jackal-god who led the deceased into the afterlife. The animal was lying on an ark while the pharaoh Amenhotep presented a conical object. The inscription stated something about giving gold and rejoicing mouths.

Another search revealed no gold, only the enigmatic white powder.

Like any competent archaeologist, Petrie recorded his findings, completed his excavation (without locating the missing altar), and continued the survey he had been sent to complete.

Having apparently reached some sort of peace with the Fund, he published a short book on his exploration, *Ancient Egypt and Ancient Israel,* in 1910. His discoveries might have caused reactions in the academic world had the real discovery not been overshadowed by the storm clouds of two world wars.

Again, like many explorers, he had set in motion forces he could not have imagined. No one in early twentieth-century Europe could have.

ONE

Stift Melk an der Donau (on the Danube)
Austria
The present

Joseph Steinburg, Ph.D., stood at the two-story entrance facing the afternoon sun. In front of him, the hill on which the first part of the monastery had been built in the tenth century dropped precipitously into the rushing gray waters of the Danube. Behind him was the library. Fifty-foot-high book-lined walls ran the three-hundred-foot length of the huge room.

From the chapel below came the vesper chants of the thirty or so monks who still occupied that part of the baroque abbey not presently used as a parochial school. He paid no attention, if, in fact, he even heard.

Were it not for the boat pushing barges upstream and the cars humming along the highway across the river, Steinburg could have been anywhere in time within the last millennium.

He wasn't thinking about that, either.

He could only ponder the strange discovery that had occupied him for the last two days.

A year ago the abbey had begun the awesome task of creating a computer index of the library, including the two thousand–plus volumes that dated back to the ninth through the fifteenth centuries. Last week one of the graduate students had discovered a number of bound parchments in ancient Hebrew, perhaps misplaced in the panic to hide all things of value that ensued when, in 1683, Kara Mustafa and his two hundred thousand Turks laid siege to Vienna, just fifty miles to the east. Although the Turks were forced to withdraw only three months later, these documents had, most likely, not been returned to their proper place, remaining with what were at the time current religious writings. The Church had asked Steinburg, part-time archeologist and full-time professor of ancient Hebrew history, to translate and date the documents.

From the heavy parchment and ink, Steinburg guessed the physical pages themselves could be as old as Melk. But the events they described were older, much older. The unusual syntax, phrases borrowed from pharaonic Egyptian, indicated that someone had painstakingly translated a chronicle from, say, 1500 to 1200 B.C. Or, to be politically correct, B.C.E., before the Common Era. In any event, before Hebrew itself was recognizable as a written language.

A cautious man, Steinburg turned around and walked back inside to one of the rolling ladders on rails, climbed to the top tier, and examined the exact area where the material had been found. Sure enough, the neighboring volumes all dated from the mid- to late-seventeenth century.

Once back on the parquet floor, he returned to the table where the parchments were unrolled. He pulled on the surgical gloves that protected the documents from any acid that might be contained in the moisture of his skin, then turned to the laptop on which he was composing a draft of his translation. He was aware of the irony of the anachronism, using electronic transcription in a place where manuscripts had been hand-copied for centuries.

But how did these documents come to be here in Austria in the first place?

If Steinburg had to guess, a pursuit he loathed as a professor but had to embrace as an archaeologist, he would say the ancient parchment had found its way to Europe as a trophy of the Crusades, most likely the third, when Duke Leopold V had held the English king, Richard the Lionheart, for ransom at his castle at Durnstein, just a few kilometers down the Danube, where ruins of its towers could still be seen. Possibly these pages had been brought to Melk from the centuries-old castle of some former crusader for safekeeping before the Turks breached the castle walls. A number of families in this area dated their ancestry back that far.

Steinburg sighed his relief at having at least theoretically solved the mystery of the papers' origin.

How the Church—or, for that matter, the world—was going to solve the consequences of his discovery was another issue.

Two hours later, he stood and glanced around the room.

Ancient or not, the facts narrated in the documents could have very contemporary implications.

Serious implications.

Implications far beyond the halls of abstract academia or the dusty pages of history.

He could simply return the documents to oblivion in their place among the top row of books and leave Melk, hoping his translation of both Hebrew and old German would likewise be lost in obscurity. But somehow that didn't seem a satisfactory option. Part of his compensation for his work was right to publish his findings in his choice of scholarly journals. The information had value to some people if published, perhaps even more if not.

At any rate, he had no intent of shunning the acclaim his work would earn. The purpose of academia was to disseminate knowledge, like a breeze laden with the parachutes of dandelion seeds. How it was used was not his to question.

He had not noticed that a frail glow from electric sconces now illuminated the cavernous room, the sun having long set. He wondered if the abbey's lightbulbs were intentionally dim to simulate the candles that had burned here for centuries.

He stood, nodding as though reaching an agreement with himself. Reaching into his computer's traveling case, he produced a disk and copied the notes he had spent the last two days inputting. Then he e-mailed the draft of his translation to his home computer. Better backup than a disk. Tomorrow he would print out both his translations along with his notes, and send it to the abbey.

But for now . . .

Well, he could look forward to at least a modicum of academic recognition, perhaps even more than his cousin, the scientist.

Then he had an idea.

Documents in hand, he walked out of the library, down several halls, and across a courtyard to where by day a gift shop sold souvenirs, books, and religious medals. Behind the shop was a small office, one to which Steinburg had been given a key yesterday when he needed to send a fax. The door to the outside was closed and bolted for the day but yielded easily to his key. If he remembered correctly . . .

Yes, the fax machine was also a photocopier. Closing his mind to the potential damage that might be done to the documents, he carefully placed them one by one on the glass plate.

His cousin in Amsterdam had mentioned a project that might make these old writings interesting. But if he sent these, Benjamin would have them for months, perhaps a year before Steinburg could publish. Not a problem. His cousin Benjamin was also a professor, but of some sort of exotic science. Analytical chemistry, theoretical physics—Steinburg wasn't sure.

He opened the desk and extracted a bulky envelope and a roll of stamps. He quickly jotted a note requesting the copies either be destroyed or hidden until he published. He estimated the stamps required, addressed the envelope, and dropped it in the sack of mail to be picked up the next day.

He smiled. That ought to get him back for the unintelligible formula his cousin had published last year, a theoretical equation that had caused a mild stirring in scientific journals. These Hebrew scrolls were going be bigger, much bigger than Benjamin's theory.

The two had been friendly rivals since childhood, and now Steinburg would be one up.

A glance at his watch told him he would be late getting home to Vienna. Locking the office, he returned to the library, exited away from the river, crossed a courtyard, and found his ancient but immaculate Volkswagen Beetle in a gravel parking lot now deserted by the daily tour buses. He drove out the gate, away from the abbey's manicured grounds, and onto the road leading to the bridge. In his rearview mirror, Melk's twin towers and dome were fading in the growing dusk.

By the time he reached the narrow bridge high above the Danube, Steinburg had an idea which publications would be given the opportunity to see his work.

His thoughts were interrupted by a pair of lights behind him. From their height above the road it had to be a truck.

Strange. Trucks were expressly forbidden on this bridge.

And the damn thing was speeding, too.

Steinburg realized what was going to happen only an instant before the crunch of metal against metal sent the Volkswagen crashing into the side railing of the bridge.

He felt a jolt of fear. No way was that rampart going to hold, to keep his car from smashing through into the void below.

He was quite right.

TWO

The White House
Washington, D.C.
0423 EST

The ringing of the telephone beside the bed brought Phillip Hansler, the president of the United States, to groggy awareness. He groaned softly as his eyes took in the time on the digital clock next to the phone. As he fumbled the receiver to his ear, he thought the obvious: He was through with sleep for the night. Only his chief of staff had access to this line, and no one called at this hour with good news.

Rather than wake his wife beside him, he sat up without turning on a light. "Yeah?"

"Good morning, Mr. President. The Iranian situation has gotten out of hand. The Joint Chiefs are on their way, should be in the situation room within the next ten minutes."

The president hung up without reply before he slipped from beneath the covers, feet groping for the slippers he had left beside the bed.

"Shall I order up some coffee?" The question came from the mound in the covers beside where he had been.

There was at least a skeleton crew manning the White House kitchen twenty-four hours a day.

The president was shuffling toward the bathroom. "No need. There'll be plenty where I'm headed."

The very mention of the place gave him chills. Far below the White House, the situation room was actually a series of rooms, including bath and kitchen facilities, that had been constructed as an emergency bunker during the Cold War in case an imminent nuclear attack did not allow enough time for the president to evacuate Washington. Equipped with the most advanced communications, it still served as a command post in times of national emergency.

Minutes later the president stood in front of the elevator just outside his private living quarters. He could already hear a cacophony of sirens growing louder. He checked his watch. The military cavalcade and its escorts would be right on time.

As the president entered the conference room, the three commanding generals and one admiral snapped to attention. The president imagined he could hear the jangle of medals. How did these guys get all that brass and ribbon on so quick, anyway? They must have multiple sets, each already pinned to fresh uniforms.

The president gave a cursory nod. "Be seated, gentlemen, please."

Four sets of pressed and starched rear ends plopped into chairs. A white-jacketed orderly appeared with a carafe of coffee and a stack of cups just as the White House chief of staff, the secretaries of state and defense, and the director of intelligence slid into their places.

"Shall we wait until we can find the vice president?" the chief of staff asked.

Not unless you intend to search every single woman's apartment in Washington, the president thought. A widower of two years, the vice president had become difficult to reach on short notice at night and on weekends, behavior that would have to be modified if the man's obvious ambitions were to be realized.

The president shook his head. "Have someone continue to try to reach him. In the meantime let's not keep everyone waiting."

The president gave a grateful nod to the coffee server and took a steaming cup from the tray. "Okay, I know you didn't get me up at this hour for the pleasure of my company." He nodded to Jack Allen, a black navy admiral in his late fifties, the first member of his race to reach that rank and only the second to serve as chairman of the Joint Chiefs of Staff.

"What's up, Jack?"

The admiral pointed to a huge flat-screen monitor displaying the Near East from the Mediterranean to the Hindu Kush. A red dot was moving east to west.

The admiral spoke in a bass so deep the president had remarked that it sounded like it came from somewhere beneath his feet, the voice of an Old Testament prophet. "The picture, Mr. President, is a real-time satellite relay, and represents six K-twelve or SUMA missiles, each capable of carrying ten or more seperate warheads, possibly nukes. They were launched from three different sites in the Iranian desert, sites our satellites never picked up. Probably underground."

"Target?"

"Israel. There's nobody else within the K-twelve's range that has a beef with Iran."

The chief of staff leaned forward to look down the table at his boss. "Mr. President, you'll recall last week the Israelis threatened a preemptive strike if Tehran didn't begin destroying its nuclear-capable missiles. Looks like the Iranians have launched first."

"Mr. President?"

A tall, rangy woman of indeterminate age was leaning forward to be seen. With her prominent nose and long, masculine walk, Susan Faulk, secretary of state, often reminded the president of a stork striding through the marsh in pursuit of a juicy frog. Avian or not, the woman was both brilliant and intuitive in recognizing the national interests of both her country and others'. She had predicted that Iran's recent war games had not been an empty show but were fully intended to prepare for offensive action against its enemy, Israel.

The president admired her clarity of thought. "Yes, Susan?"

"We can be certain Prime Minister Konic of Israel is watching, too, already preparing Israel's reply, probably a strike not only at Iran's military installations but oil fields as well. With Russia and China as Iran's biggest customers, we can expect them to jump into this if their supply of fuel is threatened."

"Both Russia and China know we stand firmly behind Israel. They know they act at their peril," the president said. With the millions of Jewish voters and hundreds of millions of their political contributions, no president could do otherwise. He turned back to the military. "How long until those things hit?"

A silver-haired man in air-force blue answered, "Seventeen minutes, ten seconds, Mr. President."

"Anything we can do to shoot 'em down?"

The air force man shook his head. "Not enough time. We'll have to rely on the Israelis for that. We sold them the hardware. Still, I'd anticipate about fifty percent of the intruders will get through."

The president didn't want to even think about the damage thirty nuclear devices could do to the United States, let alone a country as small as Israel.

"Let me make sure I have your consensus here," he said. "We've got an attack, likely nuclear, against Israel.

There's little doubt of retaliation, which will likely bring in China and Russia. Suggestions?"

The secretary of state raised her hand. "Only one choice, Mr. President. You have to contact Prime Minister Konic immediately."

"I'd guess he's sort of busy right now."

"Nonetheless, you have to speak to him, convince him not to strike back, at least not until we can speak to the Russians and Chinese."

It would be easier to convince the hotheaded Israeli to convert to Islam. But, as president, Hansler had to try.

Why the hell had he wanted this job in the first place?

As though someone had read his mind, a warrant officer appeared at the president's side. "Telephone, sir. It's Prime Minister Konic."

A pin dropping would have sounded like an explosion.

"Did you say Prime Minister Konic?"

"Yes, sir."

Skeptically, the president picked up the receiver. "Moshe?"

"Phil!" boomed a voice that sounded like it came from the same room rather than from halfway around the world.

Since becoming president, Hansler had become fast friends with the head of the Israeli nation. The two had enjoyed fly-fishing for trout on the president's Montana ranch as much as socializing at international gatherings. It had been difficult not to lose sight of the fact that all Israeli leaders made a business of getting as close to their American counterparts as possible. Israel's survival depended on it.

"How's Nancy? Your boy about through college this year? Send him over here for a graduation trip!"

The president glanced around the room, aware that Konic's voice was spilling out of the receiver. "Er, Moshe, I take it this isn't a social call?"

"Right you are," blared over the connection. "I expected to hear from you—a little matter of those pesky Iranians."

The president would have used another adjective, but he said, "We have the missiles on satellite. Hope the defenses we sent you work."

"Oh, never mind the antimissiles." The man's voice was downright jovial, as though he were telling a favorite story. "We'll be just fine. The reason I called you was to tell you just that—that we'll be okay. No need to go to alert status."

"You mean you don't intend to retaliate, to bomb Iran into the Stone Age?"

"Far as we're concerned, Iran's been in the Stone Age for decades. You checked out their politics? No, no retaliation will be necessary. Go back to sleep."

The president removed the receiver from his ear long enough to glance at it as though he might assay the sanity of the speaker. "No retaliation?"

"For what?"

"For . . ."

The four-star marine general on his left tugged gently at the president's cuff. "Mr. President . . ."

The president gave him an annoyed look until he followed where the man was pointing.

There was no longer a dot on the screen.

"See what I mean?" the Israeli statesman asked with a triumphant cackle. "Hang in there!"

"Moshe! What . . . How did . . . ?"

"Jehovah's will, Phil. Your Bible says faith can move mountains. All we did was make a few missiles go away."

The line went dead.

The air force general was speaking earnestly into a cell phone.

"What the hell happened?" the president asked.

"What did not happen, Mr. President, was a malfunction of the visual equipment. The missiles really disappeared."

"You mean the defensive system functioned better than predicted."

"No, Mr. President. The satellite showed no launch of countermissiles. The Iranian hardware just evaporated."

The president slumped deeply back into his chair. "And just how the hell did they do that?"

Silence was his only answer.

"Okay, okay," the president said. "I want to know exactly what took place, why those missiles disappeared, vanished, or whatever. And in the meantime I want a total lid on this. I hear so much as a whisper about tonight, somebody's gonna finish their career counting caribou in Alaska."

1

THREE

Blind Donkey Alley
Bruges, Belgium
2200 European Time

Even though Bruges's canal network was now scenic rather than utilitarian, the trees along the banks in front of redbrick, narrow-windowed medieval houses reminded Benjamin Yadish of his native Amsterdam.

The town was amazingly preserved from its days as a trading center for textiles, fine lace, and intricate gold jewelry some six hundred years past. The silting up of the River Zwin had largely ended its mercantile days, but it had also discouraged replacing tall town houses with more contemporary and far less charming structures, as had happened in so many European cities.

There had been the coldly charmless semidetached in Cambridge, the fourth-story garret in the Sorbonne District of Paris, the wretched and noisy rooms over a Bierstube just outside the university area of Munich, the only quarters worse than the converted barn near Bologna that still leaked hours after a rainfall. Before accepting a post as head of the University of Amsterdam's physics department, he had spent time at half a dozen institutions.

A wandering Jew, he liked to joke.

He rounded a corner, thankful to exit an alley so narrow he could have touched opposing polished doorknobs by stretching out his arms. He breathed deeply in relief.

Relief from what?

He was unsure. He was aware only of an anxiety that had no rational basis. Hardly an emotion to which any scientist would admit.

He crossed the Burg, a pleasant cobbled square consisting of several small restaurants, all closed at this hour. Now he could see the Markt, a thirteenth-century market square lined by tall, stair-step gabled houses, many with brightly painted facades. For reasons he also could not have explained, he was thankful to reach the most brightly lit place in town. Only now did he realize how claustrophobic he had felt in the confines of twisting streets and alleys too narrow for vehicular traffic.

Nonsense, he told himself. He had never feared confined spaces any more than he had standing at the roof edge of tall buildings.

The glances over his shoulder were totally unnecessary.

There was, though, something sinister about this whole trip. The unexpected phone call demanding he bring the CDs containing the protocol of his most recent experiments, a meeting at night in a strange city. Had the call come from anyone else, he would have thought he was speaking to a lunatic.

He settled at a table in one of the few bistros on the square still serving at this hour. A waiter silently materialized, and Benjamin ordered a Brugse Tripel beer. He would have preferred coffee, but caffeine at this hour would keep him awake all night.

Night.

Well after 2200.

The waiter set the beer bottle next to a glass. As was customary for such places, he also left a slip of paper on a small tray, the bill, which Benjamin could pay anytime before leaving. The waiter scurried back to the lights inside. Benjamin poured slowly, intent on the building head of bubbles.

"If you tilt the glass, you will get less of a head."

A man sat down across from him, speaking accented English. He was positioned so that his face was dark while limned by street lamps.

Benjamin squinted, unable to make out more than a featureless dark blur. "I don't recognize your voice. You're not . . ."

The head shook. "No. I am to take you to him. You have what he requested?"

Benjamin patted his inside jacket pocket as he lifted his glass. "Of course. As soon as I finish. You?"

"No, thanks."

Benjamin emptied the glass and held the tab up to the light from the street. Guessing rather than seeing, he left two euros on the table and stood. "I've spoken with him often, but we met only once. At the beginning. Why now? Why here instead of in Amsterdam, where he can personally inspect what I'm doing?"

The other man either did not hear or, more likely, ignored the questions. He was already hurrying west down Steenstraat. Benjamin caught up, curious as to the need to rush. Perhaps all would be explained shortly. A left turn down Mariastraat past the Welcome Church of Our Lady, its spire, the tallest in Belgium, stabbing the night as it glowed in beams cast by lights at its base. Right turn along the east–west canal. The steep-gabled, tall town houses had given way to modest two-story brick buildings whose steep eaves had sloughed off snow for over five hundred winters.

The man stopped and pointed to a bench under a tree with roots running down to the canal. Across a narrow street was a house with a depiction of a swan on it. A small hotel. That made sense. It was the type of accommodation the man Benjamin had come to see might choose: both luxurious and inconspicuous.

"Wait here."

Benjamin started to protest, then thought better of it and sat facing water so still that the warm light from the hotel's windows swam on the surface. On a spring night like this, sitting outside was comfortable. Perhaps the man feared some sort of listening devices might be in the walls of the hotel. Benjamin could fully understand why the man would want whatever he had to say not to be overheard. The project was best kept quiet until completed. There would be those who would very much like to see that it never was.

Benjamin heard footsteps and started to rise.

He felt something cold and hard against the base of his skull, cold and hard like steel.

Like a gun's barrel.

But why?

He heard a puff, a mere whisper, and brilliant lights exploded from somewhere behind his eyes. He felt no pain, only the firmness of the earth beneath him.

And someone's hand groping his inside jacket pocket.

Then all went black and he felt nothing.

FOUR

Manuel's Tavern
Highland Avenue
Atlanta, Georgia
8:30 p.m. EST
The Same Night

The original part of Manuel's Tavern dated back to the early 1950s. It consisted of stools along a bar and wooden booths, now time-worn and inscribed with graffiti from generations of students. Then, as now, it was a rendezvous for local Democratic politicos, university intelligentsia, and those who would like to become any of the above. Manuel had chosen wisely, locating his establishment across the street from the border of the Southern Methodist/Baptist–controlled county in which Emory University was located. The bar had been an oasis of beer and free thought on the edge of a Sahara of proclaimed abstinence and intolerance. Never mind that the greatest amount of liquor tax collected in the state at that time came from those purveyors of the devil's elixir just across that same line, stores that supplied unmarked grocery bags and boxes to conceal the potables their customers hauled back into forbidden territory.

As racial and economic diversity blurred old and perhaps outdated values, even when alcohol became legal across the street Manuel's remained quirky. While gracious lots with lovely homes were subdivided into new look-alike neighborhoods of "affordable housing," the bar remained a bit risqué, a reputation subsequent owners had done little to alter. As the years passed, it had morphed into a watering hole for not only the left-of-center but also the social contrarian and the down-right funky.

A black man wearing a clerical collar and a white man in lawyer camouflage of dark suit and power tie drew no special attention. They were steady customers, always taking the same booth, continually arguing and complaining, frequently in Latin, about the poor quality of food for which Manuel's was famous.

"*Corruptio optimi pessima*," the priest said, reaching for a half-empty pitcher of lukewarm beer.

"No doubt corruption of the best is worst, Francis," the white man agreed, signaling to the waiter as he emptied the pitcher. "But the mayor is entitled to a defense just like anyone else. *Cor illi in genua decidet.*"

"You can bet it was fear that brought him to his knees. It certainly wasn't prayer." Francis snorted.

Francis Narumba, formerly of one of West Africa's more corrupt, poverty-stricken, and disease-infested republics, had attended Oxford on scholarship, then had been sent to seminary in the United States. Either by his wish or that of a higher power, he had been assigned to minister not to the hellhole of his origins but to Atlanta's growing number of African immigrants.

As his dinner partner, Langford Reilly, described it, they were both victims of a liberal arts education and therefore unfit to do anything requiring any real skill.

Like, maybe, become a plumber.

Trapped in their own schooling, Francis had pursued a career in the church, and Lang law school. Lang's sister had been one of Francis's few white parishioners. Although tragic, her murder had brought priest and lawyer together. Before long they had become fast friends. Lang's lack of faith and, in his view, Francis's overabundance thereof provided an endless source of amicable debate.

In private, each would admit that the other, no matter how misguided, was probably the brightest mind he had known.

Lang watched their entrées' approach with interest. Regardless of what had been ordered, surprises were frequent at Manuel's. "Fortunately, the former mayor disagrees with Ovid. *Estque pati poenas quam meruisse minus.*"

Lang could see the curiosity on his companion's face replaced by suspicion as he looked at the plate set before him. The "medium-rare" filet had a very burned look to it. He sighed as the waiter shoved Lang's hamburger and fries onto the table and retreated hastily. "Fortunately?"

Lang tried to suppress a smile as Francis surveyed the cremated remains of his steak. "Fortunately for me. If he believed it better to suffer punishment than deserve it, he wouldn't pay me an outrageous fee to defend him."

Francis shook his head, reaching for a bottle of steak sauce. "I'm surprised he doesn't . . . What is it the crime shows say?"

"Plead guilty?"

"*Hoc sustinete maius ne veniat malum.* Cop a plea."

"He says he's innocent."

Francis snorted again. "His chief administrative assistant, the head of the city contract board, five others—"

"Six others."

"—have either pled guilty or rolled over on each other for corruption, bribery, racketeering, tax evasion, et cetera. What else could they charge him with?"

"Parking overtime?"

Francis sampled the first bite of his steak, chewing thoughtfully. "I'm surprised you'd take the case. For sure you don't need the money."

Lang shrugged, a tacit admission that Francis was

right. "Managing a huge charitable foundation isn't my idea of fun. Trying white-collar criminal cases is."

Francis was adding more steak sauce in a losing battle to cover up the flavor of burned meat. It had become a point of honor for neither man to admit during the meal just how bad Manuel's food could be and often was. "I still don't see why you'd want your name tied to a crook like that."

Lang wiped his face. The blood of his nearly raw hamburger—ordered medium—was running down his chin. "I seem to remember someone who spent his days with a prostitute and died between two thieves. Something to do with who should throw the first stone, as I recall it."

"You know far too much scripture for a heretic," Francis growled good-naturedly before changing the subject abruptly. "Hear anything from Gurt?"

Lang put his burger down to let it soak in its own juices, mostly blood and grease. "Not a word."

Francis started to say something, thought better of it, and renewed his assault on the steak.

"Don't expect to hear. It's been over a year now since she left, went back to Europe to work with the government."

A euphemism Francis understood to mean the Agency. Although the priest had not pressed for details, the gap between Lang's college education and his law degree indicated he had spent several years in some sort of employment. His long-standing acquaintance with Gurt Fuchs gave a clue as to where. Gurt had been the first woman in whom Lang had shown any romantic interest since the death of his wife from cancer several years before the priest and the lawyer had gotten to know each other.

"*Capistrum maritale,*" Francis said with a smile, trying to make light of the matter.

"Fine for you to bewail the woes of matrimony. Not like that's a problem you'll ever have."

Francis reached across the table to lay a hand on his

friend's arm. "I'm sorry she left, Lang. I really am. You know how much I liked that woman."

"You and Grumps. I feel for both of you."

Lang was referring to the dog he had inherited when his sister and nephew died. He had not been able to part with what was arguably the world's ugliest mutt. The animal was the only part of his family left.

The waiter was removing the remnants of dinner. He must have been a recent hire or he would have known better than to ask, "All done? How was it?"

Francis simply gave him a blank stare.

"As always," Lang said. "Overcooked steak, raw hamburger. And I just love those limp, extra-greasy fries."

"Glad you enjoyed it." With the hand not holding the plates, he deposited the check on the table. "I'll take that when you're ready."

Lang picked it up. "I suppose we may as well follow the ritual."

The two men routinely flipped a coin to determine who would pay the tab. Lang could not remember ever winning. What were the odds of that?

Maybe Francis was right: There was a greater power.

Instead Francis reached for it. "Let me get this one."

"No, no. We'll toss for it. Always *post prandium*."

Lang lost.

Francis grinned. "*Manus e, nubibus.* A lucky break."

"I think the literal translation better describes it: 'A hand from the clouds.' The consistency with which you win is enough to convert most heathens."

"Including you?"

Lang handed the bill along with a credit card to the waiter. "I have faith, just not one that's centered on a pope."

"Or anything else, far as I can see."

"I believe in a higher power, right now the highest: Judge Adamson of the Atlanta division of the northern district of Georgia. Believe me, there *is* no power on earth mightier than a U.S. district court judge. If you don't believe me, ask Dick Nixon."

"He's dead."

"Okay, so you might have to wait awhile to ask."

The credit card receipt arrived and Lang signed it, adding an undeserved tip to ensure the same booth would be available next time.

"The mayor is being tried in federal court?"

Lang pushed back from the table and stood. "Unluckily for him, yes. The feds indicted him while the Fulton County DA was still thinking about the political ramifications."

The Fulton County district attorney's office was famous for mishandling its workload. Statutes of limitation expired while county lawyers searched for misplaced files or evidence. Felons walked free after exasperated judges waited for prosecutors to show up for trial.

Both men headed toward the rear door that opened onto the parking lot.

"Too bad," Francis observed. "You'll have an opponent instead of a victim."

Lang beeped the security device that unlocked a silver-gray Porsche Cabriolet. "You're right there. Trying a case with the local guy has gotten too easy anyway. Poor bastard couldn't have convicted John Wilkes Booth for discharging a firearm in public."

The priest folded himself into the car's passenger seat. "One of these days you'll get a grown-up car."

Lang turned the key and was rewarded by a muscular rumble from the rear-mounted engine. "I did. Remember the Mercedes convertible, the malfunction mobile—had everything from the burglar alarm to the power top not working?"

"At least it wasn't a toy. Seems to me a multijillion-dollar charitable foundation would want its president to have something a little more dignified to drive around in."

Lang was looking over his shoulder as he backed out of the parking spot. "You forget, my dear Francis, I *am* the foundation."

That was true. A few years previously Lang had demanded annual payment of millions of dollars from Pegasus, an international organization, as compensation for the murder of his sister and nephew. The money funded a charitable trust in their names. Although the trust had the directors and officers mandated by tax law, Lang made the decisions that mattered. The board did, however, serve two very important functions other than satisfying the IRS: It screened the needy from the greedy, and it kept secret who really made what choices. If Lang's solitary power became known, he would drown in a sea of mendicants.

FIVE

Peachtree Road
Atlanta, Georgia
Twenty Minutes Later

Lang had dropped Francis off and was within blocks of his high-rise condominium when the BlackBerry in his pocket chirped.

Has to be a criminal client, he thought. *The foundation pays its staff way too much for someone to call me at night.*

He fumbled in his pocket for the Bluetooth earpiece before remembering leaving it on the dresser in the bedroom. With a regretful sigh he thumbed a button, wedged the phone between cheek and shoulder, and gave a grudging, "Hello."

"Mr. Reilly? Langford Reilly?"

The voice was familiar, yet Lang couldn't quite place it. He downshifted as he approached a red light. The arm movement sent the phone slithering into his lap. Modern cell phones and classic stick-shift transmissions didn't mix. He plucked the phone out of his lap.

"Yes."

"Det. Franklin Morse, Atlanta Police, Mr. Reilly. Maybe you remember me."

Lang wished he didn't. More than once the detective had been summoned to Lang's home after some deadly misadventure. "Swell to hear from you again, Detective, but it's been a quiet night. Nobody's tried to kill me so far."

"Early yet. 'Sides, ain't you, Mr. Reilly. It's Dr. Lewis."

Lang drew a total blank. "Who?"

"Lewis, professor over to Georgia Tech."

The name finally came up in Lang's mental Rolodex just as the elusive phone slipped free again. The foundation had made a rare exception to its policy of endowing medical causes in the third world. It had provided funds to persuade a professor at Oxford to move to Tech his research on a promising alternative to fossil fuel. Lang had deviated from the norm at the request of Jacob Annueliwitz, a personal friend of both men in London. The results had been sufficiently promising that the foundation was currently sponsoring parallel research both in the United States and abroad.

He retrieved the phone before it could make its escape under the seat. "What happened?"

There was a pause. Lang could hear other voices in the background. "Too soon to know 'xactly, Mr. Reilly. 'Cept Lewis is dead. Since you th' man pays his research grant, thought you could maybe help. You come on, see fo' yo'self."

"Dead? But how . . . ?"

"Tell you what, Mr. Reilly; I'm at the man's laboratory right now. Know where that is?"

Lang had overseen the installation of some very expensive equipment there just a month or so ago.

"Yeah. Just off Hemphill Avenue."

"Right."

Georgia Tech liked red brick, a fact evident in buildings as diverse as its signature semi-Victorian bell tower and the newest ultramodern box of a classroom structure. Despite a few desperate trees, the campus looked just like what it was: an urban school in a shabby part of town. Unlike its neo-Gothic-styled, verdant rival, the University of Georgia, Tech had a blue-collar, hard-work ethic about it that included Saturday classes and a very high job-placement rate. Its only real failure was its football team, which had to play schools where three-hundred-pound tackles could major in athletic education and were not required to pass calculus.

A gaggle of police car lights sprayed a symphony of red, blue, and orange across the face of an otherwise anonymous brick building. The squawk of radios roiled in the night air.

Lang showed his driver's license to the cop blocking the door. The man murmured into the radio pinned to his blouse, and Morse appeared.

The black man's slender, athletic build made it hard to guess his age. Lang guessed he was somewhere in his forties, an assumption based more on his rank than his appearance. He reminded Lang of one of those East African runners who dominated marathon competitions. The detective was also far brighter than his lazy drawl indicated.

They shook hands.

"When did you transfer to this part of town?" Lang asked.

"Figgered this'd be a quieter beat, since you wasn't on it."

Lang grinned in spite of the circumstances. "Now who's wise-assin' somebody?"

Morse held up his right hand. "No wise-assin', true." He became serious again. "Reason I axed you down here was to see if anythin's missin'."

"How'd you know I had any connection to Dr. Lewis?"

"I'm a detective, remember? I detect stuff."

Perhaps a quick check of the school's records had revealed Lang's name on the grant.

Morse headed down a short hall. "This way."

The room they entered was filled with people. A woman and a man Lang took to be crime scene technicians were using what looked like an artist's brush to sweep shards of glass into small plastic bags. A man sat in front of a computer. Another, this one in police uniform, interviewed a man in the uniform of the school's security personnel. A woman was using her flashlight to study the pages of a loose-leaf notebook.

When Lang had last left the place, it had resembled a modernized version of Dr. Frankenstein's laboratory. Now it looked like it had hatched Hurricane Katrina instead of a humanoid monster. The only things in place were two long tables that would have been too heavy to move without a crew. Loose pages, perhaps from the notebook, were scattered on the floor, which crunched with broken glass as Lang walked. Microscopes and tools he didn't recognize were thrown about as though shaken in some huge blender. He saw a spectrophotometer lying on its side. The thing had cost the foundation as much as a pair of Ferraris.

"What the hell . . . ?"

Morse pointed to yet another man, who was photographing the chalk outline of a body sprawled across the floor. "We found him there. The rent-a-cop heard sounds like somebody was tryin' to take the place apart, came in, took one look, an' called us."

"Any idea who . . . ?"

"This ain't *Law 'n' Order*, where we solve the case in half an hour so the prosecutor can have the other half for a conviction between ads. Fact is, we don't even know yet what time the vic died. We're assumin' it was 'bout the time someone was trashing the place."

"Any motive?"

"That's why I called you, Mr. Reilly. Other'n the fact that you're involved in half the mayhem in this town, I figgered you might have an idea, since your foundation funded this operation."

It *had* been the grant. How had Morse gotten that information in the middle of the night?

"I only met the man two, three times."

"Awful lotta money to give a stranger."

"Dr. Lewis wasn't a stranger," Lang said stiffly. "He was an internationally respected physical chemist." Or was it a chemophysicist? "He was doing research on non-fossil fuels."

"You mean like gas substitutes, like ethanol to run cars?"

Lang's knowledge of chemistry and physics stopped at the composition of water and the law of gravity.

"I'm not sure."

"Not sure? You're mighty careless with a whole lot o' money, Mr. Reilly."

"The foundation hires people to manage how the money's spent, Detective, as well as how much each project legitimately needs and the qualifications of the people running those projects. I assure you, the foundation watches its money a lot closer than your employer does."

A safe guess. With ability to pay bribes being the former administration's only apparent qualification for selecting city contractors, and a tax department that could not be more incompetent if operated by Moe, Larry, and Curly, both the city and county were perpetually curtailing an ever-diminishing list of services. Those most in need of those services were, of course, those who didn't pay for them.

The only true beneficiary of the system was, or had been, Lang's client, the former mayor.

Morse held up his hands in surrender. "I'm just an employee doin' my job. Think I wouldn't like to see the mayor crucified for what he stole?"

Hopefully Morse would not be on the jury panel.

"Sorry, Detective, I . . ."

Another man entered the room. Even though he had never seen the newcomer, Lang knew who he was. Slender build in a medium-priced suit, shiny wingtips. Large, over six feet, mid-thirties. Dark hair cut slightly shorter than currently fashionable, and freshly shaved, as though he had put down his razor just before coming here. Or, more likely, had an electric shaver in his government-issued Ford or Chevy.

Lang had seen him hundreds of times in slightly differing sizes and shapes. This man, or one just like him, routinely testified against Lang's clients. The names changed but that special uniformity did not.

The cop at the door followed the new man in and pointed to Morse. The man stepped purposefully across the room. Lang thought he heard a "Shit!" from the detective.

The man held up a wallet with a badge attached to it. "Special Agent Charles Witherspoon, FBI."

He did not extend a hand to shake.

Neither did Morse. "A Fibbie. Now, ain't that a surprise, the bureau workin' such late hours? I woulda sworn he'd be from the funeral home they gonna take the vic to."

Either Special Agent Witherspoon was inured to the barbs of local cops or he wasn't clever enough to recognize them. "You are Det. Franklin Morse?"

Lang could see a wisecrack flash across the detective's mind, but Morse said, "Yep. What can I do for you, Agent Witherspoon, seein' as how this is purely a local matter?"

"I'm here to offer the bureau's complete and total assistance."

That, Lang knew, translated into a statement of intent to take the case over if any possible federal grounds for doing so could be found or, for that matter, created.

Witherspoon turned to Lang. "And you are?"

"He'd be head of the foundation that funds . . . funded Dr. Lewis's research," Morse said before Lang could reply. "The doctor was engaged in some sort of non-fossil fuel research. You know, like ethanol to run cars."

The federal man was clearly annoyed that Morse had taken over the interview, and Morse was just as clearly enjoying it. Lang would not have been totally surprised to see each man start urinating around the room to mark each square foot as his exclusive territory.

Disappointingly, no bodily functions ensued.

Instead Morse asked, "And just what can I thank for havin' the bureau's offer of assistance?"

Without so much as a flicker of a smile, Witherspoon replied, "National security."

"Based on what?" the detective asked.

"I'm not at liberty to say."

"Okay, then, how did you find out about a killin' so quick?"

"Again, I'm not at liberty to say."

Morse leaned back, stroking his chin as if in thought. "Lemme see here, now. You want to know whatever we find out, you're willin' to cooperate, but you ain't an-swerin' none o' my questions. That about it?"

Lang fully expected the same response about lack of liberty to say.

Instead Witherspoon gave a chilly smile. "Detective, you and I will get along a lot better if you simply tell me what the bureau can do."

Morse appeared to give the matter serious thought. "For starters, you can reduce the number o' folks standin' 'round the crime scene by one. Gimme your card an' I'll call soon's I figger what else you can do."

This time Witherspoon understood. "Mind if I look around?"

"Long's you don't touch anythin' an' don' git in the way o' my folks."

The G-man turned to Lang. "What do you know about Dr. Lewis?"

Lang shrugged, about to repeat what he had told Morse.

"Th' man was an internationally renowned scientist," the detective volunteered.

"Your foundation funds hospitals and medical services

in poor countries," Witherspoon said to Lang. "What made you deviate into supporting fuel research?"

Lang paused before answering, again surprised at how readily information was accessible day or night. "A friend in London suggested it, actually. He was a personal acquaintance of Dr. Lewis's. The people in charge of new grants checked him and his work out and decided that finding an alternative to fossil fuels was a worthy cause."

Witherspoon shot a quick glance to someone who was taking pictures of the wreckage. "Exactly what sort of alternative fuel was he working on?"

The question was almost a statement, without the inflection of real curiosity, as if Witherspoon either didn't care or already knew the answer.

"I'm not sure. He'd been here less than six months, so a detailed progress report wasn't due yet. If you're really interested, I can—"

The man who had been at the computer interrupted. "Detective, the hard drive's been taken, along with a dozen or so pages from his research log."

Morse's head bobbed slowly. "I'd say that eliminates the possibility of the perp bein' some junkie randomly lookin' for somethin' to steal to feed his habit."

"Don't be too sure, Detective." The man held up a plastic bag. Lang had to lean forward to see a trace of white powder.

Morse took the bag and held it up to the light. "Ain't coke. It's grainy, like crumbs from some sorta crystal." He rolled his eyes. "Don' tell me, Mr. Reilly, that your foundation's been runnin' the world's most sophisticated meth lab."

Lang shook his head. "Lewis wouldn't have needed all this equipment just to cook up methamphetamine."

"How would you know that?" Witherspoon asked.

"Mr. Reilly here does criminal defense when he ain't

givin' money away to worthy causes," Morse said. "I 'spect he done come across the process."

Actually, Lang had consistently refused to represent anyone associated with hard drugs, no matter how remotely or how high the fee. He did, however, watch the local news broadcasts that regularly showed arrests at meth labs, usually kitchens in private homes utilizing quite ordinary cookware and ingredients available at a neighborhood pharmacy.

Morse pocketed the envelope. "Whatever it is, we'll know soon's the state crime lab gits through with it."

"Our lab can test it sooner," Witherspoon proposed.

Morse slowly shook his head. "I 'preciate the offer, really do, Agent Witherspoon."

"But?"

"But a year or two ago I axed you guys fo' help in a shootin' connected to an interstate cocaine operation. Nex' thing I know, my perp is in your Witness Protection Program, off somewhere 'tween here 'n' Alaska. I done had more o' your help than I can stand."

Witherspoon's jaw muscles tightened. "That mean you're not gonna share that powder?"

"Agent Witherspoon, you're an unusually perceptive young man."

The federal agent looked around the room again, as though this time he might find an ally. "We'll see about that."

He turned and left.

Lang and Morse watched him go before Lang said, "The federal crime lab really is superior to anything the state has."

Morse nodded. "I know, but ever' time I hear somethin' 'bout 'national security,' I feel like I need to duck. Somebody's throwin' a load of bullshit."

Lang was well aware of the rivalry between the FBI and local law enforcement. The federal boys tended to do what made them look good at the expense of both the case and the locals.

He said, "As I was about to say before your man told us about the computer hard drive, someone at the foundation was monitoring Dr. Lewis's work. I'll find out exactly who, and he might be able to help you."

"I really 'preciate that, Mr, Reilly. 'Fore you go, though, could you tell if anythin's missin' 'sides the computer hard drive and notebook pages, anythin' you can notice?"

Lang shook his head. "Other than the really big equipment, the stuff that costs us a lot, I really wouldn't know. What I can do, though, is provide you with an inventory of the foundation's purchases for this project and let you compare it against what's here."

As he was getting into the Porsche, Lang was thinking how very strange it was to be cooperating with Morse. Three times before, the detective had appeared on Lang's doorstep, twice in response to a violent death and once to take him to jail. If you weren't a suspect, the cop really wasn't such a bad guy.

More important, though, was the question of what relationship there was between the scientist's death and national security. What was the FBI's interest in what appeared to be a local crime? How had they found out about it almost as fast as the Atlanta police?

Lang yawned widely as he headed north on Northside Drive. For every mystery, there was a solution.

Make that *most* mysteries.

SIX

Park Place
2660 Peachtree Road
Atlanta, Georgia
The Next Morning

Grumps, the fur-bearing alarm clock, pressed his cold nose against Lang's cheek. If a dog could actually smile, this one would have laughed as his master ran a hand across his sleep-relaxed face.

"Okay, Grumps. Just another couple of minutes, all right?"

Grumps knew the game. This time he growled deeply and began methodically removing the covers.

Lang sat up. "Okay, okay, you win, as always."

The clear victor, Grumps sat and began to casually scratch his head with a rear paw. Black, with one floppy ear and the other erect, the dog had genes that contained more breeds than there were types of rum in tropical drinks.

From his bedroom window on the twenty-fourth floor, Lang could see the morning sun tinting the glass of Midtown's buildings with gold. The older structures of downtown even glowed. Like an urban yellow brick road, Peachtree Street seemed like an arrow pointing to the heart of the city. A cloudless sky roofed the vivid green of trees still in their early spring colors. The verdant carpet was dotted with splotches of snowdrifts that were dogwoods in full bloom above pink-and-white azaleas.

All of this natural beauty had a price that Lang would pay as soon as he exited the protective lobby of his building. Slimy yellow-green mist would color the air outside as well as every surface exposed to it. Cars became yellow, no matter their factory paint jobs. Black asphalt was tinted the same with dry rivers. Transplanted allergy sufferers cursed the day they left the relative comfort of Northern spring freezes.

Spring had come and reproductive romance was on the mind of every living plant, from mighty oak to tiny ragweed. Atlanta's pollen season was in full swing.

By the time Lang had pulled on a sweat suit and stuck bare feet into a pair of sneakers, Grumps was waiting anxiously by the door, leash in mouth. Outside, the dog made his usual methodical search for the perfect place to leave his mark for the next canine to come along. Once finished, he tugged impatiently to return. It was time for breakfast.

Back inside, Lang opened the cabinet where he stored the dog food and poured some into a bowl.

Only as he was returning the bag did he stop in midreach and stare.

He had fed Grumps last night just before he left to go to Manuel's. The dog food bag had been next to a cereal box. Now there was space for it only next to a stack of soup cans.

He carefully set the bag on the counter that separated the tiny kitchen from the living room. In three steps he was standing in front of the Thomas Elfe secretary, a masterpiece in mahogany and fruitwood inlay by one of America's premier prerevolutionary cabinetmakers and one of the few pieces of furniture he had taken when he sold the house he had shared with Dawn.

Behind the wavy handblown glass, his small collection

of eighteenth- and nineteenth-century first editions seemed to be as he had left them. Below, on the writing surface, though, his few antiquities had been slightly re-arranged. The time-rusted iron that had been the hilt of a Macedonian sword was now next to the Etruscan votive cup rather than the coin bearing the likeness of Augustus Caesar.

Someone had moved the objects to open the glass and look at the books. Or more likely to see if anything was concealed behind them.

Or to look through the bills aligned in the brass letter holder awaiting payment.

Five quick strides carried him into the remaining room of the small condo and in front of his bedside table. Eas-ing its drawer open, he saw the SIG Sauer P226 was as he had left it, two extra clips loaded and right beside it.

It was one of the few things he had taken with him when the fall of the Evil Empire heralded a reduction of force across the intelligence community. The next gener-ation would speak Arabic instead of Slavic languages and would do business in hot, dry places where scorpi-ons were common.

Except for one potentially disastrous trip behind the Berlin Wall, Lang's duties had never taken him from his station in the grimy building across the street from the Frankfurt am Main Hauptbahnhof. He had been with the Third Directorate, intel, where he spent his days scan-ning newspapers from Iron Curtain countries and watch-ing replays of government-sponsored talking heads reading the fiction that passed for news in the Marxist world.

Do not listen to the news broadcast from the imperialist Western democracies, only that approved by the State; the life you save might be your own.

His one experience in real enemy territory had cured forever his resentment at having not been chosen for ops, Fourth Directorate, those romantic, James Bond swashbucklers of popular fiction. Truth was, they were nuts to take the chances they did.

Informational bureaucrat though he had been, he still took the weapon issued every new graduate of the Agency's training school in Virginia, the Farm.

He looked at it as he might have gazed on his high school letter jacket, a relic of a distant time . . . if he hadn't swapped the jacket in the backseat of a borrowed Ford for the purported chastity of . . .

Her name was lost to antiquity.

Other than requisite training, he had never even fired the weapon. Years after leaving the Agency, he had shot a man with the assailant's own gun, a matter of self-defense, and he had killed another, also to preserve his own life.

Ironically, neither was with the firearm he was given for the purpose.

Out of the Agency, he had applied for and been accepted to law school, viewing the profession as just one more form of the chicanery practiced by the Agency. Grateful he was separated from employment she considered dangerous no matter how many times he explained, Dawn had supported him until he graduated.

In spite of exemplary grades, he never considered working in one of the law factories. He went into practice on his own.

His shadowy government contacts steered a certain clientele his way: a Columbian importer who had helped the Agency but had been arrested for intent to distribute the cocaine surprisingly found in his coffee shipments, an officer of a foreign bank who had simply misunderstood U.S. Treasury reporting requirements by a few million dollars.

Not like it was real money, the man had explained in an interview the day of his acquittal due to the government's inability to locate a key witness. The same witness, Lang later learned, who had chosen the week of the trial to avail himself of the use of a yacht cruising the Greek Isles. Lang had no desire to know the name of the boat's owner.

His practice flourished, and he and Dawn hoped for a child until a tumor appeared on an X-ray, stabbing into her vital parts. The end was mercifully quick for her, devastating to him. Years later he never missed a holiday placement of roses on the grave on the hill under the big oak tree, a site that now included the rest of what family he had had.

Lang left the automatic in the drawer and turned to the laptop computer that sat on a small table next to the bed. He clicked it on and punched a series of keys. The last time it had been on was 9:27 the night before.

But he had been at Manuel's then.

A few more taps revealed that the password had withstood several attempts before the machine had shut down as programmed.

Frowning, he reached for a bedside phone. "Harvey, what time did you take Grumps out last night?"

Harvey, the building concierge, not only enjoyed making a few extra bucks walking or feeding Grumps in Lang's absence; he actually liked the dog.

"Dunno 'xactly, Mr. Reilly. He was full of piss 'n' ginger, so we went for a long 'un. Here to Peachtree Battle, Rivers Road, back to West Wesley. Maybe half an hour, maybe more. I do anything wrong?"

"No," Lang said. "Nothing. Just curious."

The route would have taken a half hour at least, more if Grumps had insisted on exploring every smell he encountered.

Lang sat down on the bed, listening to the crunch of dog food from the kitchen. Someone had tossed the place, no doubt about it. The method had been different but the purpose was the same as whoever had killed Lewis.

Or was it?

The destruction and disarray of the laboratory had been intended to look like a random invasion. What was it Morse had said? A junkie looking to feed a habit. Yet the missing hard drive and notebook pages belied the scenario the killer had wanted believed.

Lang's condominium had been searched by a professional, someone after something very specific. Someone who didn't intend Lang to know.

Or someone leaving something behind.

Standing, he crossed his condo back and forth, removing every switch plate and the cover for every electrical outlet.

He found it in the telephone's receiver. It was a device about the size of the battery for a hearing aid. Not only every word spoken on the phone would be transmitted, but every sound in the apartment as well. He suppressed his rage at the invasion of his personal space and his gut reaction to remove it. Instead he left it in place.

It might be useful.

Before he left, Lang took two hairs from his head. Licking his finger, he stuck the first one to the top of the knob on the door that let out onto the common hallway. The second he put on the underside. Both would fall off at the slightest touch. Any professional would expect the possibility that he had left a telltale and would replace it.

Not many would anticipate a second.

SEVEN

Peachtree Center
227 Peachtree Street
Atlanta, Georgia
Thirty Minutes Later

As usual, Sara was already at her desk outside his office when Lang walked in. He frowned as he took the stack of pink call slips.

"The mayor said it was important," she called after him.

It always was.

To the mayor.

Unable to find work with any Atlanta firm amid the very public federal investigation at the end of his term, the mayor had joined a personal-injury group in South Florida where mere suspicion would go unnoticed among the indigenous sleaze.

But the mayor had not moved far enough away to prevent micromanagement of his defense with daily multiple phone calls and at least one trip to Lang's office per month.

The note said the mayor wanted to discuss the tax-evasion counts, possibly the toughest to beat. If you spent it, you presumably had it. Explaining the source of large sums of cash was likely to be embarrassing if not incriminating. The mayor's credit cards reflected less than a thousand dollars a year charged in spite of a publicly flamboyant lifestyle. The gambling trips, the gifts, the dinners had been paid for in cash. Cash was both untraceable and suspect. The excuse of weekly poker games in some crony's basement wasn't going to satisfy the U.S. Attorney. Those proceeds hadn't been reported, either.

The mayor blamed the failure to declare the money on his personal inability to keep adequate books. The government blamed it on his personal inability to keep his hands out of any funds being paid to contractors by the city.

The mayor's salary had been $110,000 per year. In his last twelve months in office he had taken a trip to Paris, half a dozen junkets to Las Vegas, and enjoyed very expensive seats at both the Super Bowl and the NBA All-Star Game—all paid for with cash. And he had used cash to purchase a few trinkets such as jewelry and clothing for various female companions, none of whom had been his wife.

Neither fidelity nor frugality was among the mayor's attributes.

When asked about the former by an ever-voracious press, the mayor's comment had been, "But I never missed one of my son's basketball games."

Swell. A father-of-the-year award was not a defense.

Lang wadded the pink slip and sank a three-pointer into the wastebasket beside Sara's desk.

He was almost through returning his other calls when Sara stood impatiently in his doorway.

Lang covered the receiver. "What?"

"There's a man from the FBI here to see you, a Mr. Witherspoon."

Odd.

With the arrogance that had persisted since the Hoover days, the Fibbies usually summoned people to their offices. He guessed Witherspoon wanted something.

He was right.

Before he had settled into the leather wing chair but after declining Sara's offer of coffee, Witherspoon asked, "I'd like to see a list of all persons in your organization who were reviewing Dr. Lewis's work or who might be familiar with it."

Lang thought a moment. Past experience was that the Federal Bureau of Investigation did not necessarily hire the brightest souls, but they did insist on mind-numbing thoroughness. A series of interviews of the foundation's personnel could last months, not even accounting for the duplication of whatever Morse might do.

"Detective Morse asked for the same thing. I'm sure he'll share his interview notes with you along with whatever information he gathers."

Witherspoon's eyes narrowed slightly, and he didn't move in the chair. "Detective Morse is being less than cooperative with federal authorities."

Good for him.

Lang leaned forward to put his elbows on the desk. "Please understand, Agent Witherspoon, by the time the Atlanta police get through interviewing whoever was monitoring Dr. Lewis's work and you question them again, my employees will have lost considerable time from work."

"Time loss is not a consideration in a federal investigation."

Or any other government endeavor.

Lang eased back in his chair and intertwined his fingers. This little piggy was perfectly at ease no matter how hard the big, bad wolf huffed and puffed. "I'm sure that's true. But then, you don't *have* a federal investigation, do you? I mean, only a few murders—killing someone on federal land, terrorism, for instance—are federal crimes."

Witherspoon's eyes flicked to the law degree on the wall next to Lang's desk. "I think I said we're dealing with national security here."

Lang could not have explained or defined it—the man's overbearing nature, the claim of national security that the Cold War had worn thin as a slice of delicatessen ham. There was something about Witherspoon that was the mental equivalent of seafood, glassy-eyed and with a slight aroma, that the fishmonger swore was fresh.

"I suppose if I asked how national security was involved, you'd tell me you weren't at liberty, et cetera."

The FBI man nodded. "I'm sure you understand."

Far better than you think, Lang mused. In his day "national security" was the intelligence community's equivalent to making sausage: The fewer people who knew the ingredients, the better.

"You know I can get a warrant, search all your records," Witherspoon added, making no effort to conceal the threat.

"No, I don't know. No federal crime, no warrant. No matter what you may think of the post-nine-eleven security laws, we still have a Constitution." Lang stood, extending a hand. "It's been a pleasure."

Witherspoon glared at the proffered hand and stormed out the door without another word.

Sara watched him go before leaving her desk. "He looked angry."

"That'd be a good guess."

"What did you do?"

"Do? Why, I insisted on my Fourth Amendment rights."

"Hardly seems a reason to leave in a huff."

"Hardly," Lang agreed.

He thought a moment. "Sara, would you please get the number for the FBI's Atlanta special agent in charge? I seem to remember his name as Murphy or something like that."

A few minutes later she buzzed him with the number. "And his name is O'Neil."

Lang shrugged and punched in the number.

It took a minimum of chitchat with O'Neil's gatekeeper before O'Neil came on the line. "If you're calling about the prosecution of the mayor, Mr. Reilly, you need to go through the U.S. Attorney's office."

"I'm not, but thanks," Lang hastened to say. "I'm calling about one of your agents, a Charles Witherspoon. Guy seems to be investigating a murder, and I see no federal connection. I don't mind cooperating but—"

"Who?"

"Witherspoon, Charles Witherspoon."

There was such a long pause, Lang feared the connection had been severed.

"Mr. Reilly, you sure this Charles Witherspoon is with the Atlanta office of the bureau?"

"I'm sure he said he was."

"You asked for ID?"

Lang was getting a weird feeling somewhere around the bottom of his stomach, like maybe something he'd eaten was about to seek revenge. "He showed it. Looked okay to me, and I've seen a lot of 'em."

"I'm sure you have."

Another pause.

"Mr. Reilly, I'll come straight to the point. No Charles Witherspoon works out of this office."

Lang barely heard the other man ask for a description and request an immediate call if the mysterious Mr. Witherspoon reappeared.

He spent a full minute staring at the phone after he had hung up.

* * *

Book of Jereb

Chapter One

1. And after the death of Amenhotep III the son of the king became pharaoh until Moses was cast out of the house of pharaoh and sent into Sinai, where he remained for seven years. And on behalf of the Israelites, he pleaded with the new pharaoh to free the Israelites.

2. But Pharaoh's heart was hardened against Moses, and he said unto him, "Why do you seek to take from me my people, who are the makers of brick and harvesters of wheat?" And Moses answered, "It is the will of the one God." Whereupon Pharaoh became angry and would not permit Moses to look upon him again until great misfortune had befallen all of Egypt.

3. Then Pharaoh called Moses unto him and said, "Give me proof your single god can lift from us these afflictions which our gods will not." Whereupon the priests of Pharaoh cried, "Lord, the god of the Israelites is but one while ours are legion. Tell us, how can one god defeat all others, for are they not all gods?"

4. Moses said unto them, "Show me that power your gods hath given you and the one God shall be mightier than all of them." Whereupon Pharaoh's priests threw down their staffs, which became serpents of great size so that Pharaoh cried out, "Have you brought vipers unto me so that I might perish?"

5. But Moses feared not but threw down his staff also and it became a serpent smaller than the others, but it devoured each of them in turn until none was left before Pharaoh.

6. And Pharaoh had seen what had happened and said to his priests, "Is not the god of Moses more powerful than your gods? Are not those of our people who worship this god made powerful thereby? Should we not do as Moses asks?"And the priests had no answer.

7. And so Moses said to the Israelites, "Gather your children and your wives. Take with you your asses, sheep, and other animals, for God has granted us Pharaoh's mercy and we shall leave Egypt."

8. But when Pharaoh saw how many Israelites were to depart Egypt and saw the labors that thereby would be undone, his heart became as a stone and he sent soldiers to stop the Israelites from going forth. And Moses came to him, saying, "You have decreed that the Israelites may go forth from Egypt but now you say not."And Pharaoh answered, "I do as does a god, for is not Pharaoh a god also?" And Moses went away angry but there was naught he could do.

9. And Moses went forth into the desert for forty days, during which time he spoke with the one God. And the one God directed him to a mountain where the Egyptians and their slaves labored both day and night to make great wonders with gold, some of which Moses took with him and returned to Egypt to again plead with Pharaoh.

10. And Pharaoh heard Moses and let the Israelites go forth into the desert before he again hardened his heart against the Israelites.

* * *

2

EIGHT

Peachtree Center
227 Peachtree Street
Atlanta, Georgia
11:40 EST

Lang had a lunch date.

Since Gurt's departure he had resisted the overtures of the predatory single women in his condo building. Divorced, they uniformly decried the size of their alimony checks and the injustice of their prenups while refusing to seek gainful employment. Instead they prowled Buckhead's better spas, restaurants, and social events like coyotes at the edge of a campfire. They searched endlessly for lifestyle support systems in the form of eligible men. No wealthy male was exempt. Age or infirmity of the prey was no detriment, as both potentially shortened the wait before inheritance. Many of these ladies had been trade-ins on newer models, another cruel twist of fate, but one that had paid dividends in increased settlements.

Lang was that most desirable game: wealthy, and without the inconvenience of greedy heirs.

Lang had withstood the siege like a well-fortified castle.

A week ago he had met Alicia Warner, and cracks had appeared in the wall of the keep.

A recent addition to the U.S. Attorney's staff, she had

moved to Atlanta from Denver and what she minimized as an "unpleasant" divorce.

Were there pleasant ones?

A person was more likely to enjoy a root canal.

Lang pressed for no details and she did not reveal any. They had started with sharing a coffee break at the federal courthouse and met for drinks after work.

She was refreshingly cautious; he was in no hurry.

He was busy; she was more interested in her career than in a second husband.

They were circling each other like two animals claiming the same turf.

Lang was going to make his move today: He would ask her for a real, no-kidding, adult-type date, like going to a real restaurant, where, perhaps, they would discuss something other than the criminal justice system.

Lang was not timid by nature, but the possibility of facing rejection from this woman filled him with more dread than did the several attempts that had been made on his life in the last few years. Of course, in the past he hadn't had time to brood before an assassin appeared with a knife, or a shadow government's bomb destroyed his car.

He checked his watch and pushed back from his desk. He went down the hall to the men's restroom, where he combed hair that was already in place, ran a hand over cheeks still smooth from the morning's shave, and grimaced for the mirror, checking teeth that had touched nothing since being brushed.

Although he had never served as a regular in ops, the Agency had preached to its agents to check their equipment, recheck it, and then check it again.

Training or nerves?

He straightened an already perfectly centered tie, shrugged on his tailored suit jacket, and headed for the elevators.

Other than fast-food chains and hotels, downtown Atlanta could boast of few places to have lunch. Once the office workers fled to the suburbs, the streets became the domain of druggies and beggars, the first unsightly and the second overly aggressive. Other pedestrian traffic consisted of hotel guests with great courage or greater ignorance of the city and the few hardy urban pioneers who insisted on going about their nocturnal business even if they had to step over sleeping bodies in doorways and ignore loud and accusatory panhandling.

The homeless and the needy, as termed by the politically correct, were, however, voters and therefore impervious to efforts to remove them.

Understandably, most restaurants were located in somewhat more upscale areas.

One of the few brave eateries was located in Underground, a section of the city that had been bridged by a succession of viaducts over the late nineteenth-century railroads, leaving the first floor of many old buildings subterranean.

In the late sixties and early seventies, a village of unique restaurants and bars had moved in, bringing a nightlife downtown had never seen before. Ever watchful of possible revenue, the city had subsequently taken over, with a predictable decline into low-end apparel and tacky souvenir shops, a succession of chain restaurants, and an equally foreseeable black hole of taxpayer money.

Former habitués stayed away in droves.

But the place was within walking distance, roughly between the federal building and Lang's office, and the day was warm and sunny. He stepped out with a brisk walk, futilely hoping to outdistance persistent street people. He ignored the hands shoved at him as mercilessly as microphones jabbed by the press at a celebrity or newly bereaved relative of a disaster victim.

Most of the beggars had cell phones on their belts.

Was there a panhandlers' network, exchanging the time, place, and description of easy marks?

One kept pace with him, insisting he had been robbed and only needed bus fare to get home. The story would have been convincing had the same mendicant not made the same pitch last week. It would also have helped had the man's breath not reeked of MD 20/20. At $2.75 a half pint, it was downtown Atlanta's most popular fine wine.

Lang reached the Five Points MARTA station, its entrance transformed into a shabby North African bazaar. Stands displayed everything from fresh fruit to pirated rap CDs. Two tall, suited black men preached from the pages of the Bibles they held. Passengers streamed by, unconcerned that the end was at hand and damnation certain.

As Lang turned left to enter Underground, he noticed one stand's potential customer, a man in an overcoat and watch cap who seemed occupied with an arrangement of fruit juices.

Although Lang had left the Agency almost two decades earlier, its training had become habit, as natural as sleeping or eating. Anomalies were like a missed note in a symphony: a scruffy car in an upscale neighborhood, someone running away from, rather than toward, the sound of a burglar alarm.

The day was far too warm for the coat and cap.

Possibly the man had already scored enough cash to feed whatever pharmaceutical demons he snorted, smoked, or shot up. He could well believe he was in an arctic winter.

But Lang didn't think so.

Addicts tended to move at a less animated pace, if they moved at all. This man appeared to be in a lively argument with the stand's owner.

Lang was fairly certain the man had been among those who had pounced with demands for money as soon as

Lang had reached the sidewalk in front of his building. He was the only one clothed against cold weather in late April.

Lang watched as the discussion broke off and Overcoat headed toward him. Their gaze met briefly. Lang did not see a rheumy-eyed, slack-jawed face of society's jetsam. Instead Overcoat stood erect, without the slump of an ordained loser. He was young, his beard stubble no more than a day or two old at most.

Lang had the impression that the man was going to say something to him. Instead he veered off and turned a corner.

Not surprisingly Lang had his selection of tables at the restaurant. He chose one looking down the street of old facades decorated with the carvings popular in the 1890s. He could also see two bag ladies and a street vendor of indeterminate sex who seemed to be selling used clothes.

Alicia waved to him as she arrived at the maître d's stand. Lang stood and pulled out a chair.

"Glad you could make it," he said as she straightened her skirt and sat.

She smiled up at him as he returned to his own chair. "Now, why would I miss charming company and an enjoyable lunch?"

"You've obviously never eaten here before."

"That bad?"

"Depends."

She looked over the top of her menu. "On what?"

"Whether you order anything that requires more culinary skill than throwing something on the grill." He glanced at his own menu. "I don't remember any complaints about the lunch salads, either."

"Burger or salad. You really know how to fill lunch with excitement."

He had forgotten the sarcasm that characterized her conversations.

Lang looked up, anticipating the waiter's approach. Instead he saw Overcoat striding across the restaurant floor.

"Look here," the maître d' sputtered. "You can't—"

Overcoat turned, taking something metallic from his pocket.

Lang could not see the object, but when the officious maître d' made a dive for the swinging kitchen door, he could easily guess what it was.

Even more easily could he guess where Overcoat was headed. There were no other diners.

The gun came up in Overcoat's hand, its muzzle a black hole staring directly at Lang.

Later he remembered thinking the weapon was huge. But then, almost any gun grew in size when pointed directly at the observer.

Before the pistol could be fired, Lang moved.

In a single motion he slammed his shoulder into Alicia, knocking her out of her chair, clearing their table, and propelling both of them under an adjacent one.

Two shots filled the dining room with ear-pressing roars. Lang was only marginally aware of the thump of bullets on the tabletop between him and the gunman, of the acrid smell of cordite and a scream from somewhere in the direction in which the maître d' had disappeared.

He was completely aware of footsteps retreating at a deliberate pace. He took a cautious peek over the tabletop. Overcoat was gone.

He extended a hand to Alicia. "You okay?"

"Yeah, fine."

She stood on legs that seemed none too stable, ruefully contemplating a run in her hose and a stain on her skirt that indicated the cap on some condiment on the table had not been screwed on tight. "Next time I make a wise-ass remark about lunch being filled with excitement, wash my mouth out, will you?"

Confident that all danger had passed and the police had been summoned, the waitstaff appeared in a solicitous group.

"Lunch is on the house," the maître d' announced. "You're gonna have to stay here until the cops arrive, anyway."

Lang looked at Alicia. "How 'bout it?"

"Since we have to wait, we may as well."

Lang had expected Morse. He got two bored uniforms. Apparently near misses weren't worth the detective's time. One cop carefully filled in a form that Lang knew from experience covered everything from murder to auto theft and would soon vanish into the department's clerical maw, where it would be filed away or lost, forgotten in either event. He was not surprised when one of the officers found an overcoat and watch cap in the alley outside; nor did he have any trouble identifying them as the ones worn by the assailant.

When the police had filled out every line on the report and left, lunch arrived.

Lang sampled his chicken Caesar salad. "Maybe this place's not as bad as I recalled."

Alicia grinned, showing perfect teeth. "Not bad, but I wouldn't recommend the floor show. That guy a former client? Must be real unhappy. Would have been easier to go to the state bar and complain."

"My former clients are either satisfied or in jail. I've never seen that one before."

She toyed with her fork as if trying to summon an appetite. "Then why would he want to kill you?"

He didn't, Lang almost said. At that range he could have effortlessly done so. Overcoat was simply delivering a warning.

But about what?

NINE

Lang's day deteriorated further.

He suspected it would as soon as he entered his suite of offices and saw Sara's face.

"Louis deVille called from Brussels. The Belgian police contacted him to confirm that Benjamin Yadish worked for us. He was murdered in Belgium last night," she announced.

It took Lang a moment to recall the name. "Isn't he one of the physiochemists working on the foundation's alternatives-to-fossil-fuel program?"

"That's him. He was in Brussels to meet with the European project manger. Apparently he decided to drive to Bruges for some reason. That's where he was shot."

"Any information, like who or why?"

"None yet."

Lang had never met the man, but his credentials were emerging from his memory. "Lived in Amsterdam, didn't he?"

Sara had a file open in front of her. She nodded. "Wife, no children."

Lang put down the stack of pink callback slips he had picked up from her desk. "He's the one who has a degree from just about every university in Western Europe, right?"

"That's the one."

Lang went into his office and closed the door before he reached for the phone and punched 011 for international, 32 for Belgium, 2 for Brussels, and seven numbers for the person. He checked his watch as the line bleeped and peeped. Well after 1900—seven p.m.—on the other end of the line, but he was calling one of the few remaining European countries where employees worked with both eyes on the task at hand rather than one on the clock.

" 'Allo?"

Relieved, Lang sat back in his chair. "Louis, it's Lang Reilly."

The voice, heavily French accented, sounded pleased to hear from Lang so soon. Perhaps deVille had forgotten Americans had no aversion to work, either. "*Oui*, Monsieur Reilly. Your secretary has told you of the terrible thing that has happened, no?"

Louis deVille was in charge of the foundation's European research and operations. An administrator rather than a scientist, he had the ability to unwind the varying degrees of red tape spun by individual countries. He also had a talent for recruiting the better minds in whatever field the foundation sought at any given time. Since Brussels was the seat of the European Union's economic and political arms as well as the site of the European office of hundreds of multinational corporations, locating the foundation's overseas office there had seemed natural.

"Sara said he was in Bruges and was shot. What else can you tell me?"

"The police have told me nothing more."

"Okay, get hold of his wife in Amsterdam, find out if we can be of any help, maybe expedite the return of the body, funeral expenses, any cash shortage, stuff like that."

Lang thought for a moment, dark clouds forming a pattern he could see only vaguely. "And I'll be in Brussels no later than the day after tomorrow."

First Yadish, then Lewis, followed by a clear threat. The foundation's research was making someone unhappy. Very unhappy.

But who?

It had been two years since Lang had faced real danger, two years of defending those who could afford to pay to evade justice, two years of administering a foundation that did tremendous good but offered little in the way of excitement. Even if Lang was no longer a member of the shadowy intelligence community, he wasn't without experience and assets, either. Whoever had killed those two men hadn't known that; he was sure.

They were about to find out.

"Sara, I'm taking a few days off. Tell whoever calls that I should be back in a week."

She looked up. "And the mayor?"

"Particularly the mayor."

TEN

Lang supposed others might find the ritual macabre, but he really didn't care. He rarely left the country without coming here to the oak-shaded knoll where three marble stones faced a city skyline already blurred by summer's smog. He was never sure if the trip to say good-bye again to the three people he had so loved was a habit or some ritual to ensure a safe journey.

It didn't matter; he came.

Dawn, his wife; Janice, his sister; and Jeff, her adopted son and Lang's best ten-year-old buddy. There had been times when the tears flowed on a daily basis at the thought of his wife dying as she was devoured by cancer, or of the murderous explosion that had taken the other two. Now there was a certain peace to be had here among the silent inhabitants, a few moments to think without intrusion. It was the only place where he was immune to the demands of his profession and those of the foundation.

There had been a time when the two newer graves had commanded him to seek out an organization of killers. He had known he would know no rest until he did.

Beside two of the headstones he had placed the customary dozen roses like sacrifices on a pagan altar. By Jeff's marker were sunflowers. The kid had been fascinated by the gold petals around a face as brown as his own. It had never occurred to Lang that they would serve as Jeff's funerary decoration.

He sat on the dry grass, momentarily thinking of the uncertainties that constituted life. He watched an elderly woman in black lean on a cane as she hobbled up the hill followed by a chauffeur carrying gardening tools. He guessed she was headed for the azalea bushes a few plots over.

He stayed a few more minutes, until the clacking of hedge clippers and the woman's voice reached him. Then he stood, facing the three stones, saying farewell to the only family he had had. He turned and walked down the gentle slope where the Porsche waited on the narrow curving road.

He swiveled his head for a last look up the hill before he drove away.

ELEVEN

Brussels International Airport
Zaventem, Belgium
The Next Morning

Lang Reilly stretched and yawned as he sat up on the double bed in the main suite of the foundation's Gulfstream IV. Despite a dinner served on fine china along with a bottle of a fine old Bordeaux, despite a first-run comedy on DVD for after-dining entertainment and several brandies, he doubted he had had two hours of sleep. Lang simply did not sleep well on airplanes. The time when the very spooling up of engines lulled him had been replaced by an irrational fear of not having control of his environment. He had told himself the odds were better of being crushed in the Porsche by an SUV-driving, cell phone–talking soccer mom than of dying in the finest private jet yet produced, equipped with the most modern avionics.

Still, his stubborn phobia whispered, flying was an unnatural act.

Like submitting to a colonoscopy.

His irrational and rational minds had battled the issue while he tossed and turned. They had reached a temporary truce only minutes away from the destination.

Pulling aside the curtain over the bedroom's window, Lang saw a huge arched glass structure. Concourses extended both left and right, half of which were suckling aircraft from a potpourri of nations.

"We'll be at customs in about five minutes, Mr. Reilly." The pilot's tinny voice echoed through the plane's speaker system.

Lang scrambled into the tiny head and squeezed into the shower. He was tying his shoes when the twin Pratt & Whitneys whined down and stopped.

He could have taken a commercial carrier at considerably less expense. Considerably less privacy, too. It took little talent to hack into the airlines' reservations systems and ascertain the arrival time and destination of a flight. Although the same could be done with the flight plans of private aircraft, the task could be complicated by filing a seperate plan for multiple legs of the journey, exactly why Lang had insisted on intermediate stops in New York and London, even though the Gulfstream was capable of making the trip nonstop.

There was also the matter of metal detectors, devices the SIG Sauer P226 would not pass through unnoticed. He was here to investigate the circumstances of one of two likely related murders. Being armed seemed only prudent. He jacked the action open, verifying there was a shell in the chamber, and released the clip to assure it was full, giving him a total of thirteen nine-millimeter parabellum bullets. He made sure the safety was on, pocketed two additional magazines, and stuffed the automatic into a holster on the back of his belt and covered it with a light windbreaker.

Next he stepped back into the head. He slid to his right the mirror over the aluminum sink, revealing a shallow hiding place. He took out a stack of hundred-euro bills and counted out ten before replacing the remaining money and easing the glass back into place. He stuffed the cash into a pocket.

Looking out of the window again, Lang noted wet tarmac and a steady drizzle beading on the Plexiglas. The aircraft's clamshell doors sighed open as an official car pulled up. Lang knew the crew would offer coffee and breakfast pastries to the customs officers, giving him slightly more time to get dressed than he needed.

After a brief greeting in his halting French to the two uniformed inspectors, Lang had his passport stamped, and deplaned while the arrival paperwork was being finished by the crew. His single bag would be delivered to his hotel.

At the bottom of the stairs a long, black, customized Mercedes waited, its exhaust pluming in the chilly air. It was the car the foundation used to meet VIPs. With tinted windows and a roll-up glass partition between the driver's position and the six passenger seats, it assured the privacy desirable for meetings en route to meetings.

It also would have been at home at a Mafia funeral.

Once headed southwest into the city, Lang let the metronome-like windshield wipers lull him into near sleep. Through half-closed eyes he noted street signs in both French and Flemish. The northern, Flemish part of the country had its linguistic and cultural roots in the nearby Netherlands and Germany, while the southern Walloons were similarly connected to France. In 1962 the country legally recognized what had been true for centuries and officially made Belgium linguistically schizophrenic. French was still the tongue of Brussels, however, rather than the guttural, consonant-rich Flemish.

The clutter surrounding the airport thinned, and the Mercedes accelerated smoothly to a speed Lang was certain exceeded whatever applicable limit was in place. He watched the countryside roll by with near-hypnotic sameness. Its flat character had been both blessing and curse: easy and rich to cultivate but an ideal invasion route between the sea and the rolling hills of the Ardennes since Roman times. Nearby, Wellington had vanquished Napoleon for the final time, and the German army had passed through twice to attack France in the first half of the last century.

Lang suddenly became fully awake.

The airport was less than ten miles from town, yet he saw little but fields and shallow farm canals.

He leaned forward to tap on the glass. "Excuse me, but I'm staying in the Lower Town. In the city."

If the driver heard, he paid no attention.

Lang pushed the button that lowered the glass.

Nothing happened.

He tested one of the doors. The handle was frozen.

Locked.

Shit!

He had made the mistake that had doomed more than one employee of the Agency: He had assumed. He had assumed that the car and driver were both sent by the foundation. There was little doubt the car was the same. But who was driving?

His hand touched the butt of the SIG Sauer in its holster. Even though the glass wasn't bulletproof, shooting the driver of a car hurtling along at nearly a hundred miles an hour did not seem wise. There was little to do but sit back, even if he was unlikely to enjoy the ride.

Twenty minutes later the car decelerated and exited the four-lane for a narrow farm road. It slowed even more before turning onto a rutted dirt path. There were buildings half a mile away. Cows grazed in a pasture, oblivious to the misting rain. Had it not been for a picture-postcard windmill, the scene could have come from rural America.

The Mercedes stopped in front of a small structure of gray limestone. Lang guessed it was a dwelling. The driver got out and trotted inside, leaving Lang in the car.

He did not have to wait long. The driver and two burly men carrying weapons approached. As they got closer, Lang recognized the armament: Heckler & Koch MP5s, the A3 model with the folding stocks of metal rather than plastic. The banana clips carried thirty rounds. The weapon was an international favorite of police in hostage-rescue operations, where close-range accuracy was most desirable, although you really didn't have to be a marksman to hit your target if you didn't care who or what else got shot. With firepower of over eight hundred nine-millimeter parabellum rounds a minute, those guns could fill a fairly large space with a lot of lead.

The newcomers positioned themselves on either side of the car. Mid-thirties, lean, tanned, short hair. The way they maintained their spacing and carried their weapons with familiar ease told Lang they were not amateurs but had had military training somewhere along the line.

The driver leaned over so his face was even with the passenger window. "Please show us your hands, Mr. Reilly."

The English was accentless.

Reilly held up one hand, middle finger extended. "Please tell me what the hell this is all about."

Unruffled, the chauffeur tried again. "All will be explained once we're inside."

"Tell whoever's in there to come out here where I can see him."

"You are not in a position to argue, Mr, Reilly. Someone wants a few words with you, and then you'll be taken to your hotel."

Lang nodded. "I suppose you're going to give me a bank-certified guarantee of that, right?"

Although Lang couldn't hear it, the driver looked like he sighed. "There is no reason to be difficult, Mr. Reilly. We wish you no harm."

"Right. The H and Ks are to protect me from the cows

over there. Tell your two playmates to take the clips out of those weapons, eject the one in the chamber, and toss them away. I'll feel a lot more like conversation."

The driver grimaced. "We can certainly wait, Mr. Reilly."

"But you're not going to. Sooner or later my people will figure out I haven't arrived at the hotel. Or that the car that was supposed to pick me up has disappeared. How many of these customized Benzes are around? You want to wait while the police start questioning possible witnesses, put a picture of the car on TV? No, I don't think so."

The driver said nothing. He turned on his heel and jogged back inside.

Moments later he returned, his mouth a determined line.

"Mr. Reilly, you can either get out or my orders are to forcibly remove you."

Without moving his head, Lang surveyed his situation. A man armed with an automatic weapon on either side of the car, the driver at the door to his left. No way to un-holster the SIG Sauer, let alone use it before those two weapons filled the passenger compartment with lead. He stretched slightly to see over the back of the front seat. The driver had taken the keys out of the ignition. Even if he could somehow get into the driver's seat, he'd be no better off.

No way . . . unless . . .

He smiled and shrugged, speaking up to be heard through the window. "Not much I can do. You've got the door locked, remember?"

The driver reached into his pocket, and there was an electronic squawk as the lock popped open.

Lang lunged for the door, grabbed the handle, and pulled.

Perplexed, the driver gave into his natural reflex to pull the opposite way. The door opened a crack and closed, a tug-of-war of sheet metal.

Just as the other leaned backward to pull, Lang

slammed his full weight forward, throwing the door open and smacking the driver squarely. He stumbled back as Lang lunged out of the car and on top of him. Grabbing the man by the collar with one hand, he pressed the SIG Sauer against his head with the other.

The two men with machine guns raised their weapons uncertainly.

"One of you so much as wiggles his ears and he dies!"

Neither seemed willing to take that responsibility.

Still pressing the automatic against the man's head, Lang released his grip on the collar to search the man's pants pockets. Gratified when his fingers closed around the car's key, he pulled it loose.

Keeping his hostage in tow, Lang used him as a shield against one gunman and kept the Mercedes between him and the other as he backed slowly toward the car. He reached the hand that didn't have the gun in it behind him and opened the driver's door.

He was bending to slide into the seat when a yell came from the house. He didn't understand the words but the intent was clear.

There was a short, staccato burst of gunfire. Lang felt a tug at the sleeve of his jacket, and the driver pitched forward with a grunt.

Had the driver not been there to block the bullets, it would have been Lang lying on the ground.

So much for intending no harm.

The nearest man with the H and K was lowering his weapon for another burst. Lang fired two quick shots, more to distract than to kill, and leaped into the car, slamming the door behind him.

He jammed the key into the ignition and turned, ducking a shower of glass pebbles that an instant before had been the driver's window. He jammed the shift lever into drive and floored the accelerator.

The big car fishtailed, caught traction, and lunged

ahead as the rear window went opaque in a spiderweb of safety glass.

As soon as Lang reached the four-lane highway, he checked the rearview mirror. He was not surprised to see a black car approaching fast. In seconds he could recognize it as a Land Rover, smaller than the custom job he was driving and, quite likely, faster.

Any doubt as to relative speeds evaporated as he floored the gas pedal and still the pursuing car gained on him.

If his vehicle was speed-handicapped by its size and weight, perhaps he could use those features to his advantage. Lang lifted his foot slightly.

As anticipated, the Land Rover pulled into the left lane, its occupants no doubt intending to spray him with gunfire as they drew even.

Lang looked back at the road, aware that he was going to get exactly one chance.

At least, in this lifetime.

The Land Rover behind had closed to slightly more than a single car length. Lang cut in front, the move of a man desperately trying to avoid what was inevitable.

He passed a Peugeot, pulling slightly ahead and blocking the Land Rover behind him. Driving in the left lane was illegal on European superhighways, a rule more uniformly enforced than speed limits. It was also frequently fatal.

He could see the Peugeot's perplexed driver in the mirror. Either the man was unwilling to share the road with a maniac or he had reached his destination. He took the next exit, leaving Lang alone with his pursuers.

Before Lang could return to the right lane, the car behind him pulled into the empty slot. The men in it preferred to force Lang to fire his weapon across the seat, if, in fact, he had a chance to fire at all before they did.

Lang backed off the accelerator, letting the Land Rover draw almost even before touching the brake. Before the driver of the Land Rover realized what had happened, it had shot past.

Lang sped up as the Land Rover slowed, trying to recover the best position for a shot.

As in the police chases on any American city's local news at six o'clock, Lang nudged the left rear of the Land Rover with the Mercedes's front right bumper.

The high center of gravity of the sport-utility vehicle combined with the wet surface and the German car's weight to break the adhesion between the tires of the Land Rover and the road. The British car began a slow but uncontrollable counterclockwise spin down the highway.

Lang tapped his brakes and watched the other car smash into the steel Armco barrier dividing the road.

He passed just as two dazed men were fighting ballooned air bags to climb out. He gave a cheery honk of the horn, noted the license plate, and headed back to Brussels.

TWELVE

Rue des Bouchers
Brussels, Belgium
Two Hours Later

Lang had returned the scarred Mercedes to the foundation's garage. The attendant gaped at what were obvious bullet holes. The man was staring openmouthed, too fascinated to notice as Lang dropped the keys into his hand.

"In America," Lang said, "we call it road rage."

From there he walked to the offices on the flamboyant Grand Place, the geographic, historical, and commercial center of the city. Surrounded by elaborate seventeenth-century architecture, it housed statues of saints and busts of a ducal line peering from their lofty niches high above the bustling cobblestone square. The Hôtel de Ville, city hall, with its fourteenth-century spire, competed for attention with the former palace of Belgium's Spanish monarchs.

Lang entered Le Pigeon, former residence of Victor Hugo during his exile from France. The grand old building had been converted into commercial space long ago.

Louis deVille dropped the telephone when Lang walked into his office. "Monsieur Reilly!"

He came around the desk to clasp Lang with both

hands. He was about to kiss him on each cheek when he recalled Lang's opinion of the traditional French greeting.

Instead he dropped his arms and gloved Lang's right hand in both of his own. "The police were on the phone. Someone hijacked the car and the driver called them. Since your flight crew reported you had gotten in it at the airport . . ."

Lang extracted his hand as politely as possible. "I took a tour of the countryside. I'm fine. The Mercedes needs to go to the body and glass shops, though."

Louis took a step back. "Who . . . ?"

"Good question. I have a license plate number."

Louis looked at a jeweled watch, the sort of thing few American men would wear to any event other than a pimp's convention. "It is near lunch. Have you eaten?"

Without waiting for a reply, Louis punched the intercom on his desk and rattled off a command in French.

"I have asked that the police inspector with whom I was speaking join us. He can ask his questions over a bowl of *moules* as well as here, no?"

Outside, blue was breaking through the dove gray skies. The drizzle had stopped altogether.

The two men crossed the square and walked along one of the Lower Town's main thoroughfares, Boulevard Anspach. Lang loitered, checking behind him by use of reflections in shop windows. Unlike in most U.S. cities, lunch was not a hurried affair here. It normally consisted of an hour and a half of throngs seeking good food and pleasant company. Consequently, spotting a tail in the crowd was difficult if not impossible.

A few blocks south, Louis stopped in front of the Église St-Nicolas, where a Gothic-style church marked the site of a twelfth-century marketplace. They turned left and strolled through the Galeries St-Hubert, a nineteenth-century glass-domed arcade, the location of familiar names such as Hermès and Chanel. Here it would be a little easier to discern a follower. Men hurried through; women idled in front of shop windows.

There was still no evidence that they were under surveillance.

An ornately decorated exit let out onto the Rue des Bouchers, in English the Street of the Butchers. The narrow alley was lined on both sides with restaurant after restaurant, each with an awning out front for al fresco dining and each featuring *moules,* mussels, boiled with onion, steamed with wine or beer, in sauce or butter. They were being served in the shell, in stews or cold, with horseradish, ketchup, or béarnaise sauce. Shiny, black-winged shellfish that could be prepared more ways than potatoes.

And Lang knew from experience they were all delicious.

Louis slid behind a small table around which four fragile chairs shouldered one another for room. He motioned Lang in beside him. The waiter had just delivered the menus when a thin man in a loosely cut suit approached.

"Mr. Reilly?" He extended a hand. The nails were bitten to the quick.

Lang stood, a question on his face as he shook.

"I am Inspector Henré Vorstaat." He showed a badge and sat before an invitation could be extended. "I was speaking with M. deVille about the theft of your car."

The man's face seemed too narrow to accommodate the mouth, his expression doleful. Lang guessed the tiny folds around his eyes came more from frowning than laughing.

Hercule Poirot he wasn't.

His English had the hard edge of Flemish. "I also understand Mr. Benjamin Yadish was employed by you. Having your foundation's car forcibly taken and a murder in the same week looks like a crime wave, no?"

"More like a tsunami."

"Oh?"

The waiter was hovering. Both the other men ordered without looking at the menu.

"I'll have the same," Lang said.

He waited until the waiter had retreated before continuing. "We also had an employee killed in the States, apparently the same night as Yadish. One was a physicist, the other a physiochemist."

The policeman was staring at him with eyes that Lang suddenly realized were colorless. The discovery was somehow disconcerting. Lang had the impression the inspector had used those eyes to intimidate more than one suspect.

"Do you believe the two murders are related?"

"After what happened this morning, yes."

"Tell me."

Lang did, omitting only any mention of his possession of a firearm.

As Lang completed his story, the waiter set a copper tureen and an empty plate in front of each, along with crisp brown *frites,* french fries, standing on end in tall ramekins to conserve their warmth. Lang was uncertain what was in the pale red sauce in which the mussels still simmered, but if it tasted as good as it smelled, he would be happy.

As in France, all conversation not related to food ceased once the meal was served. As each man filled the platter before him with empty shells, Vorstaat and Louis compared these mussels to others they had had here and elsewhere. Was the sauce stronger than before or weaker? Had the chef left out one of the customary herbs? Were Antwerp's mussels any fresher than those delivered daily to Brussels?

Murder took a backseat to gastronomy.

The inspector drained the last of his glass of Duvel and regarded the mound of empty shells before him with what could have been regret. He resumed the previous conversation as though there had been no interruption.

"Do you have the license plate of this Land Rover?"

Lang recited it from memory. Vorstaat had him repeat it as he wrote it into a small notebook.

The inspector leaned back in his chair, fumbled in a coat pocket, and produced a blue box of French cigarettes, Gitanes. Without offering his companions one, he lit up with a wooden match before dumping the match into the bowl formerly full of mussels, where it sizzled.

The Belgians, or at least those of Brussels, also shared with the French a total contempt for inconvenient authority. From where he sat Lang could see at least two NO SMOKING, NON FUMER, NICHT RAUCHEN signs, complete with a line drawn through a picture of a cigarette. He could also see half a dozen other smokers.

"You said you believed the murder of your employee and the attempt to kidnap you were related?"

"Yadish and Lewis were working on the same thing, an alternative to fossil fuels."

Vorstaat's nostrils exhaled blue smoke. "We might assume that the killer—or rather, killers—are opposed to the project?"

"*Really* opposed."

"And who might be both opposed to and aware of your foundation's work?"

Lang thought a moment. "Exxon? BP? Our research projects, like all the money we spend as a tax-exempt charitable foundation, are a matter of public record."

"Surely the world's major oil companies do not need to suppress such scientific research. They could conduct it themselves. Petrol is not worth murder."

"You seen the price of gas lately?" Lang shook his head, only partially joking.

The policeman sniffed. "Americans! You wail at four

dollars per gallon of fuel. Here and in the rest of Europe that would be considered inexpensive."

Lang had no intent of engaging in a debate over comparative gas prices.

Silent since his last mussel, Louis noted, "Our people—or at least Dr. Yadish—are years away from succeeding, if ever. It is hard to think someone would kill over an event that might not ever take place."

The inspector stubbed his cigarette out in an empty ramekin. The prohibition of smoking had succeeded only in abolishing ashtrays. "I've investigated many killings for far less reason, but I think you are right."

Lang was watching a particularly buxom blonde edge her way among the tables. No matter how hard he tried, she reminded him of Gurt. The memory hurt. "In Atlanta, Dr. Lewis's laboratory was wrecked and the records of his daily work taken. Do we know if Dr. Yadish's place was trashed, too?"

Vorstaat reached into his coat pocket, fishing for another Gitane, then apparently thought better of it and made a steeple of his fingers, as though to keep them from being further tempted. "We do not yet know, although I am in contact with the Amsterdam police." The self-willed fingers slid into his lap. "Do either of you know what he was doing in Bruges?"

Lang shook his head. "No."

Louis had been watching the same blonde. "He left a message that he would be in Brussels the morning after he was . . . killed. He did not give a reason, but that was not unusual. Amsterdam to Brussels is a short ride on the Eurostar. He liked to come by, report his progress, discuss what he was doing. Most of all I think he liked to come to this place to eat."

Vorstaat pursed his lips. "He ate here? I thought shellfish were prohibited to Jews, no?"

Lang shrugged. "Don't ask me. The Jews I know pretty much eat what they like. Same goes for drink, too."

Louis tore his eyes from the blonde and looked nervously around the street, as though eating mussels here might guarantee a violent death.

The inspector poised his pen over the notebook. "And exactly what was he doing?"

Louis shrugged. "I do not know. I understood little of his scientific speech. From the sound of his voice, though, he seemed excited."

"Excited or frightened?" the policeman asked.

Louis said, "I do not know. At the moment I had no reason to think he would be frightened."

Vorstaat started to say something but was interrupted by a chirping from his jacket pocket.

He stood. "Excuse me a moment."

He stepped into the street as he pulled out a cell phone.

Lang spoke to Louis, but he was looking at the policeman. "Exactly how much did you know about Dr. Yadish's private life?"

The Belgian looked puzzled. " 'Private life'? I do not understand."

Lang leaned across the table, lowering his voice to a conspiratorial whisper. "Did the good professor have, perhaps, something he would have preferred kept secret?"

Lang could almost see the cartoon lightbulb above Louis's head click on. "You mean did he have a, er, what do you call it? A woman?"

"Girlfriend?"

"Yes, girlfriend! I do not think so. All he ever spoke of was his wife and his work. He never mentioned a girlfriend."

One easy answer shot down.

"Do you have any idea why he was in Bruges, then?"

Louis shook his head emphatically. "As I told the inspector, none."

Vorstaat returned to his chair. "Forgive the interruption. While I was on the telephone I asked about automobile accidents at the place you described. The car involved, the Land Rover, was deserted. Its license plates had been stolen, as had the automobile itself. The investigating officers searched it completely."

Lang waited.

"Unfortunately, whoever took the automobile was careful. There were no fingerprints, no spent cartridges."

"In other words, nothing."

Vorstaat came as close to a smile as Lang guessed he ever did. "I did not say that, Mr. Reilly."

He also knew the drama of a pause.

"Well?"

"Something must have fallen out of someone's pocket. My men are checking with the vehicle's owner to make sure it is not his."

Lang was too impatient to endure another delay. "And it was . . . ?"

"It is torn and wrinkled, but it appears to be the bill from a bistro in Bruges."

THIRTEEN

Grand Place
Brussels
Five Minutes Later

The three men stood in front of the yellow-stone baroque facade of Le Pigeon while Vorstaat finished another Gitane.

"What are your plans now, Mr. Reilly?"

"First I'll check at the Amigo Hotel, see if they have my baggage. I'm due to change shirts sometime soon."

The policeman made a sound that might have been a chuckle had there been any humor in it. "You will be staying in Brussels how long?"

"Other than a hot shower, I have no reason to stay at all. I came to make sure the foundation's work was continuing, and Louis assures me it is."

"So you will be returning to America?" The inspector's inflection implied he doubted it.

"First I need to go to Amsterdam with Louis, see exactly where we are on Benjamin Yadish's research, then go by and offer condolences to his wife. Then home."

Vorstaat was studying Lang's face with a stare he surely knew made Lang uncomfortable. "This research, it will continue?"

Lang was taken by surprise. "I . . . I'm not sure. Our two leading guys—one here, one back home—are both dead."

The policeman dropped his cigarette and crushed it into the cobblestones with more enthusiasm than was necessary. "Has it occurred to you that these two men were murdered not just to halt their research but to steal it?"

Lang's mind flashed back to the pages torn from Lewis's notebook. "Has anything from Dr. Yadish's laboratory been taken?"

"The Amsterdam authorities tell me his wife said the CD on which he keeps his records is missing. She could not tell them what was on it, but they intend to speak to her again when she has had time to collect her . . . collect her thoughts. Perhaps next week."

Lang was hardly surprised that Vorstaat had already been in touch with the Dutch police. It was the obvious thing to do. "Did she have any idea why he was in Bruges?"

The policeman was staring at him harder than ever. "He told her he was meeting you."

Stunned, Lang said nothing for a moment. "The night he was killed I was in the United States. I have both a priest and a policeman who can attest to the fact."

That humorless grin spread across wide lips. "You may need them, Mr. Reilly. For the moment, though, I suggest you use care."

Was the man a comedian or just prone to understatement?

"You can count on it."

Vorstaat started to turn to go and then stopped. "One more thing, Mr. Reilly." He reached into a coat pocket and handed Lang a business card. "Please give me a call before you leave Europe. I may have learned more."

Lang slipped the card into his wallet. "Certainly."

Lang and Louis watched him cross the square without looking back.

"He will tell us if he learns more?" Louis asked.

"If he learns more, he will want to ask more questions," Lang said.

"He did not ask many today."

"He knows very little today."

*   *   *

Book of Jereb

Chapter Two

1. And Pharaoh sent forth his army, his archers and chariots into the desert to return the Israelites to Egypt so that they found the Israelites on the shore of the sea. The Israelites saw the army of Pharaoh; they murmured* unto Moses, saying, "Hast thou brought us into the desert and to the sea only to die by Pharaoh's hand?"

2. Moses said unto them, "Fear not in your hearts, for thy God shall save thee." And once the Israelites had passed through the shallow sea came a wave at the hand of the one God that swept away Pharaoh, his chariots, his archers and horses so that none were left to pursue.

3. And so began the forty years of the Israelites in the desert.

4. The one God commanded Moses to make unto him an ark, measuring forty-five inches long, twenty-seven inches wide, and twenty-seven inches high.** And He commanded the box to be made of wood. The Lord told Moses both the inside and the outside should be laid with the purest of gold, and gold rings at each end so that it might be borne by men. A seal should be placed upon the same so that the lid of the box should not fall off should a man stumble.

5. When the ark had been completed, Moses said to the Israelites, "Behold, your one God has created a weapon that you have never seen." And Zete, son of Zel, doubted the

---

* Throughout Exodus also, the Israelites seem to be murmuring about something: the lack of food, the harsh environment, the lack of water, Moses, even against their God.

** Rough equivalency of the measurements, given in cubits.

words of Moses, and reached to touch the ark and was struck dead by a bolt that came not from the heavens, and the people bowed to Moses, saying, "You are our savior." And Moses became angry, replying unto them, "Your savior is the one God, who hath brought you forth from Egypt."

6. While the Israelites were encamped at the base of the mountain across the sea but south of the land of the Midianites, being the mountain of the God of Abraham, the one God said unto Moses, "Come to me on the mountain and I will give you commandments I have written, that thou might instruct the Isrealites, and you shall put these commandments into the ark I commanded you to build."

7. And Moses was upon the mountain a great time, requiring neither food nor water but sustained by the one God. While Moses was on the mountain, the children of Israel began to murmur, fearing he was dead or would not return to them, and they said among themselves, "Let us make a god so that we may worship it." And they melted down their gold and constructed a golden calf and fell down before it, worshiping it.

8. When Moses returned and saw the Israelites worshiping an idol, he threw down the tablets the Lord had given him, breaking the same and rewrote the same, on tablets in his own hand.

9. And Moses cast the golden calf into the fire until it was consumed.

*   *   *

3

FOURTEEN

Centraal Station
Nieuwe Zijde
Amsterdam
Two Days Later

Lang had never seen a weather vane on a rail station, but then, he'd never seen one where the wind's direction was displayed on a clock face, either. Located along the harbor, the building featured a Dutch-Renaissance-style facade adorned with colored allegorical depictions of maritime trade, a tribute to the city's nautical past. The interior was somewhat seedier: prostitutes vying for customers among the new arrivals, and college-age kids lighting perfectly legal joints. The smell of cheap perfume and marijuana was overpowering.

Leaving the Gulfstream at the Brussels airport had been an easy decision: The proximity of the Dutch city meant a train ride could be completed nearly as fast as the necessary flight plan could be filed and approved. And the foundation didn't have to pay a thousand-dollar-an-hour fuel burn, either.

Louis was trying to ignore a woman in a dress that fit like a sausage skin. There was no room in it for most of her bosom. "Do we wish a car?" Louis asked.

Lang looked at the taxi stand. "How far do we need to go?"

The hooker was smiling seductively. Lang repeated the question.

Louis snapped to as though surfacing from a dream.

"Fifteen-, twenty-minute walk."

"It's a nice day for a stroll."

Each man was carrying a small case he had packed for no more than a single night's stay.

They walked in the shade of trees along a canal. The waterway was lined with gabled houses and long, narrow boats that obviously served as dwellings. Occasionally a craft would slowly make its way past, leaving ducks and geese rocking in its gentle wake. Although now and then a car crept past on the narrow street, bicycles outnumbered them five to one.

"The canals," Louis said, "form a crescent with the open part facing north. Almost all connect with the river, the Amstel, which goes to the sea. This one is the Singel, the innermost."

Lang craned his head back to look at a particularly steeply gabled house. "You've been here often?"

Louis stopped to let a woman on a bicycle pass. A baby gurgled from the wicker basket on the handlebars.

"I came two or three times a year to see how Dr. Yadish was coming along, yes."

The nostalgia in his voice said he would miss the free lifestyle of the Netherlands as well as Yadish.

Passing through the "new" market, an open square, they entered the Oude Zijde, the city's southwestern corner, and home to the university district. Signs everywhere advertised sex toys, peep shows, and "live" entertainment, all in English, even though lurid pictures made most text unnecessary. Scantily clad women posed provocatively in the shop windows of clubs whose neon signs, also in English, promised unimaginable delights.

English: the language of Milton, Shakespeare, and the sex trade.

Past the red-light district, they turned left past a number of university buildings to a small block of modest town houses. Beside one door a glass case displayed the names of residents next to a row of buttons. Louis pushed one, and a woman's voice replied in what Lang gathered was Dutch.

Minutes later Lang and Louis were at the door of a third-floor walk-up. The woman looked like she was in her mid-fifties, white hair tucked into a no-nonsense bun at the back of her neck. Her eyes were bottomless black pools under unplucked eyebrows. She was small, probably less than a hundred pounds, and under five feet.

Lang felt he was holding a thinly wrapped bundle of sticks when he shook her hand at the threshold. "We came to express our regrets, Mrs. Yadish."

She gave him the look of someone tired of social banalities. "Mary, please. I had just returned from saying kaddish for my husband when Louis called from the station," she said in English, ushering them into the living room. "I fear I have not had time to properly clean up or prepare refreshment."

Although worn, the room looked immaculate to Lang. "Thanks, but we ate on the train," he lied. "As I said, Mary, I wanted to personally tell you how sorry I and the foundation are. I also wanted to ask a few questions."

She collapsed, rather than sat, into a stuffed chair upholstered in a cabbage-rose print, the sort of pattern Lang saw in films set in World War II England.

Lang and Louis sat on a sofa so uncomfortable it seemed to have been stuffed with concrete.

She looked at him wearily. "Questions? The police have been here no less than three times with questions."

Lang almost bolted back to his feet. "The police have been here three times?"

She looked at him quizzically, clearly suspecting she might have said something wrong. "Three times, yes. First by an older man, an inspector, then twice more by a younger man."

"Did either of them give you his business card?"

Now she looked as though he might be deranged. "Yes, of course." She turned to a small side table and produced two cards. "The Inspector was a Van Decker. The other man's name, as you can see, is Hooy."

"The younger man, can you describe him?"

Now Louis was puzzled.

Mary Yadish was staring at the faded Oriental rug. "I suppose so. Large, perhaps over two meters tall. Dark hair cut close. Mid-thirties."

"Did he ask anything different than the first one, Van Decker?"

She lifted her eyes to regard Lang for a moment. "Yes, yes, he did. He acted as though my husband must have left something other than the CD on which he recorded his research, the one he must have taken with him when he went to Bruges, some sort of records. It was almost as though he knew it."

"Did your husband leave other notes or the like?"

She shook her head slowly. "Benjamin left only his books and his clothes. He had no interest in owning things." She looked back at Lang quickly. "Although your foundation paid him generously."

"Did your husband have any friends, know anyone in Bruges?"

She shook her head again, weary of the repetition. "No one. As I told the police, he went there because he thought he was meeting you."

Was that a tone of accusation?

"How was he contacted?"

She looked at him blankly.

Lang leaned forward. "You said your husband thought

he was meeting me. How did he get that information? Did someone telephone him?"

She shook her head for a third time. "I . . . I do not know. He simply said he had to meet you in Bruges. Two days later . . ."

Lang could not find a tactful way to ask the next question. "Do you mind if I take a look through his things? There might possibly be something there. . . ."

She stood. "The police searched the closet and the room he used as a study. They found nothing. I have already bundled his clothes to give away, but you are welcome to look. While you do I will make tea."

The clothes were in stacks of suits, shirts, and shoes, surprisingly few of each for what Yadish had been paid. Jacket and pants pockets were turned out, no doubt the result of the previous examination.

After a few moments Lang stood. "Nothing," he said to Louis.

Mary entered the room carrying a small tray. "Tea?"

Lang accepted a cup for courtesy's sake. The brew had a faint aroma of fruit. Cup in hand, he was led to a small room that struggled to contain a diminutive table and a straight-backed wooden chair. The table's surface was barely large enough to hold a laptop computer, telephone, lamp, and what looked like an antique radio. One wall, perhaps eight feet long, was lined with books.

It took Lang a single step to get a closer look at the radio, an American-made Philco with volume and tuning knobs and a numbered dial face. He remembered as a child seeing one like it at the home of an elderly relative.

"Benjamin liked to repair them," Mary said from the doorway. "Old radios. He had to make the vacuum tubes himself."

Lang turned the radio around, noting the bulbous tubes and wiring. "Made the tubes? Your husband was a chemist."

She shrugged. "He liked to play with antique electronics. The disassembled remains of a Victrola are in a closet, if you would like to see."

Lang found space enough to put his teacup on the table and turned his attention to the books. The titles were mostly in Dutch, with a few spines showing Hebrew characters.

Mary Yadish backed out of the doorway, making room for Louis. "Mostly histories, particularly ancient history. Another hobby. Take your time."

"One other question," Lang said. "Was your husband a religious man? That is, did he follow the Jewish dietary laws?"

A faint smile flickered across her face. "Benjamin was Jewish by birth only. I doubt he had been in a synagogue since he was a child." She sighed deeply. "In fact, today was the first time in years that I have been."

So much for proscribed shellfish.

Lang and Louis began to patiently examine each book, thumbing its pages before returning each to its place on the shelf.

Louis blew gently across the cover of one, sending dust spinning into the air like planets in a tiny universe. "What are we looking for?"

Lang was exchanging one tome for another that had illustrations of some sort of metallurgical process. "I'm not sure, but if the good professor kept any sort of records besides the electronic ones, this would sure be a good place."

Louis took a handkerchief from a pocket and wiped his hands. "Why would Yadish want to hide his research notes and records?"

"I'm not sure he would, but if he kept an extra set, maybe some handwritten notes, the library would be logical."

On impulse, Lang reached for the radio. He was curious to see if it worked. He turned the volume knob, half expecting to hear something from the era before television, a dialogue between Jack Benny and Rochester, or "Thanks for the Memories," Bob Hope's theme song.

Instead there was a mechanical click, and the face of the dial swung open.

Louis reshelved a book and came over to join Lang in peering into the radio's plastic case. Lang reached his thumb and forefinger in, removing a sheaf of papers rolled with a rubber band. He carefully slid the band off. He was looking at perhaps twenty or so pages in what looked like Hebrew characters.

"From his cousin Joseph in Vienna," Mary commented from the doorway. "He was killed in a motor accident not long ago."

"So he kept papers hidden in a radio?" Lang asked, truly puzzled.

"Benjamin and Joseph were very close. Benjamin went to Vienna for a service for Joseph. Just before he died Joseph mailed those papers to Benjamin, some sort of research he was going to publish. Benjamin checked his cousin's home computer. He never accepted that the accident was that—accidental. The police never found the other vehicle or driver. My husband half believed his cousin was killed for what was on those papers."

Lang put the pages down. "From where did Dr. Yadish's cousin send them?"

She shook her head. "The postmark said Dürnstein." She thought a moment. "It may be nothing, but we never knew. His laptop was missing from the wreckage, but his wife said he left with it that morning."

"Obviously your husband thought these were important."

She shrugged. "We did not know. Neither of us read Hebrew, but Benjamin said he thought they were related to some project he was working on, perhaps the one for you."

Interesting but less than helpful, Lang thought. But if

Yadish thought he needed to hide them, perhaps the papers had some answers concerning his death. Lang knew someone as proficient in Hebrew as he and Francis were in Latin. "May I borrow it long enough to make a copy?"

She shrugged, a gesture more of surrender than assent. "It could not hurt."

"One more thing and we'll leave you alone," Lang began.

"No hurry," she said slowly. "I will be alone for a very long time now."

Lang was unsure how to reply, so he said, "I'd also like a look at your husband's laboratory."

She pointed at Louis. "He can take you there. It's only a few blocks away. But you must arrive before the university locks the building for the night."

As soon as he and Lang were back on the street, Louis stopped. "Vorstaat said the woman had been visited only once by the police. That is why you asked her so closely about the second policeman, Hooy, rather than Inspector Van Decker, no?"

"Yes," Lang said, thinking about the faux FBI man, Witherspoon. Mrs. Yadish's description fit him, too. He tried to dismiss the notion as illogical. How many millions of men in their mid-thirties were over six feet with dark hair? But the idea wouldn't go away. It continued to circle his mind like a stray dog seeking a handout.

FIFTEEN

Five Minutes Later

Louis was saying something.

"Pardon?"

The Belgian pointed to a shop with a copy machine visible through the plate-glass window. "We can make a Xerox there."

Lang turned and stopped. Was it his imagination or had the corner of his eye caught the reflection of someone whirling at exactly the same time to study a handbill posted on a stand? The man was certainly there, and he certainly wasn't the size of Witherspoon. He wore a leather jacket open, with nondescript slacks and black socks under the sandals so loved by Europeans.

Lang handed the rerolled pages to Louis. "Please, if you don't mind, make us two copies of each page."

Louis looked at him questioningly before ducking inside.

Lang studied the surrounding architecture, the boats along the adjacent canal, marijuana plants growing in pots in a coffeehouse window. But mostly he studied the man in the jacket, who seemed as intent on wasting time as did Lang.

Police? Perhaps, but law enforcement officers would be unlikely to waste resources following him when all they had to do was stop him and ask questions. There was a chance, slim as it might be, that Leather Jacket was simply early for an appointment of some kind.

The coincidence that a stranger would suddenly appear idling at exactly the same spot where Lang and Louis were was unbelievable. There were also the coincidences of two bogus cops, and that both the murder victims had been working on the fringes of the same project.

Agency training had included extreme skepticism of mere happenstance. If you refused to accept similarities as flukes, you might be wrong ten percent of the time. Conversely, accepting coincidence at face value was frequently fatal.

Then there was the question of those shots fired in Underground Atlanta. He had been certain they had been a warning. If the shooter had wanted him dead, Lang wouldn't be here right now. Yet the guys who had hijacked him at the Brussels airport weren't out to just warn him.

What was the connection?

Louis emerged from the shop with a bulging paper bag in each hand. He handed one to Lang. "The laboratory is just ahead."

Leather Jacket was still inspecting a window as they left.

"This is the Oost-Indisch Huis," Louis proclaimed, pointing to an attractive seventeenth-century brick-and-concrete building. "It was the offices of the Dutch East India Company. Now it belongs to the university. You have heard of the Dutch East India Company, yes?"

Lang was not so much interested in one of the world's most outrageously successful commercial enterprises as he was in making sure they weren't followed. "Yes."

Louis stopped before an ornate entranceway, waiting

for Lang to catch up. Both men entered what looked from the street to be a series of buildings between two tree-lined canals with a block-long bicycle rack in front. As Lang soon discovered, he was in one of many passageways linking a large number of structures.

They passed through a courtyard, an outdoor café filled with students. One, a large blonde, followed him with blue eyes. Once again Gurt rose as a specter, this time dressed in motorcycle leathers, the same ones she had worn when she saved his life in Italy, her long blond hair flowing around her face. Two women, Dawn and Gurt: one his wife, one he wished had been. Both gone from his life.

He shook his head as though he could scatter the memories.

"Mr. Reilly?"

Louis was standing outside a door with Yadish's name etched on the glass pane.

Louis fumbled in his pockets and produced a ring of keys. He tried one. The click of a dead bolt signaled that he had found the right one, and he pushed the door open, ushering Lang inside. The room resembled the lab in Atlanta, except it was slightly smaller, and racks of test tubes and beakers flanking Bunsen burners occupied two long counters, instead of electronic eqipment. Another difference was that this room looked as though Yadish might return at any moment.

At the end of one counter, in front of a long-legged stool on casters, was a cloth-bound ledger, the sort of thing Lang would have expected to see in any company's accounting department before computers made paper all but obsolete. From where he stood Lang could see that a number of pages had been torn out.

Thumbing through the pages, he asked, "Did Dr. Yadish keep notes here as well as electronically?"

Louis was standing in front of a computer on the other counter. "I do not know."

Lang left the book where it was to look over Louis's shoulder as the computer hummed to life. "The ledger is a journal of sorts. I can't read the language, but the last date's less than a week ago."

Louis left the machine to boot up and viewed the open pages. "A list of purchases—nitrate of mercury, two hundred milligrams, sodium phosphate, and so on. I would suppose he kept an account of the chemicals he used."

Both men returned to the blank blue screen.

Louis tapped a series of keys and frowned. "Nothing."

Lang could see that. "Did the professor have a password, perhaps?"

Louis was still pecking away. "He may have, but we are getting nothing. It is as if the hard drive is blank."

Or gone or erased.

"Did he have any special place to put things, a particular drawer, a file cabinet?"

Louis nodded and pulled the stool behind him as he went to the far wall, where a row of cabinets crowned two industrial sinks. "Steady me, please?"

Lang held the stool as the Belgian climbed up to kneel on its seat. He opened the cabinets to reveal rows of labeled opaque jars. He moved one or two before asking Lang to push him farther to his left.

"Eureka," he said with a smile, removing a container in each hand.

Behind the row of vessels Lang could see the black face of a safe built into the wall. "Swell. I don't suppose you know the combination?"

Louis's grin widened. "No need." He handed Lang several of the containers to put aside. He held one up, however, rotating it so Lang could see a series of four numbers on the back. "Dr. Yadish could never remember, so he wrote it down. I saw him take this down to open the safe."

Thirty seconds later the door swung open. From below the cabinet where Lang stood he could see nothing in it.

"Why keep an empty safe?" he asked rhetorically.

"Not empty." Louis reached into the safe and held up two letter-sized envelopes.

He handed them to Lang and climbed off the stool. Lang opened the first. Inside was a grainy white powder similar to the traces streaked across the counter in Dr. Lewis's lab. The second contained the same.

Lang wondered if Detective Morse had gotten the test results back from the state crime lab yet. If only the stuff hadn't vanished in the APD's property room, the evidence locker that seemed to have a leak bigger than the *Titanic's*.

He'd call Morse as soon as—

He heard the door behind him shut.

"I'll take that, Mr. Reilly."

Lang turned slowly. Leather Jacket and another man stood just inside the door. Each held an automatic obscured by a silencer.

He heard Louis's surprised intake of air, something between a gasp and a grunt.

Lang mentally kicked himself. He had fallen for one of the hoarier surveillance tactics. Leather Jacket had had every intention of being spotted, of keeping Lang's attention, so that when he failed to follow Lang and Louis from the copy shop, Lang wouldn't notice a second tail.

Shit.

The two men were a good five feet apart. No chance Lang could draw the SIG Sauer from its holster and fire before at least one of the intruders could shoot.

Lang slowly raised his hands, his fingers manipulating the envelopes so that one was squarely behind the other. "What can I do for you gentlemen?"

Leather Jacket motioned with his weapon. "The envelope you have in your hand, Mr. Reilly, put it on the counter and slide it toward me."

There was a trace of an accent Lang couldn't identify.

As Lang slowly lowered the hand with the packets in it, he turned his profile slightly so the hand was briefly hidden from the intruders. He let one envelope drop into a jacket pocket. He hoped the widening of Louis's eyes didn't give the sleight of hand away.

The question was whether these two intended to take what they had come for and leave, or if the plan included making sure Lang did not trouble them further. The silencers on each gun did not suggest a happy ending. It was unlikely a man would risk carrying something that bulky if he had no intent of using it.

If Lang was going to do something, now seemed about the right time.

But what?

SIXTEEN

Headquarters, Atlanta Police Department
Ponce de Leon Avenue
Atlanta, Georgia
At the Same Time

Det. Franklin Morse read the report for a third time. It made no sense. None. Somebody over at the state crime lab been sampling the shit the narcs sent for analysis from drug busts. Either that or the place had gone loony tunes.

The powder from that professor's lab over at Georgia Tech . . . Something here was totally and terminally fucked. But then, why should Morse be surprised? Everything that had to do with that Reilly guy was equally screwed. Couple of years back a burglar had taken a dive off Reilly's twenty-fourth-story balcony. Year after that, some dude put enough sulfur nitrate and diesel fuel in Reilly's little toy of a car to reduce it to metallic confetti.

No reason, no explanation.

The worn casters of Morse's swivel chair squeaked as he pushed back from his cubicle and tried to think of something else for a second or two. This report combined with Reilly was enough to ensure a permanent migraine.

Think of something else. The hum of the office, the sound of rain.

He did not have to look out a window to know it was raining. He could hear the dripping of water from leaks in the football field–sized roof into a dozen or so buckets, trays, and whatever else could be requisitioned from a cash-strapped city. It wasn't enough to keep the smell of mildew out of the worn and soiled electric blue carpet or the faded and peeling gray wall covering.

City Hall East, they called it. An old, clapped-out, and outdated Sears mail-order center was what is was, a real estate acquisition from the venerable old retailer that rivaled only the sale of Manhattan for twenty-six dollars' worth of beads in naïveté.

The city's naïveté.

But the purchase had funneled a lot of cash in commissions to the then-mayor's friends, as well as demonstrating that his minority-participation plan would really work.

And that P. T. Barnum had been right.

The neighborhood had been so tough that female officers demanded escorts to the dark, damp parking lot. There were more winos, hookers, and small-time thieves on the streets than cops.

But that was changing. Fifty-dollar-a-week flops were being transformed into fashionable loft condos for yuppies and dinks (double income, no kids), and word was, the city was going to sell the old brick pile to developers who, no doubt, were friends of the present mayor.

Morse pushed his chair farther back, almost colliding with the woman who had the cubicle next to his. He stood and, clutching the report, made his way to the captain's office across the room. Let the brass try to make sense of this one.

If Morse couldn't solve the problem, he could do the next best thing: kick it upstairs.

SEVENTEEN

University of Amsterdam

"I said, slide the envelope toward me," Leather Jacket repeated.

Lang was now about 90 percent certain he and Louis were not supposed to leave this laboratory alive. The silencers, the fact that Leather Jacket had to have been told Lang was likely armed but made no effort to take his weapon—neither bode well.

He gave the envelope a halfhearted push a few inches.

"The envelope, Mr. Reilly."

Leather Jacket's irritation was obvious.

Lang lifted the packet and flicked his wrist, sending the envelope spinning toward the door.

The two intruders' reflexively lifted their eyes and reached, if only for a split second.

Not much.

But all he had.

Lang slammed Louis under the adjacent counter as he rolled under the other, freeing his automatic.

A string of spitting sounds filled the room as splinters, glass, and cement flooring fragments flew like shrapnel.

Lang popped up on the far side of the counter and let loose a volley of his own. Leather Jacket cursed, spun, yanked the door open, and staggered out, blood flowing down his leg. He had dropped his pistol.

His companion stood against the wall as his finger slipped from his weapon. The man started to say something as a dark red stain spread across the front of his shirt as though the bladder of ink in an old-fashioned fountain pen had leaked.

His feet seemed to take forever to slide out from under him as he sat on the floor.

Lang was beside him before the wet breathing sound stopped. He kicked the gun out of reach before a hasty search of his clothes revealed just what Lang had expected: nothing. No ID, no wallet, a total absence of anything by which he might be identified.

The trademark of a professional assassin.

The room stank of cordite and was hazy with burned gunpowder.

Louis crawled out from under his counter and wobbled on shaky knees. He looked at the dead man and quickly averted his eyes. Lang was certain the Belgian was going to throw up. Instead he stared at Lang with equal shock and horror, as if he were observing his boss sprouting a second head.

He muttered something in French, then, "Monsieur Reilly, I . . ."

Then he lost it, the old Technicolor yawn.

A man stuck his head in the door and asked something in French.

Lang followed his bewildered gaze around the devastated laboratory, then to the still-heaving Louis. "Sorry. I can't ever remember whether you can add acid to water. Or is it water to acid?"

The man left the door open. Lang could hear him shouting as he ran down the hall.

By this time Louis had recovered somewhat, although he still looked like he wouldn't be sitting down to a bowl of *moules* anytime soon.

"Louis," Lang said evenly, "listen closely. I'm going after the other guy. In a few minutes the police will be here."

He nodded. At least he understood something.

Lang continued. "You are to tell them he took me with him."

He seemed to comprehend so far.

"Those men came in here and we jumped them, *comprendez-vous pas?*"

He didn't.

"It is very important that we say the same thing. We thought we were going to be shot and killed, so we attacked first. In the scuffle one of them got shot. The other made me go with him, used me as a shield."

He might as well have been trying to explain algebra to Grumps.

He tried to keep the urgency out of his voice, although he could hear the pulsating sirens of approaching police cars.

"We had to get the guns, Louis, or we would be dead instead of this guy. You were very brave, Louis, attacking a man with a gun. The other man, the one who got away, used his gun to make me go with him."

At last, comprehension.

At first the trail of blood drops was unmistakable.

On the street they were becoming farther apart, and the sunlight was fading. After two blocks the telltale splatter disappeared. The guy must have stopped to apply some sort of tourniquet—which meant he couldn't be far away on a gimpy leg.

Lang continued down the street, rewarded by the sight of a man with an obvious limp dodging in and out of the early evening stream of pedestrians.

Keeping back, Lang followed.

Lang was thankful that Amsterdam was less than automobile-friendly. He dodged several bicycles, a tram, and one or two cars. He cleared the street just in time to see his quarry cross a canal bridge.

On the other side the trees lining the waterway spread their limbs under streetlights, making moving specters on the mottled walkways. Street signs—Dude Spiegel, Wolvenstraat—meant nothing to Lang as he followed across another canal, the fleeing figure ahead of him making no effort to conceal his direction of retreat. He obviously thought Lang would have remained behind to interrogate his partner.

Even so, there was no point in being reckless. Lang ducked into a coffeehouse with a view of the length of the street. His first breath filled his nose with the musty smell of marijuana, maybe enough to leave him stoned if he kept breathing the air. There was a time in his college days when a free high would have been appealing, but not this evening.

Lang had chosen the ideal time to hide from sight. The man ahead looked over his shoulder and slowed slightly. Lang waited for him to disappear around the next corner before sprinting past the same intersection and to the next. Flattening himself against the cold brick of a canal house, Lang peered out. As anticipated, Leather Jacket had now slowed to a painful limp, more interested in what might be behind him than in front. As he passed, Lang drew back from the streetlights' warm glow.

Halfway down the walk beside the canal, the man gave a final look over his shoulder and climbed down to one of the narrow boats tied bow and stern along the waterway. A moment later, lights appeared at a porthole.

Now what?

If there were some way to capture Leather Jacket, there was little reason to think he would yield any more information than his confederate. Professional hit men weren't known to be loquacious.

Lang noted the name painted across the stern of the boat, *Manna*, and a registration number, and decided to wait.

An hour later no one had come or gone from the boat, but police sirens seemed to be crisscrossing the city. How long before someone became suspicious of his loitering and called the cops? If he wasn't going to get any information from Leather Jacket about contacts, he might as well make certain the man didn't get another chance to kill him.

Lang waited another full five minutes before leaving the concealment of the shadows. With his hand behind his back on the butt of the SIG Sauer, he approached the boat. Since there had been no lights on before the man's arrival, it was a near certainty that the boat had only the single occupant. But how to get aboard? The craft's narrow beam ensured that even the lightest step onto the deck would produce telltale rocking. And even if he could surprise the man on board, sounds of a fight or gunshots in this peaceful neighborhood would surely draw police, who, sooner or later, would figure out that the dead man back at the university had not been shot with his own weapon.

Lang would have to think of something other than forcing his way aboard.

He watched two boats pass, neither wake sufficient to cause as much motion as climbing aboard would. He watched the sluggish current until it gave him an idea.

There was no power line from the craft to shore, no pigtail connection that would have acted like a third mooring line. The boat's electricity, then, was provided by a generator-powered battery. The lights would stay on whether or not the vessel was tied up.

Silently he crept to the stern of the boat, untying the line that moored it to the bollard at the edge of the canal's embankment and letting the rope slide into the listless water. As yet another craft passed, he did the same for the bow-line, this time holding on with one hand and keeping the other on the gun butt.

Slowly, ever so gently, the sluggish current moved the boat from the space it had occupied along the embank-ment and pushed it along at a pace Lang's slow walk could easily match. The first bridge presented a problem: Lang couldn't both hold the line and let the craft continue. He let go, following the narrow ship along the canal.

After what seemed a mile or so, Lang saw rows of bright lights ahead and perpendicular to his path. That, he guessed from what Louis had said and the brief read-ing he had done on the train, would be the Amstel, the river that crossed all canals and was the route of much of the city's commercial and industrial transportation.

The man inside was blissfully unaware he had gone from a tranquil residential canal to one of the busiest wa-terways in Europe, a highway of commerce that operated twenty-four hours a day.

Running ahead, Lang found a spot not occupied by another craft and leaned over, catching the trailing bow-line. Gently he slowed the craft until it was stopped at the intersection of canal and river. From his right Lang could see a string of barges pushed by a smaller vessel, some-thing resembling a tugboat. Patiently Lang waited until the relative positions seemed about right.

Then he let the rope go.

The canal boat edged tentatively into the river, gaining speed as the stronger current turned it abruptly to port. The sudden motion must have alerted its occupant. His head suddenly appeared through the hatch on the upper deck just as the tug saw the smaller vessel and let go a warning blast from its horn.

There was no way the multiple barges could stop in time, and the canal boat was not under power to maneuver. Lang felt the crunch of steel cutting through wood all the way to his bones.

Lang waited for nearly an hour, watching the multitude of light-flashing police craft until the divers surfaced with a limp form that was immediately zipped into a body bag. The crowd along the banks and the nearest bridge dispersed, returning to restaurants and bars.

Lang hoped he could remember the way back to the university. He was fairly certain he couldn't pronounce it well enough to ask.

As he walked, the tension of pending action was replaced by a sour taste, bile that rose in his throat at the thought of killing. In all the years he had been employed by the Agency, his most violent act had been jostling someone on the Frankfurt U-Bahn, his greatest peril, other than one foray behind the Berlin Wall, an accident on the Autobahn. Since his retirement to what he and Dawn had anticipated would be a much safer civilian life, Lang had suffered a half dozen or so attempts on his life and been forced to defend himself with deadly force.

It was, perhaps, by divine scheme that Dawn had not lived to see the ordinary American lifestyle she had so longed for become a game of life and death.

The thought gave him little comfort.

The memory of his wife, their dreams of a family, and a domestic life enjoyably dull was largely illusion, he admitted to himself. Realistically, the day-to-day predictability would have led to a tedium even spirited court battles could not have entirely dispelled. Life among normal people would have become monotonous.

On one level, he knew these truths to be evident. On another, in the place he reserved exclusively for Dawn, he refused to admit their existence. He was certain that even ennui with her would have made him happy.

Quite another compartment was reserved for Gurt, the second love of his life. He doubted she would long have tolerated a life where the only excitement was the weekly installment of *24* on television. Indeed, the prospect might well have been the reason she left despite his overtures of marriage.

So much for tripping down Memory Lane.

Lang had the present to worry about. There was no way to know who wanted the foundation's project halted, even if it meant murder. Nor could he be sure how many killers might be in Amsterdam.

He could, however, make several informed guesses.

The uniformity of armament, the Heckler & Koch automatic rifles, the silenced pistols, suggested organization. These were high-quality weapons and almost impossible to procure by civilians in the firearm-paranoid European nations. AK-47s would have been unremarkable. The most easily obtained gun on the continent, if not the world, it was a version of the Russian assault rifle once manufactured in almost every former Iron Curtain country and still plentiful on the arms black market. The variety of knockoffs carried an assortment of problems, such as jamming, misfires, and unreliable parts.

Instead, someone had the means and knowledge to acquire quality weapons.

The fact that he had been met at the Brussels airport suggested organization also. Either the group had the ability to hack into Europe's air traffic control or they had a network that extended back into the United States, where someone had reported his departure.

Once again he was the target of some ill-defined association whose chief purpose at the moment seemed to be eliminating him. Although the feeling was becoming familiar, it was far from comfortable.

EIGHTEEN

University of Amsterdam
Thirty Minutes Later

By the time Lang had returned to the university, only a couple of uniformed policemen remained in the ruins of what had been Benjamin Yadish's laboratory.

Louis stood to one side, anxiously smoking a cigarette.

"You have spoken to the police?" Lang asked pointedly.

Louis nodded. "I told them we knew we were about to die and how you threw something to divert their attention. I was not sure what happened next."

About as good as Lang could have expected.

He looked at the cigarette in the Belgian's fingers. "I didn't know you smoked."

"I quit ten years ago."

Lang Reilly: the antidote to Nicorette.

In addition to the cops in the room, a distraught little man in a seedy sweater and wrinkled corduroys was walking over. Lang didn't fully understand Louis's introduction, only that the man's name was Pierson, a professor and some sort of official at the university.

"I hope, Mr. Reilly," Pierson began in accented but understandable English, "I hope you will accept a great apology for what happened tonight. This is not a normal, er, thing to happen in Amsterdam."

"I'm sure," Lang said.

"Amsterdam is a peaceful city . . ."

It should be. Everyone was either stoned, just laid, or both.

". . . and we at the university greatly appreciate the donations of your foundation."

Now Lang understood the professor's consternation. A chemistry professor was replaceable, but a generous contributor . . .

The Dutch were a practical people.

An older man Lang had not seen before interrupted. "Forgive me. I am Police Inspector Van Decker."

Rotund but not obese, pug nose, dark eyes peering out from under bushy eyebrows like those of a small animal hesitant to leave its burrow. Other than contemporary dress, the man could have stepped out of Rembrandt's *Night Watch*, one of those burghers who paid the artist to be depicted with others of the city's volunteer police force.

He handed Lang a card. "You are Lang Reilly?"

Lang studied the card before putting it in his wallet. "I am."

"You knew Dr. Yadish?"

Lang shook his head. "Actually I never met the man. He was recommended by a friend."

Eyebrows arched like bushy caterpillars. "You hire people you do not know?"

Lang thought a moment, composing his answer. "Inspector, I am president of the Janice and Jeff Holt Foundation, a multinational charity. We support largely medical care and research for children in third-world countries, but occasionally other scientific causes such as the one Dr. Yadish was working on. I doubt I personally know a dozen of the people actually involved with our projects worldwide. We're fortunate to have people on site like Louis deVille here to keep an eye on things."

Van Decker turned his attention to Louis. "How long was Dr. Yadish employed by you before he died in Bruges?"

Louis thought a moment. "Not quite two years. But he really was not working for the foundation. He was a professor of chemistry here. We gave him a grant, money to do the research."

Van Decker's expression indicated that he was unsure of the distinction. The universal policeman's notebook appeared. "He was working on some sort of fuel?"

"A replacement for fossil fuels."

There was no doubt the inspector didn't understand.

"Gasoline, petrol," Lang volunteered. "He was looking for a substitute."

The policeman made a note. "That would be good?"

Louis nodded. "If such a fuel could be replenished like, say, hydrogen, yes."

"He was working on hydrogen?"

Louis shook his head. "No. There's already a lot of study going on in that area."

Van Decker looked up from his pad. "Then what?"

"I . . . I don't get involved in the actual research. I do ask for reports. All I know is that he was experimenting with platinum group metals."

That was the first Lang had heard of the subject of Yadish's work. But then, he could not have been specific about any of the foundation's projects.

"What are platinum group metals?" the inspector asked.

Louis shrugged. "I am not a scientist, but I understand the group has extraordinary strength, and is used in surgical and dental instruments."

Van Decker carefully wrote that down for reasons beyond Lang's imagination before he rolled a wrist over and checked his watch. "It is late and you must be tired. Other questions can wait until we finish with our examination of the room. Perhaps you would be so kind as to join me at my office in the morning?"

Surprised by the sudden concern, Lang readily agreed.

Walking back to the hotel rooms Louis had reserved, Lang asked, "What *are* platinum group metals, and what do they have to do with any kind of fuel?"

Louis, looking nervously over his shoulder every few minutes, admitted that he didn't know.

"Call whatever scientific guru you need to and find out."

"Guru?" Louis sounded as if it might be some sort of animal.

"Professor, doctor, somebody."

Louis was looking around again. "What happened to the man who ran away, the other man you shot?"

"Had a boating accident." Lang pulled out his wallet and extracted a card. "Which reminds me . . ." He scribbled a series of numbers and handed it to Louis. "This is the registration number—was the registration number—of a canal boat named *Manna*. Call whomever you need to, but I want to know to whom that boat belonged."

"Belonged?"

"It was the one involved in the accident."

Louis stopped under a streetlight. "You did this yourself?"

"OnStar service wasn't available."

"OnStar?"

Louis looked at his employer in a manner Lang had never seen in the Belgian before. Not only was there the usual respect but something else. Lang couldn't tell if it was awe or fear.

Perhaps both.

NINETEEN

Police Headquarters
Elandsgracht 117
Amsterdam
The Next Morning

Before arriving at the address on Van Decker's card, Lang had insisted on stopping at the same business store where Louis had made copies the day before, leaving the Belgian to wait on the street. Minutes later he emerged, and the two proceeded to the policeman's office.

"The store back there," Louis asked as Lang emerged. "What . . . ?"

"Unfinished business, Louis," Lang said in a tone that encouraged no more questions. "Now, let's see what the good inspector wants."

Located on the outskirts of the Central Canal Ring, the four-story building's only distinction was the red, white, and blue stripes of the Dutch flag hanging limply over the door. Inside, the place could have been a police station anywhere. People, in and out of uniform, hurriedly swirled past to the accompaniment of ringing phones and the hum of electronics. Just across the threshold a metal detector blocked entry. Emptying his pockets, Louis asked for directions to the office of Inspector Van Decker.

They were directed to the third floor, which in the

United States would have been the fourth. Europeans did not count the ground level, a custom going back to a time when homeowners were taxed by the number of stories. Lang always wondered how American cities, always cash-strapped, had missed that source of revenue.

The elevator could have been timed with a calendar. When it finally delivered them to the top floor, someone had alerted the Dutch detective. He was waiting as the doors creaked open. He greeted them with what could have been a "good morning," turned, and led them to the end of the hall.

His office was sparse even by government standards: two uncomfortable-looking wooden chairs, multiple filing cabinets, and a plank floor that had seen a lot more foot traffic than polish. A computer terminal and keyboard shared a desktop with a single file folder and a telephone. An unmistakably government-issued swivel chair squeaked a greeting as Van Decker lowered himself into it while motioning them toward the two remaining seats.

The chairs were every bit as hard as they looked.

Van Decker produced a pair of eyeglasses from a coat pocket and opened the file, a blunt signal that the inspector intended to get right down to business.

The spectacles were more for show than sight. They rested at the end of the man's nose as he continued to scan the file before lifting his gaze. "You said you shot both men with one of their own weapons?"

Lang was unsure at whom the question was directed, so he kept quiet, certain he had made no such statement.

Louis wriggled in his chair in a doomed effort to get settled against the unforgiving wood. "I said Monsieur Reilly did."

Van Decker's gaze shifted to Lang like a hawk watching its prey. "You attacked two men with weapons and disarmed them?"

"I got the gun away from one of them. It went off while

he was trying to wrestle it back. The other man was attempting to get a shot. I got lucky."

Van Decker's eyes were hooded by the heavy brows as he lifted his head slightly. "I would agree, Mr. Reilly, very lucky. Particularly since the dead man was not shot with either pistol we found. The only bullets from those weapons, we dug out of the walls and tables. And there was no indication the fatal shot was fired from the close range you suggest, no powder burns."

Now Lang understood why the policeman had been solicitous about calling it a night: He'd wanted test results before a full interview. Van Decker was sly indeed.

Lang feigned surprise. "I . . . I'm not sure what you're saying, Inspector."

Van Decker clasped his hands together, the fingers intertwined, as he leaned forward. "I'm saying, Mr. Reilly, that I know there was another gun involved, and I want to know where it is. We here in the Netherlands do not allow our citizens—or visitors—to carry firearms like American cowboys. Possession of a gun without a permit is a very serious crime. And we grant very few permits. What I want to know, Mr. Reilly, is where is the weapon that killed the man last night? If you produce it, we may overlook the crime of having such a thing on your person. If not . . ."

Lang stared back in what he hoped passed for surprised innocence. "I have no gun, Inspector. The metal detector downstairs would have discovered it."

Van Decker sighed, the sound of a man faced with a simple task made difficult. "Very well, Mr. Reilly. I think it only fair to warn you your hotel room is being thoroughly searched. If the gun that killed the man last night is found . . ."

His voice trailed off, the consequences evidently too dire to describe.

Lang slouched as much as the confines of his chair

would allow, a man totally at ease. "I understand, Inspector, but I have no reason to worry."

Louis was less successful in ignoring what he thought was surely about to happen. Lang glared at him, and the Belgian turned his head so the inspector would have difficulty seeing his concern.

"An odd thing happened last night," Van Decker continued. "As I said, we do not allow unrestricted ownership of handguns here. Yet less than three kilometers from the university there was a boating accident. The victim had been shot with a bullet that matched the one we took from the dead man at the laboratory. I have been in this job nearly fifteen years, Mr. Reilly, and I can count few evenings where unrelated shootings have taken place. Quite a coincidence, would you not agree?"

Lang nodded. "Just goes to show that gun control isn't all it's supposed to be. As we say in the States, 'When guns are outlawed, only outlaws will have guns.' "

Van Decker gave him a sour look, certain he was being made fun of, as indeed he was.

Lang stood. "If there's nothing else, Inspector . . ."

The policeman didn't bother to get up. "Not at the moment, Mr. Reilly, not at the moment. Please go about your business. For the peace of this city, I hope that business is elsewhere."

Outside, Louis had to hurry to match Lang's quick steps. "There was no . . . no point in his having us come to his office," he said petulantly. "All he did was make accusions he cannot prove."

Lang smiled. "The point, Louis, is that the wily old fox simply wanted to flush out the weapon that fired the bullets they took from the dead man and the guy on the boat."

"Flush?" Louis was clearly thinking of some sort of plumbing mechanism.

"Flush. Obviously I wouldn't be so stupid as to try to

sneak a pistol past the metal detectors at the cop shop; so, if I had such a thing, I'd hide it in my hotel room. Or ask the concierge for a safety-deposit box."

Louis stopped in his tracks, a grin dividing his face. "A safety-deposit box or a mailbox, one like they rent at the business center where we stopped."

"At the business center where we are going just before we catch the train back to Brussels. I only hope I don't get any mail that would cause them to look in the box I rented between now and then."

TWENTY

At the Same Time

Van Decker put down the phone as he stood in front of the office's single window and watched the two men cross the nearby canal bridge. He was not surprised his men had found nothing remarkable in Mr. Reilly's hotel room. The American was too smart to make things that easy.

There was no doubt in the mind of the Dutch policeman that Reilly knew more about the connection between Dr. Yadish's murder and last night's shootings than he was telling. The DNA from the man in the boating accident would likely match that in the bloody trail that began outside the university, just as the slugs from both men would surely match any weapon that could be traced to the American.

The question was not Reilly's involvement; it was, in what?

Van Decker did not like unanswered questions, and he intended to find the solution to this one. That was why he had dispatched a number of plainclothes officers. Not to follow Reilly. If the man was as sharp as Van Decker thought, the tails would be spotted. Instead, each man or woman was simply to note Reilly's passing on his way back to his hotel. If he had hidden the gun somewhere, he would likely retrieve it before leaving the Netherlands.

Once Reilly was arrested in possession of a firearm, he might be more cooperative.

The policeman sat back down behind his desk. All he had to do was wait.

TWENTY-ONE

InterContinental Amstel Hotel
Prof Tulpplen 1
Amsterdam
Thirty Minutes Later

Lang ignored the two tiers of pillars, the arches, and the gilded ceiling of the lobby as he and Louis headed for the elevators. The elegance of the suite they shared drew less attention than its condition. Drawers to period reproductions hung open, oil paintings hung askew on fabric-covered walls, and the hand-carved canopied bed in Lang's room was unmade, spilling its linen onto the rich carpeting.

Van Decker's crew had made no attempt at subtlety.

Intentionally, Lang guessed. The evidence of their search was designed to intimidate.

He was in the process of returning items to the single small bag he had brought when a cough drew his attention to the open door. A smallish man in the hotel's livery stood in the doorway, shifting his weight from foot to foot.

"Excuse me, Mr. Reilly," he said once he was certain Lang saw him. "I am Luyken, the hotel's manager. I trust you enjoyed your stay?"

The man spoke impeccably, as Lang would have expected in the city's finest hotel. He even had an English accent.

Lang nodded. "We did."

He waited, certain the manager had not come to check on the accommodations.

"This is awkward for me," Luyken finally managed. "But I must ask you to terminate your stay. The police . . . the cars, the uniforms, they upset our other guests. I'm sure you understand."

Lang closed his bag just as Louis came from his bedroom. "Of course. We'll check out as soon as you have the bill ready."

The hotel manager glanced away, embarrassed. "It is at the desk right now." He turned to go, then spun around. "And thank you for your understanding."

Louis's eyes followed the man into the hall. "What . . . ?"

"We're leaving at the request of management."

Louis eyebrows arched in a question. "The police?"

Lang picked up his bag. "We were leaving anyway." He gave the room a final inspection. "Nicest place I've ever been thrown out of."

Outside, Lang took the taxi summoned by the doorman, ordering it to the train station.

At the station he paid the cab as Louis took a bag in each hand and headed inside.

Lang grasped his arm, watching the car in which they had arrived. Instead of joining the queue of taxis outside the station, it drove off—perhaps returning to a designated area, perhaps having complied with instructions from the police.

Lang gently tugged Louis toward the line of waiting cabs. "I've never really seen the city." He signaled to the hack first in line. "And there's no time like now."

After ten minutes of aimless cruising, Lang was certain the cab was not being followed. He directed it to the copy shop, where he retrieved his weapon before returning to the station and making the next train to Brussels.

In their first-class compartment, Louis finally relaxed. "You have avoided the police now, yes?"

Lang leaned back in the seat. "For the moment, anyway."

The monotony of the steel wheels against iron rails was hypnotic. Lang was about to doze off when his BlackBerry beeped. Only Sara had that number, and it was unlikely she was calling just to see if he was enjoying himself.

"Yes, Sara?"

"A couple of matters, Lang," she began without preamble. "That detective, Morse, calls here daily. Won't tell me what he wants other than to see you as soon as you get back."

"I'm not sure when that might be."

"I am. You forgot you agreed to take part in the bar's CLE on criminal defense this Friday."

Lang groaned. "Surely—"

"Surely you'll do it. If you want to continue to practice, that is. As usual, you're behind."

Lang nodded his defeat. "Okay, okay. I'll be there."

CLE.

Continuing legal education, the Bar Association's greatest boon since Georgia had required all lawyers to become members upon passing the bar forty years ago. The association, like all bureaucracies, had taken on a life of its own not necessarily dedicated to the well-being of its members.

The bar made about four hundred dollars per lawyer a year for twelve hours of mind-numbing tedium. Most lectures were a cure for chronic insomnia. Any educational value would be—and was—equaled by simply reading current court decisions and statutes. Besides, no lawyer was likely to reveal tricks and tactics he had learned the hard way: that Judge Biddle down in Macon, Georgia, never granted attorney's fees on discovery motions, or that any questionable bit of evidence was best presented while Judge Whipple in Augusta was dozing after his lunchtime nip at the bottle.

Since the big firms largely controlled the association, they had quickly obtained the right to conduct CLE on their own, thereby avoiding an inconvenient loss of billable hours. In all his years of practice Lang had never heard an opponent from one of these legal behemoths beg off of a deposition because he was taking CLE that day.

In short, the program accomplished little other than enriching the association and presenting a less than accurate image to the public of lawyers always abreast of current developments, rather than well rested after napping through a seminar.

It was, however, possible to at least partially pay the legal equivalent of a future indulgence by participating in the program, giving a lecture in exchange for required CLE hours. Lang had promised to do just that, and now that promise was due.

Now Lang was faced with not only a sleepless night on the flight home but also an inattentive captive audience when he arrived.

While Lang had been on his phone, so had Louis.

"The boat," he began, "the registration. The craft belonged to a corporation out of Jersey."

The Channel Islands, where British law guaranteed secrecy of bank accounts and corporate ownership—the only appeal of arguably the most obscure and isolated place in Europe, along with the continent's worst weather. Without the encouragement of total business privacy, the populations of Jersey and Guernsey would soon consist only of the hardy cattle named for the islands.

"Did you get the name of the corporation?"

"Manna, Limited."

Same as the boat itself. Lang stored that bit of information away. "And platinum metals?"

"I have no answer yet."

Lang sank back into the softness of the first-class seat. Manna. As in, from heaven—god-given food for wandering Israelites. What could the people of Exodus have to do with a fossil-fuel substitute?

*   *   *

The Book of Jereb

Chapter Three

1. And the Israelites were at the base of the mountain forty days while Moses returned to speak with the one God. But they again murmured among themselves, saying, "We have naught to eat, for the cattle we brought out of Egypt have long been consumed, as has the wheat, and we shall surely starve without meat or bread."
2. And Joshua quieted their fears, saying, "Has the one God brought you out of Egypt to perish here?" And the Israelites mocked him, saying, "Does the voice of the one God speak in your ear?"
3. Upon the morning the ground and bushes where the golden calf had been burned were covered with manna*, whereupon Joshua said unto them, "This is the bread your God has given you to eat." And the Israelites likened the manna unto honey, it was so sweet, and they feasted upon it until Moses returned from the mountain.
4. And Moses bade them to gather up the manna of which they had a thousand bushels and carry the same with them.

*The Egyptian word mfkzt is used. The first-century Roman historian Falvius Josephus, a converted Jew, says the Israelites awoke to find the mysterious substance and thought it had snowed, although how people, generations of whom had lived in Egypt without the benefit of film or television, would even know of the existence of snow is anyone's guess. The Hebrew word man-hu means, "What is this?" It is more likely the term was introduced when the first drafts of what we know as the Old Testament were written, perhaps in the sixth century B.C., during the so-called Babylonian captivity. The same query comes from the Egyptian Book of the Dead, which depicts the pharaoh being served "schea food" for enlightenment and asking, "What is this?" or, "Mfkzt."

Manna, then, likely had its origins in Egypt.

4

TWENTY-TWO

Peachtree Center
227 Peachtree Street
Atlanta, Georgia
Two Days Later, 9:21 a.m.

Lang had written the day off as a total loss before he got out of bed. He would not be disappointed.

He planned to spend the morning returning phone calls and e-mails before wasting an afternoon giving what he hoped was an entertaining if not informative CLE lecture at the former Federal Reserve Building, now owned by the Georgia Bar Association.

All thoughts of the bar disappeared the minute Lang entered his office to see the former mayor sitting in the reception room.

An accusatory glance in Sara's direction only elicited an almost imperceptible shrug.

The mayor was mocha-skinned, heavy on the cream. A fringe of cropped white hair framed premature balding. He displayed a pencil-thin mustache, also gone white. As always, his suit looked as though it had never seen a wrinkle, and the crisp white shirtfront was evenly divided by a designer tie. The mayor's shoes memorialized at least one alligator.

Lang made a mental note to ask him to let Wal-Mart

supplement his wardrobe before appearing before ju-
rors, most of whom didn't make as much in a week as his
tie cost.

The mayor stood, straightening out to the six-foot
height he had used to advantage in towering over a jury
box in the days when he had been a trial lawyer rather
than a politician. He extended a hand before Lang could
think of an excuse to get him out of the office. "Thanks
for seeing me without an appointment."

Before Lang could reply, his client was in his office.

"I wanted to discuss trial strategy for a minute or two."

Lang suppressed a sigh of resignation. Lawyers in trouble with the law always wanted to handle things their
way, frequently the way that had gotten them in trouble
in the first place.

Lang shut the door, more to discourage Sara from offering coffee or anything else that might prolong the visit
than for privacy.

"I think we need to make the jury understand that
this whole witch-hunt is racially motivated," the mayor
said.

Lang plopped down behind his desk. "Racism" had
been the mayor's excuse for everything that had gone
wrong during his administration, and that was a long list.
Anyone, no matter his color, who had opposed him had
been Ku Klux Klan or an Uncle Tom, including the
majority-black city council, the governor, most of the leg-
islature, and the chamber of commerce.

The spots had just about worn off that deck of race
cards.

"An idea," Lang said in a neutral tone. "Problem is,
three of the objects of the feds' corruption investigation
are white. All three have already pled guilty to charges of
bribing you."

The mayor leaned forward, demonstrating the megawatt
smile that had looked so good on television. "But that's it,

don't you see? White economic power structure, black mayor. Hell, this is no more'n an ol'-fashioned lynching."

Lang had heard it that before, too. Despite Lang's strong advice, the mayor insisted on giving impromptu news conferences whenever he was in the city.

"Yeah, well," Lang observed, "Atlanta has had one black mayor or another since 1975. None of them has even been charged with a traffic violation."

"One of 'em's dead," the mayor said defensively.

There was a rap on the door. Without waiting for a reply Sara stuck her head in. "Important call, Mr. Reilly."

Custer could have found her useful at Little Bighorn.

Lang picked up the one line that was blinking. "Excuse me."

The mayor was annoyed but had no choice.

"Reilly."

"Morse, Detective Morse."

This time Lang made no effort to stifle his sigh. The day was spiraling downhill faster than he had anticipated. At this rate he'd have notice of an IRS audit before lunch.

He started to ask if he could call the policeman back, but realized he would only be encouraging the mayor to stay on and said, "What's up, Detective?"

"We tested that white powder," Morse answered. "An' you ain't gonna believe what we found. Or, rather, what we didn't find."

Lang was beginning to wonder if there was a conspiracy afoot to waste his whole day. "And your tests are important to me because . . . ?"

There was a pause.

"Guess I did'nt 'xactly start off right, Mr. Reilly. State crime lab tested that stuff an' came back with nothin' but craziness. Wonderin', your foundation's so generous to Georgia Tech an' all, maybe you could get 'em to look at this stuff."

Being asked a favor by the man who had arrested him for one killing he didn't commit and suspected him of another had a certain sweet irony. "You telling me the state lab people are incompetent?"

The mayor was impatiently crossing and uncrossing his legs.

"Not a'tall, Mr. Reilly. It's just that this ain't like anythin' they ever tested for before. They ain't got the equipment."

Lang's curiosity was piqued. "Exactly what did the tests they did do show?"

"Like I say, crazy. The stuff's weight keeps changin'. Hold on." There was the sound of rustling paper. "Iron, silica, and aluminum."

"So?"

The mayor was making a display of checking the diamond-encrusted face of his gold watch, apparently forgetting that he had time to spare that, quite possibly, would expand into years.

"So?" Morse repeated. "That's the part that don't make sense. Stuff wouldn't dissolve in acid."

The significance was lost on Lang, who realized that he didn't know enough chemistry to know what made sense and what didn't. "Tell you what: I'll call Tech, get the name of somebody who'll use their equipment."

"Sure 'preciate that, Mr. Reilly."

Lang put the phone down and looked up. The mayor had left.

The day showed signs of improvement.

As Lang entered the lecture hall at the Bar Association, the first person he saw was Alicia Warner.

"Hi," he said, too surprised to come up with something more original.

"Hi, yourself," she replied.

"Thought the feds had their own CLE."

She treated him to a smile that could have served as an ad for toothpaste. "We do. If you'd checked the program, you'd have seen I'm on it, too."

He did, and she was.

" 'Mechanics of a Federal Prosecution'?" Lang asked. "You're giving secrets away?"

She tossed shoulder-length red hair that Lang suspected was as real as the faint freckles makeup didn't cover. "No more than you are."

"I'd say the attendees are in for a pretty dull session."

Green eyes sparkled merrily. "And this is news?"

Lang was becoming increasingly aware that the seminar audience of thirty or so people was watching. He moved toward the podium. "I've been out of town the last few days or I would have called you."

She said nothing, watching in amusement.

"I, er, I figure I owe you a nice, quiet dinner after . . . after our lunch date."

Several attending lawyers made no effort to hide the fact that they were listening to the conversation.

Screw 'em.

Lang plunged ahead. "I'd love the pleasure this evening."

She cocked her head as though to view him from a different angle. "My Kevlar vest's at the laundry. How 'bout you just come by my house rather than we go out in public? I'll throw something together. Not only less expensive but safer."

Alicia nodded to where the program's moderator was watching, shifting his weight. She dug into a purse that could have served as a suitcase and handed him a business card. "Call me and I'll give you directions."

She turned and headed for the door.

Along with every male in the room, Lang watched her departure.

There was the clearing of a throat behind him. "Now that Lang Reilly has his social plans in place, perhaps we could entice him to speak."

Lang was not sure what a blush felt like, but suspected he was experiencing one.

TWENTY-THREE

School of Chemical Engineering
Georgia Institute of Technology
Atlanta, Georgia
Two Days Later

Like students receiving remedial instruction, Lang and Detective Morse sat in folding chairs across the desk from Hilman Werbel, Ph.D., professor of advanced chemical engineering. The man's credentials were displayed in a series of gold-framed degrees that shared the white plaster walls with photographs of the professor embracing, shaking hands with, or simply smiling beside people Lang guessed were luminaries of the scientific world. A window air-conditioning unit provided more noise than cooling, and Lang was beginning to feel uncomfortably warm as well as annoyed with himself for letting the policeman convince him to come along.

"I can't explain it," Werbel said, eyes downcast as though the admission were one of guilt. "Frankly, until yesterday I'd never heard of anything with these properties."

Morse leaned forward. Lang had noticed that the policeman's street jargon and accent had not followed him onto campus. "Doctor, had anything beyond the most basic science courses been required for graduation, I'd still be in high school. Reckon you could reduce all this technical stuff to something I can understand'?"

He had echoed Lang's thoughts.

Werbel regarded both men over half-moon glasses while his hand went to a perfectly adjusted bow tie, a gesture that he had repeated so often as to seem unconscious of it. "I'll try. First, of course, we weighed a portion of the material, the powder, to the nearest thousandth of a gram, recording that weight on the outline of the experiment you have before you." He pointed to the papers in the other men's hands. "We began with emission spectroscopy, placing the material in a carbon electrode cup and using another to create an arc. The elements in the sample ionize, revealing the specific light frequencies of the elements involved. . . ."

Lang held up a hand. "Doctor, neither Detective Morse nor I has the background to appreciate the various protocols of your experiments. Could you dumb it down a little, make it understandable to two nonscientists?"

The professor's pudgy face contracted into a quick frown, the sort of expression he might have used had been asked to actually teach undergraduate students. "But without explaining the process, the results, and my conclusions . . ."

Morse put his elbows on his knees. "The results and your conclusions, Doctor, are what Mr. Reilly and I came for." He smiled innocently. "We are far too chemically unsophisticated to understand your thorough scientific process."

The professor considered this a second and nodded. "I'll try to put all this in layman's terms. In the first few seconds, silica, iron, and aluminum were indicated, with traces of calcium, sodium, and titanium. Then, as the temperature increased, we saw what appeared to be . . . Well, without going into exotica such as iridium and rhodium, let's say the material seemed to be composed entirely of platinum group metals."

Lang's interest picked up at the words. Whatever they were, platinum group metals seemed to be a recurring theme.

"I thought you said it contained iron and aluminum," Morse interrupted.

Werbel sat back in his chair. "That's just it, Mr.—Detective Morse. The very composition seemed to change, and that isn't even the strange part."

As one, both the policeman and Lang crossed their arms expectantly.

"As the subject material heated in a separate test, it *increased* its weight by one hundred two percent. As it cooled, the mass reduced itself to fifty-six percent of its original weight. In other words, it levitated."

"Levitated?" Lang asked. "As in it rose into the air?"

"We couldn't see it actually rise," the professor said, "and there was no indication that it dissolved into the atmosphere of the chamber we used."

"But it had to go somewhere, didn't it?" Morse.

"One of physics' and chemistry's basic theorems is that matter is not created nor destroyed, so, yes, it had to go somewhere."

One of the few things Lang remembered from his brief and unpleasant exposure to the sciences. "Okay, so where did it go?"

The professor came forward in his swivel chair so suddenly, Lang thought he might be catapulted into a wall. "I'm no theoretical physicist, you understand," he said, as though apologizing for the oversight, "but my colleagues in that area speculate that the material must have gone into a different dimension."

Lang and Morse looked at each other, their expressions saying what manners prohibited: The professor was nuts!

Werbel saw the glances. "No, no, I'm not crazy—at least, no more so than anyone else who works here. Einstein as well as lesser-known physicists have long speculated that there are one or more parallel dimensions."

"Like in *Star Trek*?" Morse asked.

"We don't know—not yet, anyway. Stranger still, not only did the sample levitate, but so did its container. Further heating to over a thousand degrees Celsius transformed the subject powder into a clear, glasslike substance, which, when cool, returned to one hundred percent of its original weight."

The professor paused long enough to open a desk drawer and produce an envelope. He opened it carefully, emptying it on the desk's blotter.

Both Lang and Morse leaned forward to see what, at first glance, resembled a contact lens.

Werbel prodded it with the tip of a ballpoint, in his element of academic lecturing. Lang felt he should be taking notes. "You'll note it's flat. Unlike the glass it resembles, it is impervious to any number of acids, sulfuric, hydrochloric, et cetera. Also, you'll note the substance itself seems to magnify light." He took a pen-size flashlight from a pocket. "You'll see the size of the beam increases as it passes through and turns a richer color, yet we could ascertain no prism effect."

"What's the significance of that?" Lang asked, mesmerized by the light passing through the tiny glass disk. It had an inner iridescence he had never seen before.

The professor shook his head. "Like everything else about whatever this substance is, I don't have a clue. The only thing further I can tell you is that we reversed the testing process with another one of these bits of glass or whatever it is."

"And?"

The chemist produced another envelope and nudged its contents out with the same pen. A tiny mound of shiny yellow metal slid onto the blotter beside the glass.

"Looks like gold," Morse commented.

"It is," Werbel said, still perplexed. "Of the highest purity."

TWENTY-FOUR

The Varsity
North Avenue
Atlanta, Georgia
Twenty Minutes Later

The Varsity, just across I-85/75 from the Tech campus, had been an Atlanta institution for over seventy years. It boasted—truthfully, Lang guessed—the world's largest drive-in eatery, the world's best hot dogs, and the world's highest volume of Coca-Cola sales. It chose not to brag about its equally artery-clogging onion rings, milk shakes, and unique fried apple and peach pies. Its aroma reached for blocks and was a siren song luring the unwary onto the rocks of congestive heart failure.

Lang did not entirely dismiss the urban legend of a tunnel under the place leading directly to the nearest cardiovascular surgery center. Still, he hadn't been there for years. He rationalized that the cholesterol bomb he was consuming would do little harm as long as it was infrequent.

Besides, the earth had no better chili dog or Varsity Orange, a combination of Orange Crush and ice cream.

He and Morse had elected to leave their cars and were seated in one of several rooms featuring student lecture hall desks and a ceiling-mounted TV tuned to a local station. Lang had pulled his desk against a wall, where he could see anyone entering.

Morse's street dialect had returned like a sweater worn so often its owner never noticed it draped around his shoulders. He was heavily salting a grease-stained paper carton of french fries when he looked around to make sure no one was in hearing range. "Gold! No wonder somebody offed th' professor. Probably stole all but th' little bit we found. Least we got a motive."

Lang noted the plural first person and dismissed it as merely figurative. Unlikely that the cop was going to include him in an investigation if he could help it. He spread chopped onions more evenly along the brown carpet of chili surmounting his hot dog. "Wouldn't do a lot of good to steal the powder unless you had equipment that could raise it to . . . What did the man say, over a thousand degrees Celsius?"

"Sump'n like that," Morse agreed through a mouthful of his chili steak. He swallowed, then added, "Don' mean somebody with sophisticated equipment didn't kill the professor for it. Where he get that stuff, anyway?"

Lang shrugged. "I assume it was a product of his work."

Product of *their* work. Lang was certain it was the same powder that had been in Yadish's laboratory, too.

Morse was unsuccessfully using a paper napkin to wipe a brownish stain from his shirtfront. "Oh, well, jacket'll cover most of it," he observed before looking into Lang's face. "You thinkin' somethin', Mr. Reilly, like maybe somethin' you'd like to share with me?"

Lang shook his head in denial. "What makes you think that?"

The detective's eyes narrowed, " 'Cause I know you, Mr. Reilly. I knows there's somethin' here you ain't tellin me."

"And how do you know that?"

"I seen the shots-fired report down to Underground last week or so. Now, I don' much believe some perp takes a shot or two at you in a restaurant 'cause you with his woman." He paused. "Although you do seem to piss people off, Mr. Reilly. Some dude always tryin' to whack you. This time, though, I 'spect there's a reason—a reason that has somethin' to do with this dead professor and this powder that's really gold. Now, you wouldn't be planning on interferin' with a police investigation, would you, Mr. Reilly?"

Lang arched his eyebrows, an innocent man. The gesture, he hoped, hid his annoyance that, once again, the black detective had read him so clearly. "Me? Interfere?"

Morse shook his head in resignation. "Why I feel we done had this conversation before?"

Lang gave himself time to think by taking a swig from his paper drink cup. To tell Morse of Yadish's murder and what had happened in Amsterdam would only encourage the policeman to contact Van Decker and learn of the Dutch inspector's suspicions.

In short, there was no upside to telling what he knew.

"I have no idea why you'd think that," he said.

There was a sucking sound from the straw in Morse's cup. "Mr. Reilly, I got one homicide you kinda involved in. I don't want no more people breakin' into your house, blowin' up your car, or generally sowin' death 'n' destruction."

Lang stood, extending a hand, the meal over. "That I can understand, Detective. Believe me, I want any of the above less than you do."

TWENTY-FIVE

Park Place
2660 Peachtree Road
Atlanta, Georgia
6:27 p.m.
The Same Day

Knowing the temptations fast cars held for young men,
Lang avoided the valet and parked his own Porsche in its
assigned space and took the elevator to the twenty-
fourth floor. His mind was still on what he had heard at
Georgia Tech.

Yadish and Lewis had apparently achieved, or were
about to achieve, what had fascinated man for centuries: alchemy, the transformation of base elements
into gold. But what the hell did that have to do with finding a substitute for fossil fuels? The white powder and
gold must have been by-products. Without the notes of
their experiments, it would be difficult if not impossible
to re-create the method by which they had produced
the powder.

Another mystery: If someone wanted the gold-making
process, why kill for it rather than steal it? Lang's original
premise—that the two scientists had been murdered to
conceal something or stop whatever they had been
doing—was still the most likely motive. That was also
consistent with the attempt on his own life in Belgium.

But conceal or stop what?

Something connected to those unknowable experiments.

Then there were the Hebrew documents he had copied. Yadish had thought them important enough to hide. Could they be related to the motive of his killer? One way to find out: Get them translated. There was a professor of Hebrew history at Emory, one he had consulted before. . . .

No, he decided, best not to involve anyone nearby. Whoever had murdered the two scientists knew Lang was in Atlanta, and his consulting a local might be noted. Far better to use someone less easily ascertainable who understood Hebrew, both modern and ancient, and who was well equipped to take care of himself.

The door pinged open and Lang stepped onto the plush carpet of the foyer. Stopping to check the telltales he had left on his doorknob, he grunted his approval that they were still there. He clicked the key in the lock and swung the door open.

Grumps interrupted his twenty-three-and-a-half-hour-a-day nap to regard his master with one brown eye. His tail beat a slow rhythm on the floor.

"What a joy to come home to such enthusiasm," Lang said, reaching for the leash beside the door. "If you think you can spare the time . . ."

Outside Lang made two decisions: First, the chances for anonymity were better if he left the Gulfstream for a commercial flight, even if that meant leaving his weapon behind. Second, he would see if Alicia was willing to make last-minute plans for tonight.

He frowned as he and Grumps headed back for the high-rise condo. The woman was popping up in his mind with increasing frequency. It wasn't the deep love that had grown between him and Dawn, his wife; nor was it the lust at first sight Gurt had inspired. His feelings for Alicia were . . . well, different, if undefined.

Quit introspecting and start dialing, he told himself, *or the woman will already have made dinner arrangements.*

TWENTY-SIX

Middle Temple Inn
Fleet Street
London
1022 Hours
Two Days Later

Lang was still red-eyed from lack of sleep. Even multiple drinks and the made-up beds into which the first-class seats had been transformed had not cured his aircraft-induced insomnia. Arriving at Gatwick Airport along with the dawn, he had randomly chosen a taxi rather than picking one up at the hack stand. He wanted no replay of Brussels.

The cab dutifully deposited him at the Stafford, a small hotel on a cul-de-sac in St. James's. He was in time for an ample breakfast in a lobby that resembled a parlor Queen Victoria might have visited.

A telephone call, shower, and change of clothes later, he had decided to enjoy the sights of London on foot. Crossing in front of Buckingham Palace, he strode across St. James's Park and Horse Guards to Trafalgar Square, where he paused, ostensibly watching pigeons and traffic swirl around Nelson's Column, an activity that gave him reason to look around like any gawking tourist should anyone be following him.

No one showed him any particular interest.

A short walk down the Strand, past the Savoy, and he stopped again, this time looking at the playbill posted by the theater in front of the hotel. If Lang were being followed, he was unable to detect it.

A block or so farther along was a brief section of old Roman wall that marked where the city of Whitehall ended and the city of London began. It also marked the place where the Strand became Fleet Street, once the center of the city's newspaper and publishing industry, enterprises long ago farmed out to the suburbs, former colonies, or anyplace where labor unions had little sway.

In the twelfth century, the Knights Templar had had a temple here. A short, unmarked path led from the street to what remained of it. Just past that was the ant hill–like Temple Bar, home to most of London's barristers. They located here because of its proximity to the Old Bailey, for centuries past the site of the principal criminal courts.

Lang trudged up a flight of stairs, pausing to flatten himself against the stone wall to make way for a distraught young lady in heels, a black gown, a starched white split dickey, and with a white periwig held atop blond curls by the hand that didn't have the briefcase in it. She gave Lang a baleful stare, muttered something that might have been, "Thanks," and hurriedly clattered on her way down.

Being late for court apparently was just as uncomfortable here as in the United States.

About halfway down a dingy hall, Lang stopped in front of a door bearing a plaque that announced, J. ANNUELIWITZ, BARRISTER. There was no bell, so Lang knocked.

"Enter," came a voice from the other side just before the sound of an electric bolt sliding back.

Once he was inside the door swung shut, the only sound being that of the lock returning to its place. J. Annueliwitz, barrister, like Lang, had old habits that died hard.

Lang stepped into what could have been the wake of a tornado: Papers were piled, not stacked, on every flat surface, including the floor. An occasional leather book cover peeked out from the debris. Roughly down the middle of the room a path had been cleared, and in the middle of it stood an older man.

"Lang Reilly," he observed, pushing spectacles back up on his nose. "You must be sorely oppressed to come to me for help."

Lang returned the ensuing bear hug as best he could. "Aren't most of the people who come in here?"

The man stepped back as though to inspect his visitor. A fringe of white hair encircled an otherwise pink scalp. "Oppressed or lost."

He was wearing a starched white shirt unbuttoned at the collar. Part of it hung outside gray trousers held up by bright red suspenders. Turning, he led Lang into a tiny inner office that was, if possible, more littered than the room they had left. Like icebergs, a computer monitor and rack of briar pipes on the desk towered above an arctic sea of paper.

Jacob Annueliwitz surveyed one of two Naugahyde chairs before stooping and gathering up a file folder, spilling its entrails onto the floor. "Sit, sit." He retreated behind the desk. "Sit and tell me your life's story since I saw you last. Is Gurt well?"

The unintentional wounds are the most painful, Lang thought as he gingerly sat. "Don't know. She left me almost a year ago."

"Can't say I blame her, nice girl that she is." He was reaching for a pipe. "And such a bounder you are."

Lang watched the pipe being packed with tobacco from a leather pouch. "I thought Rachel had finally gotten you to quit."

He nodded as he struck a wooden match. "And so she has . . . at home, at least. That's why I still have this wretched office: to have a place where I can enjoy a pipe or two in relative calm."

Calm was hardly this man's life story. Born to Holocaust survivors in Poland, he and his family emigrated to the new state of Israel after the war. As a young adult Jacob had come to university at Oxford after his obligatory military service. For reasons known only to him, he had preferred the dank English climate to the Mediterranean sun of Palestine and had become a citizen, then studied law. His new citizenship did not deprive him of his Israeli one, and he had been contracted by Israel's intelligence agency, Mossad, to keep an eye on Arab embassies and diplomats.

Both MI5 and the resident CIA had been aware of his activities and, if not approving, did little to interfere. After millennia of shifting attitudes toward them, the Jews felt compelled to spy evenhandedly on friend and foe alike. What had not been so widely known was Jacob's expertise—some said artistry—with explosives, learned during his time in the Israeli army. He was the nuncio of nitrates, the pundit of plastique, a technician of T4.

He and Lang had met while Lang was briefly assigned to the Agency's London office and had become fast friends, a relationship further cemented when each had had a chance to save the other's life.

Lang inhaled deeply before the blue cloud of foul-smelling tobacco smoke reached where he was sitting. "Does Rachel know you still smoke here?"

Jacob took the pipe out of his mouth long enough to survey the bowl. "As you know, the source of all law lies in its enforceability. I think Locke made that observation."

"He probably didn't have a wife who wanted him to quit smoking."

"Quite likely. Now, what, besides my scintillating wit and brilliant powers of observation, brings you here? Or, in the vulgate, what crack have you gotten your arse into now?"

Jacob listened without interruption, poking and prodding his pipe with what looked like a nail. When Lang finished, Jacob made a sucking noise on the pipe before tapping it against an already overflowing ashtray.

"Bloody hell! I'm sorry to hear about Professor Lewis. Seemed a nice chap. For a goy, anyway. Handled a really nasty divorce for him. He wanted to get as far away from his ex as possible. Atlanta was as distant as I could do for him."

Lang didn't reply.

Jacob extended a hand across the desk. "These Hebrew writings, you think they may contain clues as to who is after what?"

"They're one of those stones I'd hate to leave unturned."

"I suppose you want me to translate them for you."

"You bragged you could read the language."

"No brag, lad. I can and do." He moved his fingers in a give-it-here gesture. "Let's see."

Lang reached into his coat pocket and produced them. "You understand those are only copies. The originals are somewhere in Austria."

Jacob was pushing his glasses up again. "I'll bear that in mind if it becomes bloody relevant." He looked up. "What's your stake in this, anyway?"

"Somebody tried to kill me, remember?"

Jacob was sucking on an empty pipe. "Happens daily to someone in your country, if what I see on the telly is correct."

"This wasn't in the U.S.; it was in Brussels and Amsterdam."

Jacob looked up. "I can see why any number of blokes would be interested in the process of making gold, if that's what your two murdered scientists were really doing. I'm a bit at a loss as to what an ancient manuscript would have to do with it."

"That's what I hope to find out."

Jacob was inspecting the copies carefully, as though they might contain something toxic.

"Quite thick for a truly old manuscript," Jacob muttered, running his free hand across a shiny scalp. "Not something I can do in an hour or two. Have to consult references and the like." He made a vague motion toward the debris of his outer office.

"I don't think I'm in a rush."

Jacob put the papers down and produced a cell phone. "Excellent! I'll ring up Rachel and tell her to put a little more water in dinner's soup."

Lang felt a jolt of near panic.

In the tight intelligence community, Rachel Annueliwitz had been famous as the world's worst cook. Excuses to avoid her dinner parties were as creative as they were varied. Some merited Pulitzer prizes for fiction. The last time Lang had been cornered into eating one of her concoctions had been over two years ago, and he still could not decide whether it had burned most going in or out. Either way, he had been reduced to a state of flatulence that would have rivaled a Greyhound bus for emissions.

"You were kind enough to feed me last time."

"Loaned you the Morris, too," Jacob added, referring to the diminutive automobile he had driven as long as Lang had known him. "So what?"

"Last time I didn't exactly feel free to be seen in public. Seems only fair that Rachel not have the burden of feeding me again. Let me take you both out."

Jacob had put the phone down and was using the nail-like thing to scrape the bowl of his pipe, producing a crunching sound. "Fair? What else does the woman have to do? Besides, I'll bet you eat only takeaway, haven't had a good home-cooked meal in a bit."

And not likely to have one tonight, Lang thought. *Not only is love blind; it has no taste buds.*

The prospects were bleak either way. The average London pub or restaurant provided only marginally better fare, usually featuring stringy beef burned beyond recognition and vegetables so thoroughly boiled that they offered little color and less taste. Lang had a theory that this small island had established an empire and dominated the world because the Drakes and Hawkinses, the Wellingtons and Nelsons, the Churchills became morally and mentally tough by enduring English cooking, second only to Aleut Eskimo whale blubber as the worst cuisine in the world. A man who could enjoy steak-and-kidney pie was unlikely to flinch at an enemy broadside. Faced with eating Yorkshire pudding or charging emplaced cannon, who would not choose the guns? The onslaught of the Luftwaffe was nothing compared to a lifetime of blanched peas.

Waterloo was not won on the playing fields of Eton. It was won at the English dinner table.

The quality of British food, or lack thereof, was the reason Chinese and Indian establishments flourished in London. In the last few years one or two French eateries had opened, with great success.

Lang had an inspiration. "Why don't we try Mirabelle's?" Although the food wasn't a whole lot better than the city's dismal average, the checks were astronomical. The theory, Lang guessed, was, Who was going to complain about a dinner that cost more than Great Britain's average weekly salary? "It'll give Rachel a chance to put on some nice clothes."

Jacob grinned, agreeing. "The bird does like to tart up a bit. You'll stop by for a tot or so before dinner?"

Lang tried not to show his relief as he assented.

That evening Lang took the tube's Waterloo Line to St. George's Circle at South Dock, where contemporary high-rises peered at Westminster and the Houses of Parliament across the Thames. Since the addition to the skyline of the London Eye, a huge Ferris wheel along the Embankment, the view was different, perhaps slightly disconcertingly so, from the one Lang had known. The

subway, or "tube," had its own amusement system of as-
piring musicians, singers, jugglers, and magicians. Lang
paused a few minutes at his stop to see an attractive
young lady contort her body into what he had thought
were anatomically impossible positions before dropping
a pound coin into her bowl and heading up the stairs.

Once on the surface, he walked a few blocks to Lambeth Road. Ahead of him were the massive naval guns
that marked the Imperial War Museum. He turned left
and entered the foyer of a glass-and-steel tower indistinguishable from its neighbors.

The Annueliwitz living quarters were nothing like Jacob's office. Chrome and glass furniture threatened to be
a great deal less comfortable than it was. Several pieces
of modern sculpture displayed on acrylic stands looked
as though they had been machine parts in a former life.
On the walls were squares of earth-toned canvas that
could have come from a military shelter, each a testament to the gullibility of collectors of modern art.

If monochromatic cloth qualified as art.

Rachel met him with a hug and a kiss that smelled of
gin. "Langford! How delightful to see you again!" She
pressed a frosted stem glass into his hand. "A very dry
martini! See, I remembered!"

Lang was reasonably certain he had had his customary
single-malt last time. He had quit martinis ever since
Dawn, his wife, had described them as "silver mumblers—
have two and you're mumbling."

He accepted the drink as gracefully as possible, looking for a potted plant that might surreptitiously enjoy it
more than he. Or at least not show the consequences of
imbibing straight alcohol. "Rachel! You have not aged a
day. And am I mistaken or have you lost a few pounds?"

Neither was remotely true, but one of the very few
things Lang had learned about women was that those
two phrases were always appreciated. Actually, losing

weight was the last thing Rachel needed to do. He had often thought that if she turned sideways, she would present no shadow. He supposed she maintained that figure to enjoy the miniskirts she favored, one of which she was wearing tonight. With blunt-cut hair the color of midnight and a face Lang was certain had put at least one plastic surgeon's children through college, she could have passed for Jacob's daughter.

"Only pounds she's lost is at sodding Fortum and Mason." Jacob grumbled as he entered from the bedroom.

Lang noticed he had a glass of Scotch.

Rachel whirled away toward the kitchen. She did not walk, step, or move by any mundane means; she danced, tiptoed, pirouetted, or spun. Lang supposed a ballet teacher had also been enriched by knowing her.

"Oh, I have some very special hors d'oeuvres I made just for you," she called over a shoulder.

A potted plant was now a necessity.

Seeing none, Lang stepped over to the sliding glass doors, opened them, and stepped onto the narrow ledge that Jacob generously referred to as a balcony. The last time Lang had been out here he had been hanging underneath by his fingertips.

"Do you mind?" he called inside. "It's a pleasant night, and your view of Westminster is the best in the city."

The darkness permitted him to jettison both martini and the hors d'oeuvre Rachel insisted he sample. He feigned sipping at an empty glass until Jacob announced it was time to leave for the resaurant.

All three shoehorned into the Morris. Lang soon regretted his gallantry in insisting on riding in the car's mere symbol of a backseat.

"Bloody hell!" Jacob growled. "I left my bleedin' wallet in my office!"

"No problem," Lang said, feeling as if he were speaking between his knees. "It's my treat, anyway."

"You'll not want to pick up the chit if I get stopped by some sodding copper wanting driver's permit and insurance card."

"The Middle Temple Inn isn't so far out of the way," Rachel soothed.

"No, but parking's a problem, and driving round the block's a bother with the one-way streets. You two'll have to sit in the car while I dash in."

Although one way, Fleet Street wasn't wide enough to accommodate curbside parking. A blare of horns from usually polite Londoners when Jacob stopped made it clear another plan was in order.

Lang resisted the temptation to remind his friend that he had suggested the tube.

Jacob sighed in resignation. "There's a car park a block over."

Lang and Rachel made listless efforts to make conversation before becoming quiet.

After what Lang guessed would be ten minutes, she stirred. "Shouldn't take him this long to find his wallet."

"Have you seen his office lately?"

She chuckled. "Heavens, no! Last time I went in there I was afraid something would fall on me. Besides, the dear man guards the place as if it were top-secret. It's his exclusive domain."

Ten minutes later Lang squeezed out of the car. "Exclusive domain or not, I think I'd best see what's taking so long."

Rachel pulled the key out of the ignition. "I'll come along."

The old Templar temple was dark, the surrounding grounds more shadow than light. Only one or two office windows were illuminated. A single bulb on each landing showed the way upstairs. English barristers did not work the hours of their American counterparts.

The dimness of the second floor made the light from under Jacob's door all the more visible. Lang was reaching for the knob when he stopped. The voice he had just heard was not Jacob's.

Using one hand to put a finger to his lips, he used the other to gently push Rachel against the wall before putting an ear against the wood of the door. It gave slightly. Whoever had last entered hadn't pulled it completely shut.

Lang tried to recall whether the hinges had squeaked that afternoon.

He pushed it open only wide enough to put his face to the crack. Jacob was facing him, speaking to a man whose back was toward Lang. From Jacob's expression, the visitor was no friend.

"Again," Jacob said, "I have no bloody idea what you're talking about. You've jolly well tossed the office and haven't found whatever you're looking for. . . ."

The man said something Lang couldn't hear and gestured with a gun in his hand.

Then Jacob saw Lang. Or at least, Lang thought he did. Not wanting to alert the intruder, he had given only the slightest twitch of an eye.

Lang shifted slightly, trying to see as much of the room as possible. His choice of action was going to vary if there was another person in the office.

"What . . . ?" Rachel asked.

Lang made a hushing motion.

"Look," Jacob was saying. "You've simply made a mistake. Since it's only you, why don't you—"

He had answered Lang's question.

Jacob stepped forward. His visitor's reaction was a step backward to keep the space between them. The man motioned menacingly with his weapon. He wasn't going to retreat farther. This was as close to the door as he was going to get.

Something—a slight groan of the floorboards, a puff of

air from the opening door—gave Lang away before he had reached his adversary. The man had been trained. Instead of the normal reaction of spinning around and exposing his back to Jacob, he attempted to sidestep before turning.

But not in time.

With his left hand Lang got under the other man's gun arm, shoving it upward as he cupped his chin in his right hand and simultaneously brought up a swift knee to the groin. His opponent grunted with pain and doubled over in time to take a second knee to the face.

Blood from the broken nose made abstract patterns on the papers scattered on the floor.

The two blows had taken sufficient strength from the intruder that Jacob easily wrested the gun from his hand. Before he could bring it to bear, the interloper was out the door, a bloody hand holding his crushed face. Jacob stepped outside and leveled what Lang could now see was a massive weapon.

"Jacob, dear, be more careful where you point that thing." Rachel stood between her husband and the sound of rapidly receding footsteps. "Whatever did you do to that poor man?"

Lang crossed the room and took the pistol from Jacob as he lowered it. "IMI Desert Eagle."

Jacob nodded. "Fifty-caliber Magnum, the one designed in America and developed by the Israeli military. Bit of a cannon, that."

Lang turned the heavy automatic over. Only seven shots in the fifty-caliber version. Short on firepower, too large and heavy for most who simply needed a firearm, but more easily concealed than a carbine with similar hitting force—no amateur's gun. The Desert Eagle's cavernous bore inflicted "magnum flinch" on those not used to its mule kick of a recoil.

"Whoever your visitor was, he was a professional. What did he want?"

"Thanks to you, we never got specific. He just wanted to know where 'it' was."

" 'It'?"

"Don't think I misunderstood. That's what the bloke said, 'it.' "

Rachel crossed the room, taking the heavy automatic from Lang. She carried it into Jacob's office with two fingers in much the same way she might have disposed of a dead rat. "Gentlemen, our dinner reservations won't wait all evening."

The woman was a seasoned intelligence operative's wife. But the look she gave her husband clearly said the interrogation would begin when they were alone.

Once they were all back in the car, Lang's mind went over the last two days. Rather than risk his reservations appearing on an airline's easily hacked computer, he had shown up at the airport and paid cash for the ticket, thereby also avoiding a credit card's all too traceable charge, if guaranteeing a thorough search of him and his single suitcase by zealous airport security.

He would, of course, be on the aircraft's manifest.

The fact that he had been traced to London and followed to Jacob's office meant several things, all unsettling. First, whoever was out to end the alternate-fuel program probably had contacts in the United States. That was hardly surprising in view of the shots fired in Underground and Lewis's murder. Second, this unknown entity was well organized, able to gain information on one side of the Atlantic and use it on the other. He had surmised that if not known it.

The gun he had just held, though, told him something new: This . . . this unknown was composed of at least some professionals, trained men, as opposed to a band of wild fanatics. To leave such a clue was a surprise. Anonymous groups involved in violence usually took pains to use sanitized equipment, weapons like the Russian AK-47 and its progeny, the U.S. Colt .45 automatic, or any of several Berettas, firearms of such universal use that they were no longer attributable to any particular location, country, or organization.

Either someone had gotten careless, or whomever he was opposing didn't worry about leaving clues.

He spent most of dinner trying to figure out which.

TWENTY-SEVEN

Middle Temple Inn
London
The Next Morning

Lang sat across Jacob's littered desk from the barrister. They were both sipping hot tea the color of strong coffee as Jacob thumbed through the copies Lang had given him the day before.

"Can't really say when I'll be through translating," Jacob said. "Not a good idea to keep them about the house. Our friend from last night might pay a call. At least here I can hide 'em in the general clutter—like a pebble on the beach."

Lang took a tentative sip from his mug and winced at the bitterness of the brew, only increased by the wedge of lemon Jacob had offered. "Any preliminary ideas?"

"A few. I'd say someone copied a much earlier document—copied it out in verse, like your King James Bible. Like the so-called Dead Sea Scrolls, these were likely used in synagogues rather than available to the public at large. They appear to be an effort to reduce Jewish history to the written word sometime after the Roman sack of Jerusalem in 70 A.D. This particular lot claims to be a copy of a much earlier chronicle by the scribe

Jereb. Superficially it resembles the Book of Exodus. The operative word here is *resembles*. The original might even predate Exodus."

"By how much?"

Jacob shrugged as he put his mug down on a stack of legal pleadings. "Possibly from the time of Moses. If I had to guess, I'd say from the little bit of content I can understand without a closer look that someone translated these from another language. It's likely that they were again copied, possibly in the first millennium. It would be helpful if I could see the material itself, judge the ink and writing surface."

"That's not possible."

Jacob picked up his tea and took a long sip. "Pity."

"I mean, I don't have a clue where the copy I used to make those came from, other than Dr. Yadish's cousin in Austria."

Jacob was regarding the contents of his mug. "The tea, I mean. A pity. Time was we got excellent leaf from Ceylon. Now it calls itself by some other name, natives too bleeding busy with some sodding revolution to tend the bushes, and I have to make do with Indian leaf."

Lang hid a smile. Jacob's current zeitgeist was sometimes limited. "Can you at least give me some idea?"

"What does it matter? India's effing India, not Ceylon."

"The manuscript. Can you give me an idea what it's about?"

Jacob looked mildly surprised that the conversation had gone astray. "Some rot about Moses, powder, perhaps like the lot you told me about. And the Ark of the Covenant. Or so it seems."

Lang forgot the tea. "As in Exodus?"

Jacob shook his head. "Like but not the same. Someone else is telling this particular tale. I was told by those more educated on the subject than I that what you call the Old Testament was probably first reduced to Hebrew sometime during the Babylonian Captivity, 500 B.C. or thereabouts, a collection of Jewish oral history and stories in more ancient languages. What you have is probably one in a series of sequential copies, this one, as I said, much earlier than 500 B.C."

Lang was leaning forward in his chair. "But what you're looking at isn't in the Old Testament?"

Jacob was reaching for a pipe. "Not in your book nor mine. Torah either, I suspect."

"But . . . ?"

Jacob had the leather pouch out, pinching stringy tobacco into the pipe. "Just as you Christians picked four Gospels out of any number—a new one seems to pop up every year or so—I suspect my people did, too. I'd speculate this one didn't . . . what do you Yanks say? Make the cut. This one didn't make the cut."

Jacob cocked an eyebrow as he puffed the flames of a match into the bowl, well aware that Lang's Southern upbringing frequently made him bridle at being called a Yankee. "So, what do you do now?" he continued. "After last night I wouldn't think you'd want to be about while I work on your manuscript."

Lang hadn't considered that it would take any length of time to translate the papers. "Don't know exactly. By the way, I apologize for exposing Rachel to what might have happened last evening."

Jacob watched a ring of blue smoke shimmer across the desk. "Apologize to me. I'm the one who caught bloody hell for it. Now she thinks I'm somehow back, connected to the lads over at the embassy."

The British headquarters of Mossad.

"You didn't tell her about . . . ?"

Jacob put up a restraining hand. "Tell her you gave me something that turns out to be dangerous enough to get us killed? Not bleeding likely! She'll simmer down, thinking I'm doing my part for the homeland. She knows it's just a favor for a friend, albeit a jolly good friend. Otherwise I'd be takin' my sleep on that bloody awful settee you saw in my parlor. Less a woman knows, less she has to complain about."

That idea, Lang thought, had damned near gotten him killed.

"Speakin' of favors for friends." Jacob put the pipe down long enough to open a desk drawer and remove a pistol in a belt clip holster. "When you called yesterday, you asked what I could do about gettin' some protection. I guessed right off it wasn't condoms you were lookin' for. I remembered you favored one of these."

Jason took the proffered weapon, a SIG Sauer P226 just like the one in his bedside table at home. "Thanks, Jacob. I'm surprised you could come up with this so quickly."

Jason held up dismissive hands. "I still know a few secrets some lads would just as soon I keep to m'self. Now, it's been lovely chatting you up, but if you'll leave me be I'll get on these papers."

Lang walked back to his hotel, careful to watch for anyone who might be following. He was still unsure of what came next when he checked the telltales on his door and let himself in.

He sat on the bed and picked up the phone after checking his watch. Then he put it down again and left the room. At the concierge's desk in the lobby he exchanged bills for coins before stepping back outside.

It took a while to find a pay phone in St. James. The signature red booths had long ago disappeared into American chain restaurants, to be replaced by simple plastic bubbles, if there at all. The cell phone had made the coin-operated variety an endangered species.

Although almost any call on the planet had been subject to monitoring long before the fact became a political issue, a public-telephone conversation would be buried in unmined data. If they—whoever "they" were—had sufficient sophistication to hack into the FAA's flight plan database to meet him in Brussels, they possibly could piggyback the Anglo-American spy system to pull up any calls made from his cell, a number they would surely be watching.

He toyed with the idea of simply going to a post office, a place that always had pay phones, since the British postal system owned the phone company. But it was too crowded and too easy to overhear conversations in the ordinary post office.

Past Picadilly Circus, he spotted what he was looking for and counted out a handful of change. He patiently listened to the hisses and squeaks of a transatlantic call, wondering why the sounds were just the same as when the old Atlantic cable was the sole means of communication.

"Hello?"

At least the quality had improved. The voice on the other end could have come from across the room rather than an ocean.

"Francis! It's your favorite heretic!"

Pause.

"Lang?"

"You don't recognize my voice?"

"Of course I do," the priest snapped. "You're just not among the people I'd expect to be calling at seven in the morning, *ante lucem*."

"*Qui male odit lucem.* That's because it's noon here. Surely I didn't wake you up."

"Obviously not, since you called my office, not my cell phone, hopefully for some other purpose than to announce the time of day, wherever you are."

Lang was about to quote Virgil again until he noticed a young cherub-faced and uniformed nanny giving him an odd look over the long handlebars of the pram she was pushing. "It's all right, dearie. I always practice my Latin on the phone."

She retreated at a pace that might have exceeded the baby carriage's safety limits.

"What?" Francis said. "*Unis dementia . . .*"

". . . *Dementes efficit multos*," Lang finished. "Insanity is catching. But I didn't call just to chat. I've got some questions about the Bible."

"You apostates always have questions about the Bible. That's why you're infidels," Francis said dryly.

It was an old and good-natured barb.

"The Ark," Lang began, "tell me about it."

"Noah's?"

"Of the Covenant."

The cockney-accented voice of the operator interrupted to request more coins.

"The Ark of the Covenant," Francis mused after the additional deposit was made. "Just what endeavor has sparked this interest?"

"I'll tell you about it when I get home. Do we know where it is?"

Francis snorted. "We pretty well know where it's not, Indiana Jones notwithstanding. That tale, as you recall, had it located in Africa. There are those who believe that Solomon gave it to his son by the Queen of Sheba, Menyelek, who took it to what's now Ethiopia. There's a sect of Ethiopian Jews who claim to have it."

"But you don't believe that."

"Just a minute." There was the sound of something being moved. Lang could visualize his friend dragging one of his biblical reference books to the center of his desk. "No. Solomon himself tells us he sat a place for the Ark in the Temple, One Kings eight: twenty-one. The Old Testament mentions it a number of times after Solomon, particularly its being hidden from Nebuchadnezzar when his Babylonians invaded. Then reference to it simply stops. Where it is now is anyone's guess. Some make a strong case the Templars found it under the temple in

Jerusalem and carried it back to Europe. There's something to that."

Lang shifted the receiver to the other ear. From his own experience he knew the former organization of religious knights had at least one biblical treasure. "Oh?"

"Chartres was one of the several Gothic cathedrals in France begun fairly close to one another in time, sixty years. Notre Dame, Chartres, Reims, Amiens. All associated with the Templars."

"So, the Ark might be in one of those?"

"Not so easy. All have been associated with the Templars. Where else but from the East could have come the knowledge to build something so spectacular? Flying buttresses, thinly ribbed vaulted ceilings towering hundreds of feet high. The world, or at least the Western world, had never seen anything like it. For that matter, no one at the time had the skill to do that sort of building."

"I don't take your point." Lang was getting uncomfortable. Standing at a pay phone was not conducive to changing to more relaxed positions.

"Perhaps I'm straying a bit, *celeritas.*"

"Promptness would be appreciated. Truth is, Francis, I'm standing out on a public street."

"But why would you . . . ? Oh, I get it. Anyway, all of these Gothic cathedrals are associated in one way or another with the Templars: the skills, the knowledge, whatever. Most important, no one had a clue as to how to build what, by the standards of the day, must have seemed to defy gravity. That power had to come from somewhere. This becomes significant when you consider Chartres has the last known contemporary reference to the Ark."

Lang forgot his physical discomfort. "And that is . . . . ?"

"On a north column there's a small stone carving showing the Ark being moved. Underneath is a Latin inscription, *Hie amittitur archa fedris.*"

Lang ran a hand across his face, unconscious of the gesture. "I'm not sure I know what that means. Something about something being let go or sent. Must be some sort of medieval corruption of the language."

"That, plus centuries of accumulation of grime, erosion from the weather, and perhaps help from French revolutionaries chipping away at the words. I'd put it at, 'Here the Ark is sent forth or yielded up.' "

"Sent to where?"

"That, my friend, is the problem. To Scotland when the Templars perhaps fled there? To the Languedoc region of France when it was a Templar stronghold?"

Lang turned around, looking for anyone showing an interest in him. He was well familiar with the Languedoc and its connection to the medieval monastic order of Templars. Too familiar. "Okay, so much for the Ark. Do you know anything about a sort of powder connected with it somehow, a very peculiar white powder that melts into a strange, almost self-illuminating glass?"

There was a pause.

"Funny you should ask right after we spoke of Gothic cathedrals. If you look at the few parts of the stained-glass windows original to those places, sections that haven't fallen out or been destroyed by wars over the centuries, you'll see what's called 'Gothic glass,' a sort of iridescent glass in which every color seems to glow. It was made during the hundred years or so after the cathedrals were begun; then it disappeared. The process for making it seems to have disappeared also. One wonders if that beautiful glass was the same as mentioned in Revelations."

"Glass in Revelations?"

"Just a . . . Ah! Here it is: 'And the city was pure gold like unto clear glass. . . .' Revelations twenty-one: eighteen. Frequently the Book of Revelations is difficult to comprehend."

Gold like unto glass. The writer of the last book in the Bible understood something Dr. Werbel at Georgia Tech did not. Neither did Lang. The two, glass and gold, had been connected in antiquity. But how?

"Lang? Lang? You still there?"

Francis's voice brought his attention back to the conversation. "Does Revelations mention the Ark?"

"Not that I know of. As I said, references stop fairly abruptly about the time of the Babylonian invasion. What's this all about?" Francis asked. "I don't for a minute think a heathen like you has suddenly become interested in the Bible preparatory to seeing the truth."

"I'll tell you when I get home," Lang promised and hung up.

He could imagine his friend's frustration at having his mind picked and not being told why. But then, weren't Christians taught to forgive?

TWENTY-EIGHT

Hotel Stafford
St. James
London
An Hour Later

The telltale was missing.

Either the hotel's housekeeping staff had already made its daily visit or Lang had an uninvited visitor. He stepped back from the door and reached behind his back to grip the butt of the SIG Sauer as though to make certain it had not somehow escaped.

This was one of those situations that simply had no safe solution. If anyone were in the room, the sound of the key in the lock would give them all the advance warning needed. Kicking in the door and entering with gun blazing worked great in action films but left a lot to explain, particularly if the room turned out to be empty. Besides, real doors tended to be somewhat less destruction-prone than the plywood of the movies.

He took his cell phone from his pocket. Reading the number from his room key, he called the hotel, requesting that room service deliver an early lunch. With the aplomb of the better British hotels, no one inquired why he was using an outside line to make such a request.

Lang backed down the short hall and waited, watching the door to his room.

Within fifteen minutes a liveried waiter was balancing a tray as he hurried from the opposite end of the hall.

Lang waited until he knocked, announcing himself as room service. By the time he was knocking again Lang was beside him, key in the lock and his other hand again resting on the concealed weapon. Arguably, any occupant of the room would not realize Lang had returned.

Gently pushing the young waiter aside from a potential line of fire, Lang eased the door open.

The room was empty.

The maid had not yet been there.

Lang took the linen-draped tray, thanked the lad, and handed him a five-pound note.

The lunch was typically British: attractively cut, nicely served, and without an iota of taste or flavor. Who but the English would put butter on a ham sandwich? As he munched what was at least fresh bread, Lang tried to remember exactly where he had placed things: Was his shave kit exactly where he had left it? Were the shirts in the dresser in the same order?

He stopped, staring at an upholstered chair. The chintz of the seat didn't match the back. He stepped to the chair, removed the cushion, and gave it a ninety-degree turn so its design was now aligned with the back. He was certain he would have noticed the aberrant pattern.

Whoever "they" were, they had found him.

But how?

And exactly what were they looking for?

He had paid cash on arrival, only slightly raising the eyebrows of a front-desk crew well adjusted to the idiosyncratic behavior of the hotel's guests. Perhaps an unspotted tail. Or . . .

The thought made him uncomfortable. This hotel had been his choice, what, three or four times in the last several years? In the past he had paid with the foundation's credit card. If someone's computer had traced that card number, it would have revealed where he stayed when in London.

Like it or not, the Information Age was privacy's funeral notice no matter how many people were fruitlessly trying to revive the corpse, an effort not unlike unscrambling an egg.

In fifteen minutes Lang was on the street, suitcase rattling along behind him like some dutiful animal. He visited a number of shops before reaching the block occupied by Fortnum & Mason. He entered, took an elevator as far as it went, took another halfway down, and walked the rest of the way to street level, exiting opposite where he had entered and hailing a roaming cab.

In London, as in most large cities, the traffic made it difficult to spot a following vehicle.

Lang directed the taxi to Knightsbridge in Kensington and from there to the Marble Arch Hotel. He was not surprised there was no doorman to greet him. Inside a lobby that was as dreary as the exterior, he waited while a platoon of Japanese tourists formed ranks behind their leader and sallied forth into the world of the *gaijin*, snapping pictures at every step.

A tired clerk took Lang's money in exchange for a key and explained that, on a cash basis, all room service requests would have to be paid for upon delivery. He made no offer to have someone show Lang to his room, nor was he ashamed to explain that there would be no refund were Lang to vacate before the next morning.

Named for a London landmark nearby, the Marble Arch had the worn-at-the-elbows look of a destination for tourists on a budget, traveling salesmen on commission, or a spouse on a lark. Lang's view was of a brick building perhaps five feet distant, but the room was clean and utilitarian.

He didn't intend to be there long, anyway.

He consulted a phone book and left the hotel. At the entrance he paused for a full minute, as though uncertain where he was going. He could see no one loitering in doorways, and there were few store windows to attract shoppers. A stroll around the block revealed a dark-skinned woman haggling with a greengrocer, a young mother walking twins, and a liveried chauffeur sneaking a quick smoke as he listlessly wiped the hood of a vintage Bentley free of imaginary spots.

Lang assumed he was alone.

A walk up to Knights Bridge Road took him past the part of Hyde Park known as Speakers' Corner, once the site of public executions, where the condemned were allowed to speak their minds, adding to the general entertainment before mounting the thirteen steps of the gallows. The gibbet was long gone, but the tradition of radical and unpopular speech lingered. Two men, both unshaven with long hair, were shouting at unconcerned passersby.

A block farther and he turned into a building flying the Union Jack. A small sign outside announced its function as a library. Inside, Lang stopped to whisper to an elderly man, who pointed him to the computer room.

Seated in front of the latest equipment, Lang called up Google and typed in *alchemy*, the quasi-scientific quest of a method of turning base metals into silver and gold. He was overpowered by the number of references. He was going to be here a little longer than he had planned.

Five hours later he only reluctantly left his machine at the prodding of the same old gentleman, this time announcing the closing of the facility for the day. Once back on the street, Lang stretched his arms and arched his back, surprised at how quickly the afternoon had retreated.

What he had thought to be simply misinformed medieval science was more, much more.

First, the practice of alchemy had its origins somewhere before Aristotle, a philosophy by which the soul or being of man could be enriched, life prolonged, and enlightenment achieved. He had tried to hurry through the purely ideological theories to spend more with the scientific.

Medieval scientists, or "philosophers," as they were called, had included no small number of charlatans, as the practice might suggest. It had, though, attracted some of the more serious minds of the time, including Roger Bacon, and Isaac Newton of falling-apple fame. Also Robert Boyle, whose observations, Lang was informed, were viable today and dealt with volume of gases. Lang was unsure what kinds, but unlikely those generated by Rachel's cooking and Mexican restaurants.

In Sir Isaac's time, the prevailing theory had been that all matter was composed of a combination of the four basic elements: fire, water, air, and earth. By correctly altering the proportions of these elements in, say, lead, gold would result.

There were scraps of writing from alchemists that seemed possibly relevant: John French, in his 1651 *The Art of Distillation*, described fire that would keep more than a thousand years unless its container were opened. What containers? Like the ones in Lewis's and Yadish's laboratories? Under *definitions* in one article, *comminution* was "reduction of a substance to powder by means of heat."

There were also bibliographies numbering hundreds of volumes, books Lang would never have time to read in a lifetime, let alone before his pursuers caught up with him. He settled for four names of people who maintained Web sites concerning alchemy. He discarded the first two upon browsing their sites and finding one published a small magazine on Wiccans and alchemy. He could do without witchcraft, although his subject was only marginally more distant from the black arts. The second described himself as "sorcerer extraordinaire." Lang passed for the same reason. The third site had not been updated in over a year, and Lang's query to the e-mail address was undeliverable. The fourth, a Dr. Heimlich Shaffer in Vienna, displayed a more comforting curriculum vitae as an archeological chemist, whatever that was.

Outside the library, Lang tried the phone number given by the Web site and understood most of a message recorded in German that said he should leave a message. Lang decided against it, wondering if Wiccans and warlocks used answering devices or if astral impulse sufficed.

Once back at the hotel he called Jacob and listened to a very normal request that he leave a number. If the professor in Vienna was going to be any help, having all the facts possible was going to be necessary: Templar cathedrals, a new, or unknown, version of Exodus . . . Were they related, and if so, how would two scientists seeking a new energy source an ocean apart come up with the same powder that levitated and became glass and gold? The answer, if there was one, might lead him to who was trying to end the energy project and kill him in the process.

At least, he hoped it would.

He had no other means of ending a chase that had already become deadly.

*   *   *

The Book of Jereb

Chapter Four

1. And Nadab and Abihu, sons of Aaron, died from the fire from the Ark, for they had made to carry the Ark without wooden staves nor breastplates of gold, nor had they removed their shoes and washed their feet.

2. But the Levites carried the Ark ahead of the Israelites and into the Lands of the Moabites and Ammonites and Amorites, who fled before its power and were slain by the commandment of the one God.

3. But Moses did not cross the River Jordan but looked across into the land of the Canaanites and anointed Joshua to lead the people.

4. And Joshua sent forth the Levites with the Ark to Jericho, wearing gold breastplates and rings and having washed their feet but leaving sandals behind with the rest of the people.

5. Seven priests went before the Levites, blowing trumpets each day for six days. Upon the seventh day they marched seven times around the city. There came forth from the Ark lightning, which destroyed the walls of Jericho. And the children of Israel slew the people thereof, sparing only the family of Rahab the harlot, for she had given aid to the Israelites.

6. Then Joshua led the Israelites farther into the land of the Canaanites and unto the mount of Abraham to place upon it a throne of the House of Judah to rule over the Israelites.

5

TWENTY-NINE

Schwechat International Airport
Vienna
Three Days Later

The Vienna airport terminal is small compared to those in London, Paris, or Rome. Rather than overpowering architecture, gently curving sides of shining blue glass give passengers the sense of being embraced upon arrival.

At least, Lang thought so as he peered out of the window of the foundation's Gulfstream IV. The aircraft had left the United States to deliver a team of pediatricians to Greenland, bound for the Arctic Circle and a rumored outbreak of some strain of measles among children of one of the Eskimo tribes. The mission complete, Lang had arranged for the plane and crew to proceed to Scotland.

He was fairly certain his arrival was unknown to the mysterious group who apparently wanted to kill him. He had had to show no identification to purchase a British rail ticket from London to Glasgow, meet the plane, and depart minutes later.

Both England and Austria were European Union countries. No passport nor customs were required, and no official note of his arrival was made other than the aircraft's manifest or general declarations. Since these documents were rarely verified, Lang had donned the gray suit with epaulets on the shoulders worn by the foundation's flight crew. The general decs would show pilot, copilot, and two cabin attendants, one male, one female.

He hoped he had successfully concealed both his departure from London and his arrival here, although a careful check of the departure documents would show one fewer crew member when the plane returned to Atlanta with a very perplexed MD on board who would never guess his urgent summons to the foundation's headquarters was no more than camouflage for the Gulfstream's side trip to Vienna.

With a single suitcase containing two copies of Jacob's translation, the SIG Sauer, and a change of clothes, Lang joined the other crew members in a casual stroll through the terminal along glossy tiles the color of butter as they reflected brightly lit shops and overhead lighting.

As far as Lang could tell, no one paid them the slightest bit of attention.

They parted company at the transportation exit, the crew taking a bus to a nearby hotel and Lang a taxi. Twenty minutes later he was on the Karntner Ring Strasse, if a swath that included tram tracks, four lanes of traffic, a middle green space, and four more traffic lanes could simply be described as a road. A tram's bell rang angrily as the cab made a U-turn to stop at the door of the Imperial Hotel.

Of the two Belle Epoch hotels of Vienna, the Sacher Haus was better known to tourists, but the Imperial boasted a guest list that had included Richard Wagner as well as the triumphant Adolf Hitler, in town to celebrate the 1938 Anschluss.

It was not the sort of place one would expect to house itinerant flight crews, but the man in the long-tailed coat behind the highly polished mahogany desk did not seem to notice the uniform. Lang gave him a foundation credit card, one that did not have his name on it, along with his passport, and signed the registration with an intentionally illegible signature, declining an offer for assistance with his single bag. Passing through the heavily carpeted lobby, Lang turned left into to a small vestibule housing ornate elevators.

His room, wallpapered a tasteful green, was furnished in a style that elsewhere would have been garish. Here, the gilt-edged furniture, swagged drapes, and elaborately made-up bed seemed perfectly in place, a memory of nineteenth-century Hapsburg grandeur. Lang was relieved to see the theme did not carry over to the bathroom. Modern fixtures and a multiheaded shower stall gleamed under operating-room brightness.

Checking his room's door and windows for security, Lang took out his cell phone to call Dr. Shaffer, who should be expecting him. The phone was answered on the second ring by a voice that Lang recognized from two previous conversations.

"Dr. Shaffer?"

"*Ja?*"

"Lang Reilly. We spoke a couple of times."

There was an almost imperceptible pause, the short delay as the mind switched from one language to another. "You are now here in Vienna?"

"The Imperial Hotel. Maybe you could drop by, have a beer or two, and we could talk?"

Another pause, this one longer.

"I would prefer another place, one where I will be able to recognize strangers as strangers. The Koenig Bakery. Do you know it?"

There were hundreds if not thousands of small restaurants in Vienna.

" 'Fraid not."

The professor gave him directions.

Twenty minutes later Lang was walking beside the baroque buildings of old Vienna. Mozart had lived and composed within a block or so, written *The Marriage of Figaro* in an apartment on the dead-end Blutgasse. Johann Strauss had formed the world's first waltz orchestra nearby. Both Beethoven and Schubert had died here. The last Hapsburg emperors, including the kindly Franz Joseph, who described himself as the empire's chief bureaucrat, had worshiped at the Stephansdom, whose Gothic spires were visible over the rooflines.

Even the little restaurant to which the doctor had directed Lang was in historical context. He paused to read the menu posted outside one of several side-by-side eateries. Through open doors he could hear the murmur of conversation. Inside were three small rooms separated by white plaster walls contrasting with beams darkened by centuries of smoke from tobacco and candles.

Just inside the door a smallish man with a beard streaked with white took Lang by the arms. "Langford Reilly?"

"How'd you guess?"

"As I said, I wanted to meet in a place where strangers would be obvious."

Lang thought of the menu outside. Unlike in most European establishments, there was not one in English. Other than Dr. Shaffer, no one was speaking it in here, either.

Lang had an uneasy feeling. "Any reason you're concerned about people you don't know?"

Dr. Shaffer was leading Lang to the back of the restaurant, the one place tables weren't close enough to touch. "Within an hour of the time we first spoke," the professor said in Oxford-accented English, "a man appeared in front of my house. The next day another. I feel I am being followed because of our conversation. Why would that be?"

Lang didn't answer immediately. "They" had retrieved or intercepted the call from his BlackBerry, a feat requiring a fair amount of sophistication—or sharing of information from the Anglo-American Echelon, the worldwide listening station in northern England that automatically recorded every conversation involving a satellite, which included most phone conversations, e-mails, and other communications. Having the communications was one thing. Being able to find one of interest among millions of others was another. Even if access to Echelon by someone other than England, Australia, New Zealand, Canada, or the United States were permitted—something unheard-of in Lang's days at the Agency—the sorting-out process would still be daunting. But what if . . .

"Mr. Reilly?"

Dr. Shaffer was peering at him curiously, as though Lang might have suddenly contracted some exotic disease. "I was hoping you could tell me why I am being watched."

Lang shrugged. "I have no idea," he said, hoping the lie was believable. "As you'll see, these documents are of scientific and historic interest only."

He hoped.

Without taking his eyes off Lang's face, Shaffer stuffed a copy of Jacob's translation into a briefcase beside him. "In that case, you would have no objection to my going to the police?"

Lang picked up a menu, trying to recognize the German he had once known. Four of the six pages were handwritten specialties of the day. "I would think that would be the thing to do. Could be a disgruntled student . . ."

"I have not taught in years. I work on a job-to-job basis for foundations and museums, usually doing chemical analyses of archeological finds." He reached into a pocket somewhere, producing a pack of Marlboros. "Do you mind?"

The only benefit of Gurt's departure had been that Lang had finally gotten the stench of her Marlboros out of his life. The damn smoke still lingered in the condominium and his clothes like a memory that would not go away. He wondered if the smell would have been as offensive if he hadn't missed her so much.

He sat back in his chair and flip-flopped a hand—*I don't care*. The place's patrons all seemed to be puffing away. One more would make little difference.

"You are not a smoker?"

"No."

Shaffer returned the pack to wherever it had come from and waved at the proprietor/waiter. "I will wait, then."

Rare. A smoker deprived of his vice who didn't think he was being imposed upon.

"I recommend the pancake noodle soup. The Wiener schnitzel, goulash, and *Tafelspitz mit G'roste* are equally good."

From his years in Frankfurt, Lang remembered that German food was as filling as it was hearty, something that not only stuck to your ribs but made you feel it was still stuck a day later. "The goulash sounds great. I'll pass on the soup. And whatever beer you're drinking."

Shaffer relayed the orders.

When the proprietor walked toward the kitchen, Shaffer asked, "Just what are these papers you have given me?"

The couple at the next table were leaving. Lang waited until they were headed out. "I'm not sure. I've only had a chance to glance at them, but they seem to deal with some ancient process involving a powder that levitates and turns into gold or fine glass."

Shaffer looked at him blankly. "You are referring to the manna of the Bible, I take it."

"Apparently not the Bible we know. This is an unpublished account of Exodus."

"The Melk parchments?"

"Melk?"

Shaffer waited for two Krugel half-liter beers to be set upon the table.

"A *Kloster*, monastery, in the Wachau near here. A very persit . . . er, persistent story, rumor, says some ancient Hebrew documents were found in Jerusalem during the Third Crusade and wound up in the library there. Supposedly they contained ancient secrets long ago lost. Most people took them as legend, not fact, since they have never been found. Then a former colleague, a man named Steinburg who taught ancient history when I was still at the university, was killed in a motor accident. The police never found the other vehicle. Steinburg's wife was convinced it wasn't an accident, because her husband had been talking about something that had been discovered at Melk, something he said could affect the world." Shaffer took a long sip. "Are you still certain you know of no danger I may be in, Mr. Reilly?"

Lang shrugged as he reached for his beer. "As I said, I just looked at the papers quickly, didn't see anything earthshaking. You mentioned the biblical manna?"

Shaffer had both hands around his glass, staring at the bubbles. "You called me because of my Web site dealing with alchemy, a hobby for a chemist who analyzes ancient artifacts." He looked up at Lang. "Alchemy was both the curse and the mother of modern chemistry. Did you know that, Mr. Reilly?"

Lang was unsure whether the question was rhetorical or not. Either way, he had never given alchemy a thought until recently. "Can't say I did. How so?"

Shaffer's eyes narrowed, the expression of a man relating a personal slight. "While scientists of the seventeenth and eighteenth centuries—philosophers, as they were called—were making quite accurate observations of the physical laws of the universe, and botanical discoveries were common, chemistry was limited to alchemists' quest to create gold and silver. Although a few important findings were made, chemistry really became a legitimate science only in the early to mid nineteenth century."

Had it waited another century or so, Lang's junior year in high school would have been a lot happier.

Shaffer continued. "The medieval practitioners had it backward. After the fall of Rome, a lot of true science was either lost or suppressed by the Church, which saw, correctly, science as its enemy. What was saved was kept by the Muslims who from time to time occupied parts of Europe. With the beginnings of the Crusades, some of that knowledge was reintroduced, particularly in mathematics, astronomy, and medicine.

"Somehow the memory of your powder lingered. It is referred to in the old texts as 'the philosopher's stone' because it resembled stone dust, but the writers of those works got turned around. The Egyptians used gold to make the powder they called *mfkzt*. Among other uses, pharaohs ate it. It was thought to prolong life."

Lang watched plates being set down on the table. Judging by the size of his portion, he had been wise not to order the soup. "Ate it? Ate gold?"

Shaffer leaned over, savoring the aroma of his meal. "Gold, Mr. Reilly, has little intrinsic value, yet it is prized all over the world. Why not, say, iron or copper? Because the ancients used a gold product as a life-prolonging substance. The rest of the world developed some sort of atavistic fascination for that element, forgetting its purpose. Because of its properties it aids in health and generates a unique energy."

"Levitation?"

"That is part of it, of course."

Lang forgot his goulash. "And the other part?"

Shaffer returned his attention to his plate. "Who knows? That, too, is lost. There are those who believe that, under certain circumstances, the powder has huge energy potential."

Lang put down his fork, the connection between Yadish, Lewis, and the mysterious white powder beginning to come into focus like a figure emerging from thick fog. Details were still blurry, but the form was visible.

"What sort of energy potential?"

The doctor used the side of his fork to surgically dissect a dumpling. "No one really is sure of the details, but we can be certain of some generalities. A few years ago an English team attempted to duplicate the erection of one of the smaller pyramids using the means the Egyptians would have had available. As the structure grew, they surrounded it with a sand incline, a road around the perimeter to drag stones into place—the same method archaeologists have assumed for years was used to build the pyramids. It didn't work. At some point, the pile of sand was too high for its weight and it collapsed—not once but every time they repeated the effort."

Lang took a pull at his beer, watching Shaffer's face through the wavy lines of the glass. "And?"

The dumpling was apparently sufficiently satisfactory to merit another incision. "It became obvious the Egyptians used an alternative method to lift stones weighing tons."

"And you think the powder . . . ?"

Finished, Shaffer regarded his plate regretfully. "I only speculate, Mr. Reilly. The Emerald Tablet of Hermes, considered the founding work of alchemy, is an ancient Egyptian text, so the two—alchemy and the mysteries of Egypt—are . . . are . . . intermingled? No, intertwined. Are you going to finish that goulash? It really is not so good cold."

Lang pushed the plate across the table. "But how could a powder be used to lift that sort of weight?"

The goulash was also to Shaffer's satisfaction. "I am unsure; I do not know. Physics is not my territory. But I might know someone who does. Or might. A man who is named bin Hamish, in Cairo, with whom I've occasionally worked." There was a squeaking noise as he scraped the platter with the edge of his fork. "As you Americans say, tell you what: Let me read over these papers tonight. We'll get together tomorrow. I cannot imagine a better way to start the day than with a Sacher torte and coffee. Perhaps you will join me there?"

No doubt as to where "there" was. The hotel's apricot-jam-and-chocolate confection was served with a generous dollop of *Schlag*, rich, melt-in-the-mouth whipped cream.

Enough calories, cholesterol, and unsaturated fat to make a cardiologist weep.

The good doctor's dietary habits would have felled an Olympic athlete, yet he was smallish, perhaps plump, but not obese. Europeans seemed to eat as they pleased, yet few were fat. The older he got, the more Lang hated every one of them for that.

Lang stood as the proprietor exchanged the empty glasses and dishes for a small square of paper that was the check. If he saw it, Shaffer made no move to pick it up.

Lang lifted it, glanced at the surprisingly low total, and put several euros on the table. "Around when, seven or so?"

"The cafe opens at eight."

"Eight, then."

Outside, Lang realized he was still hungry. Small wonder, since Dr. Shaffer had eaten all but a couple of bites of both dinners.

Lang checked his watch. Early for Vienna, where few dined before 2100 hours, nine o'clock. He could get a sausage at one of the mobile *Würstelstand* and enjoy one of the city's more attractive sights a few blocks over.

Closed to most vehicular traffic, Stephansplatz and the adjacent bars and restaurants on Backerstrasse and Schonlaterngasse were in full party mode. In front of the church, acrobats in white tights performed flips and midair spins for tips. Nearby a mime held several small children spellbound. Winding his way through the crowd, Lang briefly stood in line to get a beer and what closely resembled an American hot dog.

He retreated to one of the public benches to enjoy both his meal and the spectacular cathedral, spotlighted as bright as any day could illuminate it. It was built in the thirteenth century, but all that remained of the original structure were the Giant's Door and the twin Heathen Towers, so called because they had replaced an earlier pagan shrine. The main *Steff*, tower, a fourteenth-century Gothic addition, stabbed four hundred fifty feet into the night's belly. Lang was particularly enchanted by the roof, a mosaic of over a million glazed tiles displaying the double-headed Hapsburg eagle.

He resolved to visit the church again in daylight. From years ago he remembered the twisting passages of the crypt, where the bodies of centuries of Hapsburgs were entombed under iron statuary that could have been designed by Stephen King. The helmeted skulls and contorted forms were made all the more grisly by the knowledge that the corpses below had been eviscerated so that heart and entrails might grace two other churches, a gory custom of the times not peculiar to Austrian royalty.

Hardly thoughts for enjoying his sausage, Lang thought as he stood to toss his empty beer bottle and paper napkin into a nearby receptacle. He had taken a single step when he felt cold steel against his neck.

"Just sit back down, Mr. Reilly."

The voice behind him was low and accentless.

Lang sat slowly, eyes darting from left to right. Two men, one on his left, the other on his right, seemed interested in what was happening. They looked very much like the type, if not the actual men, who had shanghaied him in Brussels.

They moved closer as he sat.

A man in a windbreaker slid around the edge of the bench, letting the weapon he held reflect the square's light for the briefest of moments before covering it with his jacket. One of the other two circled behind, reached over the top of the seat, and removed the SIG Sauer from its holster in the small of Lang's back.

"That's better," the man beside him said. "Now you will come with us."

"My mama told me never to go with strangers," Lang said, not moving.

Stall. Stall for time; stall for opportunity. Basic Agency training years ago. These people had demonstrated what they would do given the chance. *Let time pass and watch for a break.*

If it didn't arrive soon, though, he was in deep shit.

Getting into a vehicle with them or walking to some dark alley was like driving his own hearse.

"We only want answers to a few questions," the man said amiably. "That is all."

"You'll forgive me if I choose to stay here." Lang was trying not to be obvious as he searched the square for a cop, one of the olive-drab uniforms of the *Polizei*. No doubt they were all busy handing out parking tickets.

"We can go peacefully or forcibly. I fear I cannot be responsible if you anger my comrades by being uncooperative."

Lang shifted and put his hand in a pocket. "Try another bluff. You're no more going to drag me off kicking and screaming in front of all those people than you're gonna jump over the church there."

He was touching the BlackBerry, trying to remember . . .

The man beside him sighed and nodded to one of his comrades. The second man's hand came out of a pocket. Something twinkled briefly, something . . . like a hypodermic needle. "If you insist . . ."

One-three-three! One-three-three was the police emergency number in Vienna. Lang hoped his touch was not betraying him, that he was pushing the right keys. He thumbed the thing to silent, fearful these men might hear its dial tone and guess what he was doing.

"I'm highly allergic to a lot of medication. If that kills me, you'll never get your answers."

Stall, delay.

"A risk I fear we'll have to take." He nodded to the man with the needle to proceed.

Lang stood, edging toward the center of the square. "C'mon, man. I hate needles. Surely we can do something. . . ."

One of the men standing shoved him roughly back onto the bench. The man with the needle held it up, squirting silver liquid into the air to make sure there were no bubbles.

Lang took small comfort from the precaution. They weren't going to kill him right now, right here.

Lang had run out of stall tactics. "Look, I'll come along; just put that thing away."

He never knew if the local cops had the world's quickest response time or he was just lucky. A pair of white BMW motorcycles rounded the church, heading slowly toward them. Flashing blue lights reflected from the cobblestones.

The man next to Lang muttered something Lang understood only as unlikely to be a blessing, and stood. "Nothing funny, now, Mr. Reilly. My men are armed and have no problem dealing with the police. Unless you want to get innocent people hurt, you will let me speak."

Lang was certainly attentive to the safety of the ever "innocent" people, but even more so to his own welfare. If he was going to make a move, now was the time.

He rose slowly, as though to meet the approaching officers. He still had the beer bottle in hand. The instant the man beside him shifted his gaze to the oncoming motorcycles, Lang jerked erect, smashing the glass on the edge of the bench.

The man in the windbreaker saw what was coming and tried to raise his weapon. With his empty hand Lang shoved the gun's muzzle down while his other brought the jagged stump of the bottle up in a slashing motion.

The man screamed, the gun dropping as he threw both hands to his face to stanch a river of blood from shredded cheeks and nose.

Lang was certain he had seen teeth through the ripped flesh.

Lang scooped up the dropped weapon and threw himself over the bench. Something tugged at his sleeve as he heard the coughs of sound-suppressed weapons followed by shouts in German.

More sputters, two loud shots, and the clatter of motorcycles falling onto the street.

By now Lang was at the edge of the square's light. A brief glance over his shoulder showed two policemen sprawled beside their bikes and two men headed straight for him.

He did not take the time to place the one he had attacked. The man would be *hors de combat* for some time.

Lang sprinted into the darkness, the sound of footsteps in his ears.

In his hurry he was aware only that he was running in an easterly direction. The white walls of the Hofburg Complex, the area of palaces of Austria's nobility—now largely offices, embassies, and fashionable apartments—as well as the Stallburg, once a royal residence, home to the Spanish Riding School.

He was walking now, the hand with the gun in it under his jacket as he looked over his shoulder. A brief glance told him he was on Kohl Markt, which, he could see, dead-ended into a small *platz* in front of a domed building he recognized from the neoclassic facade as the Michaelerkirche, the Hapsburgs' parish church.

One of the city's main streets should be only a block or so to his left, an avenue that, even at this hour, would be crowded enough for him to disappear among the evening's diners and strollers.

The thought had barely formed when his two pursuers emerged from the shadows, one on his left, the other to his right.

There was nothing in front but the church.

THIRTY

Sonnenfelsgasse 39
Vienna
At the Same Time

Dr. Heimlich Shaffer had lived in the second-floor walk-up behind the Academy of Sciences since his divorce eight years ago. He loved the wandering, narrow streets of the Old Town. The baroque sixteenth-century facades had a soul that was sadly lacking in the faux–Vienna Woods cottages of Nussdorf, where he and Analisa had raised their two children. He didn't miss the commute by crowded U Bahn into the city, either.

He had gotten the apartment cheap—he preferred *inexpensively*—when a colleague at the university had retired to somewhere in the Tyrol. Bedroom, bath, small kitchen and office, the formal living room. All his. His books, his computer with only his stuff on it, his bath with no drying panty hose dangling from the shower curtain like snakeskins.

His.

He supposed he was lonely from time to time, but his work was engaging, and he had to account to no one other than those who hired him.

Which reminded him—he hadn't asked the American

about his compensation for reading the translation of these remarkable documents spread before him. The dinner had been nice, but it was hardly going to pay next month's rent, no matter how enjoyable an alternative it had been to the snacklike meals he fixed for himself. The man, Reilly, surely didn't expect advice for free. That was hardly the purpose of maintaining the Web site in four languages. It would be reasonable . . .

The buzzer for the street-level entrance to the building interrupted his thoughts A visitor? Unlikely. Shaffer's only visitors were his two children, and then only on occasional weekends. Someone pressing random buttons to gain entrance, then.

A year ago, thieves had gotten in this way and taken old Frau Schiller's TV set as well assorted valuables from other tenants. Some fool had pushed the button that let them in, expecting someone else. After that the landlord should have installed an intercom so residents could identify who was pressing the buzzer on the street.

The irritating noise sounded again as he got up and checked the locks on his door.

Secure.

He was returning to his reading when the annoying sound came again.

Ignore it.

But what if it were the American with more questions? He would call, though, wouldn't he?

The damned buzzer rasped again.

Reilly or thieves?

No matter. The door onto the street was heavy oak, and he wouldn't open it all the way, just peek around to see who was causing all that racket.

THIRTY-ONE

Michaelerplatz
Vienna
Minutes Later

There was no place to go but the church.

The main doors were closed, no doubt locked at this hour. To the right was a smaller one, one Lang hoped was kept open for parishioners with late-night spiritual needs. A dash across the small *platz*, a snatch on a brass handle, and he was inside.

The interior was dimly lit. The tumbling cherubs and sunbursts of the ornately carved choir loft threw sinister shadows, and the figures of the Renaissance frescoes of the fall of the angels were only malevolent hints of human figures.

Something about this church prowled the fringes of his memory, something from his last visit to Vienna years ago. . . .

No time for a senior moment.

He turned to the door through which he had entered and lifted his eyes in thanks for a bit of luck: The entrance had both latch and dead bolt. He lowered the latch and strode quickly the length of the nave.

What was it about the Michaelerkirche?

The rattling of the locked door was followed by the thumps of silenced bullets. The old hinges wouldn't withstand an assault of that magnitude long. The whole door would fall into the entrance in seconds.

The sight of an iron railing to the right of the baroque altar sparked a memory to life. Now he recalled what he had known about this church.

In a second he was descending into the crypt. A very special crypt.

At the bottom of the stairs he ducked his head and shut an all too flimsy gate behind him.

The light from the single low-watt bulb overhead was swallowed by the uniform grayness. Gray bones were stacked in gray arches like gray firewood, the stump of a single candle melted on each brick ledge. Tibias, ribs, femurs, humeri, all clinically arranged by type. To his left he was observed by the empty sockets of countless skulls stacked in their niches like some pagan display.

Wooden caskets, gray with age, were in neat rows across the floor. Some had come open, displaying their occupants in gray funeral finery. A grinning mummy's face above a gray vest or lace collar, flesh-covered arms across the breast of a gray burial dress. A nightmare's bounty of corpses that had been entombed under the church in the seventeenth and eighteenth centuries and been preserved by a freak of nature: the constant temperature and dry air of this particular crypt.

Footsteps in the church overhead.

Lang glanced around and made one of the more macabre choices of his life. Moving to the edge of the light, he chose a coffin just beyond the overhead lighting's penumbra. He hoped the protesting shriek of old hand-forged nails being pried loose wasn't as loud as it seemed to him.

The corpse he dispossessed grinned up at him, black eye sockets still rimmed with bushy brows, now gray. The face had gray skin stretched over it, much like the pictures of Egyptian mummies unwrapped after millennia.

Lang dumped him on the gray stone floor. "Sorry, old pal, but unless I'm gonna join you sooner than I'd like, I need this more than you."

He could hear someone tugging at the gate.

He rolled the former occupant behind another casket, arms and legs seeming to disintegrate into dust as it moved.

He had time only to grasp in both hands the weapon he had taken before squeezing into the confines of the coffin. Although the weight of the gun should have prepared him, he was surprised to note he was holding another IMI Desert Eagle, identical to the one held by the intruder in Jacob's office.

Whispers at the head of the stairs told him he didn't have the time to consider the significance of his discovery, only to make sure a round was in the chamber and the safety was off. He had chosen the largest box he could find, but he couldn't straighten out his legs. No time to look for another. The best he could do was to turn the casket on its side so only the bottom was visible from the direction of the gate.

He hoped he didn't have to wait long. He thought he could see small, furtive shapes scooting along the gray floor. He could hear gentle scurrying and the occasional squeak of rats that had not feasted on a new body in two hundred years.

He heard a whispered conversation, then slow footsteps down the stone stairs.

Lang twisted his head as far as possible, giving him a limited view through a crack between the planks of the casket.

One man, gun with bulbous silencer in hand, was carefully picking his way in front of a bone-filled arch. From his constant glances to his left, Lang was certain his com-

panion was across the room, if out of view. They were set-
ting up a cross fire. If Lang had entertained doubts he was
dealing with professionals, he no longer did.

At some point they would be at the row of coffins
where Lang was concealed. His protruding knees would
give him away. Better to use whatever bit of surprise he
could, to make his move.

Then his BlackBerry beeped.

THIRTY-TWO

Sonnenfelsgasse 39
Vienna
At the Same Time

Adel Schiller thought at first that she had left her television on, the new color model that had replaced the old black-and-white stolen last year. She had been watching an American film when she had dozed off. Sometime later she had woken up, seen the movie was over, and gone to bed.

Then something had awakened her again.

The TV?

Slipping blue-veined feet into the furry slippers her grandchildren had given her this past Christmas, she pushed the covers aside. A long-haired dachshund hopped to the floor from the foot of the bed. Ignoring Fritzie's growl of displeasure at being disturbed, she stepped into the small living room. No, the television was off. Something else had awakened her.

With a clatter of hardware she undid the three chain locks and single dead bolt on her door and peered into the hall through the narrowest of cracks. She wasn't nosy, of course, didn't really care what her neighbors did, but after being robbed it simply made sense to know what was going on around her. That was why she peeped out into the hall every time she heard the door downstairs open, just for her own safety.

Oh, she had learned that Frau Grafner on the floor above had occasional visitors, all-night visitors, when Herr Grafner was out of town. That might have been the reason for the horrible fight she had heard right from this same doorway. And then there was that nice young man, Manfred Kellner, the one who always spoke to her. At least, she had thought he was a nice young man until she had stood at this very door and seen him kiss another young man leaving his apartment one morning!

But neither the Grafners nor Kellner had her interest at the moment. Instead, two men she had never seen before were standing in front of Herr Dr. Shaffer's door, using a key to get in. Dr. Shaffer never had guests. Oh, his *Kinder* paid infrequent visits on Sundays, but he never had *night* visitors. And even if he did, why didn't he let them in himself? She knew he was home, had seen him enter at an hour later than usual.

One of the men in the hall started to turn around, and she gently shut the door, puzzled. Where was Dr. Shaffer?

From Fritzie's low growl, he must be wondering, too.

THIRTY-THREE

Michaelerkirche
At the Same Time

The sound of the BlackBerry froze the two men, each turning his head like a wild animal trying to ascertain the source of a predator's scent.

The BlackBerry beeped again, the sound's origin difficult to determine in the confines of the crypt.

A third beep would surely give Lang away, as would any movement to turn the infernal thing off.

He had no choice.

Move now!

He rolled out of the coffin, the heavy Desert Eagle in both hands. He extended both arms, locking elbows against the anticipated recoil, and fired.

The silencer still on his weapon spared Lang's ears the concussive roar of a large weapon in confined space. Instead there were two spitting sounds. The man on his left flinched as a skull next to his head exploded like a hand grenade, sending fragments into his face and neck. He yelped in pain and surprise as he turned to bring his pistol to bear.

Long-past Agency training slipped into place as comfortably as an old shoe. Lang made himself forget the man on his right for an instant, ignore his own exposure as he looked down the muzzle of his adversary's pistol wavering under the weight of the silencer.

Although Lang rationally knew he was acting in split seconds, it seemed to take forever to place the stubby sight of his own Desert Eagle on the target's belt buckle, where even a near-miss would take the man out of the fight.

He ignored another puff of a sound suppressor and the sting of brick fragments on his hands and cheek.

He squeezed off a shot, and the man on his left was screaming on the floor, a rivulet of blood coursing its way across old brick.

Lang thought he heard the damn BlackBerry buzz again as he rolled to his left just as there was another puff, and the coffin in which he had been hiding splintered.

The remaining man was not visible. There were more than enough places to hide, and he had chosen one of them, Lang guessed. On his belly he was using the rows of caskets for a shield as he crawled toward the only exit, his arms crossed commando-style.

He paused and listened, unsure whether he could hear anything among the muffling effect of wood and brick.

He could clearly make out the moans of the man he had shot.

He turned his head to glance over his shoulder. Would the weakening cries for help draw out the remaining gunman? Not if he were a professional.

Lang crawled on.

After what seemed an hour of scraping elbows on brick, Lang was at the foot of the stairs. He had little doubt his adversary was waiting for him to try to escape that way, to expose himself.

But how else was he going to get out of here?

Lang was next to one of the open caskets. Still flat on his stomach, he reached inside. What he touched felt more like leather than human skin. He probed until he found the head. A gentle tug of the hair was enough to pull it free from its long-desiccated body.

The head in his left hand, he rolled onto his back, avoiding looking at what he held. Instead he concentrated on carefully aiming the big pistol at the naked lightbulb overhead. One more whisper of a shot and his area of the crypt went dark.

It would be obvious to his opponent that Lang was going to use the darkness for a rush up the steps.

Instead Lang, still on his back, threw the skull toward the opposite wall as hard as he could. Over the edge of the casket he saw the muzzle flashes of one, two shots in the direction of the skull's trajectory.

Jumping to his feet, Lang pumped two bullets into the area from which the gunfire had come. Two coffins exploded, emptying their contents. A third shot brought a scream of pain.

There was no return fire.

Weapon with the remaining round extended, Lang approached slowly, feeling his way with the hand not holding the Desert Eagle. His fingers touched something upright, cold, and smooth. A search of his pockets produced the slim matchbox he had taken from Mirabelle's.

He might be taking a chance, but if he couldn't confirm his adversary was down, using the stairs would be a greater risk. Holding the matchbook in the same hand as his pistol, he struck a match and pressed against the wall. The sudden glare in the deep darkness almost blinded him, but he managed to light the stub of candle his fingers had touched.

Ears attuned to the slightest sound of movement, he held the light aloft.

Beside the debris of old wood shattered by the shots, a man sprawled across the floor. The bottom half of his face was a bloody pulp, evidence of the damage a fifty-caliber Magnum round could do.

Lang stooped over and looked through the pockets of the man's windbreaker. He was not surprised to find them empty except for a full clip of ammunition.

He removed his own near-empty magazine and put it in a pocket before slamming the full one into his own gun. He was headed for the stairs when his BlackBerry beeped again.

"Yes?" he snapped.

There was the briefest of pauses before the voice of Sara, his secretary, asked, "Am I interrupting something?"

THIRTY-FOUR

Südbahnhof Police Station
Wiedner Gürtel
Vienna
0920 the Next Morning

In twenty-two years of service, Chief Inspector Karl Rauch had never experienced a night like the one just past. A former professor shot at the common entrance of his ransacked Sonnenfelsgasse apartment, an emergency call to the Stephansplatz, where a man had been raked with a glass bottle and two officers shot, one in serious condition.

Then, this morning, before the paperwork had been completed, a hysterical call from the sextant at the Michaelerkirche. Coffins ripped apart, the dead scattered across the crypt, and two very recently deceased among those who had reposed there for centuries. The man had been more upset about the violation of his charges' last resting place than the two additions.

More carnage than had ever taken place when Vienna had been the meeting place of East and West, the battleground of Soviet and Western spies. At least they had been tidy in their rare executions of one another.

Since the fall of communism, Vienna had been a relatively quiet place. No militant Arab émigrés with their endless sectarian violence, no former African colonials demanding this and that. Oh, there were the pickpockets and the occasional fight in the Prater and problems in the nearby red-light district.

But multiple shootings?

To add to the mystery, no one had heard a single-shot—fifty-caliber shots. Rauch had not seen a fifty-caliber weapon since his mandatory military training in his youth. The two *Polizei* had been shot from two different guns, ballistics had told him. The two bodies in the church with a third, and the professor with yet a fourth. More slugs had been dug out of the bricks of the crypt but were too badly crushed to add a fifth gun to the melee. Handguns, judging by the several shell casings at the Stephansplatz and church crypt.

All from weapons like the two monstrous automatics found with the dead men in the crypt.

Who would want to lug around something that big?

The uniformity of weapons and the fact that no one had heard anything suggested silencers had been involved all the way around, again like the ones in the old burial ground. Professional assassins acting in concert. Professionals also judging by the total anonymity of the corpses in the church, men whose clothing had even been stripped of labels.

But to what end?

What did two professional gunmen have in common with a divorced university professor of . . .

Rauch pushed aside a stack of papers on his desk, sheets that included yesterday's newspaper, last week's reports, and, quite likely, the wrapper for the pastry that had been breakfast.

A tidy desk was symptomatic of a small, if not sick, mind.

He found what he was looking for on top.

A professor of chemistry, now in business as an archaeological chemist, whatever that was.

The investigating officers had found the professor's apartment a wreck, obviously searched. He regarded his own office, where paper covered everything. Well, most likely searched, anyway.

For what?

The phone on his desk rang. It took two more rings for him to find the thing under—what else—a stack of papers on the credenza behind his desk. *"Ja?"*

He listened carefully. He might not waste his time with useless order in his office, but his investigations were not only orderly, they were organized and thought out. Already men were at the bank denoted by check stubs at the professor's apartment to look at deposits, ascertain who had paid Herr *Doktor* for what lately. The fingerprint crew was working on the shell casings, and the area around the church searched for anyplace a weapon might have been dumped. Even this early, one of his men had found what might be a clue.

The inspector took his suit jacket from where he had tossed it onto a chair and headed downstairs.

In the basement he entered a windowless room with a table and four chairs bolted to the cement floor. The room stank of stale sweat and tobacco smoke, although no one had dared light up, in view of the inspector's feelings about cigarettes. Two *unter* inspectors were watching a third man draw on an easel as a fourth described a face. The two policemen displayed eyes rimmed with red, and beard stubble, testimony to being roused out of bed and given assignments in the small hours.

In front of each person was a paper cup containing a brownish liquid that passed for coffee at the station. Rauch was certain it was poisonous—or, at least, not proper Viennese coffee, which amounted to the same thing.

"Am Morgen," the younger of the two policemen murmured without enthusiasm as Rauch entered the room.

"This is Herr Jasto Schattner, the owner of the Koenig Bakery restaurant near the Stephansplatz. He knows—knew—Herr *Doktor* Shaffer. The professor had dinner there last night with someone."

Rauch nodded to the drawing pad.

"That's him, according to Herr Schattner, the man who had dinner with the victim last night. He spoke only English."

Rauch said, "See that a copy is circulated. If he is a foreigner, I am particularly interested in your taking it to the hotels."

Both younger inspectors slumped slightly. There must be a thousand hotels in and around the city.

Hans and Fritz, the inspector thought. The original Katzenjammer Kids, these two. Any assignment that involved leaving the meager comforts of the station house was greeted as a form of privation. "Not so glum, lads. Antiquated as we may be, we do have a fax machine."

The pair brightened noticeably.

"And the various *Bahnhof und Flughof.*"

Even though there were only a limited number of train stations and one airport, the two returned to expressions of being imposed upon like a host whose guests wouldn't go home.

Rauch turned to go, stopped, and looked over his shoulder. "*Danke*, Herr Schattner."

Rauch was relieved to depart the stench and confines of the room.

THIRTY-FIVE

Peachtree Center
227 Peachtree Street
Atlanta, Georgia
The Next Afternoon

Lang Reilly scooped up a stack of pink message slips from his secretary's desk with the hand not holding his briefcase. Without meeting Sara's eyes, he slunk into his inner office and shut the door, a warning that he was in a foul mood.

Pissed off and tired would have been a more accurate description. As he had made a hasty exit from the crypt of the Michaelerkirche, Sara had been explaining via BlackBerry why his presence was needed in Atlanta, a departure from Vienna that, under the circumstances, had a certain appeal. The real reason for his immediate return home was that Judge Adamson had chosen today for a hearing on those few motions in the mayor's case he had not already denied out of hand.

Lang had paused only long enough to wipe the Desert Eagle clean of fingerprints and deposit it in the first trash bin on his way back to the hotel.

As usual, he had arrived home in a state of sleep deprivation. This morning he had climbed into the Porsche and noted the odometer had mysteriously crept forward, no doubt a result of entrusting the keys to the condo's carhops.

He would have to remember to retrieve the extra set of keys.

His first stop had been at the federal courthouse, where his day took a decided turn for the worse.

Lang had never grown accustomed to the fact that a man could practice law for twenty years and, when, Christ-like, he ascended to the bench, chew out one of his former fellow practitioners for doing the same thing the judge had done for his own clients: filing a multitude of motions in hopes that denial of one or more might be grounds for a future appeal should trial not prove fruitful. Lang knew it was going to happen, had come to expect it, but a tongue-lashing from a man who, until a year ago, had been a mere mortal, one far less successful (if more political) than Lang, was not recommended as an enhancer of the spirit.

It was enough to ruin the disposition of a saint.

If any had been members of the Atlanta bar.

Lang's travails had not ended there. Before he could escape to his car, he had to endure the critique of his perpetually displeased client.

It was quite understandable that Sara peeked around the door rather than entering. "Don't forget tonight. You need to get your tux from the cleaners and pick up Ms. Warner at eight."

She disappeared before Lang could react.

Another item to try his soul: In his absence Alicia had called to invite him to some charity function, where the recipient foundation would receive some small percentage of the costs of drinks and dinner.

And no part of whatever the ladies spent on new gowns, coiffures, and manicures.

Somehow Alicia had enlisted Sara's connivance to

search his calendar and confirm the date. Sara had always been protective of his personal life. It must have taken true advocacy to sway her over to Alicia's side.

He was secretly delighted he would see her again, but forced to feign outrage lest Sara commandeer his future social life.

Once the mayor finally departed, Lang walked to the door, opening it. "Sara, I'm taking the rest of the day off. If you really need me I'll be trying to overcome jet lag at home."

Hours later, resplendent in a shawl-lapeled tuxedo and alligator dancing pumps, Lang pulled the Porsche under the granite-sided porte cochere of Atlanta's oldest and most prestigious club, the Piedmont Driving Club. A bastion of father-to-son, male-only WASPs for over a hundred years, the club had finally relented to the social conscience only the rich could afford and admitted Jews, blacks, women, and people whose last names ended in vowels—even some whose ancestors might have arrived a bit late to serve under Bobby Lee during the War of Northern Aggression. Or worse, Yankees. So had political correctness slain another quaint and relatively harmless tradition.

The problem with a tardy rush to apparent diversity had immediately become apparent: The wealthiest of Atlanta's black community had already joined other formerly all-white organizations. The hefty initiation fees made becoming racial tokens multiple times less than attractive. A scramble by the more liberal members to find suitable new initiates finally produced a ratio of black members that, compared with other, lesser Atlanta clubs, was still minuscule.

When her door was opened by the uniformed attendant, Alicia alighted with more grace than most Porsche passengers by swinging both legs out simultaneously. Lang wondered where she had learned that.

They entered a marble-floored entranceway filled with what looked to be Federalist antiques. Three stair-steps at the end and to the right and they stood in a marble foyer. The baroque molding lining the twenty-five-foot ceiling could have stood up to any Lang had seen in Vienna. A massive crystal chandelier was a galaxy of diamonds overhead.

It was only as Lang and Alicia were following the sound of music down another marble corridor that he noticed how very well her gown fit. He had no idea of its brand name, but it was one of those jobs that was enticingly short on top and very long on bottom, a sort of sea green material that resembled spun sugar. A double strand of pearls draped just above enticing décolletage.

Ahead was the ballroom, the huge, high-ceilinged dance floor polished by the feet of the city's elite for generations. To their right was a small oak-paneled bar where a few hardy members clutched their bourbon-and-waters as talismans against the intrusion of the great unwashed.

The money the club made from rentals to groups like tonight's was received somewhat more graciously.

Several hundred people were seated around the ballroom's perimeter, while a band played from a stage at the far end. A tuxedo-clad maître d' showed them to their table and signaled a waiter who had a tray of champagne flutes.

Alicia was gazing around the room.

"Come here often?" Lang asked.

"Once or twice a year some organization I belong to has a party here. You?"

"I've been here before."

She was looking at the band. "But it's so . . . so *elegant*. It was founded in 1889 as a place for members to drive their carriages. Piedmont Park next door was a part of the property. The club gave it to the city for the Great Cotton Exhibition in the 1890s. The president attended, had lunch here. So did John Philip Sousa."

Lang smiled. "You're certainly knowledgeable."

"Clark Gable and Vivien Leigh were entertained here after the premiere of *Gone with the Wind*."

"I'll bet Hattie McDaniel, who played Mammy, wasn't."

Alice looked at him disapprovingly. "Retroactive political correctness. It's unfair to impose our mores on yesterday's institutions."

"Like slavery?"

Ignoring him, she exchanged her empty glass for a full one from another champagne-bearing waiter. "It's one of the few places left in the city with any historical significance. Plus it's so . . ."

"Elegant?"

"I think I said that."

"Elegant surroundings, impeccable service, abysmal food."

She treated him to bottomless green eyes. "Surely there's more to this place than food."

"Thankfully." He cocked his head as the band began a tune Frank Sinatra had made famous, one slow enough not to require terpsichorean exploits. "Dance?"

As they moved around the floor, he nearly stumbled over her feet as she insisted on trying to lead.

"Sorry I'm not Fred Astaire," he apologized sarcastically.

"I'm not exactly Ginger Rogers, either."

He gently tugged her in the opposite direction from that in which she was heading. "At least she let him lead."

She nodded. "Yeah, but remember: Everything Fred did, Ginger did backward."

"Feminist!" He sniffed.

"Okay, okay." She giggled. "Enough of the old movies."

He stepped back to lead her from the dance floor. "And enough dancing, before I break your foot."

When they returned to their table, an Asian woman of indeterminate age was placing salads at each place. She looked up with a wide smile. "Eve'n, Mista Reilly!"

Lang pulled Alicia's chair out and smiled back. "Evening, Lo Sin."

Seated, Alicia looked at the departing back of the waitress, then at Lang and back to Lo Sin as the light dawned. "You're a member!" It sounded more accusation than question. "You didn't tell me!"

Lang picked up his salad fork. "You didn't ask."

She regarded him quizzically for a moment and then burst out laughing. "Here I was touting this place and you belong here."

"I'm not sure I fit, let alone belong."

Mischief twinkled in those emerald eyes. "You mean you're not an heir of one of Atlanta's oldest families?"

He made quotation marks with his fingers. "I didn't go to the 'right' private school, either."

"Then how . . . ?"

"Through absolutely no merit of my own, I became CEO of a large charitable foundation. Members here are mostly old money, a few new money. Best of all is lots of money. Or, at least, access to it. I was actually asked to join. It's a nice place to take clients for lunch, but I wouldn't want to eat dinner here."

"Clients? You mean those . . . those . . ."

"Criminals?"

"That's a polite word, yes."

"They aren't criminals until a jury says so."

"A fine point."

"No, the United States Constitution. Now, are we going to argue or are you going to finish your salad? Trust me, it's likely to be the best part of dinner."

It was.

Shortly after midnight Lang drove up the condominium's drive and, waving off the carhop, down the ramp to the residents' parking.

"Wouldn't it be easier to let the boy park your car?" Alicia asked.

Lang nodded as he pulled into the space where his unit number was stenciled on the wall. "Easier but not wiser."

She gave him an inquiring look, which he ignored.

Once they were upstairs, Grumps enthusiastically inspected the visitor, tail wagging furiously.

"You'll get dog hair on your dress," Lang cautioned as he poured from a Scotch bottle.

Alicia was squatting, bringing her eyes level with the dog's. "That's why dry cleaners are in business."

She stroked Grumps's long nose and began scratching his chin. "How did you come up with the name?"

Lang handed her a glass, the ice tinkling an invitation. "My nephew named him."

Though it was unintentional, there was something in his tone that said further questions on the subject were off-limits.

She stood and slid open the door to the narrow balcony. "Wow! What a view!"

Later Lang was never sure what happened or how, whether she stumbled and he grabbed her or he had his arms around her before she moved. It didn't matter. They held each other for a long time.

"I never could resist a man in a tuxedo," she finally whispered. "Maybe you'd better take me home before I do something foolish."

Lang stepped back, holding her at arm's length. "Alicia Warner, assistant United States Attorney, do something foolish? Inconceivable!"

"I was married once, remember."

"That's foolish?"

"To him, yeah. Downright stupid, maybe even insane. You ever been married?"

"Once. She died."

"Oh, I'm sorry!" She looked like she meant it.

Lang never understood why people said that when he mentioned Dawn. Were they sorry they had asked or that she was dead? Or both?

Either way, the mood of a few minutes ago had evaporated like morning fog in sunlight.

She put her glass down and looked around the way a woman does when she couldn't recall where she'd left her purse. "Home, James."

Lang was unsure whether he was relieved or disappointed. Grumps was definitely the latter.

"He hopes you'll come back and spoil him further."

She reached a hand behind Grumps's head, gently rubbing his neck. "So do I."

If all Lang had to do was ask, she would.

THIRTY-SIX

Südbahnhof Police Station
Wiedner Gürtel
Vienna
The Next Afternoon

Haupt Inspector Karl Rauch was in mid-*Jause*, that after-noon break the Viennese took to enjoy coffee and pastry. Today the inspector was alternately nibbling at *Bischofs-brot* as he sipped coffee from Eils, the coffeehouse pa-tronized largely by government officials and lawyers. Where else but in Vienna would such places exist, sepa-rate from establishments frequented by such diverse groups as writers, actors, bridge players, musicians, stu-dents, artists, and athletes?

He had cleared a space on his desk for three pieces of paper: the artist's drawing, a copy of a bill for a room at the Imperial Hotel, and a reproduction of an American passport issued to one Langford Reilly from the hotel's guest registry. The quality of the latter was too poor to definitely match the passport photo and the sketch. He swiveled his desk chair to face a computer monitor and sighed, knowing his next cup would be the swill from the machine downstairs, and licked his fingers free of the last trace of sponge cake filled with nuts, raisins, fruit glacé, and chocolate chips.

It took only a few minutes of searching the international crime database before Herr Langford Reilly's name appeared. Kidnapped in Belgium? Involved in a shooting in Amsterdam? All within a week or so of having dinner with a murder victim in Vienna? Herr Reilly seemed to tow violence behind him like the wake of a ship.

A few more taps of the keyboard brought up the American FBI's criminal data index. Rauch was less than surprised to see Reilly's name there, too. Over the last four or five years a number of people in the world had wanted Mr. Reilly dead.

Why?

Half an hour in cyberspace provided no answers. Langford Reilly was . . . What was the American word? A lawyer—a lawyer who defended people accused of high-dollar crime: embezzlement, fraud, bribery. That might incite someone to try to kill him. But half a dozen people? Reilly also headed the Janice and Jeff Holt Foundation, a charity specializing in medical care for children in third-world countries and, lately, doing research in alternatives to fossil fuel.

Laudable goals.

Hardly an inspiration to murder.

So, what was it about the American that brought death and chaos?

The Dutch and Belgian authorities had had no reason to detain him, but Rauch did: He was possibly the last person to see Dr. Shaffer alive. Unfortunately, Herr Reilly had concluded whatever business he had in Vienna and, according to the desk clerk at the Imperial, checked out in the late evening, even though he would be charged for the night. The doorman remembered the generous tip he received for summoning a cab to take Reilly to the airport.

An abrupt departure from an expensive hotel was hardly a crime, but certainly suspicious.

Rauch swung back around to gaze out of the window

at nothing in particular. Was that suspicion sufficient to start the mass of bureaucratic paperwork for an extradition warrant? If Reilly proved innocent, Rauch would have to justify the cost of a round-trip ticket from America to tightfisted superiors. Alternatively, he had no other leads and was unlikely to uncover any.

Rauch knew the answer of government employees worldwide: Let his immediate superior make the decision.

THIRTY-SEVEN

Park Place
2660 Peachtree Road
Atlanta, Georgia
That Evening

A glass of single-malt Scotch in hand and clad in a sport shirt rather than a clerical collar, Father Francis Narumba stood on Lang's balcony, gazing south across the city. "*Deorum cibus est*, Lang. Best meal I've had since . . ."

He intentionally left the sentence unfinished.

"Since Gurt left?" Lang was wiping his hands on a dish towel. *Amantes sunt amentes.*"

"Lovers may be lunatics. I obviously wouldn't know. But anytime you want to talk about it . . ."

Lang shook his head as he joined his friend in viewing the panorama. "Don't spoil a good meal."

"It was that. How'd you improve your culinary skills so quickly?"

Lang reached behind him, producing a highly varnished wooden box. "Easy. Instead of cooking, I pick up a couple of prepared dinners at Whole Foods or eatZi's."

He was referring to two of the neighborhood's more

upscale groceries/delicatessens, where shoppers listened to opera as they selected applewood-smoked bacon and Jarlsberg quiches at $12.50 a slice.

Lang opened the box, revealing a row of cigars. "Would you like to finish off dinner with a *Cubano*, a Montecristo number two?"

The priest made a selection and held it out while Lang clipped and lit it before his own.

"It's a good thing we do this only every month or so," Francis commented between puffs. "I wouldn't want to declare myself a smoker the next time I filled out an insurance application."

"You mean the Church doesn't provide health insurance?"

"Even the Church can't afford catastrophic health problems. It buys insurance for its employees like any other business."

"I guess relying on prayer and the laying on of hands is a little risky."

"*Mus non uni fidit antro*, or, in the vernacular, a wise person always has a backup plan."

The two men enjoyed the aroma of fine tobacco for a moment before Francis asked, "I suppose you got these illegally."

"A mere peccadillo against an unreasonable government."

"*Facinus quos inquinat aequat.*"

"Okay, so I'm a criminal no matter how slight the offense. I suppose you don't want to further enjoy the fruits of unlawful activity."

Francis contemplated the tip of his cigar, a red period on the night's page. "I didn't say that. Besides, I can always confess my sinful complicity, a measure unavailable to the apostate."

Lang watched the smoke drift in the breezeless evening

for a moment. "Now that I've furnished food, drink, and a fine smoke . . ."

"The necessities of life."

"Whatever. I've got something I'd like you to look over."

Francis gave a theatrical groan. "By now I should expect quid pro quo, particularly from a lawyer and a heretic."

Stepping across the room, Lang moved the telephone to a place in front of one of the speakers for the CD player, selected a disk, and turned up the volume. *Hope they enjoy Vivaldi*, he thought to himself.

"Hey," he said to Francis, "you're the one learned in church history. Presumably that includes the Old Testament."

Francis looked from Lang to the CD player and back again. He had long ago conceded he would never understand some of the weird things his friend did—like turning the sound up instead of down before beginning a conversation.

"Even a heretic can learn," Francis said good-naturedly, reaching for the papers.

Inside, Lang fussed with the dishes while Francis read the translation of what Lang had come to call the Hebrew parchments.

When Francis stood to refill his glass, Lang asked, "Well?"

The priest measured his drink with the care of one fully aware of just how much liquor he could safely hold. "You never cease to amaze me. For a heathen you unearth some of the most startling religious relics. Who translated this?"

"A friend in London, a Jewish friend."

"And the provenance?"

"So far, unknown."

"What makes you think they're genuine?"

Lang almost answered that he doubted people would be getting killed over a historical practical joke, but he

shared as little of the more violent side of his life as possible. Even though he was sure his friend would understand, Lang was never in a mood to hear the string of
homilies on the virtues of nonviolence that would follow.

"You're the one in the faith business. Assume they're
real."

Francis looked around to make sure he wasn't stepping on Grumps and sat down.

He read for a few minutes. "First, it's no surprise that
Moses was no Jew. Exodus two:nineteen, I think."

"Moses, the Jews' great lawgiver, not a Jew himself?"

"Exodus says not."

Fascinated, Lang sat at the kitchen bar, facing the
small living room and his guest. "Then who was he?"

"A good question. Akhenaten, son of Amenhotep III by
Queen Tiyre, a descendant of Esau, elder brother of Jacob, who became Israel."

Lang took a drink. "You've lost me."

"Sorry. As your documents state and some biblical
scholars have long thought, Moses was actually of royal
blood. In fact, the Egyptian word *Mose* means 'royal.' The
ancient Greek is *Mosis*. There are only clues. For instance,
he was raised in the royal household of a pharaoh."

"I thought he was found in a basket, where he'd been
hidden to avoid the killing of Israelite babies."

Francis winked over his glass. "You'd never make that
stand up in court. To accept it, we must also accept that
Pharaoh's daughter conspired to frustrate her father's orders, and that Moses's sister just happened to be nearby
when he was found, even though she is never specifically identified. Later on, we learn of a Miriam who is described as a sister of both Moses and Aaron. The basket
story is most likely an explanation of how an Israelite
grew up in the royal household. Within a few years the
new pharaoh, Akhenaten, rejected the polytheism of
Egyptian religion, worshiping a single god represented

by a sunlike disk. The new king closed the temples, infuriating the powerful priests. The swell of public opinion forced his abdication at a time about ten years before Moses's reappearance, still giving allegiance to the single god with no name. Could Akhenaten and Moses be one and the same?

"The Israelites might be willing to follow a former pharaoh, even one who lacked the usual oratorical skill attributed to most biblical leaders. See Exodus three:twelve."

"Wait a minute," Lang said, his cigar dead and forgotten in an ashtray. "Are you telling me that Moses was actually an Egyptian pharaoh?"

Francis was looking around for a relight for his own smoke. Lang tossed him a box of wooden matches. "The dates for Akhenaten, who became Amenhotep IV, match, as do the dates when the new king closed all the temples. Consider that the single-god king was deposed about the same time Moses was banished and returned about the same time. Then there was the snake thing. Moses obviously knew the tricks of the court magicians, knowledge the royal court would have been unlikely to share with some maker of bricks.

"Look at the papers you've given me. They use 'Moses' and 'Pharaoh' interchangeably."

"So, they were the same?"

Francis shrugged. "No way to tell for sure. But there is a certain logic: Egypt forced a monotheistic ruler out. From the dates on the various stelae in front of tombs and obelisks, we know the dates fit Amenhotep Four, previously known as Akhenaten. Interestingly, his tomb has never been found, although those of his predecessor and successor have. Perhaps because he was buried in Sinai by his new followers. Anyway, the Israelites, historically monotheistic, would have followed such a person."

"And you call me a heretic."

Francis smiled. "I don't think the Church cares a lot about the genealogy of Moses, only that he was one of many Old Testament figures who set the stage for the coming of the Messiah."

"But why would a former king want such a following? I mean, the Israelites were slaves, right?"

"No, not if we read Exodus. Joseph, the man of the many-colored coat, you may recall, was sold into slavery in Egypt, but he did well, became a confidant of that particular pharaoh, and invited his family to join him. Over the years between Joseph, who became Israel, and Moses-slash-Akhenaten, they were one of the many groups that had immigrated."

"Like the U.S.," Lang said, standing to refill his glass at the sink. Grumps gave a low growl of displeasure at having to move from under his master's feet. "Like all immigrants who came here."

Francis held his glass out for a refill also. "One more and I've got to go. But yes, sort of like having Israelite-Egyptians, Nubian-Egyptians, all those hyphenated things some people use today because it feeds some sort of insecurity, as though simply being American isn't enough. One difference, though: The Egyptian immigrants probably became part of the country over many hundreds and hundreds of years, not just a couple of centuries. I'm afraid I have no comments on the gold and manna part of your papers. You'll need a chemist or physicist."

Lang wasn't about to mention the fates of the ones who had already been involved.

"Again, though," Lang persisted, "why would a former king want followers who were just brick makers?"

Francis drained his glass and stood. "Have you ever seen a politician refuse a constituency? Besides, he believed in the one God, as did they."

He moved to the door, extending a hand. "Fine food, good cigar, great company. As always. Thanks."

"Sure you won't have another wee tot?"

The priest shook his head. "God may be my copilot, but if I get stopped I'm the one who gets the DUI. The diocese frowns on the bishop having to get his minions out of the slammer at strange nocturnal hours."

Lang stood at the door until he heard the chime of the elevator.

An hour later Lang lay on his back, listening to Grumps's snores. Reflections of passing traffic below played across the ceiling like some abstract black-and-white film.

Moses, who was not an Israelite but a king.

Israelites who were not Jews but Egyptians.

The form that had begun to emerge from the fog in Vienna still had no face, but it was getting clearer.

Vienna?

What was the name Shaffer had mentioned?

Bin Hamish in Cairo, a man who supposedly could explain the energy potential of the white powder.

Lang got out of bed and went into the living room, where a laptop sat on the desk part of the Thomas Elfe secretary. It took nearly an hour before Lang found the man he was certain Shaffer had had in mind.

THIRTY-EIGHT

Park Place
2660 Peachtree Road
Atlanta, Georgia
The Next Morning

Lang was on the phone before he was dressed, making airline reservations to Vienna via Paris. When he was finished he called the foundation's pilot and requested he prepare the Gulfstream for the same trip.

Whoever had placed the bug in the condo would not know he had no intention of going to either place.

Showered and dressed, he removed a panel from the back of the bedside table's drawer and removed a passport with his picture and the name of Joel Couch of Macon, Georgia. It purported to have been issued five years earlier by the United States Department of State. Only the picture bore any relation to the truth. In fact, the document had been issued at Gurt's request by the Agency's Frankfurt office three years ago, when she and Lang had both needed to travel under names other than their own. With it were a driver's license, a membership card to a health club, two credit cards now expired, an ATM card, and a wallet-size snapshot of a little girl he had never seen, presumably Couch's daughter.

Patting the passport against the palm of a hand, he wondered if the intruder who had left the listening device had found the false back of the drawer and noted the Couch name. It was a chance he'd simply have to take.

He drove out of the condo and turned north instead of south toward downtown and his office. Stopping at a branch bank, where he made a substantial cash withdrawal, he drove a mile or so farther and parked the Porsche at Lenox Square, a high-end mall that included a Delta Airlines reservation office. The shopping center's doors were just opening for the day.

He was aware that paying for tickets in cash was sure to invite the attention of the Transportation Safety people, but a search of his baggage and person was the price he would pay for leaving whoever might be watching behind. He was fairly certain the Agency's passport would pass scrutiny both in appearance and in verifying the number.

He would, then, be traveling as Joel Couch, an eccentric who abhorred that most American of conveniences, the credit card.

Ticket in the pocket of his jacket, he stopped at a Starbucks to watch the mall slowly fill. He could see no one who showed any interest in him. He emptied his cup of a liquid that tasted more like confection than coffee, as well it should.

He smiled as he walked out, imagining one of the inner city's panhandlers: "Hey, mister! Can you spare five bucks for a large chilled Kenyan mocha?"

That evening he had dinner at Alicia's. She lived in a small town house in Vinings, a residential community across the Chattahoochee River. It had a past as a semi-rural locale that included a few quaint cottages and a train station. The station was now an expensive boutique. Condos and gated subdivisions, equally indistinguishable, had reduced whatever bucolic aesthetic there might have been to a single rambling clapboard cottage reminiscent of another age. The house had survived only as the site of an upscale restaurant specializing in entrées cooked in fruit jellies.

In jeans and a T-shirt designed to display her figure, Alicia met him at the door. Her hair, shoulder-length, framed her face. A emerald in the shape of a heart sparkled on her finger.

Lang gave her a perfunctory hug. "Don't you look nice! I don't remember the rock."

She let him in, closing the door and holding up her hand for inspection. "Don't usually wear it. It was an engagement ring, only good thing left of a bad marriage."

Lang followed her toward the back of the house, noting tasteful contemporary furniture punctuated with an occasional antique. "So why wear it tonight?"

She stopped so suddenly he almost ran into her. Turning, she took both of his hands in hers. "Because I'm through brooding about a failure. I'm in a new house in a new city and with a man who's fun and entertaining."

"I'm being damned with faint praise? Is that the female equivalent of, 'All the girls like her,' or, 'She's a great cook'?"

"I'll bet it's the first nice thing anyone's said about you all day."

"Maybe. But my dog loves me."

She dropped one of his hands and led him to a small deck; a view of Atlanta's skyline serenely floated on a sea of trees. "Single-malt Scotch, if I recall."

He took the sweating glass she was offering. "It's clear to me there's nothing wrong with your memory."

There was an energy between them, the electricity a woman projected when she had something in mind more than an affectionate embrace. In college dorms Lang had participated in the ageless debate of whether a woman decided she would bed a man when she first met him, playing out the event like some sort of drama. Lang never knew the answer, but he had come to recognize the signals when a decision had been made to implement the choice. Tonight, as the saying went, he would get lucky.

The meal, fish poached in a wine sauce with steamed vegetables, would be act one.

Lang sipped a glass of chilled white wine. "A California chardonnay?"

Alicia was peering over her glass. "You can't tell me the vineyard and vintage?"

"I'm not that much of an oenophile."

She put her glass down. "Oh? Then how did you know . . . ?"

"I saw the bottle as we came through the kitchen."

She studied his face a moment. "Do you always notice the details?"

Lang was looking back at her. "I try. You know as well as I do that winning a case often depends on it."

"I have a confession to make."

"I have a friend who hears them professionally."

She shook her head, sending a wave of red hair flying. "You're going to hear this one."

"Do I get to choose the penance?"

"Depends."

"On what?"

"On whether I want to serve it or not."

Lang pretended to gravely consider this for a moment. "So, confess."

"I had a conference call this afternoon, a really boring one with the Justice Department in Washington."

"A bunch of Department of Justice lawyers are tedious? That's not a confession; it's fact."

She waved him silent. "I had nothing better to do than an occasional 'uh-huh' or 'uh-uh' and to play with the computer. So I looked you up on the bar's Web site. There's a big gap of time between college and law school."

Lang tried not to let her know he was getting uncomfortable. "Lots of people try to earn an honest living before they become lawyers."

"True. But I thought about that . . . that bit of excitement in Underground. Made me wonder if you were involved in something . . . something shady."

"What criminal lawyer isn't?"

She grew serious. "I used my DOJ creds to get into lists of former government employees. At various times you were listed as being a trade attaché, a chargé d'affaires, diplomatic researcher, and in charge of cultural exchanges."

"Job instability: It's one of my less attractive features. Besides, I was never in charge of anyone's affairs. They did it all on their own."

She was staring at him as though he had suddenly dropped out of the sky. "Lang, I've been with the government long enough to know those positions are phony, usually used as cover—albeit thin cover—for intelligence agencies. You were some kind of spy."

He held up three fingers. "Scout's honor, I never spied on anyone."

"Would you tell me if you still were?"

"I wouldn't be much of a spy if I did, would I?" He saw her face fall. "But I'm not."

"Sure would explain someone taking a shot at you."

"So would a jealous husband."

Her mouth twitched, and she failed to straighten it before breaking into laughter. "Do you take anything seriously?"

"Only those things that deserve it."

"Do I? No, wait, I don't think I want the answer."

"Hear it anyway. Yes, Ms. Warner, very seriously. Now, do I get to set your penance?"

"As I said, it depends."

"How 'bout we have dessert in bed?"

She stood. "Direct, aren't you?"

"I try."

"I suppose I should worry that you won't respect me in the morning." She was already moving inside.

He stood. "Don't forget 'I don't know you well enough.' "

She turned with a malicious grin. "Why is it I feel that if I knew you better, I wouldn't do this?"

Lang didn't leave the town house until the next morning.

His mind was too occupied with promises unspoken and consequences just now considered to notice that the landscape crew paring already manicured grass was the only one he had seen in years that included no Hispanics.

It was only after he was almost a mile away that the workers, four large, muscular men who acted with the concert of military personnel, packed up their equipment and crossed the street to Alicia's residence.

6

THIRTY-NINE

Near Intersection of Hassan Sabry and Sharia
26th of July
Zamalek District
Garden City
Cairo, Egypt
0920, Two Days Later

Gezira had been a mere sandbar in the Nile until it was built up as an island site for a royal palace. The northern part, Zamalek, was now a leafy, upscale residential district much like those found in Paris, London, or Rome. It was far enough away that little of the noxious air and even less of the noise of the Central City invaded its neat, palm-lined streets. Lang's first impression of the Egyptian capital had been seemingly random traffic, the stench of animal offal combined with exhaust fumes, and air so dirty it made Los Angeles's worst days seem pristine.

He sat on a rickety stool at the bar in Simonds, one of the oldest European-style cafés in Cairo, trying to ignore eyes stinging from both lack of sleep and pollution. He munched a croissant that rivaled any he had enjoyed in Paris. He hoped the bitter, black Turkish coffee would help clear a head still dusty with two days of jet lag, even if it was stripping away his stomach lining. Atlanta–Dallas–New York–London–Cairo, all with tight connections. If anyone had been following him, they would have been obvious as he passed briskly through one terminal after another.

At least he had been lucky: Only one screaming child, and no seatmates exhibiting what might be the symptoms of a terminal and highly contagious disease. Not bad, considering each aircraft had contained, what, one hundred and fifty–plus passengers? All those people, with the only commonality being that no two of them had paid the same price for their ticket.

The Couch passport, multiple reservations, and having the Gulfstream fly to Stockholm had reduced to negligible the chances of his being followed to Egypt.

Before leaving Atlanta, he had used an Internet café to e-mail Amid bin Hamish to confirm that he had the right man, the name given him by Dr. Shaffer, and made an appointment. Bin Hamish had suggested meeting here.

Lang glanced aground the dimly lit interior. Although the savage desert sun had not yet risen completely above the cluster of modern office buildings across the river, the cafe's louvered blinds were already lowered, giving a zebra effect to the newspapers of the few remaining breakfast patrons. Dust motes spun for seconds in the streaks of light before disappearing into darkness like planets out of orbit. The hum of air-conditioning muted but did not block the cries of muezzin, recorded, amplified, and blasted from the minaret of a nearby mosque, calling the faithful to the second prayer of the day.

As far as he could tell, Lang was just one more European in the most Westernized part of a Muslim city.

That was precisely as he wanted it.

He used a linen napkin to wipe the last crumbs from his mouth.

The waiter behind the bar pointed to Lang's nearly empty cup. Lang allowed him to refill it.

His mind went back, what, less than two days since he had sat on Alicia's deck in Vinings? He saw her face in the highly polished wood of the bar's surface, heard her laugh in the wheeze of the AC. For the first time since Gurt had left, he was not just looking forward to coming home; he was excited. Love, lust, attachment—he knew better than to try to quantify what he felt. Just enjoy it, just . . .

"Mr. Reilly?"

Lang turned to look into eyes almost as dark as the coffee. A round face perched above a pink knit shirt displaying an alligator on the left breast and buttoned to the chin. Even seated on the stool, Lang was half a head taller. The man's dark skin made guessing his age difficult, even if a few gray strands were clearly visible scattered among the jet-black.

"Langford Reilly?"

Lang nodded. "Amid bin Hamish?"

White teeth were made even brighter by the dark skin as the man extended a hand. "As you English say, Any friend of Dr. Shaffer's . . ."

"American. And Dr. Shaffer is dead."

The smile disappeared. "Dead?"

Lang slid off the stool and groped in his pocket for change. "I'm afraid so. Murdered in Vienna. Were you close?"

Bin Hamish shook his head slowly. "We never met, just exchanged ideas on the Net, wrote each other."

Lang was grateful to come up with a handful of piastres, one hundred of which made up the Egyptian pound. He had already learned the hard way that so few coins were in circulation that exact change was rare. He started to leave them on the bar top, thought better of it, and left an Egyptian note instead. At the current exchange rate, the coffee had been a bargain compared to, say, Starbucks.

"You have euro, dollar?" the waiter asked hopefully.

Egypt's chronic currency problems caused many hotels and restaurants not to accept the national money.

Bin Hamish snapped something at the man, who sulked as he picked up the Egyptian bill.

The little man turned his attention back to Lang. "Murdered? By whom?"

Lang noted the correct grammar. "I'm afraid I don't know. I'm sure the Austrian authorities are working on finding out, if they haven't already."

Bin Hamish glanced uneasily around the café, as though one or more of the killers might have followed Lang to Cairo. "Perhaps we should talk elsewhere, perhaps my house."

Why meet at the café if they were going to bin Hamish's house to talk?

As Lang took his light jacket from the back of the stool and started for the door, bin Hamish put a hand on his shoulder. "No, this way."

They walked out the back door into an alley fetid with garbage that smelled like it was a permanent part of the environs. Flies buzzed angrily at the disturbance, and rats boldly surveyed them from atop piles of refuse. An occasional skeletal dog paused in rooting through piles of waste to snarl territorial claims.

As though by magic, a turn at the end of the alley brought them onto a street that could have been in Beverly Hills or Palm Beach.

Cairo, it seemed, was unaware of modern zoning. Or public health.

Lawn sprinklers made rainbows over lush grass medians lining high walls. Through the occasional gate Lang could see lavishly landscaped grounds with driveways winding to tile-roofed mansions.

The preferred mode of travel was by chauffeured Rolls-Royce, the less fortunate making do with highly polished Mercedes limousines.

The contrast was enough to make Lang look over his shoulder to be certain he had not imagined the squalor of the alley. "Any reason we couldn't take the front door?"

Bin Hamish turned to look up and down the street behind them, a gesture performed so frequently, Lang was beginning to think of it as some sort of nervous tic. "They would have followed, just as they would have noted your arrival at my home."

"They?"

Bin Hamish left the question unanswered. "We are almost there. Good thing, hey? I remember what your English poet said about only mad dogs and Englishmen going about in the midday sun."

"I'm American."

Bin Hamish ducked down what Lang had thought to be another driveway. After a turn to the right, he realized they were approaching the back of a house. Slightly smaller than its neighbors, judging by the perimeter of the wall, it still would be a large estate by most American standards. Whatever its size, Lang would be glad to get inside and out of soaring temperatures that promised to soon become unbearable.

They stopped at a small wooden door while bin Hamish fumbled with a jingling set of keys. When the portal swung open, Lang was treated to perhaps an acre of rampant flowers, citrus trees heavy with fruit, and towering date palms that obscured most of what appeared to be a two-story stucco house, each floor with the arched, elaborately columned loggias favored in Muslim architecture. At the back of the building the blue waters of an Olympic-size pool sparkled.

Bin Hamish relocked the gate. "It is my oasis."

Lang hoped it was an air-conditioned oasis.

Lang followed his host to the house and through huge mahogany doors that opened and closed soundlessly. He stopped for a moment to let his eyes adjust to light low enough to reveal furniture only in silhouette. He followed bin Hamish up a short flight of stairs to what Lang guessed was the foyer. Reception hall would have been a better description. Lang was surprised to see the screen of a TV set flickering above more massive mahogany doors.

Bin Hamish pointed. "As you can see, they are watching."

Looking closer, Lang realized he was observing the sweep of a security camera mounted somewhere outside. Two men sat in an old Mercedes and stared back through sunglasses. Neither made any effort to appear interested in anything other than this residence. Since they were in the only car parked in the area, Lang assumed they knew their presence was no secret.

"Who are your pals?" he asked.

"Mukhabarat."

Lang turned away from the television to look at the little Egyptian. "What are you doing that would interest the state security police?"

Bin Hamish smiled again. "Ah! You recognize the name of the Mukhabarat! Most Englishmen would not."

Lang gave up. It would be easier to be British.

Bin Hamish motioned. "Come, I will show you."

As they passed along one dimly lit corridor into another, Lang had the impression that they were not alone. Twice he was certain he heard gentle footsteps, but when he turned no one was there. Once he recognized the swish of fabric against the wall. Again, no one was to be seen.

Stopping in front of an arched doorway, bin Hamish ushered Lang inside. From one of the beams high overhead, a slow-moving fan stirred the dry air around the paneled room. Upholstered cushions surrounded a low table floating on the muted colors of an Oriental rug. On the table were several bowls and a teapot, steaming as though just set in place by some invisible jinni.

"Tea?" bin Hamish asked, pouring into a small cup without handle or saucer.

The idea of hot liquid was less than appealing. Lang shook his head. "No, thanks."

His host shook his head, too. "Arabs begin conversations with coffee or tea, Mr. Reilly." He pointed to the bowls. "Perhaps a few dates, almonds, or pastries?"

Lang helped himself to a date the size of a pecan, nibbling carefully to avoid the pit. "I certainly did not mean offense."

"None taken. Another Arab custom is a long chat before getting around to business, something you English are loath to do. Why did Dr. Shaffer send you here? What is it you want with me?"

Lang decided not to correct the impression that Shaffer had actually sent him. Instead he reached into the pocket of the jacket he had been carrying over an arm and proffered the papers Jacob had translated. "I'd like your thoughts on this. Dr. Shaffer said you might be able to help."

Lang never saw the switch, but a light from the ceiling suddenly beamed down onto the table in front of his host. Bin Hamish read, his eyebrows coming together in a near scowl. When he finished, he began again.

At last he looked up. "Where did you find this?"

"Hidden in an old radio," Lang said, and explained what had happened.

Wordlessly, bin Hamish rose and went to the wall at Lang's back. Soundlessly a panel slid back, revealing nothing but dark space. It suddenly became ablaze with such light Lang had to shield his eyes after the dimness of the rest of the house.

When he moved his hands from his face, he was looking at a laboratory of glass and stainless steel. A number of machines occupied the single counter, some of which he recognized from Georgia Tech.

They entered and the door silently slid back into place.

"I thought you were with some university," Lang said.

"I was until . . . Well, as you Americans say, that is another story."

He walked over to a box about the length and width of those Lang's cigars came in, but much thicker and made from a shiny metal. "The Ark in your document, Mr. Reilly, has certain dimensions. This has proportionately the same."

Lang waited for him to continue.

"You will note that, like the Ark, this is made of gold and wood."

Lang waited again.

"Are you familiar with superconductors, Mr. Reilly?"

Lang stepped closer to take a better look. "Only that it's some kind of new theory of physics."

Bin Hamish sighed, disappointed. "Superconductors are no longer only theory. Among other things they can create a highly conductive path along certain molecules or even DNA strands. The medical implications for treatment of cancer and other diseases are endless.

"Additionally, in a superconductor, a single-frequency light flows at *less* than the speed of light but absorbs magnetic energy, enough to repel both positive and negative poles. . . ."

Lang thought he remembered something from long-ago physics classes. "But if both poles are repelled . . . ?"

"Then the superconductor can cause material to weigh less without losing mass."

"Levitate?"

"Exactly."

"Good. That's about all the science I can call up from high school."

Bin Hamish seated himself on a long-legged stool in front of the counter and motioned for Lang to take the one remaining. "I will try to keep it simple. Much energy either loses potency over space or is conducted by some means. Electricity, for example, is conveyed by wires. A superconductor has no such limitations, so . . ."

Lang held up a hand. "Whoa! Electricity, superconductors—we're talking about 1500 or so B.C. They didn't have such things."

Bin Hamish wagged his head dolefully. "Of course they did, Mr. Reilly. Electricity was not invented; it was discovered. The same with gravity. The physical laws of the universe were in effect long before the pharaohs. The ancients were aware of many and knew how to use some. Much of that knowledge was lost during the Dark Ages. A lot of that wisdom remains to be rediscovered."

Lang had a hard time taking his eyes from the gilt box. "That's what you do, rediscover ancient secrets?"

"I suppose you would call me an archeological physicist. At least, that was the subject I taught at the University of Cairo until . . ."

Lang waited.

"Until the government uncovered my secret."

Lang leaned forward, the box momentarily forgotten. "Which was . . . ?"

Bin Hamish inhaled deeply, a man about to dive not into water but the past. "Would you be surprised if I told you my real name was Hamish, not *bin* Hamish?"

"You're Jewish?"

Bin Hamish nodded. "Once that was discovered, I was removed from my teaching post lest I contaminate Muslim youth."

"But I thought Egypt and Israel settled their differences."

Bin Hamish snorted sardonically. "After Israel seized the Sinai, bombed the Egyptian air force into oblivion, and destroyed almost all the Egyptian tanks, it was very easy to make peace. Your President Carter could broker the Camp David Accords because Egypt had essentially lost the war and had no means to continue or get its territory back. The Arabs' hatred of Jews, though, continues and will continue as long as one of each is left on this earth."

He paused and swallowed. "That is why I am under constant surveillance, also. At any time the government could have me arrested as an agent of a foreign power." He laughed bitterly. "All Jews in Egypt are agents of a foreign power, particularly those whom the government suspects might be useful."

"Useful?"

He was inspecting his hands as though looking for flaws. "Before I was forced to leave the university, I published a number of papers in archeological and scientific journals dealing with ancient and lost sciences."

"So, why not leave? I'd bet one of Israel's schools would love to have you."

"Not that simple," he said dully. "My specialty is ancient Egypt. Once I left, the Egyptians would always find a reason to deny me reentry. Besides, my wife is Arab and has no desire to leave her native land."

The soft footsteps?

"But I stray," bin Hamish said. "We were talking about superconductors."

"I still have a hard time believing such things existed."

Bin Hamish rubbed his chin and got off the stool. "Very well. Please indulge me."

He left the room, the door sighing closed behind him. A minute later he returned, a manila folder in hand. Opening it, he placed several photographs in front of Lang.

At first Lang was uncertain what he was seeing. He recognized the stylized Egyptian figure of a man, face in profile, torso in frontal view. He squinted and picked up the picture.

"It's a photograph of a relief from the temple of Hathor in Dendra, dating back about forty-five hundred years," bin Hamish informed him.

"But what does . . . ?" Lang stopped in midsentence,

suddenly aware of what the figure was holding. "Looks like an elongated lightbulb with a snake for the filament."

"Not a lightbulb, a cathode tube."

"Or a vacuum tube."

Bin Hamish was puzzled. "A vacuum tube?"

"As in old radios."

Like Dr. Yadish liked to tinker with.

Lang picked up another picture, this one of several large jars. One had been cut in half vertically. Inside, a rod of some sort had been inserted, held by a stopper.

He held it up. "And this?"

"Look closely, Mr. Reilly. That jar is in the National Museum of Iraq in Baghdad. A copper cylinder was inserted into the neck of a clay jar and fixed with tar or asphalt and topped with lead. In the middle of the cylinder was an iron rod. That particular jar and a number like it have been dated to 1200 or so B.C."

Lang thought a moment. "I was never a science whiz. What's the significance of the jars?"

Bin Hamish spoke slowly, as though addressing a dull child. "A battery, Mr. Reilly. A battery or electric cell."

"But how . . . ?"

"After the Second World War, a man named Willard Gray of General Electric's Pittsfield, Massachusetts, plant built an exact replica of what you see, using nothing more than the material I've described. With only a little citric acid—the acid in, say, a lemon—the jar produced two volts of electricity. If you doubt me, check the April 1957 issue of *Science Digest*."

There was a knock at the panel that served as a door. Unhurriedly bin Hamish walked over and spoke through a narrow crack. Lang could not make out the words. Shutting the panel again, bin Hamish returned with a tray bearing what looked like the same tea service and bowls.

"A little refreshment?"

This time Lang accepted a small cup of bitter tea while the professor continued. "Those other pictures are of copper utensils from ancient Sumer. They had been electroplated with silver. Then there are more pictures of your 'vacuum tube' at other places."

Lang almost expected his host to next produce Egyptian tomb drawings of a pharaoh watching a TV set, or one of his wives or concubines using a hair dryer. Either the man and those like him were lunatics or the current view of ancient world history needed serious revision.

He was inclined to the latter possibility.

What he had just heard and seen, though, was the stuff of fantasy, Lovecraft, Vonnegut, and H. G. Wells. He could not have been more dumbfounded had Grumps suddenly quoted Shakespeare.

He took a sip of tea and set the cup down. "Assuming all this is true, what is the significance of the Ark being a superconductor?"

"When fueled by orbitally rearranged monatomic elements, such as the pure gold mentioned in your papers—"

Lang held up his hands in surrender. "Try to keep it simple, Professor, something a mere English major might understand."

Bin Hamish thought for a moment. "Simply put, or oversimplifying, actually, once a superconductor is fueled, it keeps on doing whatever task is set for it, sort of a perpetual-motion machine. The way the Ark is constructed is to transport energy over any distance for any length of time. Basically, when fueled by pure gold, the manna of your papers, that energy could well take the form of unimaginable power directed at a specific target."

"Like Jericho."

"Like Jericho."

Lang reached toward the box. "All from a box like—"

"No!" Ben Hamish knocked Lang's hand away. "You would die instantly, like those mentioned in your papers. Let me show you something."

Stepping down from his perch on the stool, bin Hamish placed a rubber mat under his feet. "They had no rubber in biblical times, but the Ark's handlers washed and thoroughly dried their feet, thereby removing moisture or anything else that might act as a conventional conductor. Their clothes would have been of the finest cloth, so as to generate as little static electricity as possible."

He pulled on a pair of rubber gloves and then moved the golden box slightly before walking across the room and opening a cabinet.

He removed a piece of metal and tossed it to Lang. "Slug iron."

Lang looked at the heavy ingot in his hand. "So?"

"Place it at the end of the counter, if you please."

Lang did as instructed.

Bin Hamish returned to stand by Lang and adjusted the box.

What happened next wasn't quite clear. A bolt of light, the brightest Lang had ever seen, seemed to leap from the box and disappear faster than lightning, so fast Lang wasn't sure he had seen it at all. There was no sound. The slug of metal was gone. Not melted, not transformed, but gone without fragments or a wisp of smoke.

"Shit!"

Bin Hamish was peeling off his gloves. "Exactly so."

"But what happened to the metal?"

Bin Hamish shrugged. "There are any number of theories, including transportation to a parallel dimension."

"Yeah, Dr. Shaffer mentioned that. Can you bring it back?"

"So far, no."

Lang inhaled deeply, still not completely sure he

wasn't dealing with a madman or a talented trickster. "I'd guess a lot of governments would like to have that in their arsenal."

Bin Hamish chuckled. "What makes you think they do not?" He raised a hand to stifle Lang's next question. "Let me tell you a brief story: In 1976 near Phoenix in the state of Arizona, there was a cotton farmer named David Hudson. In that area, the soil has a high sodium content, a condition Mr. Hudson attempted to lessen with high amounts of sulfuric acid. Do you understand?"

Lang nodded. "Using an acid to dilute a base, right?"

"Just so. Now, after one such treatment, Mr. Hudson sent soil samples for analysis. When dried by the hot Arizona sun, some particulate in that soil sample would burst into flames and totally disappear. Do I have your attention?"

Lang helped himself to a pastry, a sugary substance that literally melted in his mouth, leaving a pleasant but unidentifiable flavor. "You do."

"Mr. Hudson had more analyses done over a period of years. Each time the substance tested as different elements at different temperatures. . . ."

Lang remembered what the professor at Georgia Tech, Werbel, had told him and Detective Morse. "Let me guess . . ." He related as best as he could recall.

"Precisely. You have already had this . . . this manna subjected to tests. But Mr. Hudson's story is not yet ended. He spent a fortune trying to develop this marvelous material into an energy source by use of superconductors. The sudden flame, the weightlessness, all had tremendous potential. First he was denied a building permit for a plant in which to work, and then fault was found with every plan he submitted. Then came zoning delays. Then came an unexplained explosion that leaked tons of toxic material. Your government people, environmental, employee safety . . ."

"OSHA," Lang supplied.

"Whoever they were, they imposed fines and other penalties. Then your military appeared and closed the man's research on superconductivity on grounds of national security. Frankly, Mr. Reilly, I was surprised your much-touted democratic government could act in such an arbitrary manner."

Lang wasn't. Once a motivated coalition of bureaucracy and military was formed, law, Constitution, and individual rights might not be suspended, but they could be made so expensive that only the wealthiest could afford them.

"You're saying the military intervened?"

Bin Hamish nodded. "Just so."

"So, they were interested in the weapon's potential," Lang mused.

"Not potential," bin Hamish corrected. "Very real."

"Real?"

"Mr. Reilly, surely you remember your President Reagan's Star Wars proposal, the idea of building a series of killer satellites that would knock Soviet missiles out of the sky? You will recall it was never built, but the mere threat caused such a surge in Russian defense spending that within a year or two the communists went broke."

Lang remembered clearly. It was the collapse of the Evil Empire that had precipitated his departure from the Agency. "You're telling me that Star Wars was actually a version of this . . . this whatever it is. Superconductor?"

Bin Hamish smiled and gave a slight bow. "Precisely. The talk of killer satellites was just a red fish."

"Red herring."

"A ruse by any name."

"So, the United Sates, at least, has this technology?"

"I am fairly certain, yes."

"Who else?"

Bin Hamish shrugged. "Who would know? Only the few

physicists who are aware of the unique powers of the Ark realized what your president was actually describing."

"But the Egyptians must have some inkling of it. Otherwise why the surveillance?"

"From my published work they would know I am studying something that could be a potential weapon. I also am studying something that, if properly harnessed, could literally move mountains."

Lang settled back on his stool and refilled his teacup. "Or tons of rock to build a pyramid."

"Just so."

"But how?"

Bin Hamish was checking the backs of his hands again. "That I do not yet know. What I do know so far is what you have seen. The only material not affected like the slug of metal is pure gold."

"What happens to gold?"

"Gold, Mr. Reilly, does not burn. It melts. Your papers tell of Moses burning the golden calf. The only way he could have done that is by using a force similar to the one the Ark projects. It turns gold into the white powder. Manna, if you will."

"Let me get this straight." Lang was trying to reduce the process to one he could understand. "The white powder, manna, fuels the Ark, and the Ark turns gold into the white powder. Why?"

Bin Hamish moved his head slowly from side to side. "That is, so far, unknown to me. That is a law of the universe that is yet to be rediscovered."

Lang slid from the stool, standing. "Dr. bin Hamish, I appreciate your time. What can I do . . . ?"

Bin Hamish crossed the room and somehow opened the panel. "It is unnecessary for you to do anything. As you can see from this house, I have no need of money. An inheritance and investments outside Egypt have seen to that. Having a chance to talk with you is recompense enough. I rarely have visitors." He nodded in the direction of the street and his minders. "You can understand why few if any of my former colleagues come to call."

Lang left by the same rear door through which he had entered. When he reached the street, the same two men were still in the same Mercedes.

FORTY

Lang had gone from the airport straight to meet bin Hamish, detouring only to entrust his single bag to the hotel's concierge before heading across the river. Now he had returned to a flurry of excuses and promises as to when he might occupy his room. His expectations were not enhanced by the marble-pillared lobby's growing line of disheveled arriving guests who were also looking forward to a shower, a shave, and perhaps a nap to bring their frayed psyches more in line with local time.

Although Lang had spent little time in the Arab world, he understood far better than most of his tired, jet-lagged, and irritated fellow travelers how things worked. Deeply apologetic, the desk clerk pleaded an abnormal number of late checkouts and the lack of trained help.

He leaned toward Lang conspiratorially. "It is difficult to get these people to work," he confided with a patronizing smile that said he was sure someone of Lang's sophistication would understand the abhorrence with which local women regarded labor. "But we do have the presidential suite available right now. Only a few hundred pounds more than yours."

Lang wasn't falling for the old upgrade trick, one common throughout the Middle East. Instead he crossed the ornate lobby to press against the concierge desk so that those behind him could not see the ten-Egyptian-pound note he spread out on the varnished wood.

Smiling, he said, "I would like my room as soon as possible."

"Of course," the man said with an oily grin as he reached for the bill.

Lang stepped back, returning the money to his pocket. "It will be yours when you deliver the room key. I'll be in the bar."

Lang was uncertain whether the hotel's bar was supposed to be contemporary with an Egyptian flair or was just overdone. A round window of dark blue was reflected in twin crystal obelisks. He sat in one of the gold-lacquered chairs that vaguely resembled something he might have seen at Versailles.

A waiter who looked like he might have just left a meeting of the local Shriners, complete with fez, appeared as though from Aladdin's lamp. Already full of caffeine so early in the day, Lang ordered a large orange juice, leaned back, and went over the meeting he had just left.

Add to a Moses who was not Hebrew but a king and Israelites who were not Jews but Egyptians a weapon of ancient origin that, quite likely, had toppled a modern empire. Was it this device that the unknown "they" sought? More likely they were trying to suppress it. If someone were trying to prevent its proliferation, presumably that would be a power that already had it.

As far as Lang knew, that included only the United States.

But weapons systems tended to be like popular songs: Once performed, everyone whistled or hummed along. If America had the Ark . . . what? Ray? Laser? Whatever. Star Wars. If the United States had it, it was certain to have been tested; and, if tested, its existence was at least known to the other major players.

But which ones?

"Mr. Reilly?"

The smarmy concierge was looking down at him, suitcase in hand. "Your room is ready."

The view of the river one block west and the island he had just left were impressive, but Lang pulled the curtains against the glare, took a long shower, and stretched out on the king-size bed. He tried to take up the thought process that had been interrupted in the bar but was soon asleep.

He had no idea how long he had slept. The sun was now making the room brighter despite the curtains. For an instant he hung between the reality of this world and the gauzy consciousness of dreams. He had been . . . somewhere, and there had been a sound . . . a noise. But what?

A very real knock came from the door to his suite.

"A minute!" Lang called, struggling into his pants and shoes. "Who's there?"

"Room service."

Lang stopped halfway to the door. He hadn't ordered anything, nor was he going to. Another common scam in this part of the world was to post room service items at one price while charging nearly double that for delivering them.

Lang pressed an eye to the peephole. Outside his door was the concierge. Now what?

The instant he unlocked the door it flew open. Two burly men stepped into the room from the hall and slammed the door shut while the concierge, his mission complete, slunk away.

Both men wore dark suits despite the heat; both faces were hidden behind sunglasses.

Tweedledum and Tweedledee.

They could have been the men outside bin Hamish's house. The two took their time inspecting the room and Lang's suitcase while Lang cursed himself for not making arrangements for the weapon he could not have carried past airport security.

"If you gentlemen are from the tourist bureau, I'm perfectly satisfied with the room."

Neither intruder gave a sign of having heard.

Instead they completed probing the lining of Lang's single bag before the shorter of the two turned and asked in accented English, "What did you discuss with the Jew bin Hamish?"

He made no effort to conceal the butt of a pistol in the holster under his left arm.

Lang pursed his lips and squinted, a man desperately trying to recall something. "We spoke of many things: of shoes and ships and sealing wax, of cabbages and kings."

The blow came so fast Lang barely had time to roll with it, an openhanded slap that made Lang see double. Apparently these goons weren't fond of Lewis Carroll.

The man was immobile, as though he hadn't moved at all. "Once again, Mr. Reilly . . ."

"My name is Couch," Lang snapped. "You've obviously gotten the wrong room."

The man allowed himself the beginnings of a smile. "We are aware of the name on the passport you presented upon arrival at this hotel, Mr. Reilly. Now, for the last time, what did you and the Jew talk about?"

If the man were anything other than a hired thug, he would not have stood quite so close. Nor would he interrogate a possibly hostile subject with his gun still in his shoulder holster, where Lang could get at it.

"Go fuck yourself."

This time the blow was with a closed fist, delivered with the assailant's full weight behind it.

Just as Lang had anticipated.

Easily sidestepping the fist, Lang placed his leg across the man's knee as he grabbed the wrist, using his opponent's forward inertia to jerk him forward. An almost simultaneous twist of his own leg bent the other man's knee backward, sending him stumbling with a yelp of pain. As he fought for his balance, Lang's hand was inside the man's jacket, emerging with the automatic.

The whole thing was over before the other man could clear his weapon. Instead he was now looking down the muzzle of what had been his companion's pistol. He warily moved his hand away and held both out in front of him.

Lang edged toward the door, the pistol's barrel alternating between the two. "Okay, guys, here's what's going down. First, you." He gestured toward the man with his hands outstretched. "You. Take off your suit coat and throw it on the bed. Then, using only your left thumb and forefinger, remove that gun from the holster and toss it on the bed. Now!"

The man sneered at him. "Come take it. A shot in this hotel would draw the police like a dung heap draws flies."

Lang knew he was right. He took a step closer, as though he were, in fact, going to get within range of an attack. Instead he delivered the toe of his shoe into the man's crotch with as much force as he could.

With a single grunt, the man folded like a beach ball from which the air had suddenly escaped.

Lang knelt over the writhing, moaning form on the floor, sighing as he reached into the jacket and removed the pistol. "Well, I tried it the easy way."

He stood, a gun in each hand, and motioned to the one favoring what was quite likely a shattered kneecap. "You: Pick up the stuff you took out of my bag and repack it. Unless you want to join your pal there in indefinite celibacy, I suggest you make it quick."

He did.

"For your continuing amusement, gentlemen, our next game is going to be a contest to see who can tie the other up most securely. Start ripping the bedsheets into strips."

Five minutes later the two intruders were secured firmly to the bed.

Lang let himself out the door, carefully pulling it shut until he heard the lock snap into place. He slipped one of the two pistols out of his waistband and started to put it under the cushion of a chair, part of a furniture grouping in front of the bank of elevators. He stopped and stared. He was holding a Desert Eagle.

Damn. He'd seen more of the bulky automatics lately than he had in a lifetime. Some arms merchant must have had a sale—a real sale to convince the Mukhabarat to switch over from the Russian knockoff of the Walther PPK, the Stechkin. Unreliable, but cheap and plentiful.

In the lobby he stepped to the front of the line of protesting guests waiting to register.

A ten-pound note in hand, he spoke to the clerk. "An emergency checkout. My passport, please."

The increasingly angry queue was still grumbling as he quickly strode across the lobby, noting the surprise on the face of the concierge, who quickly disappeared into a room behind his stand.

On the street the afternoon's heat hit Lang like a hammer's blow. Sweat plastered his shirt to his back as he searched for a cab, surprised there were none at the hack stand outside the hotel.

He was trying to decide the quickest way to the airport when his mind was made up for him.

Tweedledum and Tweedledee shoved through the hotel's revolving door. The sheets must not have been spun from the finest Egyptian cotton, and the blow to the knee must have been much less severe than Lang had thought.

Lang was running just as they spotted him.

Without surprise, he stood little chance against both of them unless he used the heavy automatic, something that would quickly bring the police.

Straight ahead was the opera house, and across the street the red *M* in a blue star, the emblem of Cairo's Metro.

Lang nearly knocked a woman and child over as he took the stairs two at a time.

He was in luck: A train was stopped, disgorging passengers. Even in his rush he noted how much cleaner the station was than the streets above. Thankful he had conserved his change, he slid coins into a slot until a ticket appeared with a whir and a click. He knew the price varied depending on how many stops he intended to travel, but he didn't care. Jumping the turnstile would have alerted the uniformed policeman on the platform.

He lunged for the nearest car and stopped, realizing the first two were reserved for women. He gave the now interested cop a weak smile, the look of a Western tourist making a typical cultural error.

He wedged himself and his suitcase into the third car and turned just in time to see Tweedledum and Tweedledee burst into the station. One pointed to the window through which Lang was looking. Lang couldn't resist a wave as the train jolted forward and gained speed.

Lang had no idea where he was going, only that he was putting as much real estate between him and those two as possible. At the next stop he edged through the packed car to inspect the diagram of the Metro system, labeled in Arabic and English. He gathered he had boarded at the Gezira station, the one closest to the opera house. Ahead, the two legs of the system intersected. He could transfer to the other or remain on the present line. He saw no indication that either went to the airport.

A man in a worn business suit stood to get off at the next stop, and Lang took his seat.

Something wasn't right.

If the two Mukhabarat men knew he was on the train, why didn't they simply have it boarded at the next stop?

One answer was ominous: They didn't want the law enforcement people to know anything, thereby preventing inconvenient questions if Lang disappeared into the black hole of some secret prison.

Or perhaps they simply hadn't had time to position the police at the various stations.

Either way, it seemed expedient to get off while he could.

He was stepping down from the car when Tweedledum and Tweedledee came down the steps from the street. No doubt they had been more successful than Lang in finding transportation, and it had taken them this many stops to get ahead of the train.

Too late to wish he'd gotten off earlier.

Shielding himself amid the exiting horde, Lang almost made it to another set of stairs before one saw him and they both broke into a run.

Shoving cursing passengers aside as he galloped upstairs, Lang made it to the top and glanced around.

He still didn't know where he was. He bolted for the nearest corner and the one after that.

He was standing in the middle of a souq, a large Arab bazaar. Small stalls crowded the narrow street, compressing the crowd of tourists, merchants, and customers into a space less than five feet wide. The mixture of languages was straight out of the biblical Tower of Babel. A woman wearing a soiled chador squatted in front of him, offering a drink with one hand and shooing flies from it with the other. Several were floating in the rose-colored liquid. From where he stood he could see copperware, blown glass, spices, and tacky souvenirs for sale. Manure, rotting vegetables, and wood smoke were the three smells he could identify.

There was a tug at his pants leg. "Scarab, Mista 'merican?"

Lang looked down to see a young boy, sans front teeth, in traditional bedouin headdress and robes, proffering a small carving of the Egyptian dung beetle that symbolized resurrection.

"Come from tombs in the valley. Very, very old. Only five dolla 'merican."

Lang shook his head and started twisting his way down the street. He paused to let a procession of earphone-wearing American tourists follow the leader, a woman carrying aloft a handkerchief tied to an umbrella as she spoke into a headset.

The stop was enough for the young scarab seller to catch up. "Three dolla, Mista 'merican. You take for three dolla?"

Lang shook his head and started off again.

A series of what were undoubtedly curses made him look over his shoulder. Tweedledum and Tweedledee had knocked over the old woman's drinks, and she was expressing her disapproval in what Lang guessed was most unladylike terms.

His small bag held like a football to a running back's chest, Lang shoved aside a tourist in shorts and hideously European sandals as he ducked between two stalls, but not before the young souvenir salesman approached the newcomers.

"Scarab, mista? Only five dolla 'merican."

The souq was a maze of rickety stalls and sagging tents. Lang had little room to run, but his determined pursuers could go no faster. He ducked between a wooden kiosk where turquoise jewelry was hanging and the ropes holding up an adjacent tent under which dates were stacked in boxes.

Then he stopped.

One of the men was no longer there.

A quick look told him where he had gone. Somehow he had gotten in front. Lang was hemmed in by stalls, canvas, and two men who certainly bore him no goodwill. His hand went to the Desert Eagle in his belt.

No. Too crowded. Customers or purveyors were as likely to get hurt as his targets.

FORTY-ONE

2110 Paces Ferry Road
Vinings, Georgia
7:38 a.m.
Two Days Earlier

Alicia was humming an old show tune as she stepped out of the shower. Last night with Lang had been every bit as wonderful as she had fantasized. Smiling at the thought, she swaddled herself in the thick terry-cloth robe from the Willard Hotel in Washington, the one she had swiped the time the cheapskates at the Department of Justice had allowed her to stay there instead of the usual out-of-the-way Sheraton or Marriott. She was wrapping a towel into a turban around her hair as she walked into the bedroom and stopped.

For an instant she thought Lang had come back to reclaim some forgotten item. But there were two men she had never seen before standing between her and the door to the hall.

The one closest was of slender build, over six feet, mid-thirties, dark hair cut slightly shorter than currently fashionable, and freshly shaved, as though he had just put down his razor. He looked out of place in the landscaping service's uniform he wore.

Her first reaction was anger rather than fear. "How did you get in . . . ?"

He held up a thin black wallet with a badge fixed to one side, a photo ID on the other. She had seen hundreds just like it. "Special Agent Witherspoon, Federal Bureau of Investigation."

The other man was holding up similar creds.

Her anger not even slightly mollified, she snapped, "You're not from the local office. I hope to hell you've got a warrant."

Witherspoon returned the black wallet to a pocket. "We understood Langford Reilly was here."

She stepped to the bedside, reaching for the phone. "I don't care if you thought Osama bin Laden was here— you don't have a warrant, your ass is grass, as you're about to find out."

She picked up the receiver and had punched in the first four digits of the local FBI office, a number any assistant U.S. Attorney knew by rote, when she felt a slight prick in her arm.

"What the hell do you think . . . ?"

Her knees suddenly gave way and she was lying on the floor, looking at a pair of men's shoes. Above her she heard the phone being replaced on its cradle.

Then her world went black.

Should a neighbor have been leaving his house for work a minute or so later, he would have seen nothing unusual at 8:10. Two men from the community association's landscaping service were carrying a large bag, no doubt full of grass cuttings or fallen leaves, to their truck. The only thing unusual was that the sack seemed to weigh more than such material should. Both men were struggling with the weight. It would have been comforting to know residents were getting their money's worth.

FORTY-TWO

Khan al-Khalil
Cairo

Lang didn't see many options. Even if he could literally push through the crowd, he would wind up confined by more stalls. The only good news was that for whatever reason, the Mukhabarat men had not yet called for backup or summoned the local police to join in the chase.

Lang moved sideways under the tent, pretending to examine a small carton of dates. The tent's proprietor smiled, showing yellowed teeth, and extended a hand with one of the fruits. He was offering a sample of the merchandise.

Tweedledum and Tweedledee, anticipating success, had slowed to a walk. As they approached, the angle for an escape right or left, never good, diminished even more.

Lang accepted the proffered date, nibbling tentatively as he backed slowly to stand beside one of the ropes supporting the canvas. Four guy lines wrapped around rocks held the tent against a peaked pole that looked less than steady. Lang guessed it was rigged for easy removal once the day's business was complete.

Tweedledee ducked as he stepped under the edge of

the tent. From where he stood, Lang watched as Tweedle-dum did the same.

With a forced nonchalance, Lang took a step, as though to speak with the date seller. The two men antici-pated his move and came further under the canvas.

Lang suddenly spun, exiting the shade of the sailcloth, and snatched the rope from its tethering rock. One cor-ner of the canvas now hung limply. Repeating the move, he slipped the second line free, cutting himself off from the view of the two. He gave the corner a hard pull and the entire structure collapsed, to the screams and curses of those inside, who were blindly shoving one another to get out from under the confines of the enveloping canvas.

Lang fled.

Two blocks away he finally succeeded in waving down a cab and was on his way to the airport. He would take the first flight out to anywhere.

Then he had some very specific questions he needed to have answered.

The sound of his BlackBerry's beep startled him. It could be only one person.

"Yes, Sara?"

"Lang? I can't hear you."

Cairo's traffic intruded even through the cab's win-dows rolled up to contain air-conditioning of doubtful value: horns honking, as many mufflers missing as were still working, the driver's radio blaring something Lang supposed was music. He tapped the man on the shoul-der, motioning him to lower the volume.

"Okay, Sara, try again."

"Lang, someone slipped a package through the mail slot last night."

"The mayor can't afford stamps?"

"Lang, I'm serious."

"Okay, what's in it?"

"Makes no sense. A ring with an emerald in the shape of a heart."

It took Lang three tries to Alicia's personal office number before someone else answered.

No, Ms. Warner was not in her office. No, she had not called in. The anonymous coworker was certain Alicia had an appointment out of the office and had simply forgotten to tell anyone.

Lang was less sure.

FORTY-THREE

British Airways Flight 721
Somewhere over the Mediterranean
That Night

Lang usually enjoyed British comedy, with its under-
stated humor and cleverly absurd situations. Tonight,
though, he watched the Hugh Grant movie on the individual screen without really seeing it. Instead he saw the
shadow in the mist, a figure now recognizable.

Maybe.

His rush from the Khan al-Khalil to the airport had gotten him there only twenty-five minutes before a departure for London's Heathrow. When he'd been told by an
unconcerned ticket agent that the plane was full, a wad
of bills provided enough baksheesh to purchase not
only a ticket but also an avoidance of time-consuming if
indifferent security. The ease with which he evaded supposed protection against bomb-toting candidates for Islamic martyrdom du jour did little to make him feel safe,
but it did get him to the gate in time. A bored glance at
his forged passport, a nod from the accompanying ticket
agent, no doubt signaling a willingness to share the new-
found wealth, and he eased himself into a first-class
seat.

He tried not to think of the righteous indignation of whomever he had displaced.

Instead he utilized his flight-induced insomnia to review the few facts he knew about whoever it was that wanted him dead. He had concluded that the reason was the white powder, the manna, or whatever it was with such amazing chemical and physical properties. The stuff simply didn't answer all the questions, though. If two scientists working for the foundation an ocean apart had discovered it, it could not have been such an impossible secret. In his mind he replayed the morning's conversation with bin Hamish and the revelations of Dr. Shaffer in Vienna.

Perhaps it was not the powder; perhaps it was . . .

He shook his head to decline the offer of a beverage by a flight attendant, regulation smile in place. The noun *drink* apparently did not exist in the airlines' lexicon.

The scene at the marketplace had added another riddle: Why didn't Tweedledum and Tweedledee call for backup from the local police?

There was only one reason he could think of in retrospect.

Somewhere between that thought and the glare of the next morning's light, the weariness that was the dregs of the day's adrenaline surge took over.

FORTY-FOUR

New Scotland Yard
Broadway
London
The Next Afternoon

Inspector Dylan Fitzwilliam scowled at the grainy photograph on his desk, the product of an airport security camera. The man tendering his passport might have been traveling under the name of Joel Couch of Macon, Georgia, but face-recognition technology revealed him to be Langford Reilly.

IRA terrorism of the seventies and eighties had spawned the know-how of storing facial features in data banks. With cameras all over Great Britain, the average Englishman had his picture taken almost daily, a Londoner three times a day. The Irish killers had long since swapped bombs and guns for pin-striped suits and negotiating sessions, but the cameras remained. Like any other government intrusion, once begun, the program was unlikely to end nor the technology to be scrapped.

Mr. Reilly had appeared on one of the cameras at Gatwick a week or so ago, and again the same day on another that scanned London's streets. Although Fitzwilliam had been alerted, there was nothing to be done. In spite of the suspected murder in the West End, the shooting of two unknown thugs on the streets of South Dock, and the surprising discovery in Portugal a few years ago, the American had been cleared of any wrongdoing. There had been no reason to detain him.

Innocence, of course, had no place in data banks.

That had been before the Yard had received notice from Interpol that Reilly was wanted for questioning in connection with a murder in Vienna.

Fitzwilliam exhaled wearily as he turned to the computer terminal on his desk. Some people simply could not shake off the violence that followed them any more than Patel, the inspector's immediate subordinate, could rid himself of the smell of curry.

A few taps on the keyboard and a list of names appeared. The inspector squinted over half-moon glasses at the screen. It seemed each year the font became harder to read, no doubt some space-saving economy by the Yard's accounting boffins. He refused to accept that age had anything to do with the matter.

There it was: Annueliwitz, Jacob, wife Rachel. A flat on Lambeth Road on South Dock. A barrister, unsurprisingly with offices at the Middle Temple Inn.

He printed out the addresses before summoning Patel.

The man appeared silently with the smile that perpetually lit his dark face. Even dressed in a suit and without a canteen, Patel reminded Fitzwilliam of a modern-day Gunga Din. The inspector mentally chastised himself. Let a word of that slip and it would be sensitivity training instead of police work for a fortnight at least.

The policeman handed both addresses and the picture across the desk. "Send a couple of lads to watch both these places. If this Reilly chap shows up, I want him brought in. There's an international warrant on him."

Patel, grin still intact, reached for the papers.

"No, on second thought, send four men to each." He caught himself in another politically incorrect gaffe.

"Officers. Men or women. And make sure they're armed. The bloke has been implicated in some pretty rough activity."

Patel nodded his understanding. "Like the killings a few years back? Should I have vests and rifles issued?"

Fitzwilliam regarded his subaltern for a moment before deciding the man was serious. "Hardly a way to avoid attracting attention, wouldn't you say?"

Grin undiminished and gentle reprimand ignored, Patel turned and left the inspector staring at his office's walls. Sodding rotten luck, having Reilly show up, unbidden as Banquo's ghost, on the night Shandon, his wife, had booked theater tickets.

FORTY-FIVE

Middle Temple Inn
Fleet Street
London
Minutes Later

Jacob listened patiently as Lang brought him up-to-date.

Removing the dead pipe from his mouth, he stared into the bowl as he reached for the nail-like tool. "So, your guess is that those sods in Cairo weren't Mukhabarat at all?"

Lang nodded. "Otherwise they would've called in backup."

Jacob was busily excavating the pipe's bowl. "So, who were they?"

"I think they were Jews. In fact, I think there's some Jewish organization behind this whole thing."

Jacob stopped, his hands for once still as his glasses slid down the bridge of his nose. "You're cocking me a snook."

Despite what Churchill described as the barrier of a common language, Lang guessed at the meaning. "No. I'm serious."

"But why . . . ?"

"Okay, let's look at the facts." Lang held up an index finger. "One, the only way those people could have known I'd contacted Shaffer, the Austrian, was by intercepting a call from my BlackBerry."

"They could have tapped his phone," Jacob argued.

"How would they know to do that? Other than the one call, I'd never spoken to the man before he felt he was being followed, as he clearly was."

Lang flinched at the memory of the corpses in the crypt.

Jacob used the stem of the briar to push the spectacles back into place. "Cell phones are subject to interception."

"Odds of any specific phone are, what, less than hitting the sweepstakes?"

"But the only other way your call could have been intercepted—"

"Would be Echelon," Lang finished the sentence.

Jacob shook his head. "But that's strictly Anglo-American. No one who isn't American, British, Canadian, Australian, or Kiwi has access."

Lang stared at his friend for a few moments.

Jacob finally looked down, running a hand along the edge of the desk as though looking for flaws in the wood. "Dash it all, okay. So, an occasional scrap gets shared with Mossad." He looked up. "But you don't think . . . ?"

"That Mossad's involved? No, I don't. I do think someone *in* Mossad may be, though. In fact, *has* to be. The Israelis are the only people outside the club who ever have access to Echelon. Plus the weapons . . ."

Jacob snorted. "The Israeli army discarded those Desert Eagles years ago. Too heavy."

"I'd be interested in knowing how they disposed of them."

"You can bloody well bet they didn't hand them out as sodding gifts at bar mitzvahs. The army usually destroys obsolete weapons."

"Humor me; call up old pals and see what you can learn about who was supposed to melt down the guns and who has access to Echelon. I'd bet it turns out to be the same person or persons."

It was clear Jacob wasn't happy but that he'd do it. "Anything else on your great bleeding laundry list?"

"Yeah, what I think is the clincher—"

There was a knock on the door, the one between the outer office and the common hallway. "Police! Open up!"

Jacob looked ruefully over his glasses. "This, as you Yanks say, is where I came in, what with the coppers about to beat the door down just like at my flat the last time you got involved with the wrong people."

Lang stood, but not before more blows fell on the outer door. For once he was thankful for his friend's paranoia that had resulted in the locking mechanism.

"Open up before we knock the door in!"

Lang desperately glanced around the office; the only exit was into the outer office. "I haven't done anything."

Jacob nodded calmly. "Same thing you said last time before you wound up hanging off the bleedin' balcony sixteen floors up. Maybe this time you'd like to explain your innocence?"

There was the sound of something hard smashing into wood.

For whatever reason the police wanted him, Lang wasn't about to surrender, to render himself incapable of movement. It was all too easy to arrange an "accident" once someone was incarcerated.

"Where?"

Another smash.

"Where indeed?" Jacob replied.

FORTY-SIX

At the Same Time

It was like pushing to the top from the bottom of a very dark pond: Light was visible but far away. No, not a pool—the ocean, because consciousness kept coming and going like the tide, leaving a bitter, salty taste in her mouth.

It had been like this for . . . ?

Perhaps hours or years; there was no way to be sure. Too many tides had risen and fallen.

Alicia had only hazy memories, fragments from some nearly forgotten dreams that came as regularly as the waves. At first she thought she could hear them murmuring against a distant shore, but she decided it was only the sound of her own pulse pumping in her temples.

But she knew she had not been in the sea forever, because there was one thing she knew was true, a single bit of memory unclouded, clear, and focused: She had come out of her bathroom in her house, the same way she had every day since moving to Atlanta, and . . .

What?

There had been strange men in her bedroom?

The idea seemed absurd, but no more so than the sounds and smells of an airport she thought she remembered. Yet maybe she had been in the hospital. She knew she was in a bed with side rails while a tube of some sort was in her arm. And she couldn't move. There were straps around her arms and legs. But at the same time she was certain—as certain as she could be about anything right now—that she had been in an airplane.

Was that possible?

She supposed it was, that she could have been medevaced somewhere.

But why?

Had she been in some sort of accident on the way to work?

No, she thought it all had more to do with those men in her bedroom.

And Lang. Had he been there?

She sorted through the misty images, tried to put the pieces together to make a single picture, like a child's jigsaw puzzle. No use. There were too many parts missing. Some things, like starting out at home, she was sure of. Others, like the nurse or person whose dark silhouette showed up to replace the tube in her arm, she was not sure were real. One thing she was sure of: The pitch of the engine sounds had changed slightly, and the pressure on her ears told her the plane was descending.

And she seemed closer to reaching the surface of the ocean than before.

The familiar shape was beside her bed. It extended an arm, and lights went on. She tried to shield her eyes before she remembered she could not move her arms or legs.

Even through eyes held almost closed, she could now see a face on the figure. She had seen him somewhere before.

In one hand he had what she recognized as a small recorder. The other held a single sheet of paper.

"Ms. Warner," he said in a voice she also recognized, "I want you to read these lines into the recording device."

The first words she had heard since . . . since she had found herself at the bottom of the ocean.

FORTY-SEVEN

Middle Temple Inn
London

The only other exit from Jacob's office was two windows behind his desk, the old-fashioned kind that actually opened. In a step Lang slid one pane up and looked out. Two floors down to a concrete walkway that would surely shatter a bone or two on impact. At each end stood a man in a suit with the unmistakable look of a cop. A tree's branches beckoned, but Lang discarded the idea. The sound of him grabbing a leafy bough would alert the pair below.

Another blow and the groan of hinges unable to hold much longer sent Lang through the window to a tenuous perch on the keystone of the arch framing the window below. Face pressed against the building, he extended the fingers of his right hand to claw for purchase in the cracks and crevices of the ancient stone, while his left maintained a death grip on the sill of the window he had just exited.

Another window was to his right, across a tantalizingly short chasm three or four feet away.

Lang forced himself not to look down as his left shoe

crept along the extrados of the arch below until it found a narrow hold where centuries of weather had eroded one stone slightly more than the other.

Once, twice, he pawed the air with his right foot.

Inches short.

Lang took one, two deep breaths.

Just as he heard Jacob's voice followed by harsh commands, he lunged. His right foot teetered on the adjacent arch as both hands scraped the sill of the window above. His fingers met impassive stone and began to slip as he pushed with his feet.

At what he would later regard as the last possible second, his fingers grasped a niche running along the sill, a crack perhaps left when the medieval opaque glass shutter-type panes were replaced with ones that opened from the top and bottom.

Mentally offering thanks to a deity of whose existence he was less than certain, Lang worked his fingers underneath the bottom pane and pushed upward. Next door he could hear a voice asking questions in a raised voice. He could not make out Jacob's answers.

He wriggled over and across the sill, falling to the floor inside. He was in an office similar to Jacob's, though far more orderly. He paused, hardly daring to breathe, as he waited for the occupants to raise an outcry. As he glanced around the small room, he realized he was alone. The computer terminal on the desk was turned off, as was the gooseneck lamp beside the keyboard. An old-fashioned brass hatrack stood sentinel by the door to what Lang supposed was the outer office. From it hung a barrister's black robe.

Lang stood up and glanced around the space from where he stood, desperate for anything that might be of help when the police began their inevitable search of the building. A small leather box sat on a battered tea table between two club chairs across from the desk. In a step he had the box in hand. He had seen one like that before, seen it . . .

Opening the hinged top he was rewarded with what he expected: a periwig, the white wig of short hair on top and curls down the sides worn before English juries, just like the one he had seen in Jacob's office a few years before.

Feeling more than slightly silly, he perched it on his head and slipped on the robe. A bit short, but it would have to do.

He grabbed a briefcase before fumbling with a cranky dead bolt on the front door and letting himself out into the hall.

A group of what he gathered were the building's tenants was gathered around the open door of Jacob's office, curious as to what had caused the police to interrupt the centuries of scholarly discourse and professional courtesy at the Middle Temple Inn. No one was interested in a lone barrister, briefcase in hand, scurrying for the staircase and the Old Bailey across the street. The two men guarding the entrance were too busy speculating what was going on inside to notice a barrister late for court, head down, searching the depths of his attaché for some critical paper as he hurried along.

Once across Fleet Street, Lang submitted to the metal detectors of London's oldest criminal court and entered the rabbit warren that had been in use for four hundred years, although most criminal cases were now heard in newer quarters. He paused at a door marked with a primitive figure of a man above the letters *WC* and went inside. Making sure he was alone, he deposited wig, gown, and briefcase inside one of the toilet stalls and left the building by a side door.

Lang ducked into the first London Underground entrance he came to. He wished it were later in the day, making it easier to hide among the commuters who would flood the system in an hour or so. As it was, he felt conspicuous sharing a nearly empty car. His only companions were a pair of nannies conversing in some African dialect over the howls coming from matching prams, and a single man, intent on a racing form advertising the services of Murphy and Quint, Turf Accountants.

As he changed to the Picadilly line, one of the infants was still managing to voice its outrage around the bottle with which his nanny had unsuccessfully tried to quiet him.

Had the British had to deal with their own squalling offspring, they would never have had time to raise the Union Jack over half the world.

Mary Poppins: the cornerstone of empire.

In a car filled largely with American tourists headed for London's largest shopping and entertainment district, Lang felt oddly alien. He envied them their laughter, the fact that they were here purely for the pleasure of travel.

How had the cops known where he would be? Most likely because of the incidents a few years ago, when Jacob had been identified as a contact in the city. Okay, he told himself, but how had they even known he was in the country? His passport had drawn no more than a perfunctory electronic scan upon arrival.

He had only to glance up at a camera attached to the car's ceiling. Surveillance equipment. As common in London as fish and chips. He had been made before he even left the airport.

But why?

As far as he knew, a passport violation would have been handled by Her Majesty's immigration service, not police. So there must be another reason, one he was fairly certain was not going to make him a happier man.

He got off at Picadilly and walked over to Regent Street and paused to inspect the equestrian stature of William of Orange dressed as Caesar. Or in drag. The thing always made him smile when he envisioned some American politician similarly represented. They tended to straddle issues, not horses.

As he surveyed the sculpture, he looked for the surveillance camera, finally spotting it almost hidden by the pediment of what he guessed was a Victorian's idea of a Greek Revival facade. He picked up a newspaper from a nearby kiosk and pretended to read so that the paper was between his face and the cameras as he circled the block.

Although he was fairly certain he was alone, he stopped long enough to use a shop window as a mirror to make sure.

Then he crossed over to 47 Jermyn Street and stood before an unmarked door beside which were a column of names, each above a bell button. Below was a speaker.

The odds were that, sooner or later, at least one thing would go his way today, and it did. Nellie was still in business.

During his years with the Agency, Lang had an all-too-brief assignment to the London Station. Nellie had been carried on the payroll as a psychological therapist.

Her actual job was slightly less academic if greatly more successful in aligning psyches along the right track. She ran a stable of call girls.

When a defector from one of the Eastern European workers' paradises made it safely from behind the Iron Curtain, he usually wanted three things immediately: a woman, decent whiskey, and American cigarettes.

Nellie could provide all three.

On more than one occasion it had been Lang's job to go to Nellie's place, select a woman, and bring her back to whatever safe house was serving as a debriefing center at the time. Nellie had often chided him for not wanting to sample the merchandise, even tempting him with an occasional freebie.

"I'll just look and not touch," had been his constant refrain. He had not wanted to offend such a valuable asset by explaining that he had a strong aversion to the potential health problems just then beginning to enter the public domain: AIDS and herpes had taken the place of the generic clap that would succumb to two or three shots of penicillin. Lang was not about to take a chance of having to try to convince Dawn, his then-fiancée, that the Agency's toilet seats were infected.

Plus, should the shit ever hit the congressional fan, using his employment to get freebies from a brothel keeper would be regarded with great disapproval.

Still, he and Nellie had maintained a friendship, one she had renewed a couple of years before, when, as now, Lang needed a friend not stored in any law enforcement records.

He pushed the buzzer.

His felt a slight chill begin to creep up his neck when there was no response. Then he realized Nellie and most of her crew were probably just now beginning to stir. Their working day would not begin for an hour or two yet.

The third try produced a drowsy, " 'Oos there?"

Lang looked around, reluctant to speak his name aloud. "Tell Nellie the guy who just looks is back."

He was fairly certain the comment would be assumed to be an announcement of some sexual perversion by the woman on the other end, but he was rewarded by a voice he recognized.

"Lang, you have come back! Perhaps now . . . ?"

"Just buzz me in, Nellie."

There was a click and Lang opened the door.

At the top of a staircase stood a woman he knew was well past fifty. But she didn't look a day beyond thirty. Her profile was clean, unblurred by the sags and wrinkles time inflicted, a testament to the plastic surgeon in Switzerland she regularly visited. Her eyes still had the slight Asian slant of the Eastern European, perhaps the only clue that she had come to London as Neleska Dwvorsik, wife of a Hungarian defector whom she soon dumped for the oldest of capitalistic enterprises.

As he reached the top, he was standing in what could have been the lobby of a modestly priced hotel. Sofas and chairs were scattered about, most in front of TV sets. What wouldn't be seen in public accommodations was the group of young women lounging about in various states of undress. Of every race and most nationalities, they paid little attention to Lang, even though most customers never came here; this was home base for work all over the city.

Nellie embraced Lang with a strength surprising for her size, and wet lips touched his cheek. "You have decided it is time to quit just looking, Lang? We even have an American girl or two, but I'd recommend one just arrived from Hong Kong."

Lang shook his head slowly, as though in regret. "Not this time, Nellie. Can you put me up for a couple of days?"

She laughed evilly, taking his hand and leading him farther into the room. " 'Put you up'? What is this 'put up'? Is something my girls can do in bed?"

"No, Nellie. As inviting as the prospect might be, I need to, er, hide out for a day or two."

"The place is yours, Lang. If you want anything, or any person, ask."

FORTY-EIGHT

Dizengoff
Tel Aviv
The Next Morning

Theli Yent was no beautician, even though she arrived every morning (except Shabbat, of course) at the same beauty parlor in the Dizengoff, once the city's most fashionable neighborhood. The area still boasted coffee shops, discotheques, and boutiques, but it was showing its age like bald patches on what had once been an exquisite fur coat. The shop catered to an older clientele, those who had enjoyed it here in the vicinity's heyday. Most had been born in Western Europe or the United States and were therefore accustomed to the luxury of trying to replace youth with facials, massages, and sculpted hair. Early on, Theli had noted that no matter how much the other girls in white jackets rubbed perfumed salves into leathery skin, irrespective of the quantity of eye shadow and lip gloss or the subtle arrangement of thinning hair to conceal bare spots, the only thing that really improved was the coffers of the shop. And maybe, just maybe, the attitudes of its refurbished customers.

Theli had been working at the building for two years now, ever since she had returned to Israel with a degree in computer science from Southwestern University, a small school for electronic and math geeks within blocks of the Mississippi as it lazed through Memphis, Tennessee. She had been home only a day when she had been approached by a charming young man who had told her he was recruiting persons skillful both on the computer and in English. She never knew how high she had scored on the tests she had taken, but they were far more difficult than any she had taken in school.

Then he told her whom he really worked for.

At twenty-four, she had been willing to trade the sugarplum visions of high salary for the equally evasive excitement of working for Israeli intelligence, Mossad. When it turned out she would do all her spying from a computer terminal, she was disappointed, of course. But, after all, it would count as her mandatory military service.

So, she came to work six days a week to the building with no street number that looked like one of those Bauhaus multistoried buildings whose no-nonsense utilitarianism had appealed to the wave of immigrants of the 1950s. That had been when the city itself had been newly created from a few settlements and the old port of Jaffa, the same port from which Jonah had commenced one of the strangest voyages ever recorded.

Every day she would speak to the girls already snipping hair or smearing ooze on customers for a facial as she passed through the salon. She had no idea if they were actually cosmeticians or worked for Mossad, too. Once across the mirrored, brightly lit room, she opened the door marked OFFICE and descended several flights of stairs to another door, this one flanked by two armed men in uniform. Inside was a long room consisting entirely of a double row of computer screens. Even if the place was well lit and never varied from a constant twenty degrees Celsius, it reminded Theli of a dark cave dug into a mountainside, a place in the desert where Elijah or another Hebrew prophet might have lived.

This morning a man she had never seen before was waiting at her workstation. His windbreaker displayed the authorized visitor's badge. He was tall, tanned from the sun, and inclined to exhibit a perfect set of teeth. British, judging by the accent of his Hebrew. "I've got a favor to ask of you."

Theli was instantly on guard. Hardly a day passed without . . . without—what was the American phrase?—her being hit on. Men hit on her regularly. They frequently wanted favors that caused problems. She said nothing as she sat down and turned her machine on.

"I need some information," the man said, unfazed by Theli's lack of response.

She was entering her password, which appeared as a series of *X*s across the screen. "Information requests come from the head office."

He hovered over her shoulder. "True. But this request comes from an old friend of the company, something he wants run down outside of channels."

Theli swiveled around in her chair, switching to English. "Let me get this straight: You appear unannounced, no introduction, and want me simply to drop what I'm doing to go outside established procedure to get you information you might or might not have clearance to see. Is that about it?"

He was reaching inside the pocket of his windbreaker. "I apologize." He handed her a folded, letter-size piece of paper. The first thing she noticed was the embossed seal at the top, along with the word *secret* stamped in red right under it. "I really should have started with this."

"That certainly would have expedited things," she commented dryly, reading and returning the sheet. "Exactly what is it you want?"

"Sharing your next coffee break would be nice."

It would have been churlish not to reward the clumsy effort with at least a smile. "Let's get started on the information you want."

A few minutes later the stranger was about to leave. "What about the coffee break?"

"Don't take them."

For the first time the perfect teeth disappeared.

"But I usually leave here about seventeen hundred."

It was only after he had gone that Theli realized she still didn't know his name.

FORTY-NINE

Bull & Rose Public House
Abington, Gloucestershire
Northwest of London
A Day Later

Lang sipped his room-temperature pint of ale, admiring the meticulously landscaped rose garden, typical of those surrounding each lock of the Thames. The lock itself was crowded with small pleasure boats, each equipped with weekend mariners and one or more dogs. Most of the former wore swimming attire that showed off skin the color of fish bellies. Lang wondered if the English ever had enough summer weather to tan.

Across from him, Jacob was making rings on the weathered wooden tabletop with the bottom of his black and tan, a half-and-half of beer floating on stout. "No bother?"

Lang shook his head. "Not a bit. Had a friend drive me to Victoria Station and buy a ticket while I stayed out of the way in the men's WC, and caught the first train. Was here in less than an hour. Why'd you choose this place, anyway? Doesn't seem to be much going on."

Jacob glanced around. The sluggish river crept right to left, then narrowed to pass under an arched stone bridge that seemed to be buttressed by a grove of willow trees.

In the other direction was the domed town hall, one of the few buildings erected during the rule of Cromwell. "You've answered your own question, lad. Far as I know, farming's all that's up around here. There's a county fair every summer and that's it. Few coppers, fewer surveillance cameras."

Both men were silent for a moment, as though contemplating the rarity of such pastoral surroundings.

Jacob was reaching for what Lang suspected was a pipe when Lang spoke. "You said your folks found something?"

The pipe stopped halfway to Jacob's mouth. "I did indeed. Using your premise that the rotters in this case are somehow connected to Israel . . ."

"*Had* a connection to Israeli intelligence," Lang corrected.

Jacob was patting his pockets in the search of the tobacco pouch. "Just so. I had some friends at Mossad start with the Desert Eagles. The army swapped them in four years ago. Chap by the name of Zwelk, a former colonel in the quartermaster's corps, handled that. The old guns were to be melted down. You can imagine what a dilemma that was, choosing between destroying several hundred thousand dollars' worth of equipment or selling it in the same international arms market that equips Hamas and that lot."

Lang smiled at the thought of the quandary that must have posed. "And?"

"Appeared to have been a discrepancy between the number turned in and the actual number receipted by the smelter. About forty weapons in all."

Lang had forgotten his ale. "Too many for a clerical mistake. Was there any follow-up?"

Now Jacob was conducting a pocket-by-pocket search for matches. Despite the view, Lang was wishing they had chosen a table inside, where smoking was forbidden. "Oh, there was a proper ruckus, an exchange of e-mails, but that was about it. Zwelk was about to retire to a kibbutz, anyway. It was an election year, and the government wasn't too keen about making a public brouhaha of it."

Compared to Israeli politics, those in the States were calm indeed. In such a small country many of the constituents knew their representatives and were passionately pro or anti. Accusing one of the many factions, cults, or sects of something could easily upset the precarious balance of power based on the thinnest coalitions between groups disparate in culture, ethnic origin, or belief. Alienation of the smallest group could bring down the government.

Lang sat back in his chair, waiting.

Jacob found his own Mirabelle's matches, and puffs of evil-smelling smoke dissipated into the air. "I pulled some strings, as you Yanks would say, and got a peek into the man's service jacket. Seems the pistols weren't the first things nicked on his watch. A dozen or so A-model Heckler & Koch MP5s vanished the year before."

The same model Lang had seen far too well just outside Brussels.

Jacob took the pipe out of his mouth and inspected the bowl, a gesture Lang recognized as a dramatic pause before revealing the more important part of what he had to say. "He was still being investigated for that when the Desert Eagles went missing. Had the cheek to deny he knew anything about it."

"Amazing the man could be so careless," Lang commented dryly.

Jacob nodded. "Seems Colonel Zwelk had had a past with Mossad. There was a spot of bother there, too. Suspected but never convicted of sharing classified with unauthorized. Rather than cause problems, transferred to the quartermaster corps of the army."

A definite demotion. Like going from naval intelligence to galley duty.

Lang tried to mask his impatience. "Any reason given?"

Jacob took a full five seconds applying another match. "No. But I did find that, while he was there, the good colonel had whatever Echelon access Mossad could beg from the Americans or English."

"So, it's possible that he kept a contact there."

Jacob eyed Lang over his glass. "Possible his contact passed on an occasional transmission, but how would he know which ones?"

Lang remembered the glass in front of him and emptied it before waving to the waiter. "Once you're into Echelon, you're into the filter system. You can key in words, names, phone numbers."

Jacob mouthed a perfect smoke ring that spun into the still air a moment before dissolving. "Well, then, there's your answer as to how they knew where you were. Whoever the sodding 'they' might be."

Lang knew his friend well enough to know there was more. "I can't imagine you stopped there."

Jacob applied yet another light before continuing. "You know me well. The lad's background's seemed worth a glance. He was born into a sect of extremely conservative nationalistic Jews who call themselves the Essenes."

Lang thought a moment. The name sounded familiar. "Weren't they the group that lived out in the desert, out near Qumran, where the Dead Sea Scrolls were found?"

"Had quite a settlement: water conduits, huge meeting rooms, their own coinage. They settled in the desert before Christ's birth, were displaced by an earthquake, and moved back to the same place about the time of Herod the Great. They were one of the three philosophical Jewish sects, the others being the Pharisees and Sadducees."

"And they're still around?"

The pipe had gone out and would not rekindle. "So it would seem. Though that lot no longer live in isolation, they are intensely loyal to their order, are extreme Zionists, have their own kibbutz, and still hold to many of the old ways. Think of them as Jewish Amish crossed with your VFW."

Use of the most sophisticated eavesdropping devices the world had ever known, theft of modern weapons, and attempted and actual murder did not exactly comply with Lang's concept of peaceful, if eccentric, Pennsylvania farmers.

Lang thought a moment before asking, "I don't suppose this colonel of yours has any connection to Bruges?"

Jacob stopped in the middle of reaming the pipe bowl with the nail. "Bruges? As in Belgium?"

"As in."

"Odd you would ask. Bruges happens to be the only place outside of Israel where there are any of them to speak of. Understand a small colony is still there, remains of the many who migrated during the Middle Ages, when Jews were the only banks in Europe, what with you Christians finding it sinful to lend money for interest. This lot financed the lace and weaving trades all over the Spanish Empire, which, of course, included Belgium. Just like their cousins back home, they keep pretty much to themselves."

"That's an odd bit of information."

"Mossad keeps track of factions of Jews that might be militant at home and abroad. But why . . . ?"

Lang slowly nodded. "And if we were to check out Benjamin Yadish, I'd bet he had been an Essene."

They both thought of that before Jacob stood. "Seeing how many these sodding bounders, if it is them, have killed, I'd say being a Jew isn't a primary requirement." He glanced over his shoulder back into the pub. "Too many black and tans. I've got to go to the loo."

Lang watched him retreat inside without really noticing. Loyal. Sect. Zionist. It had happened before: silencing a member of the faction deemed disloyal. Once one was emboldened by one or two murders, killing as a means of silencing people who had no relationship to the group became progressively easier, a progression from warning shots in Underground Atlanta to permanently silencing someone.

Of course, the Essenes could be just one of many of the small and various types of Judaism, and Zwelk simply a thief or a very poor administrator.

Could be.

But Lang didn't think so.

The murdered scientists had not been killed because of what they were discovering, but because of what that discovery might include.

He was so deep in thought, he didn't notice the young boy park his bicycle at the curb, walk across the pub's lawn, and stop at the table.

"Mr. Reilly?"

Lang turned his head to see a redheaded, freckle-faced, pudgy child of eleven or twelve.

"Yes?"

The youth handed him an envelope. "This is for you."

Reflexively Lang reached for it. "From whom?"

The kid pointed to a dark Audi idling at the far curb. It drove off immediately, its tag too far away to read.

Lang opened the envelope. At first he thought it was empty. Then a ringlet of red hair fell out.

It was not the messenger's.

The emerald ring Sara had mentioned and Alicia's unexplained absence from work came together in a revelation that almost made Lang gag.

He grabbed the boy's wrist. "Who are the people who gave you this?"

The child struggled but could not break free. "I don' know, honest I don'. They give me five quid and th' envelope, point to you. You're hurting me!"

Lang realized he was telling the truth and let go. The child was rubbing his wrist as he backed away, as though afraid Lang would seize him again.

Lang was on his BlackBerry when Jacob returned, no longer caring how many people tracked the call. "Sara? Yeah, it's me. Hate to bother you on the weekend. Listen: Monday, I want you to drop whatever you're doing. Call the DOJ, find out if Alicia Warner has been to work in the last week." He nodded as though his secretary could see him. "Yeah, I know, but use whatever pretext you can. Thanks."

Jacob slid into his chair. "A bit dodgy, y'know, using that thing. The Essenes, or whoever, could trace you here if they're still tapped into—"

"They already have," Lang said, shoving the envelope and its contents across the table.

FIFTY

New Scotland Yard
Broadway
London
At the Same Time

Inspector Fitzwilliam was trying to control the foul mood working on weekends always produced. He recognized as irrational his feeling of guilt as he had kissed his wife, Shandon, good-bye as he left the flat this morning. He should have been disappointed at not being able to join her on the trip to Manchester to see the new grandchild. But then, squalling, projectile-vomiting, and excreting babies were not his favorite creatures, no matter how close the kinship. Let nannies, or even the parents, do the necessary. He preferred to wait at least a year, until the child had some semblance of humanity, to make the acquaintance.

Even more illogical was the hostility he was feeling for his assistant, Patel, the author of the morning's balls-up.

Patel, eternally bright smile dividing the dark face, reeking of curry, stood behind the two chairs that faced the inspector's desk. If giving up his weekend bothered him, he didn't show it.

For the third time Fitzwilliam glanced at the report, the single paper on the faux wood of the government-issue desk. "I don't understand how you could have lost him."

Patel shrugged. "He is cunning, sah. As you know, I was one of a pair observing the barrister, Annueliwitz. We saw him come out of his residence at oh-seven-twenty-one. Or at least, a person wearing a man's overcoat drove the man's vehicle out of the car park. Naturally, sah, we followed, followed all the way to Notting Hill, sah. When the vehicle stopped in another car park, a woman later identified as Rachel Annueliwitz got out. Naturally I called in, and two more men were dispatched to watch the Annueliwitz residence, sah. So far we have not observed Mr. Annueliwitz."

Nor is it bleeding likely you will, Fitzwilliam thought, recognizing the onset of a headache. He could be out of the country with the American, Reilly, by now.

He sighed in resignation. "Very well. Keep the observers in position and let me know if anything happens."

"Sah!"

Patel did a near-military about-face and headed for the door.

"And Patel?"

He stopped in midstride and looked over his shoulder. "Sah?"

"Next time, try having one man follow the family auto and one man stay in position. Or, better yet, call for backup."

Fitzwilliam was treated to that infuriatingly good-natured smile. "Yassah!"

The inspector watched the door shut before he began the search for the aspirin bottle he kept in a desk drawer. He was not looking forward to informing his counterpart in Vienna, Rauch, that Scotland Yard had lost contact with its only lead to Reilly.

He found the bottle and took a tablet before he picked up the telephone. As he waited for the connection to be completed, he wondered just how much of a furor he would incur if he transferred Patel to one of the Yard's more remote offices in London, Wapping, for instance. If the man were white, not a word would be said.

But he wasn't, and the diversity people denied the existence of incompetence unless it was wrapped in a white skin.

The inspector took another aspirin before a voice came on the line.

FIFTY-ONE

Bull & Rose Public House
Abington
At the Same Time

Jacob looked at the lock of hair, puzzled. "I'm afraid I don't quite understand."

Lang explained to him while the replacement for his empty glass finally arrived. He was gratified to see Jacob putting his pipe away along with its assorted impedimenta.

Jacob held his own empty glass up for the waiter. "I look forward to meeting your new bird."

"I hope you do. First we've got work to do. Obviously Zwelk and his people have her."

"If he's the heavy in all this. Either way, I'd guess you'll be getting some kind of a demand shortly."

Lang leaned forward, elbows on the table. "Why, do you suppose, didn't I get one with the envelope?"

Jacob pursed his lips for a moment and then pointed to the BlackBerry still on the table. "I'd venture they want you to use that thing, verify the chippie has disappeared, before they start making demands."

"But that means they'll have to keep me in sight."

"No, that means you bloody well will want them to keep you in view rather than lose contact."

Lang thought about that. "I suppose they're watching now."

Both men resisted the impulse to turn around.

"Doesn't mean we can't start," Jacob said, standing as he drained his glass in a gulp. "Come along."

Lang followed suit. "Where?"

"On a bleeding holiday, lad."

Minutes later they were strolling along the river's grassy bank. Shortly past the lock, Jacob stopped at a dock to which five or six gaily painted rowboats were tied, each with a tiny outboard motor bolted to the transom. A cloth banner overhead advertising boats to rent by the hour hardly moved in the still air.

"Ever cruised the Thames?" Jacob asked.

"No, never thought about it."

"Great pity. The fact that just above London it narrows into little more than a stream with a slow current makes it an ideal day trip or a week's excursion, depending on how far you want to go. Boats have the right to tie up anywhere along the banks, and you can cruise from Maidenhead all the way to the bogs in Hertfordshire. Great way to visit Hampton Court, Oxford, et cetera."

Lang was watching Jacob hand a credit card to the man on the dock. "I'll remember that."

He glanced around, unable to distinguish anyone suspicious among the boaters, picnickers, or others out to enjoy a beautiful day.

Once on the river Jacob opened the little motor all the way, propelling the craft at what Lang guessed was slightly less than three knots. The river was as crowded as the lock. Racing hulls, rowboats, and other small craft, along with an occasional long, slender canal boat, all traveled at the same stately pace. Lang noted the number of houses along the water, as varied as the boats on it. A small cottage there, a Tudor mansion here.

From his seat in the bow, he turned to where Jacob

was steering with one hand and talking into a cell phone held by the other. "This is swell, but I don't see how a river cruise is going to—"

Jacob took a hand from the motor's handle to wave him into silence. The little boat rocked dangerously.

Without speaking, Jacob made a sweeping U-turn and continued to retrace their course for a minute before turning back around. Lang was about to risk another near swamping when he realized Jacob was making straight for a willow-framed boathouse in front of a white-frame Georgian. The door swung upward and the rowboat's motor went silent as the little dinghy's momentum carried them inside. Immediately the door came down again.

Lang was letting his eyes adjust to the relative gloom that had replaced the bright sun reflecting from the river when Jacob spoke. "Guess you thought I'd gone round the bend, turning around out there."

"The thought crossed my mind."

Jacob was tying the craft to a cleat next to the slip. "Wanted to make sure our friends hadn't had the time to rent their own pleasure craft and crash the party." He climbed onto a wooden deck. "C'mon inside."

Lang did as he was bidden. "But I thought we wanted them to know where I was."

"They'll find us soon enough once we return the boat. Come along, now."

Lang followed his friend along the tree line to the house. A door opened as though by magic as they approached. Inside, a man held the door open. Despite the warmth of the day he wore a tatty wool sweater. The white of the shirt underneath showed through a network of holes. Wordlessly he led Lang and Jacob along a corridor devoid of furniture or furnishings. The rooms were equally empty.

Safe houses all had a certain barren similarity, Agency or Mossad.

At the end of the hall their guide opened a door, revealing a flight of stairs. Halfway down a wave of cool air washed over them. They entered a room totally dark other than the flickering screens of banks of computers. In the murk Lang got only the impression of operators.

Jacob seated himself in front of one, motioning Lang to sit beside him. Their guide disappeared into the darkness.

Jacob began booting up. "Nice country estate, don't you think? Office extension for those weary of the city."

How a computer room in the English countryside differed from the one at Mossad's part of the Israeli embassy in London escaped Lang.

Jacob's machine flickered to life. Lang watched the screen. To his surprise Jacob called up the Internet just as anyone with the capability might do.

"Don't tell me we're shopping on Amazon."

Jacob didn't turn his head from the monitor. "Nothing that complicated. You'll note I'm calling up Google."

"You're going to Google Zwelk?"

"Not exactly. But I am using a site any bloke connected to the Net can use."

Lang watched as what appeared to be a satellite picture of brown earth filled the screen. "What are we looking at?"

"Israel. More specifically, a part of it near the Gaza Strip."

Lang watched as Jacob narrowed the focus with each click of the keyboard. He could see the brown of the desert that was Palestinian Gaza meet the green of Israel's cultivated fields and orchards. Many people remarked on the success of Jewish agriculture in the desert while the land across the border remained empty sand. The reason, he knew, was not a difference in desire or ability; it was the irrigation system that fed Jewish farms but was denied their Arab neighbors.

A cluster of ten or so flat roofs was now clearly visible,

with a little whitewashed wall showing. The angle of the satellite was directly overhead so that shadows, rather than profiles, defined objects.

"Maximum resolution," Jacob announced. "This is Zwelk's kibbutz in real time. If he has your lady friend, she's in one of those buildings."

Fascinated, Lang stared at the screen. "You mean anyone with a computer can look down anywhere?"

"If he has the coordinates or, in the civilized world, an address. Of course, the system isn't so helpful at night or on cloudy days."

Privacy: available only during the evening hours or inclement weather.

Silently the two men watched a small herd of animals, Lang guessed sheep or goats, being driven somewhere. A person, sex undeterminable at this angle, walked out of one of the houses and into another.

Jacob pointed to a building in the middle of the compound. "See the extra vehicles? Something's going on in there. Unusual for Shabbat. I'd guess if she's there, those cars belong to her guards."

"That or they're celebrating the Sabbath."

"Possible," Jacob conceded, "but these people are ultraconservative, believe in strict observance. That would prohibit all work, including driving. I'd bet those cars and trucks have been there since sundown yesterday, and there's only one reason I can think of why there would be more than one per house: alternating guard duty."

Lang agreed. "Can you print this out?"

"Better. I can print out what you're seeing as well as everything within a couple of miles. Surely you're not thinking what I think you're thinking."

Lang grinned. "Of course I am. You coming along?"

Jacob sighed as he centered the cursor on the print icon. "Why not? I haven't been back home in a long, long time."

"What about Rachel?"

Jacob looked into Lang's face. "You don't really think I'd tell her where I was going and why, do you? Why, the old love would have a fit."

Or worse, Lang added mentally, insist on coming along.

7

FIFTY-TWO

Ben Gurion International Airport
Lod, Israel
Fifteen kilometers south of Tel Aviv
Monday Evening

The Gulfstream slid down the glide slope in the early evening darkness. The western horizon still bore the angry red scar of the desert sun. Across the aisle, soft snores came from one of the seats that reclined to horizontal. Lang had offered Jacob the use of the single small bedroom suite on board the aircraft, but he had protested that flying in such luxury was too unique an experience to be so wasted.

An hour out of Marseille, he was sound asleep.

In view of the police's interest in him, Lang had insisted on driving from London to Dover, then through the Chunnel to Paris, where they met the foundation's jet at a fixed base operator at Charles de Gaulle rather than risk the scrutiny of security in the main terminal.

Israel was another matter.

Without Jacob, no matter whom Lang's passport declared him to be nor how large the private jet on which he arrived, he would be subjected to identification by thumbprint, facial recognition scanning, and other procedures of which he would be unaware. The Couch identity on his passport was backed up by the best false information the Agency could provide when it had been issued two years ago.

Israeli security rarely stopped at the obvious, though. Lang knew that even the most cursory investigation of worldwide computer records would show that, for at least twenty-four months, Joel Couch of Macon, Georgia, had used none of his credit cards, made no bank deposits, and incurred no utility bills. Without the intercession of Jacob's Mossad friends, facial identity and fingerprints alone would match those of a man in whom the Vienna police had an interest.

Despite Jacob's assurances, Lang could not dispel the jitters until the two men were ensconced in a Mercedes limousine dispatched to fetch them by Jacob's former employer. He would have preferred the anonymity of simply meeting the Egged Bus Cooperative line at its exit on Sharon Street in Airport City and riding the shuttle that ran to Tel Aviv's Hotel Row.

"Don't be daft," Jacob had said. "You take the bleedin' bus an' Zwelk'll know you're here before you even get into town."

"He's not expecting us," Lang said.

Jacob shook his head. "If he has access to Echelon, he's got somebody in Mossad, somebody who might trip to the search I had run on him. And who's to say he doesn't have access to the photo that's taken of every arrival?"

Good advice, Lang recalled from his Agency training. One of the best ways to cease being a living fool was to assume the ignorance of your opponent.

You likely became a dead fool.

The Mercedes exited the airport road in the middle of the city. The windshield was filled with high-rises, modern buildings picketing the blue Mediterranean now turning an oily black in the twilight. They turned away from the sea to proceed down Rothschild Boulevard, lined with large and expensive-looking town houses and towering office buildings. Lang recognized the logos of IBM and AT&T among other letters of American industrial alphabet soup. The inhabitants' driving reminded Lang of Rome or Naples: Horns were preferred to brakes.

The Mercedes glided across three lanes of aggressive traffic and slid down an entrance ramp under a glass-and-steel tower, which turned out to be a residence building that would have fit unnoticed into Manhattan's Upper East Side.

Once out of the elevator, Lang followed Jacob down a hall of identical doors until he stopped in front of one distinguishable only by its number. Lang suspected the similarity with its neighbors stopped at the door as he set down his single bag. Few apartments on the street were likely to have door locks as sophisticated as bank vaults, nor would they have steel mesh just inside the windows, letting in light but screening out unpleasant items such as grenades that might somehow make their way through glass that was probably bulletproof.

In a corner of the unfurnished living room were two packages. Jacob inspected each carefully and started to carry the larger toward the back of the apartment. "Like something left by Saint Nick, what? You'll be wanting to open yours."

Lang did so. Inside were two SIG Sauer P226s, two spare clips, loaded, and a belt clip holster.

A pistol in each hand, he walked back to where Jacob was unwrapping what looked like a child's chemistry set. "I appreciate somebody's thoughtfulness, but *two* guns? That somebody must have thought I was the Lone Ranger."

Jacob straightened up from his package and came over to inspect both weapons carefully. "That makes me . . . ?"

"Tonto."

"Sodding Tonto." He took the automatic in Lang's right hand. "This is for me."

"There's a difference?"

Jacob told him.

"Sounds like you have a plan."

Jacob nodded. "That I do, lad. But first let's see what in the nature of sustenance might have been left for us."

In the small kitchen Lang started to ask about the meat in the sandwiches but thought better of it. From previous experience, he knew the cold beer had to be better than the astringent Israeli wine.

Jacob spread a map on the Formica of the tabletop, anchoring it north to south with a plate and a beer bottle. "Here we are"—he pointed—"and here's Zwelk's kibbutz."

Even though he was aware of how small Israel was, Lang was surprised at the proximity. "Looks like it's not more than sixty, seventy kilometers."

Jacob squinted. "Pretty close. It's less than one kilometer from the Gaza Strip."

"Why would anyone want to live there? I mean, you're right next to a bunch of Palestinians who want to kill you."

Jacob swallowed the rest of a sandwich. "Which means you don't have a lot of Jewish neighbors to snoop into whatever you're doing. Besides, since the government removed Jewish settlers from Gaza and put up a fence, the Arabs have been more or less peaceful. Then there was the war in the summer of 'oh-six. Although that was mostly along the Lebanon border, it brought in U.N. peacekeepers, quieted Hamas and Hezbollah down a bit. All in all, I'd say Zwelk has got himself an ideal place."

Lang was still studying the map. "Ideal defensively, anyway."

His BlackBerry beeped.

"Yes, Sara?"

"I spent the morning following up on tracking Ms. Warner."

"And?"

"She hasn't shown up for work since a little over a

week ago. Two days after anyone there saw her she called in, said her mother was in the hospital after a car wreck and she wanted to take vacation time to be with her."

"And that's it?"

"Not exactly. I called the DOJ in Denver, the city where she worked before coming to Atlanta. I said I was her mother and was trying to locate her."

"And?"

"Her mother was in an auto accident, all right. Only it was ten years ago and fatal."

Lang sat down at the kitchen table. "As always, you've been very helpful. Thanks."

"That's not all," Sara's voice protested before he could disconnect. "You got a very strange e-mail today."

"I get strange e-mails every day, mostly from spammers trying to sell worthless stock."

"Not this one. It said . . ." There was the sound of tapping keys. "Yeah, here it is. I quote, 'Alicia asks you come soonest.'"

"That's it?"

"That's it."

Lang thought a moment. "Reply. Ask where I should come and when. Anything you can do to delay."

"Like saying you're out of town and will respond when you return?"

"That's as good as any other reply."

Lang glanced at his watch, estimating how long the conversation had lasted and wondering if Zwelk's eavesdropper was recording it. "Call me if anything else happens."

"Lang, before you go, the mayor said to tell you—"

He disconnected.

Jacob put down a beer bottle. "Bad news?"

"Only a confirmation that the woman's been missing from work."

Jacob lifted a shaggy eyebrow and Lang explained.

Jacob raised the beer bottle to the light. "Already

empty. Don't understand why we Jews can't bottle it in a proper pint." He looked at Lang. "At least you know she's alive. If Zwelk intended her harm, there'd be no reason to keep her once he had your attention."

Lang finished his beer. "You're a real comfort."

"I try." He paused. "Oh, I forgot to give you this. Our limo driver handed it to me as we got out."

He extended to Lang a photograph of the kibbutz.

"It was taken this morning."

Lang studied it for a full minute. "So? What's different?"

Jacob came around the table and pointed to the lower left corner. "See?"

Lang moved the photo back and forth. "See what?"

"There's a figure of a person there. From the high angle we can't be sure if it's a man or a woman. But look at the color of the hair."

Red.

Alicia Warner red.

Jacob was fumbling for his pipe. "Unless there's an abnormal incidence of Jewish carrottops, I'd say we may have found your lady friend."

FIFTY-THREE

Südbahnhof Police Station
Wiedner Gürtel
Vienna
The Next Morning

Chief Inspector Rauch reread the e-mail from Scotland Yard and shook his head. Langford Reilly had been in England only long enough to disappear again, slipping through the much-heralded fingers of the world's most famous police organization. Of course, in dealing with British or American police, suspects frequently went free even after being captured. Writs of habeas corpus, jury trials, rights against self-incrimination—it was a wonder the English-speaking justice system convicted anyone.

Nonetheless, Rauch's superiors had authorized Reilly's extradition for questioning, and the inspector's life would go a lot easier once he had been found, interrogated, and either charged or released. It was as if Rauch himself were responsible for English incompetence.

The one bit of useful information from the Englishman—Fitzwilliam was his name—was that Reilly had entered Great Britain under the name of Couch. A few minutes at the computer confirmed that no such person had passed through customs and immigration anywhere in Europe in the last week or so.

Undaunted, Rauch called up the Web site for Reilly's charitable organization, the Janice and Jeff Holt Foundation. A few minutes later he learned the corporation had a private jet. Another site and a few more minutes revealed that the aircraft was a Gulfstream and its most recent trip had been Paris–Marseilles–Tel Aviv–Atlanta.

Now he was getting somewhere. The Israelis kept careful records of those entering their country.

He stared at the screen, unable to believe what it told him. The jet's international flight plan had been duly recorded and promptly closed on arrival at the noted time. But the space for names of the persons on board was blank. Either the plane had made the trip with no passengers or . . . or somebody with something to do with Israeli national security had been on board.

What could Reilly have to do with . . . ?

Rauch slid his chair back from his desk and glared at the computer's screen as though it were the one withholding the information.

With almost any European country he could simply call some official, explain his interest in the passengers on that flight, and, more likely than not, get the information.

Not necessarily with the Jews.

First, the Israelis had a bit of a prickly personality to begin with, trusting no one.

Second was the Kurt Waldheim matter.

Kurt Waldheim had been secretary general of the U.N. and was elected president of Austria in 1986. He had become friendly with a number of world celebrities, including a young Austrian who was a minor American movie star, Arnold Schwarzenegger, along with his American wife, a member of the politically connected Shriver family. Waldheim had been in office a short time when someone came up with papers that demonstrated he had not served in the Wehrmacht, regular army, during the war, been wounded, and come home to go to law school, as he claimed. Instead he had served a full five years in the SS. Worse still, in an *Einsatzgruppe* that had specialized in rooting out and deporting "undesirables."

It had been a diplomatic disaster.

After forty years of Austria's painting itself as the land of pastries, Mozart, and *The Sound of Music*, the old and hopefully forgotten connection with Nazis had been resurrected. The world started to recall that, although the von Trapp family were Austrian, so was Hitler.

The Jews worldwide screamed bloody murder. The United States listed the president of the sovereign state of Austria as a person to whom entry would be denied.

The Austrians took the view that they and only they elected their national officials. One woman was shown on international television, saying something to the effect that the Jews wanted to run everything but they wouldn't run Austria.

Some wag noted that that was because there were so few left.

World opinion was less than sympathetic.

Austria's relationship with the state of Israel did not benefit. Forty-plus years hadn't done a lot to dim the memory, and relations with Israel were diplomatically correct but far from cordial.

Even so, surely the Jews wouldn't deny a request for extradition of someone involved in a murder investigation, particularly someone who was hardly in a position to claim political persecution or some such. If he were to act as though he knew Reilly was on that flight, surely even the Israelis would be obligated to honor his request.

He picked up the phone.

FIFTY-FOUR

Kibbutz Zion
Near Sderot on the Gaza Border
The Next Morning

Alicia's days and nights seemed to merge. Perhaps it was the narcotics that had kept her knocked out for a period of time she had yet to measure. More likely it was the sameness of each day here.

Wherever "here" was.

Oh, she knew she was in Israel; the white flag with the blue Star of David told her that. And she surmised she was on some sort of kibbutz of about a hundred and fifty very devout Jews.

When the glassless window in her room was unshuttered, she could see the gullies of eroded hills as barren as those on the moon and, beyond, a very tall wall, behind which she guessed was the sea. The wall seemed to stretch into infinity, as though defining a border. Somewhere between the sandy hills and where she was, the land went green, like an oasis in the desert, which she guessed this was, artificial or natural. She could also see neat rows of towering date palms, arranged in ranks like so many soldiers. Sort of like a pecan grove in Georgia, but the trees here were taller and had leaves only at the top.

So, she guessed this kibbutz was a date farm.

She tried to remember what little she knew about kibbutzes, or, rather, kibbutz*im*. They were collective farms, communism in practice, where each person, kibbutznik, owned a share of the whole and got a share of the profits. Many, like this one, were populated by a specific sect of Jews. The men here wore hats or those little beanies, had long curls that hung by the sides of their faces like sideburns, and were unshaven. The women rarely appeared outside without scarves covering their heads. Whether this was for religious reasons or only a defense against the constant hot, gritty breeze, she didn't know.

She did know that the long, tin-roofed building was the communal kitchen and dining hall, and that all the other buildings she could see were white stucco with flat roofs. She knew many of the inhabitants spoke English, but none would answer her questions about why she had been brought here.

"Here" wasn't exactly the greatest place she'd ever been, either.

They'd given her clothes, ill-fitting khaki desert shorts, a T-shirt, and underwear, all of which were clearly hand-me-downs.

Like everybody else's.

Not exactly Club Med.

There was no air-conditioning to combat the heat of midday, temperatures so high that even the hardest workers retired to whatever shade they could find or sought a spot under a rotating fan.

No Caribbean cruise, either.

At least the evening brought coolness if not a downright chill.

There was no running water, only a well or cistern filled by some sort of irrigation system, as best she could tell. Every morning she was shaken awake by an old woman. She got up from the cot in her otherwise bare,

cell-like room and trudged to the edge of the little settlement to take her turn waiting for a place in the communal women's shower and privy.

Wet herself, turn off the water, soap up, turn the water
on to rinse, and shut off the water again.

Like Girl Scout camp.

Two men followed her from her sleeping quarters to
the shower house and back again. If the showers had
had a window, she might have thought of escape.

But there was no window and no place she knew to escape to.

So, once she dried off and dressed, she was escorted
back to her quarters, where the old woman served what
Alicia guessed was goat's milk, bland yogurt with chips of
fresh fruit in it, and some bitter, black stuff that was supposed to be coffee.

She could leave her room only to go back to the
women's privy to go to the bathroom. From the proximity
of the desert she guessed water was too valuable to waste
on a sewer system, even if the smell was enough to make
her dizzy if she had to use the facility in the day's heat.

Her captors did provide her with week-old copies of
the *International Herald Tribune, USA Today,* and some
British newspaper. She read every word of each, knowing that once she finished, there would be little else to fill
the hours other than looking out of the one window.

For the first few days she had wept continuously,
whether as an aftereffect of the drugs, pure despair, or
both, she never knew. Then she resolved to quit acting
like a ninny, as her mother used to say. She wasn't going
to give these people the satisfaction of seeing her weep.
Instead she adopted a haughty manner that expressed
contempt for her captors—as much contempt as her situation allowed, anyway.

The change in her manner produced no ascertainable
change in their treatment of her: courteous but aloof. The

women still gave her brief smiles, and the men nodded or averted their eyes. Still, no one would tell her where she was, nor why she was here. She supposed that if they meant her any harm, she would have already been subjected to it.

She guessed it was her fifth or sixth day of captivity today. For lack of anything better to do, she was looking out of her window, waiting for the stack of newspapers. She could see the only road to this place, a sandy two-lane that looked as though it had had oil or tar spilled on it regularly to keep down the dust.

In fact, it looked like that was what was happening now. Two men, their clean-shaven faces announcing that they weren't from the kibbutz, were in an old tanker truck, driving slowly along the fence that separated kibbutz property from the road.

Odd.

She had assumed the dirt track was all part of the collective, since she had seen men from the kibbutz working on it. But the men in the truck were definitely spraying something on the sandy surface.

The one in the passenger seat turned, looking in her direction. Too far away to make out the details of his face, yet . . . There was something familiar about him, something she couldn't quite place.

If he wasn't from this kibbutz, maybe he could help if he knew she was being held prisoner here. Should she scream? Try to climb through the window and make a run for it?

Something moved behind her, and the old woman entered the room, scowling. In a step she was at the window, reaching out to close the wooden shutters.

Alicia had to try very hard not to start weeping again.

"I swear, that was her," Lang said.

Jacob was too busy keeping the truck on the narrow

sand road. "It's eyes like a bleedin' hawk you'd have to have to recognize her at this distance."

Lang sank back against the tattered upholstery. "If it wasn't her, why would they be so quick to close the shutters?"

Jacob took a hand from the wheel and started to explore his shirt pocket. The truck lurched to the side before he grabbed the wheel with both hands again. "Damn me if I know. These kibbutz Jews are peculiar sometimes. Maybe this lot doesn't believe in women showing their faces to outsiders."

Lang leaned forward to adjust the holster in the small of his back. "So far, no surprises. The layout is just like the satellite picture, jammed up against the Gaza wall. Except it didn't show the wire fence, and I had no idea those hills, sand dunes, whatever, were so high."

Jacob found a place to turn around and did so. "I hope they appreciate our oiling down their road for them."

"They should. It cost us enough. Paying those road workers to 'lose' their truck for a couple of hours wasn't cheap."

Jacob was straightening out the wheel before resuming the same slow pace. "Right you are, but at least we know where the irrigation pipe comes in."

"Incredible," Lang said, "bringing water in all the way from the Jordan River! That's, what, fifty miles or so? Looks like a desalination plant would be more effcient."

"I'm sure they have one of those, too. Problem is, a desal plant big enough to water the crops and supply those blokes' needs would have to be as large as the kibbutz itself."

Lang shook his head. "Still, bringing water all that distance . . ."

"Making the desert bloom, lad, that's what this country's all about. Besides, the Roman aqueducts carried water farther than that." He stopped and pointed. "There's some sort of pumping mechanism that lifts the water up into that water tower so that gravity creates enough pressure to irrigate the crops and support these people."

Lang looked at the tower. It could have come from any small town in America except for the Hebrew characters painted on the side. "What does the Hebrew say?"

"Zion, the name of the kibbutz."

"Zion?"

"Historically, a citadel that was the nucleus of Jerusalem. Also, the ideal nation or society envisioned by Judaism."

"Good choice by nationalist extremists."

This time Jacob succeeded in finding his pipe. He was clenching it between his teeth.

"I wouldn't recommend stopping to fill that thing," Lang said.

"Why not?"

"Because there's a truck right behind us. I'd guess Zwelk wants to know why we're spraying his private road."

Jacob leaned forward, the better to see the rearview mirror. "And he's blinking his lights. Think he wants us to stop."

Lang withdrew the SIG Sauer from its holster and slipped it beneath the seat. "You aren't going to outrun 'em. May as well stop and see what they want."

Looking in the passenger-side mirror, Lang saw two bearded men, one on each side, approach the truck. From the way they held the Uzi machine guns, he would have guessed they knew how to use them. This close to Palestinian territory, it would be unusual if they had not been armed. The one on the right stopped a few feet short and wide of the passenger door, a position where Lang would have to fully turn in his seat to make a hostile move. It was a maneuver taught in every police academy in the world.

The other man was speaking with Jacob in what Lang assumed was Hebrew. The tone was even, perhaps friendly. Finally Jacob shrugged his shoulders and rolled his eyes heavenward, the universal Jewish gesture that could mean anything from sudden enlightenment to total frustration. The man on the other side of the driver's door laughed, shook his head, and started back to his own truck.

"What the hell did you say to him?" Lang wanted to know.

"He wanted to know what we were doing here. I told him we had been assigned to oil down the dirt access roads along Road Four Seventy-seven all the way to the Gaza Strip."

"But we came here on Four Seventy-seven. We turned off a mile or so back."

"That, basically, was what the chap said. He thanked us for slicking down the kibbutz's road." He turned to Lang. "Think I convinced him I'd made a mistake?"

Lang watched the two men in the truck behind. Through the streaked windshield he could see one was talking into a cell phone. "I sure as hell hope so."

FIFTY-FIVE

Near Kibbutz Zion
Seventeen Minutes Later

"You're sure, then, that's her?" Jacob asked from his seat in the sand on the shady side of a hill.

Lang took the binoculars from his eyes. The morning sun was heating the metal quickly enough to make them uncomfortable to hold to his eyes. "Pretty damn sure."

He could hear Jacob tapping the pipe against the heel of his shoe. " 'Pretty sure'? Bravo! That's bloody swell! We go charging into this kibbutz, fight our way through the rotters to where you saw this woman, and presto! We find out you made a sodding mistake. Almost worth trying just to hear your apology."

Lang had the glasses to his eyes again. "You're the one who suggested we come out here after seeing a satellite photo of a redhead. Besides, that's why I'm roasting in the sun—trying to make sure we don't screw up."

He heard the sound of a striking match. And then, "You never explained what made you think that lot trying to kill you were Jews. Almost any country might be interested in the powers described in that old manuscript."

"The superconductive abilities aren't what they're after."

Lang took the binoculars down again long enough to use a sleeve to wipe the sweat from his face. "As I think I mentioned, I'd bet something very much like that was the basis for the Star Wars defense program President Reagan suggested twenty-five years ago."

"If not the weapons capability, then what?"

"For what the Book of Jereb says."

Jacob briefly pondered that. Then, "What does it have to say that's worth killing people for, other than the secret of the Ark, which you're telling me is no sodding secret after all?"

"It's . . ."

"It's what?"

Lang had put the glasses to his eyes again. "That's her! She's walking between two men, carrying what looks like . . . looks like . . . a towel. Yeah, that's it. She's got a towel and what could be a change of clothes." He reached backward, motioning. "Here, come see for yourself."

"To what end?" Jacob growled. "I've never seen the bird, wouldn't recognize her if she was standing on the balcony at Buckingham Palace."

In his excitement Lang had forgotten. "Of course you wouldn't. Take my word for it, though; that's her."

Jacob's breath whistled through closed lips as he checked his watch. "I make it nearly nine hours before sunset, a long time in the heat."

Lang was still staring through the binoculars. "We can't very well drive back in daylight. Someone'd get suspicious if they saw us there again."

Jacob got to his feet, dusting himself off. "There's a little town, Sderot, about two kilometers the other way, a place we can at least get something cool to drink while we wait. And I've got a bit of tinkering yet to do."

Lang didn't ask; he was well aware of what Jacob's tinkering usually involved.

FIFTY-SIX

Central Police Station
Ibn Gabrel and Ariozroy Streets
Tel Aviv
An Hour Later

Captain Kel Zaltov paced around the long table rather than sitting at it. His shirt was showing sweat stains at the armpits despite the frosty chill of overefficient air-conditioning. "I still don't understand why we have to cooperate with some neo-Nazi cop from Austria," he complained. "We owe those krauts nothing; and, far as I can tell, this goy Reilly has done nothing. Besides, he has the blessing of King Solomon Street," he added as an afterthought.

The other man in the room looked as though he might have just stepped from the pages of *GQ* or *Esquire*. His dark suit was tailored, his white shirt unwrinkled, and his toe caps shined to a military luster. "I'm not here on behalf on our friends on King Solomon Street," he replied calmly. He intertwined his fingers, resting his hands on the table. "My authority is higher than that."

Zaltov scowled. "I'm a policeman, not a diplomat or politician."

He spit the last word as though it had a bad taste.

That, thought the man in the suit, was one thing they both could agree upon.

The policeman was notorious for his distrust, if not downright hatred, of anything Germanic or Russian. During the decade between 1935 and 1945, each of those two World War II combatants had exterminated the larger part of his family: first the Stalinist purges, then the Nazi pogrom. It was amazing that a man could be so angry over the murders of relatives he had never known. But then, these Jews of Eastern European descent tended to hold grudges for centuries rather than generations. Zaltov was still probably pissed off at the Romans for destroying the temple in Jerusalem in, what, A.D. 70?

"Although unnecessary, I have explained the government's position," the man in the suit said. His voice was becoming frayed along the edges, the sound of a man letting his frustrations show. "Need I do so again?"

Zaltov sat down and stood up again. "Why do I give a shit what a bunch of ass-kissers from the State Department think?"

"That depends on whether you want your pension when you retire next year. You serve, after all, at the pleasure of the Israeli government, ass-kissers included."

The policeman sat again, this time staying put. "Okay, explain again. Maybe I'll listen this time."

The man in the suit nodded slowly, acknowledging the wisdom of the other's decision. "Very well. This Inspector Rauch wants to take into custody a man named Langford Reilly, an American. It seems Mr. Reilly may know something about one or more shootings in Vienna. . . ."

"Like that is our business," Zaltov sneered.

The man in the suit silenced him with a lifted eyebrow. "As our friends from King Solomon Street tell us, Mr. Reilly is accompanied by one of their former employees, a Jacob Annueliwitz, hence the cooperation so far. Both Monsieurs Reilly and Annueliwitz have shown more than a passing interest in a man named Zwelk."

The policeman stood, resuming his pacing. "A patriot, from his file."

"A patriot perhaps. The leader of what amounts to a private army, an armed military force literally next to the Gaza border wall."

"Sounds like a good place for an army to me."

"The government is less than sanguine about troops it does not control, particularly in such a sensitive area."

The policeman snorted. "You mean someone not afraid to stand up to a bunch of fanatical murderers of women and children, someone who doesn't piss their pants for fear the United Nations might speak ill of them? If he's such a threat, why is he allowed to continue?"

"You are aware of the political situation, the narrow coalition by which the prime minister governs. Any action against a right-wing group would precipitate every Arab-hating Jew in the country screaming for the prime minister's head. Or worse, joining this man Zwelk's cause."

"And this is a bad thing because . . . ?"

The man in the suit paused a second, perhaps the indecision of whether the conversation was worth continuing. "The man is an extreme Zionist, a frequent embarrassment to Israel's stance of moderation on the Palestinian question. He was bitterly opposed to the surrender of the occupied territories and the Lebanese cease-fire. . . ."

"Last time I looked, this country allowed freedom of expression."

The other man continued as though he had not heard. "He's suspected in a number of preemptive raids against Palestinian communities, raids that provoked rocket attacks against our citizens."

"Since when did those people need provoking?"

The man in the suit sighed. "Not every rocket launched into an Israeli town, not every suicide bombing is without cause. You've been a policeman long enough to know the news doesn't always tell the whole story."

"And you've been with the government long enough to know it's very careful what it tells the news."

The man in the suit didn't disagree with the observation but continued. "From what I understand, Annueliwitz and Reilly are reconnoitering Zwelk's kibbutz right now."

Zaltov crossed his arms over his chest, body language that didn't exactly signal acceptance. "So, you want me to arrest Reilly the minute he enters the kibbutz and have a look around while I'm there, use the arrest as an excuse to snoop."

"I would prefer not to phrase it that way, but yes. Once you have a legitimate reason to enter private property, you can certainly follow up on anything you find suspicious."

"Like the Gestapo or NKVD."

The diplomat shook his head in resignation. "I don't think they compare."

The policeman smiled, an icy grin without humor. "I'm using my right of free expression."

FIFTY-SEVEN

Terminal Three
Ben Gurion International Airport
That Afternoon

As he stepped into the terminal, Chief Inspector Karl Rauch was met by a man and a woman. They could have been brother and sister, Hansel and Gretel. Each treated him to brilliant, orthodonticaly perfect smiles; each wore what, in the United States, would have been described as "business casual": polo shirts over khakis with knife-sharp creases; and each had that well-scrubbed look of youth, along with optimistic expressions that told Rauch neither had yet learned much about the world they lived in.

The man reached for the inspector's carry-on bag, his only piece of luggage. Though he rarely flew, Rauch had frequently been advised of the capricious nature of baggage once entrusted to the airlines.

The woman shook his hand while holding an ID wallet up for his inspection. "Come with us, Inspector," she said. "No need to waste time standing in line with all the tourists."

"Your German is perfect," Rauch observed as he walked beside her. "Your accent sounds like Berlin?"

"Very close. Potsdam. My grandparents, actually. If you

remain long in Israel, you will note that almost every family speaks at least one tongue besides Hebrew. We are a nation of immigrants. Do you make a specialty of languages?"

"In my line of work, it is sometimes useful to recognize a particular dialect."

If the man, Hansel, understood German, he gave no sign of it. Instead he headed into the concourse, Rauch's bag in hand.

Rauch and the woman followed his suitcase. She politely asked the usual meaningless questions required of someone meeting a recently disembarked stranger. This was not exactly the reception a visitor on police business expected. Rauch felt more like a distant relative arriving at a family reunion.

The man in front eased his way past multiple lines of arrivees waiting their turn with customs and immigrations and, probably unknown to most, computerized facial scans by cameras concealed in the ceiling. Just short of the officials' glass booths, Hansel held open an unmarked door. Although the inspector was glad to bypass the bureaucratic traffic jam, he wished he had known the visa he had spent an hour or so securing would not be needed after all.

They entered a room without windows. There were six molded plastic chairs with legs and backs of chrome. Rauch wondered why anyone would go to such effort to make furniture look both so ugly and uncomfortable. Against the far wall was a Formica-topped table. The walls had a yellowish tint, a color someone might have thought cheerful when originally applied. It had since faded to the pigment of old nicotine.

The girl turned to him. "Forgive me for failing to introduce myself earlier. It seemed unwise in public. Lt. Heidi Strassman, Tel Aviv police."

Rauch felt a strong but not exaggerated grip. "You

obviously know my name." He faced the man, hand outstretched. "And you?"

The smile was long gone from the young man; nor did he seem interested in shaking hands. "I speak no German," he said in English. "Aaron Gruber. Shin bet, national security."

Rauch withdrew his hand, frowning at the prospect of speaking English. It was not one of his greater achievements. With verbs randomly scattered about instead of neatly stacked at the end of each sentence, verbs that had no real endings, and nondeclension nouns, the language was oral chaos.

In Rauch's experience national security usually equaled some sort of intelligence operation. Why couldn't these people just admit it up front? "Might I ask what your interest in Mr. Reilly is?"

Gruber and Strassman exchanged glances before he spoke. "Your friend Reilly seems to be interested in a person also of interest to Israeli security services." She motioned him to a chair that was every bit as uncomfortable as he had anticipated. "What can you tell us about the American?"

Nothing they didn't already know, as it turned out.

"We intend to execute your request and arrest Mr. Reilly this evening," Gruber continued. "He is near a kibbutz near Gaza. Would you care to join us?"

Actually, Rauch would much rather find a hotel room with a hot shower, cool air-conditioning, and a decent dinner. He was not looking forward to the long return flight with Reilly in custody. But he said, "Of course. Thank you for asking me."

"We will go by helicopter," Gruber announced like a threat.

And it was.

Rauch was hated helicopters. From his limited experience they seemed unstable, bouncing around in the sky so that a man's stomach was in his throat as often as not. Worse, the main rotor was attached by what he understood was called the Jesus nut: If it came loose, you were going to see Jesus very soon.

"Helicopter?" he asked, hoping they could not see the blood he imagined was draining from his face.

"Helicopters," Gruber repeated. Rauch was sure the young man was enjoying his discomfort. "We have three waiting for us if you're ready, Inspector."

Thoughts of helicopters eclipsed those of dinner. In fact, Rauch was feeling a little nauseated already.

FIFTY-EIGHT

Just Outside Kibbutz Zion
An Hour Later

Prone in the sand, Lang and Jacob watched the kibbutz from a slight rise that gave them a view of most of the compound. Family by family, the inhabitants walked to the dining hall, the last arriving just as the day's last light leached from the western sky. Almost immediately the date trees began to speak, with fronds rustling in the breeze that sprang up from the ocean.

Both men waited a few more minutes until it was totally dark before standing.

"I didn't see anyone on lookout duty," Lang observed, dusting off as much sand as possible.

"This close to the wogs, they'd jolly well have some sort of sentry," Jacob said. "Most likely electronic sensors—visual, motion-detecting, or both."

"I looked pretty close when we drove by in the truck this morning. Didn't see any."

"You wouldn't. They'd be concealed, most likely in those two palm trees at the entrance."

"Easy enough to take care of. And from seeing someone carry three lunch plates from the mess hall, it's also likely that Alicia has a couple of guards around the clock. Just like we guessed from the satellite shot."

Jacob stooped to pick up a backpack and shifted it onto his shoulders. "As we planned, you handle them. I'll handle diverting everyone else."

Lang took a last look at the lights spilling from open windows before both men started down the hill. He savored the familiar tingle of his scalp, the chill down his spine, the almost narcotic high of pending action. It was a feeling a lawyer and head of a charitable foundation did not often enjoy.

He had missed it.

Just outside the entrance they stopped. Silently, Jacob made a circling motion. Each man walked in a wide arc before returning to the point of beginning.

"You're right," Lang said. "There's something in that tree besides coconuts."

Jacob was studying the trees with the night-vision goggles. He pulled them up on his forehead. "Two small cameras on each, angled to cover anyone going or coming."

Lang squatted, bringing the outline of the kibbutz into focus against the starry sky. "And I suppose the fence is either electrified or has a trip wire."

Jacob put the goggles on again to have a look himself. "Bloody unlikely the fence is charged—too great a risk of killing someone's livestock. We can cut through it."

"That's sure to trip whatever alarm system they have."

"Right you are. Perhaps we can dig under it."

The two approached the triple strands of wire, careful to keep out of the field of view of the tree-mounted cameras.

Lang stooped to reach under the fence. "Shit! Concrete—they've poured cement under the fence. We'd need a jackhammer to dig under it." He stood and looked across the kibbutz. "But I bet their date orchard isn't inside the fence."

"So what?" Jacob asked. "We're not here to steal effing dates."

"Maybe not," Lang conceded, "but let's see."

Keeping low to prevent presenting a silhouette, they skirted the fence line as it turned a corner. Minutes later they could see the stately palm trees against the night sky. As they got closer it became clear the palms would be on their left and the fence to the right.

"Now what?" Jacob asked. "You planning to climb a tree like some sodding monkey?"

Lang was moving along the fence line. "Exactly."

"And do what, jump? Fit to fight we'd be, what with broken legs."

"I don't think that's necessary if we can—"

Lang stopped so suddenly Jacob almost collided with his back in the dark.

"There!"

A number of the date palms, pushed by years of sea breeze, were leaning drunkenly toward the fence.

Lang selected one bent almost horizontal. "This should do."

"Do what?" Jacob protested. "We can't even see how far it is off the ground where it crosses the fence."

"I doubt it gets any farther off the ground than we see here. Besides, feel how soft this sand is? Makes a great landing surface."

Jacob mumbled something before inhaling noisily. "I suppose this is the only way in."

"Unless you have another idea."

Jacob shook off his backpack and tossed it over the fence. "If I can't find that in the dark, we've made a fruitless trip."

Lang held out a hand. "Need a boost up?"

"Keep yer sodding boost to yerself. I may not be as young as I used to be, but I bloody well can still climb a tree."

Two attempts later he was breathing hard. "Well, okay, then, perhaps a wee boost would be in order."

With Lang behind pushing, Jacob made the ten to twelve vertical feet before the tree bent toward the fence. The trunk was wide enough to permit easy movement along it.

"This should do," Lang announced, swinging over the side. He hung by his arms for a moment before dropping with a barely audible thud onto the sand below. "Softer than I thought," he whispered up.

It took perhaps a full minute to locate Jacob's backpack.

"Okay," Lang said. "I'll wait for you to do your thing. Try to get to where they're holding her. We'll take one of the cars outside to get out of here once we have her."

Without a reply, Jacob disappeared into the darkness.

Using the lights from the buildings, Lang navigated to the one from which he had seen Alicia exit that morning. There were three vehicles in front, a Range Rover, Mercedes's boxy version of the same automobile, and a Toyota pickup.

Lang waited in deep shadow until he was certain no one else was in the area. Keeping the cars between him and the building, he crawled to the pickup, knelt to open the door, and popped the hood latch. Seconds later he had the distributer cap in hand, which he threw as far away as he could. He repeated the process with the Range Rover before withdrawing again to the shadows to wait.

He was never sure of how long it took, only that the explosion came much quicker than he had anticipated.

He saw a flash, an orange cloud limning the water tower as its two front legs buckled like an animal kneeling to drink. He felt a blast of hot air, and only then did he hear the sound, a noise that cracked like a roll of thunder, followed by the diluvial slosh as the toppling tank ruptured when it hit the ground, releasing thousands of gallons of water.

He watched as figures jammed the mess hall's doorway just in time to watch the pyrotechnic display of what Lang guessed had been a fuel storage facility erupting in a greasy orange-and-black firestorm.

Men were outside the mess hall now, some firing Uzis blindly toward the conflagration, believing they were under attack by their Arab neighbors. Others screamed for firefighting equipment, which, Lang guessed, would be quite useless with the loss of the water supply.

The general impression was like kicking over an anthill.

Lang positioned himself beside the door of the building in whose shadows he had been waiting.

Two men carrying Uzis, Alicia's guards, stepped outside. The noise of general pandemonium as well as the roar of the flames devouring the shed made it impossible to hear what was said, but it was obvious they were as surprised as their comrades in the mess hall.

Lang stepped into the doorway behind them so that, should anyone look this way, the two would block sight of him. The SIG Sauer was in his hand. "This way, gentlemen."

They whirled, one beginning to raise his weapon until he saw the muzzle of Lang's pistol only inches from his forehead.

This sect might well be fanatics but they weren't suicidal.

Both men slowly raised their hands, and Lang took both Uzis before returning his automatic to the holster in the small of his back.

With one machine gun under his left arm, he pulled the bolt back on the other just far enough to make sure the weapon had a shell in the chamber and was ready to fire.

He gestured inside. "If you will, gentlemen, please. After you."

What he saw stopped him cold.

He had entered what he supposed was the main room, off of which there were one or two smaller ones. It was bare except for a rough wooden table and a pair of bent-wood chairs. Alicia sat in one. Next to her was a small man with the side curls and beard of the orthodox Jew, like the men Lang had seen at the kibbutz. He held one of those massive Desert Eagles to her head.

"Lang!" She gasped in surprise.

"Ah, Mr. Reilly! I've been waiting for you," the man with the pistol said in slightly accented English. "I was beginning to fear you were unable to put all the clues together and were not coming."

The Uzi relied more on rate of fire than accuracy. Trying to shoot the man with the gun to Alicia's head, he was just as likely to hit her. Even if not, there was no guarantee the man couldn't pull the trigger before he died.

Lang put both Uzis down on the table. "Sorry to keep you waiting. You are Mr. Zwelk?"

The man nodded as he gestured to the two guards, who began a none-too-gentle search of Lang's person. "Quite correct. I must confess a small disappointment you didn't find me sooner."

Lang held up his arms as he was patted down. One man tugged the SIG Sauer free and placed it on the table. "Trust me, I came as quickly as I could."

"Lang," Alicia began, "this man—"

Zwelk silenced her with a glare. "If you want out of this alive, you would be wise to remain quiet."

"You have no intent of either of us leaving here," Lang stated.

Zwelk gave a chilly smile, nodding his head toward the flickering shadows caused by the flames outside. "I certainly have just cause if I choose not to let you live."

"But why . . . ?" Alicia asked.

"Because Mr. Reilly is in a position to release a secret, one that could do my people great harm."

"Why don't you let your government decide that?" Lang asked.

Zwelk wrinkled his nose in disgust. "Government!" he spit. "The government is nothing but a harlot, prostituting itself for this interest and that. The government of the state of Israel was originally intended to be of the Jewish state. But what has it become? A society of material greed rather than Zionism!"

"I thought all Jews are welcome—the zealot, the conservative, as well as those who are Jewish by birth, if not particularly religious."

Zwelk curled a lip in disgust. "Not religious? Israel was to be a nation of religion!"

"Like your friends the Arabs? You would have a clerical rather than secular state?"

Agency training: Keep your opponent talking; delay as long as possible.

Zwelk snorted. "Like the ever-materialistic, antireligious United States? No, Mr. Reilly, there are those of us who have higher hopes for our nation. A nation, by the way, to which you pose a great danger. The force your institution has found could be the ultimate weapon."

"I'd guess it already is—was long before I came along. Besides, you're not referring to the powers of the Ark," Lang said. "You know that as well as I do."

Alicia's puzzled voice interrupted. "Lang, what are you two talking about?"

Zwelk paid her no attention. "Ignoring the weapon's potential? Really? He stroked his beard, a gesture that Lang guessed was more habit than conscious gesture. "Then what exactly do you think I'm talking about?"

"The Book of Jereb, those scrolls you took after you had Professor Shaffer murdered in Vienna. It wasn't what was said about the Ark; it was what was said about Moses and the Israelites. That's what you want to remain a secret."

Alicia had been turning her head as each man spoke. "What power? What Book of Jereb?"

This time it was Lang who didn't respond to her question for the moment. "How did you know the copy of Jereb had been found?"

"We knew it was buried somewhere among the medieval manuscripts at Melk. We couldn't just walk in and rummage through them. So, when the abbey decided to sort them out, create a computer index, we simply hired someone to keep a close watch. We never dreamed that man Steinburg would actually reproduce a copy of the book and send it to his cousin. By the time our man at Melk told us what had happened, it was too late."

"You kidnapped me and are threatening to kill us over some medieval manuscript?" Alicia asked incredulously.

Lang didn't break eye contact with Zwelk. "Not just any manuscript. This was a copy of a much older one, an alternative to the Book of Exodus."

"I still don't understand."

"This book, like Exodus, states that Moses was an Egyptian. It went further, telling of a king deposed because he was monotheistic—put the priests of the various gods out of work, as it were. But it went on. The Israelites were Egyptians, too, Egyptian believers in a single god, not Jews. Mr. Zwelk figured that anyone researching superconductors similar to the Ark might be lead to the Book of Jereb or come across the real story: that Egyptians, not Jews, wandered in the desert and settled in what is now Israel. He couldn't take that risk, so he had everyone connected to that research killed."

Alicia was clearly perplexed. "So, what does that have to do with . . . ?"

"Our friend Zwelk here wants to make sure no word of the Israelites' true origins gets out to the world at large. See, if the Israelites were not Jews, but Egyptians, Arabs—"

Zwelk interrupted. "The state of Israel cannot afford to have the legitimacy of its claim to Palestine disputed, particularly by the Muslim world. It is the land promised to my people by their God."

"Not unless your people happen to be Egyptians," Lang observed.

Zwelk's face screwed into a scowl. "And that, Mr. Reilly, is why you won't be leaving."

Alicia gave Lang a frightened look.

"Don't worry," he said. "He isn't going to—"

He stopped in midsentence.

The three men in the room had heard it, too: the distinctive thump of helicopters in flight.

"Whoever that is," Zwelk announced, "I assure you they are too late to be of help to you." He reached for Lang's SIG Sauer on the table. "They will find that you shot your lady friend here in an attempt to kidnap her from the hospitality of our community."

"Won't work, Zwelk," Lang said, mentally measuring his chances of successfully lunging across the table. "Nobody is going to believe she was here by her own will."

Zwelk stepped back, gun arm extended. "Why not? Neither of you will be alive to contradict it. In any event, I will not be here by the time whoever is in those helicopters arrives. I have known for a long time that my devotion to the purity of the Jewish religion would provoke the authorities and planned accordingly."

"Reminds me of rats and sinking ships," Lang said.

Lang took a deep breath as he watched Zwelk's trigger finger tighten.

He could only hope Jacob had known what the hell he was doing.

FIFTY-NINE

Three Kilometers from Kibbutz Zion
At the Same Time

Another few minutes of bouncing around like a cork in rough water and Inspector Rauch would have embarrassed himself by getting sick, loosing his last meal all over the other five men in this infernal device, including the Israeli policeman, Zaltov. The bastard actually seemed to be enjoying the flight. The security man, Gruber, had explained that the cooling of the night air over the sun-warmed desert caused irregular heating and, therefore, the updrafts—thermals, he called them—that had rocked the Bell helicopter. The meteorological information had not made the ride any less terrifying.

For the first time in years, Inspector Rauch thanked God. They were descending, and this ride from hell was about over. He risked a peek through the Plexiglas. The aircraft's spotlight showed what looked like a small village with what might have been a pond in the middle. No, not a lake, but the smashed remains of some kind of huge container in the middle of whatever liquid it had contained. A water tower, he could now see. He could almost hear the desert sand greedily drinking up the available moisture.

And there was a fire; one of the buildings was burning. He could smell smoke.

The light moved to an open space, and the helicopter began a vertical descent that left Rauch's stomach somewhere above. On either side the other two machines were also settling.

Now he was close enough to the ground to see a group of men and women. The men wore hats and were all bearded, with the side curls of Hasidim. Several were pointing upward.

Rauch swallowed hard and spoke for the first time during the trip, asking Zaltov, "How do we know this man Reilly won't escape before we land?"

The policeman gave what Rauch supposed was a laugh had he been able to hear it over the clatter of rotor blades. "Escape? Where? This kibbutz is sealed off from the sea by the wall along the Gaza border and is in the middle of the desert. No one in his right mind would want to wander around out there."

Rauch was tempted to point out that Zaltov's ancestors had, according to their own tradition, done just that. And not just "wandered." After forty years of meandering, they had managed to select one of the few places in this area of the world that had no oil under it.

Instead he concentrated on mastering his heaving stomach for a few more minutes.

Rauch was surprised when the helicopter touched down with the lightness of a ballerina. In seconds Gruber was standing at his elbow, shouting orders over the dying whine of turbine engines and slowing rotor blades. The dozen or so uniformed and armed men fanned out, knocking on doors before opening them, while two of their number disappeared into the darkness, presumably to cover any exit. To the Austrian it looked like a military maneuver by well-trained troops. He was a little surprised that none of the residents seemed either surprised or upset that their kibbutz had been invaded. He supposed that, this close to hostile territory, the appearance of friendly forces at any time was welcome.

One of the soldiers had an old man by the arm, gently leading the white-bearded elder toward the place Rauch and Gruber stood. It was clear to Rauch that more respect than coercion was involved. Although the Austrian policeman could not understand the language, the tone indicated polite questioning rather than harsh interrogation. Finally the old man pointed toward one of several bungalow-like buildings just beyond the shrinking perimeter of light from the waning fire.

Gruber pointed to the same place. "He says he knows of no strangers here other than a red-haired woman who is visiting the chairman of the kibbutz and his wife. That's their house." The security man took off at a trot. "Come on!"

Rauch had not taken his second step when he heard shots. They seemed to come from the very house to which he was headed.

SIXTY

The SIG Sauer exploded in Zwelk's hand, sending shrapnel-like fragments into his face.

For an instant his eyes protruded from a blood-splattered face as he contemplated the shreds of flesh that had been his hand moments before.

Then he grunted with shock and grabbed for the stump at the end of his arm as though he might stop the geysers of red his ulnar and palmar arteries were pumping.

Lang doubted Zwelk had even begun to feel pain as he heard the first note of a scream from Alicia.

The shock that had frozen the two guards passed. They both lunged for their weapons on the table, but Lang was closer.

Shoving Alicia aside, he dove across the table, sweeping up both weapons. He brought his hands up, the Uzi in each spitting bullets that stitched both men across the chest with ragged red flowers blooming larger and larger until they merged into a single crimson stain.

It had all taken perhaps three seconds, three ticks of a clock. The small room so stank of cordite, blood, and death that Lang nearly gagged. He was deaf from the shots in such close quarters, and his eyes wept from acrid wisps of burned gunpowder.

He dropped the Uzis and turned to pull Alicia to her feet. She looked straight at him without seeing, a catatonic stare of stunned fright.

Holding one Uzi, Lang took her hand in the other, speaking words he himself could not hear. "Come on, Alicia; we can't stay here."

On legs as uncertain as those of a newborn colt, she stood and transferred her stare to someplace over Lang's shoulder.

At first he thought he might be hallucinating.

Blocking the doorway was a tall man in his mid-thirties, clean-shaven and with a recent haircut.

Witherspoon.

The would-be FBI man spoke words Lang's ringing ears could only partially hear, but there was no mistaking the Desert Eagle he held in his hand.

With a shove Lang pushed Alicia out of the line of fire, a motion that diverted Witherspoon's eyes just long enough for Lang to raise one of the Uzis.

He felt, rather than heard, the dull click of the hammer on an empty chamber. The damn clip had been half-empty when he grabbed the gun.

Shit.

Witherspoon had heard it. Lowering his weapon, he moved with the grace of a professional fighter. He smashed his Desert Eagle against the side of Lang's head, sending him slipping across the blood-slicked floor. The force of impact with the far wall knocked the second Uzi from his grasp.

Ears ringing both from the gunshots and the blow, Lang did not have to hear all the man's words as he stuck his own weapon into his belt and charged. The murderous gleam in his eye said it all: Witherspoon intended to literally kill Lang with his bare hands.

Before Lang could regain his feet, Witherspoon's heavier weight was pinning him to the floor while large hands sought to choke the life from him.

Tugging at the ever-closing fingers was useless. Witherspoon was not only larger; he was stronger. Already Lang was desperately sucking at what little air his hungry lungs could ingest.

Lang groped for the gun in the man's belt and realized the effort was hopeless. Instead he used all of his remaining strength to arch his back into a wrestler's bridge that lifted his shoulders and shifted both his and Witherspoon's weight slightly forward.

The pressure eased slightly, allowing Lang to twist quickly to his right, free his left arm, and roll violently back, smashing the point of his elbow against the side of his adversary's head. As Witherspoon recoiled from the blow, Lang scrambled out from under him and began to stagger to his feet.

Witherspoon was on him before Lang was fully erect. This time, though, Lang was able to get his arms inside his enemy's outstretched hands, shunting them aside. With his arms spread for just an instant, Witherspoon was vulnerable.

Lang put every ounce of weight and strength into a strike not of his fist but of fingers cupped to fit just under Witherspoon's sternum, driving the wind from his opponent's diaphragm with the whoosh of a deflating balloon.

Lang had intended to snatch the automatic from Witherspoon's belt before the man could gasp his next breath. Instead the force of the contact had knocked the gun loose, sending it clattering across the floor.

Without hesitation Witherspoon reached into a pocket. As his hand swung forward there was a metallic snick. The long dagger of a switchblade glistened evilly. From the way he held it—blade up, arm bent—Lang guessed the man had had some experience in using it.

"You're not in your office, now, Reilly," he sneered. "You won't be ushering me out like some salesman."

He was tossing the knife from one hand to the other and back again.

"Learn that at the FBI academy?" Lang asked, surprised he could now hear his own voice.

Witherspoon was moving in a semicircle, taking side steps so that he always maintained his balance. Lang was reminded of the dance of a fighter looking for an opportunity to deliver the knockout punch. "All that matters to you, Reilly, is that I learned it."

Lang was also moving to keep squarely in front of Witherspoon. "There's no point in this, you know. You heard the helicopters. The Israeli police will be here in seconds. I wouldn't want to have a weapon in hand when they burst through that door."

Witherspoon's lips curled back from his teeth in a cruel parody of a smile. "So what? I didn't come all the way back to Israel to surrender, to let you undermine my people's right to their own land. If I die for that cause, I'll be happy."

"Oh, come off it! Even your Muslim neighbors get multiple virgins in paradise for martyrdom."

"Less talk, Reilly. It's time for you to die."

Retreating a step, Lang groped behind him, his hand touching one of the chairs. He snatched it up by the back, holding it out like a circus performer confronting a ring full of snarling lions.

Witherspoon shoved it aside and feinted a stab to Lang's right before slashing at Lang's left.

The chair was too heavy to use as a weapon. Stepping back, Lang simultaneously slammed it against the floor. As he had hoped, the legs broke free. Still watching Witherspoon, he scooped one up. Now he at least had a club.

Witherspoon, still pacing, snorted. "A piece of wood won't save you."

The chair leg had snapped off, leaving a sharp point where it had been attached. Lang jabbed. "Like the song says, Witherspoon, 'a little less talk and a lot more action.' Much as you'd like to, you can't talk me to death."

Lang knew his best chance lay in either stalling until help arrived or forcing Witherspoon to commit himself. A broken chair leg was better than no weapon, but not by much.

Lang's eyes fastened onto those of his antagonist. He was aware that even the most experienced knife fighter must at least glance in the direction of attack.

Thrust and parry, thrust and parry. Lang blocked each jab with solid wood, retreating a step with each move. He felt the wall at his back, a fact Witherspoon must have noted, judging by the victorious smile on his face.

But the man had given himself away. His eyes shifted quickly to the opposite side before he feigned an attack. This time Lang was ready. Witherspoon's eyes darted to Lang's right as he jabbed futilely to the left. When he moved right, arm extended for what he anticipated would be the kill, Lang spun aside, bringing the chair leg crashing down across Witherspoon's wrist, smashing the ulna.

Witherspoon howled as the knife spun like a sparkling comet across the room. He bent over, cradling the shattered bones of his wrist. Lang was tempted to swing the chair leg down on the man's head. Too risky. Such blows reliably rendered only film villains unconscious. In real life the skull was frequently too thick to allow more than temporarily dazing an opponent.

That was one of the reasons the Agency had taught the seven kill spots on the human body.

Lang jabbed upward, stabbing the wooden point into the area just below the chin. Witherspoon's head snapped head back with sufficient force that Lang could hear the vertebrae snap.

Witherspoon dropped lifelessly to the floor.

"What a sodding mess!"

Whirling, Lang faced the source of the voice as he raised the chair leg for another blow.

Jacob stood in the doorway, surveying the carnage inside. "Put that silly stick down and come outside."

Lang grinned. "Remind me not to let you near any weapon I own. What would have happened if it had been me instead of Zwelk pulling that trigger?"

"If you had had to shoot it out with two Uzis, what happened when you pulled the trigger would be sodding irrelevent."

Lang held Alicia's hand as he followed Jacob. They had almost reached a place where neither the pale light of the fire's embers nor that from surrounding buildings could reach them when Lang heard an order in English to stop.

There was just enough illumination to make out four men. One, the oldest of the group, wore a rumpled suit and tie. Another was dressed in shirt and pants as though for the golf course; a third was in the uniform of the Israeli police. The fourth, in military uniform, held an Uzi at bay, not pointed at Lang but not far from it, either.

Jacob immediately stepped forward. "Yosi, is that you? Yosi Gruber, the lad I knew was bright enough but never had the discipline to make the intelligence service?"

The one in the polo shirt stepped forward, grinning. "Jacob Anueliwitz! What is a retired old goat like you doing here?"

" 'Old goat,' is it?" Jacob laughed. "Well, I'll be telling you youngsters something: While you were farting about, I've found an arsenal here."

"So what?" the policeman said. "It's not uncommon for these kibbutzes to be ready to defend themselves."

"With rocket and grenade launchers?" Jacob asked,

grinning evilly. "I'd bet ten quid you'll find the last few attacks by the wogs on 'tother side of that wall started when some bloke lobbed explosives into their villages. A provocateur is what you have here."

Rauch was at a total loss. He was expecting to make an arrest, and what he was witnessing more resembled a family reunion. He stepped forward, facing Lang. "Mr. Langford Reilly?"

"Yes?"

"You are arrested."

Lang looked quizzically at Jacob and then to Gruber. "By whom and what in the hell for? Or is that a secret?"

"I am Chief Inspector Rauch of the Vienna police, and you are for questioning wanted in regard to the murder of Dr. Heimlich Shaffer."

"Heimlich Shaffer?" Lang asked. "The professor I had dinner with? He's been murdered? By whom?"

"That, Mr. Reilly, is what we hope you can tell us."

"Then you're about to be seriously disappointed."

A man in an Israeli army uniform appeared out the darkness as though by a magician's trick. He spoke hurried Hebrew to Gruber.

In turn, the intelligence man turned to Rauch. "I'd like to borrow your prisoner for a few moments, Inspector."

The Austrian was hardly in a position to refuse.

Lang looked at Alicia. "You okay?"

"Oh, sure," she said. "Just peachy keen. And why not? After all, I've been within seconds of being killed, treated to a marvelous display of testosterone, and splattered with someone else's blood. No reason to worry about me."

Sarcasm was one of her less attractive features.

Lang, Gruber, Jacob, and two Israeli soldiers crossed to a small hut on the far side of the kibbutz. Rauch, unwilling to let his prisoner out of his sight, followed a pace or two behind.

The interior of the building was déjà vu for Lang. A

long table was lined with scientific equipment resembling the laboratories at Georgia Tech and Amsterdam. There was a notable addition: an oblong, boxlike device clearly made of a combination of wood and gold, decidedly out of place among the gleaming gauges, scales, and machines.

Gruber pointed to it. "Mr. Reilly, I have a feeling you might know what that is."

"Whatever gave you that idea?"

Gruber frowned. "It is getting late, and I have little patience for games. I think you did not spend the time reconnoitering this kibbutz as a possible place to vacation. I think you were interested in this object."

Jacob spoke for the first time. "Actually, old man, he was looking for the lady, the red-haired bird you saw. Seems Zwelk nicked her as bait to force Mr. Reilly to come here. Truly ill of the man, what?"

Gruber was unconvinced. "Why would he do that, want to force Mr. Reilly to come here?"

Jacob shrugged. "Who knows the mind of someone that irrational? You yourself said the man was a fanatic."

Gruber's expression said he was certain he wasn't hearing the whole story. Jacob's expression said he had told all he intended to.

Gruber shook his head slowly. "It is unlikely anyone in government will mourn Zwelk's death. He was a threat to any possible peace with the Palestinians." He jerked his head toward the wall. "The cache of arms here far exceeds any need to simply defend the kibbutz. The man was prepared to provoke a war."

One of the men in uniform with a sergeant's chevrons on his sleeve spoke excitedly in Hebrew. Gruber stepped over to where the man was pointing and held up a test tube and a beaker.

"Some sort of white powder and . . ." He looked closer at the test tube. "What looks like gold dust." His face wrinkled into that of a man perplexed. "What would these people be doing with gold dust?"

Jacob and Lang exchanged glances.

"Struck gold on the Jordan River?" Lang suggested.

"Not likely. It is fifty miles away." Gruber's glare told him the man had no sense of humor.

"I say, looks like something you might want to refer to your superiors," Jacob offered.

Gruber looked skeptical.

Jacob spoke in Hebrew, apparently repeating the suggestion before switching back to English. "I cannot tell you how deucedly clever it would be to take all this equipment, gold, and that white powder back to Tel Aviv. I'd speculate someone there will be very interested in the whole lot."

Gruber shook his head. "But I can't just . . . just take kibbutz property because someone back at the office might be interested."

Jacob puffed his cheeks and exhaled loudly, the sound of exasperation. "I'd give a monkey to a monkey wrench that this kibbutz is about to go out of business once the government sees what's in this building."

He reached into a pocket, producing a pipe. Another hand held the tobacco pouch. Under Gruber's glare he shook his head and put both away for the moment, turning to Rauch. "Inspector, I'm no copper, but I'd suggest you take a close look at the arsenal these people have here. Another wager: You'll find either the weapon that killed your Dr. Shaffer or its mate. No point in putting Reilly in the coop when it's clear that Zwelk and his lads had every reason to kill the professor."

Rauch had a mental picture of returning to Vienna without Reilly after what had been spent to get here, life-size and in natural color. He'd be back in uniform, foot-patrolling the Karlsplatz Bahnhof for drug dealers or chasing Gypsy beggars out of U-Bahn stations.

"I will certainly be interested in what you have to show me," he said noncommittally. "I have been sent for questions to bring Mr. Reilly to Vienna. My superiors will decide what acts to take."

The German syntax reminded Lang of Gurt. Too bad the inspector lacked her humor.

And looks.

Gruber intervened. "Hate to disappoint you, Inspector, but I have a feeling my government will want to speak with Mr. Reilly before he leaves the country."

And they did.

SIXTY-ONE

Tel Aviv
Two Days Later

Lang spent the days with a man Jacob later identified as Mossad's master interrogator. He was mostly interested in just how much Lang knew and how far along Zwelk's work with gold might have gotten. The word *weapon* was never mentioned, but the progress of the foundation's research was. Although not specifically told, Lang came away with the definite impression that it would be wise to stick to matters of a medical nature.

It was an idea he would definitely consider.

While Lang was occupied with answering questions, Jacob gave Alicia a view of the city, a fast-paced walking tour that left her begging for time-out and an afternoon nap. With her back at the hotel, Jacob moved much more leisurely and directly into the Yemenite Quarter, the city's oldest. Narrow streets were lined with Arab-type dwellings competing for space with newer Art Deco homes, many decorated with tile panels. He turned into Nakhaler Binyamin Street, where fashionable boutiques and cafés did a brisk business despite the afternoon heat.

He passed several outdoor tables under an awning

and a sign announcing the premises as the Camel's Hump in Hebrew and English before slowly turning around. As though unsure of his surroundings, he surveyed the nearly empty street before backtracking to the café and sitting across a table from a man whose face was hidden by a newspaper.

"Try the konafa," said a voice from behind the pages. "It's freshly baked."

Jacob nodded his assent to a waiter who had appeared as though by magic and vanished just as quickly. "I assume you didn't ask me here to sample the pastry."

The paper dropped to the table and Gruber shook his head. "No, but it's good enough to make the trip worthwhile."

Jacob waited until a tiny cup of black Turkish coffee was placed next to the small plate holding roasted pistachios wrapped in crisp strings of fried dough and the waiter had retreated.

Gruber folded the paper with a great deal more care than a day-old tabloid merited. Jacob wondered idly whether Mossad budget cuts had mandated reuse of newspapers.

"We owe you and your friend Reilly," the security man said.

Jacob was reaching for his coffee. "And just who might 'we' be?"

Gruber folded his arms on the table and leaned forward. "All of us Jews, the government."

Jacob refrained from pointing out that the two were far from synonymous.

"We needed to get rid of that nutcase on the Gaza border. He would have provoked the Palestinians into another war."

Again Jacob kept quiet, not mentioning that everything from an Israeli prime minister's casual visit to the Temple Mount to security precautions against suicide bombers seemed to have that unfortunate effect on the Palestinians and their beneficent, peace-loving Islamic brethren.

"Or worse, much worse. And the politicians would never have allowed us to storm in there without a reason. How'd you steer Reilly to that kibbutz, anyway?"

Jacob sampled coffee that had the consistency of used motor oil. He ameliorated its bitterness with a nibble at his pastry. "I didn't. Zwelk did it for us."

Gruber nodded knowingly. "I should have guessed. Not even you could have arranged for the girl to be kidnapped and taken there. But you did do a hell of a job trashing the place."

"A specialty," Jacob said uncomfortably.

Although he was happy to have the Israeli government owe him a favor, he would not want Lang to even suspect he had been manipulated.

"He never questioned how that oil truck just happened to be in the right place, how you just guessed the satellite coordinates for the kibbutz, or . . . ?"

Jacob was definitely ill at ease, his coffee and konafa in midair. "Just so happened your interest and his coincided."

He wished this circuitous conversation would reach its intended destination, but he did have a question. "I'm curious: How did you make sure Zwelk learned about the Melk manuscript?"

"Easily enough. Its existence had been rumored for centuries. The problem was finding it and making it disappear without causing an incident. Zwelk had someone at the monastery. The guy worked for us, too."

"And you guessed he'd do whatever it took to make sure it never became public."

A statement, not a question.

"Pretty much a given. Our historic claim to this land is the moral right we have to a nation of our own. Any true Zionist would die, if need be, to protect that."

"So, your double agent tipped you the chase was on."

Gruber nodded affirmatively and glanced around as though fearful of eavesdroppers before leaning forward, ready to finally come to the point. "How much does Reilly know?"

Jacob put down the pastry and stared innocently. "Know about what?"

Gruber frowned. "Don't fuck with me! The weapons system, of course! You're the one who suggested I take that powder and the box to King Solomon Street. Does Reilly realize what it is, how it works, what it can do?"

Jacob took another sip of the viscous coffee to give himself a moment to think before answering. He had little doubt what would happen to Lang if he told the truth. "I think he swallowed that trash you fed him about not caring about the historical origins of the country."

Gruber's eyes glistened with irritation Jacob knew could become lethal. "That wasn't the question."

Jacob shrugged. "If you're asking me specifically if he knows about the power that can be generated from the dimensions of the Ark, I'd say he hasn't the foggiest. The man's a sodding barrister, not a scientist."

Gruber leaned back against his seat, a man relieved. "Glad to hear it. He's not a bad sort for an American. But national security comes first, right? You'll let us know if he figures it out, right?"

Jacob took another bite of pastry. "Right."

Right after I make a dash across Trafalgar Square in the buff.

Gruber's chair protested against the pavement as he pushed back and stood, tossing shekels onto the table to cover Jacob's tab. "Glad to hear that, too." He picked up the newspaper. "And so will be King Solomon Street. They would do whatever was necessary to keep the secret."

The warning was far from idle. The Royal Canadian Mounted Police bragged of always getting their man;

Mossad did. Even if it took years. Retribution for the murders of the Israeli athletes at the Munich Olympics was completed nearly fifteen years later.

Jacob watched Gruber walk away, wondering if Lang, too, had just been threatened.

It was on the way to the airport in a limousine offered by Gruber that Lang decided to ask Jacob a question that wouldn't go away.

"The Ark?"

Jacob turned from staring out of the window, his teeth grinding in resentment of very explicit warnings that smoking was not, repeat, not allowed in government transportation. "What about it?"

"Israel has made some sort of weapons defense system out of it, hasn't it?"

Jacob looked forward, making sure the glass between the driver and passenger compartments was up before he replied, "Trust me—you don't want to know."

SIXTY-TWO

Südbahnhof Police Station
Wiedner Gürtel
Vienna
Three Days Later

Lang stood in Rauch's office with his hands clasped behind him, gazing out of a window as he waited for the inspector.

Somewhere out there, somewhere in Vienna, Jacob was showing Alicia the city. Or at least that part of it the three had not seen yesterday. They had started with a brief train ride to the Hapsburg summer palace, Schönbrunn. Here the last real Austro-Hungarian emperor, Franz Joseph, had put aside one day a week when his subjects might meet their ruler and personally express whatever grievance, real or fancied, they might have against the imperial government. The man had lived to see his armies shift from horsepower to airpower, finally dying in 1916.

Then they had visited the Kunsthistorisches Museum to view an incredible collection of sixteenth- and seventeenth-century masters. Afterward, they lunched on local dishes at Do & Co overlooking the Stephansdom.

If appetite were any indication, Alicia seemed to have forgotten—or at least not been overly traumatized by—her experience at the kibbutz. She did, however, admit to leaving the light in the hotel room on at night. Lang had enjoyed her company but sensed he was a long way from being invited back into her bedroom. He took that as a clear indication that she held him responsible for her ordeal. How long would it be before they resumed—

The sound of a door closing behind him scattered a potentially erotic memory.

Inspector Rauch motioned Lang into a chair in front of the desk as he sat behind it. The two men looked at each other across a sea of paper before the Austrian nodded briefly. "Good morning, Mr. Reilly."

"*Am Morgen, Herr Inspector,*" Lang replied in what little German he remembered from his days at the Agency's Frankfurt station. "*Wie gehts?*"

"Very well, thank you," Rauch countered, wondering how long the bilingual conversation would continue. "I hope you our city yesterday enjoyed."

Lang smiled. A less than subtle team of plainclothes cops had followed him all day. Clearly the inspector viewed him as a flight risk. "Very much, thanks. By the way, thanks also for allowing me to be outside of your custody."

Rauch nodded an acknowledgment. The decision to let Reilly roam free pending a conclusion of the investigation had not been his. It had come from Number 3 Minoritenplatz in the Hofburg, the chancellor's office itself. The Israeli government's hand in this was obvious. Before they were allowed departure from Tel Aviv, Reilly and the Jew Annueliwitz had spent an entire day behind closed doors with Gruber and a number of people Rauch gathered were Israeli intelligence. Years of police work left the inspector with the definite impression the American knew something the Jews did not want disseminated.

Then, most unusual, Rauch had received not permission but orders to return with Reilly in the suspect's private jet. It was like asking a prisoner to drive both himself and police officer to jail. Once aboard, who knew where they might end up?

Once again, Rauch saw Jewish interference with Austrian affairs. That and the Vienna police's desire to save airfare.

"You've completed your investigation?" Lang asked hopefully.

Rauch nodded wearily. Actually, there had been little investigation at all, other than what had taken place the day after the shootings in the Stephansplatz and Michaelerkirche. A few ballistics tests had confirmed the same sort of weapon, the huge MI Desert Eagle, had fired the shots that hit the policemen and killed Dr. Shaffer, but the specific weapon that had fired each had not been located. True, that sect of Jews . . . What did they call themselves? Essenes, that was it. The Essenes had had a rather large collection of the weapons in their arsenal, but that proved little. No, there was more, a lot more, to this whole affair—a lot that the higher levels of government had decided to relegate to the trash heap of obscurity rather than make public.

Somehow politics had become involved. When that happened, Rauch's superiors—and theirs in the Hofburg—called the shots, not a mere inspector. Shaffer's killers as well as those who had shot two police officers would be permanently designated "unknown" and the case hurriedly closed.

Not good police work, perhaps; but, then, politics seldom were.

Rauch stood and reached across the desk. "You are free to go, Mr. Reilly."

Lang stood to take the proffered hand. "Thanks, Inspector."

After a cursory shake, he turned toward the door.

"Oh, Mr. Reilly? A favor, if you please?"

Lang stopped, his hand on the doorknob. "If I can, sure."

"Enjoy your stay in Vienna."

Lang smiled. "That's hardly a favor."

Rauch nodded. "True. But I wish you to enjoy it enough not to return for three years."

Lang's smile widened. "Just three years?"

"I shall be by then retired."

EPILOGUE

Lang succeeded in keeping his mouth shut while the mayor treated the media to a stinging denunciation of the racism, bias, and unjust system that had resulted in his conviction on two counts of tax evasion.

Even when a pretty but empty blond head shoved a microphone in his face, Lang managed a mild, "We are very disappointed in the verdict."

"Do you intend to appeal?"

"That is under consideration."

He was thankful when the mayor, never content for the spotlight to shine elsewhere, resumed his tirade.

Actually, Lang had been astonished when the equally racially divided jury had acquitted on the racketeering, bribery, bid rigging, and other counts. The mayor's time as a guest of the federal government had been reduced to a small fraction of the original potential. It was even possible that probation, not time, might be given at next month's sentencing hearing.

Finally sated, the newsies dispersed, no doubt in search of other carrion to strip from the bones of the day's events. A black limousine that had hovered discreetly out of camera range slid to the curb, and the passenger door swung open.

"It could have been a lot worse," Lang observed.

The mayor turned a rage-contorted face to him, something no news camera would ever capture. "Oh, yeah? You're not the one who will lose his law license, are you?" he snarled. "You're not the one who has to live with the humiliation."

Nor the one who bilked the taxpayers out of millions in inflated contracts, Lang thought.

"If you think that's a performance to be proud of, Mr. Langford Reilly, think again! Consider yourself fired!"

Even the mayor's back conveyed indignation, righteous or otherwise, as he took the few steps to the street and got inside the car.

Lang slowly shook his head. Gratitude was a rare commodity in criminal practice. If your client got convicted, you hadn't done your job. If acquitted . . . Well, then he was innocent and hadn't really needed you anyway.

"Unappreciative bastard!" said a voice behind him.

Lang spun around to see Alicia standing there.

"Goes with the territory," he said. He noted the briefcase in her hand. "They let you out early?"

"I was coming back from a witness interview," she explained, "not leaving."

"Wouldn't want the taxpayers shortchanged."

They openly stared at each other for a moment. Since returning from Vienna she had not returned his calls. He guessed he represented a memory that would be slow to fade.

"Speaking of unappreciative," she began slowly, "I don't think I ever thanked you for saving my life."

"Or putting it at risk," Lang added.

"That, too," she admitted. "But I don't think you had reason to think seeing me would put me in danger."

"No idea," Lang agreed. "For that matter, I had no idea they were after me."

She jerked her head toward the building. "Got a minute? I'll stand for a round of coffee."

He shrugged. "Why not? Looks like I'm not going to be handling the mayor's appeal."

"Swell," she said. "I'm delighted to present an acceptable alternative."

It was then that Lang realized he might, just might, be around her enough to get used to—and even enjoy—that sarcasm.

AUTHOR'S NOTE

I am no physicist. The parts of this book that deal with the Ark as a superconductor come from Laurence Gardner's *Lost Secrets of the Sacred Ark*, as does the theory that Moses and the single-deity-worshiping pharaoh, Akhenaten, were the same person. What little I actually learned about superconductors came from a very patient friend who teaches at Georgia Tech. He, understandably, would rather remain anonymous.

Had chemistry been a required course, I would not be a high school graduate. The explanations of alchemy come largely from an article in the *New York Times* by John Noble Wilford, "Transforming the Alchemist," August 1, 2006.

G.L.

December 14, 2006

CPSIA information can be obtained at www.ICGtesting.com
260023BV00002B/2/P